"Shockingly beautiful. . . . Seth Kantner's *Ordinary Wolves* is to the mind what a chunk of pemmican made from dried caribou, cranberries, currants and rendered fat is to the body: It's going to stick to your ribs for a long time." —**SARAH T. WILLIAMS, *MINNEAPOLIS STAR TRIBUNE***

"A land and its life. . . . If the emotional terrain is universal, the physical one is uncharted: farther North than Jack London, deeper into hunting than Ernest Hemingway."
—**JULIE BRICKMAN, *SAN DIEGO UNION-TRIBUNE***

"A lyrical yet unflinching look at the clash between modern and traditional values in Bush Alaska. . . . Haunting."
—***ANCHORAGE DAILY NEWS***

"Kantner's language flashes across the page like the northern lights themselves. . . . [A] mesmerizing debut novel." —***DENVER POST***

"What a story of Alaska. . . . Here is the remote Far North captured from the knowing perspective of someone who was born in a mud igloo and home-schooled there, too. . . . A compelling read."
—***SEATTLE POST-INTELLIGENCER***

"In the small but growing genre of ecological fiction, the great challenge is to balance political and environmental agendas with engrossing storytelling. This riveting first novel sets a new standard, offering a profound and beautiful account of a boy's attempt to reconcile his Alaskan wilderness experience with modern society. . . . A tour de force and may be the best treatment of the Northwest and its people since Jack London's works." —***PUBLISHERS WEEKLY* (STARRED REVIEW)**

"*Ordinary Wolves* has scope and a style to match its subjects, the wide-open spaces of Alaska and youth. . . . Kantner, who was born and raised in the Alaska wilderness, manages along the way to touch on the dissolution and devastation visited upon the state's native population, the youthful yearning for experience and guidance and the abiding love of an odd, isolated frontier family. His novel comes across as smart and authentic. It's hard to imagine a better start."
—**MARK KAMINE, *NEW YORK TIMES BOOK REVIEW***

"Readers hungry for a new perspective will fall into this extraordinary novel, panoramic as the arctic tundra on which it begins and ends. If you want to update your romantic conceptions about igloos, the arctic winter, and Native respect for nature, start here. . . . Cutuk's view of America will break your heart." —***BLOOMSBURY REVIEW***

"Beautifully subtle writing. . . . Interspersed throughout this thought-provoking story are short chapters written in the voices of wolves, either hunted or hunting. Through their eyes Kantner movingly underlines the passion he feels for the Arctic wilderness." —***BOOKPAGE***

"Beautiful. . . . Despite the harshness of life in Alaska, this is a gentle book, one that, no matter how much or how little in it is autobiographical, no one else could have written. . . . Kantner's descriptions are vivid, precise, distinctive, and full of awe—making *Ordinary Wolves* no ordinary book." —***RAIN TAXI***

"An episodic, avidly detailed, and many faceted tragicomedy of Alaskan life. . . . An exciting and potentially riling debut."
—***BOOKLIST* (STARRED REVIEW)**

"A man's novel full of nature lore and the mechanics of hunting and surviving, but also richly poetic and emotionally engrossing."
—***KIRKUS REVIEWS***

"Once in a great while a novel comes along that can shiver right down your bones and show you the world was always larger than you knew. This is just such an astonishing book: exotic as a dream, acrid and beautiful and honest as life, it sweeps back the material curtain of human contrivance to reveal what lies panting behind it. A piece of your heart and some longing, I promise, will stay on in that other place forever."
—BARBARA KINGSOLVER

"Seth Kantner's novel, *Ordinary Wolves,* is a magnificent and dramatic evocation of what it truly means to be a human being on North America's last real frontier. *Ordinary Wolves* is an original and beautifully written novel by a fresh new voice in American fiction. Hurrah for Seth Kantner and for Milkweed Editions in continuing to publish outstanding fiction." **—HOWARD FRANK MOSHER**

"Each year as booksellers, we hope that a novel like *Ordinary Wolves* will come along, a story crackling with truth about places both foreign and familiar. Native Alaskan Seth Kantner has written a vivid and stirring coming of age story about a white boy raised with Eskimos in the harsh Alaskan tundra. When he tries to reconcile his upbringing with the exit ramps and Taco Bells of the modern world, he's drawn back to the North." **—THE PACIFIC NORTHWEST BOOKSELLERS ASSOCIATION AWARD COMMITTEE**

"Best novel I've read in a year." **—COLIN REA, TRADEBOOK BUYER, UNIVERSITY OF OREGON BOOKSTORE**

"I truly 'lived' this book and by the end was sad to let go of the characters."
—ERIN BALCH, WASHINGTON STATE UNIVERSITY BOOKSTORE

"I loved *Ordinary Wolves.* I couldn't put it down! . . This is the kind of book I want to give to lots of people I know and a handseller's dream! And always—the wolves."
—SUE RICHARDSON, MAINE COAST BOOK SHOP

"Seth Kantner's *Ordinary Wolves* is a beautiful, complex novel of our northernmost civilized land. Full of beauty and danger, *Ordinary Wolves* tackles ecology, ethnography, and cultural imperialism without ever ceasing to be a sharp poignant story of real people with real emotions. The few old people who cling to the old ways are unforgettably depicted and the Great North in conflict with the differently civilized western world brings forth a melancholy sense of loss that can bring tears."
—PAUL INGRAM, PRAIRIE LIGHTS BOOKSTORE, IOWA CITY

"Three reasons to buy this book:
1. the characters truly inhabit a different and mesmerizing place;
2. it makes use of Iñupiaq language and culture without degrading it;
3. it's dazzling. Trust me, please."
—MICAWBER'S BOOKSTORE, ST. PAUL, MINNESOTA

"With writing as luminous as the aurora borealis and as raw as a tundra blizzard, Seth Kantner delivers a great first novel. The recent winner of the Milkweed National Fiction Prize, *Ordinary Wolves* tells the story of Cutuk, a white boy raised in a sod igloo in the Alaskan wilds. Through Cutuk's struggle to define himself, Kantner explores the contrast between the traditional Iñupiaq culture and the 'Everything-Wanters' of our consumer culture. Kantner deserves a place beside writers Tim O'Brien, T.C. Boyle and Andre Dubus III. I can't wait for his next book."
—MARY JUDE, BOOKIN' IT BOOKSTORE, LITTLE FALLS, MINNESOTA

ORDINARY
WOLVES

ORDINARY WOLVES

SETH KANTNER

MILKWEED EDITIONS

The characters and events in this book are fictitious. Any similarity to real persons, living or dead, is coincidental and not intended by the author.

Published 2005 by Milkweed Editions
Printed in Canada
Jacket and interior design by Christian Fünfhausen
Cover photograph by Denis Felix/Getty Images
Author photo by Stacey Glaser
The text of this book is set in Jenson.
07 08 09 5
First Edition

Milkweed Editions, a nonprofit publisher, gratefully acknowledges support from Emilie and Henry Buchwald; Bush Foundation; Cargill Foundation; Timothy and Tara Clark Family Charitable Fund; DeL Corazón Family Fund; Dougherty Family Foundation; Ecolab Foundation; Joe B. Foster Family Foundation; General Mills Foundation; Jerome Foundation; Kathleen Jones; Constance B. Kunin; D. K. Light; Chris and Ann Malecek; McKnight Foundation; a grant provided by the Minnesota State Arts Board, through an appropriation by the Minnesota State Legislature, a grant from the Wells Fargo Foundation Minnesota, and a grant from the National Endowment for the Arts; Sheila C. Morgan; Laura Jane Musser Fund; National Endowment for the Arts; Navarre Corporation; Kate and Stuart Nielsen; Outagamie Charitable Foundation; Qwest Foundation; Debbie Reynolds; St. Paul Companies, Inc., Foundation; Ellen and Sheldon Sturgis; Surdna Foundation; Target, Marshall Field's, and Mervyn's with support from the Target Foundation; Gertrude Sexton Thompson Charitable Trust; James R. Thorpe Foundation; Toro Foundation; Weyerhaeuser Family Foundation; and Xcel Energy Foundation.

Library of Congress Cataloging-in-Publication Data

Kantner, Seth, 1965-
Ordinary wolves / Seth Kantner.— 1st ed.
p. cm.
ISBN 1-57131-047-9 (paperback : alk. paper)
1. Young men—Fiction. 2. Rejection (Psychology)—Fiction.
3. Loss (Psychology)—Fiction. 4. Wilderness areas—Fiction.
5. Arctic regions—Fiction. 6. Inupiat—Fiction. 7. Alaska—Fiction. I. Title.
PS3611.A55O73 2004
813'.6—dc22

2003024025

This book is printed on acid-free paper.

TO MY MOTHER, WHO WAS THERE

ORDINARY WOLVES

IÑUPIAQ GLOSSARY

aachikaaŋ	*watch out! danger!*
aana	*grandma*
aaqqaa	*something stinks, smells bad*
aarigaa	*an expression of satisfaction*
aatchuq	*to give*
adii	*an expression of hurt, disappointment (modern pronunciation)*
aiy	*ugh*
akutuq	*Eskimo ice cream, whipped fat with berries and fish*
alapit	*to black out, to be drunk, to be unaware, as when delirious*
alappaa	*it is cold, to get cold*
arii	*an expression of hurt, disappointment (elder pronunciation)*
atchiq	*to name*
atchit	*to lend something to someone*
atikłuk	*traditional pullover shirt*
babiche	*rawhide strips (French word)*
bart	*buddy, friend*
bun	*daughter (slang) (Iñupiaq word: "panik")*
guuq	*it is said, someone once said (an ending to a sentence)*
ichuun	*skin scraper, flensing tool*

igamaaqłuk *half-dried fish or meat*

iġitchaq *pluck feathers*

iŋaluat *blind intestines*

iññuqun *unknown prowler or woodsman, commonly confused with "iñugaqałłigauraq"*

iñugaqałłigauraq *small, strong, troll-like mythical men*

iqsi *to be frightened*

itchaurat *lacy intestinal fat*

ittukpalak *whipped fish-egg and cranberry pudding*

kaŋiqsivich *do you understand?*

katak *to drop, to fall*

kinnaq *a dumb person, a crazy person, a fool*

kuukukiaq *common snipe*

maatnugun *soon, in a little while*

malik *follow, accompany*

mamillak *waterproof mukluks (modern usage, plural: "mamillaks")*

masru *roots, Eskimo potato*

miġiaq *to vomit*

milluk *breasts (modern usage, plural: "milluks")*

mukluks *skin boots (slang) (Iñupiaq word: "kammak")*

muktuk *whale skin and blubber (Iñupiaq word: "maktak")*

naataq *great horned owl*

nallaq *go to bed*

naluaġmiu *white person (modern usage, plural: "naluaġmius")*

niqipiaq *Eskimo food*

nulik *to have sex, mate*

pakik *ransack, dig in someone's stuff*

paniqtuq *dried meat, dried fish*

patiq *marrow*

qaatchiaq *skin mattress, traditionally caribou hide (modern usage, plural: "qaatchiaqs")*

qanisaq *entranceway, storm shed*

qayaq *small Eskimo hunting boat (English word: "kayak")*

qilamik *quickly! hurry!*

quaġaq *fermented sourdock*

quaq *frozen meat or fish, often aged or fermented*

qusrimmaq *wild rhubarb*

siġḷuaq *cold storage built in the ground, cache on the ground*

siulik *northern pike*

suvak *fish egg (modern usage, plural: "suvaks")*

taaqsipak *black person*

taata *grandpa*

taikuu *thank you*

takanna *down there*

tiktaaliq *mudshark*

tinnik *bearberry*

tulugaq *raven*

tupak *to scare, to be frightened*

tuttu *caribou*

tuuq *ice chisel*

ugruk *bearded seal*

ukpik *snowy owl*

ulu *women's curved knife*

uqsruq *seal oil*

usruk *penis (common usage: walrus penis bone)*

utchuk *vagina*

uvlaalluataq *good morning!*

yuay *lucky you*

ORDINARY
WOLVES

PROLOGUE

ON THE DRIFTED SNOW of a lake in the tundra a wolf lies dying. Blood splotches her trail down a bluff, out onto the lake. Her punched tracks zigzag. She lies on her side, panting, one eye open to the sky. A ski plane soars against the blue. It swoops low, a giant buzzing eagle coming to pluck the wolf away. The tundra glares brighter and brighter in the wolf's eye until land and sky have no detail, and then a wing slides to a stop over her. Its shadow is black. The buzzing is insane now, a tiny angry blizzard, drifting snow. It stutters to silence. In the silence the wolf hears her pups of the spring, their howls yipping mournful and confused, across the land, and the distance of death.

Two humans bend over her. The larger one is dressed in down overpants. A down parka spans his barrel chest and stomach. A wolf ruff is sewn on his hood. Moosehide mittens hang from wool strings around his neck. The female beside him wears caribou *mukluks* with *ugruk* bottoms, and she too has a strip of wolf fur on her parka. She is skinny, her hair black and her face gaunt. Her eyes shift and water, and flick south to the orange horizon, impatient to climb back into the sky, to escape to lands the sun doesn't abandon.

The man leans and touches the wolf's eye. "She's dead." The eye doesn't blink but the man wonders if she can still see out. He's wondered about other wolves, hundreds. He scratches his throat. He pulls a down engine cover from the fuselage and toggles it over the cowling. "Long flight ahead. Don't got room for you and this hundred-twenty-pound animal. Best skin her." His glance runs along the skyline, and then over at the woman. He flicks open a knife. "Coupla' more days, sun will be gone. Then the damn Darkness." He bends and slits the wolf from front foot to elbow and across the chest.

The woman turns away, uninterested in him or his commentary. She thinks it ironic that this man named for the coldest month of the year, with a home at the northern tip of a free country, should complain about winter. She's shivering. She jogs across the lake to keep from freezing while he skins. Her steps crunch in the snow. She hates snow. She pulls back her hood, holds her breath, listens a last time—she hopes—to the tundra.

To her surprise, she hears wolves. She sees specks, running and stopping. Young wolves, waiting for their mother. A sob catches her unaware. Her heartbeat roars in her head. She runs, back toward the dot of the ski plane, her only doorway to civilization here on a planet of wilderness, cold, and encroaching night. She hums, to keep from hearing their cries, and, instinctively, to protect the wolves from the pilot. Far away the narrow shapes turn north and run.

PART I **THE LAND**

ONE

IN THE BAD MOUSE YEAR—two years after magazines claimed a white man hoofed on the moon—Enuk Wolfglove materialized one day in front of our house in the blowing snow and twilight of no-sun winter. His dog team vanished and reappeared in the storm. Abe stood suddenly at the window like a bear catching a scent. "Travelers!" He squeezed out his half-smoked cigarette, flicked it to the workbench, wiped ashy fingers on his sealskin overpants. We kids eyed the cigarette's arc—we could smoke it later, behind the drifts, pretend we were artists like him.

"Poke up the fire?" Abe grinned like an older brother, our best friend, no dad at all. "And hide the vanilla." His head and broad shoulders disappeared as he squirmed into his shedding caribou-calfskin parka. He banged the door to break the caribou-skin stripping loose and jumped into the storm.

Jerry pocketed the cigarette. He glanced up through his eyelashes. "I'll share," he mumbled. Iris and I paced the floorboards, excited about travelers. We were barefoot and red toed. It was getting dark, and stormy, or we'd all have dressed in parkas and hurried outside. Jerry lowered a log into the barrel stove. He got the second log stuck and had to wrench it back out, sparky and smoking. "Goddamn son of a biscuit!" he said, practicing with Abe absent. He was tall and ten—twice my age—and had the good black hair. Also, he remembered cities and cars and lawns, red apples on trees—if that stuff was true. Jerry left the draft open until flames licked the pipe red and smoke leaked out the cracks. He tracked down each spark, wet his finger, and drowned it. He wiped his finger on a log, peered at it, and wet it again. Abe was spanking-strict about fire. That, and no whining.

"It's Enuk Wolfglove!" Iris said. "Only one traveler!" Through the flapping Visqueen window we watched Abe and the man hunching against the wind, chaining the dogs in the willows near our team. Enuk lived west, downriver in Takunak village, but like wind he came off the land each time from a different direction. Iris squinted, myopically counting his dogs. Abe would be too generous, offering too much fish and caribou off our dogfood pile that needed to last until Breakup. Iris felt bad if our dogs got narrow and had to eat their shit. She was eight now, black hair too, and with blue eyes—but they were weak. She had gotten snowblind, the spring before last when she didn't wear her Army goggles on the sled back from the Dog Die Mountains. Someday, Abe meant to mailorder glasses.

I broke a chunk of thin ice off the inside of the window and sucked it. "How come they hitchin' 'em there?" The ice tasted like frozen breath and wet caribou hair.

Jerry peered over our shoulders. "You're talking Village English. Company isn't even off the ice." His voice was tight. People made him nervous. People made all of us nervous, except Iris. Our family lived out on the tundra. Abe had dug a pit, old Eskimo style, and built our igloo out of logs and poles, before I even grew a memory. Eskimos wouldn't live that way anymore, but for some reason we did. The single room was large, sixteen by sixteen, and buried to the eaves in the protective ground. In the back, over our beds, trees reached into the soil on the roof, and in the storms we heard their roots groaning, fighting for their lives out in the wind. Our walls and roof Abe insulated with blocks of pond sod. In the sod, mice and shrews rustled and fought and chewed and built their own homes, siphoning off warmth and mouthfuls of our food and winnowing it down to tiny black shits. Abe had escaped something, roads and rules possibly. Little things didn't bother him; Abe liked his meat dried, cooked, raw, or frozen. He didn't mind fly eggs on it—as long as the tiny maggots weren't moving.

Once we had a mom. She wasn't coming back. That's what Iris said she told Jerry the day she flew away. She had a twelve-string guitar and apparently liked music more than caribou and bears and a moss roof that leaked. She'd left us alone with none of those thousand warm things children with mothers don't count. Abe never talked about it. He never painted it. Her leaving was the back wall of my memory.

Iris scraped at the ice on the window with her fingernails inside her sleeve. Her bony elbows stuck out of her shirt. "They're chaining below the willows so the drifts won't bury his dogs." She flitted away to hang our parkas on pegs over the wood box, push *mukluks* and clothes tighter into the corners and under our bunks. Caribou hairs clung to all our clothes. She whisked hair and Abe's plane shavings and sawdust into dirt corners with a goose wing.

The north wind swept the open tundra and howled into the spruce on the bank where our sod home was buried in the permafrost. The skylight shuddered. Snow laced over the riverbank. The gray wool of moving snow hid the horizons. Overhead the frozen sky purpled with night, and above the wind and frantic branches clung watery stars. Out under the ice, the wide Kuguruk River flowed past the door, through the arctic part of Alaska that our mail-order schoolbooks called *barren icy desert*. That shamed me, that quick, throwaway description flung from the far rich East, printed in the black-and-white validation of a textbook. My protests only made Abe shrug.

The homemade Visqueen window shivered and whacked. The men chopped a frozen caribou for the dogs. The dogs ripped the skin off the meat and swallowed chunks. They guarded the skin, pinning it down with their claws. When the last bone and meat crystal was sniffed off the snow, they chewed the hair off the skin, ate the skin. Then they curled up to protect their faces and feet.

We heard the men trudging through the drift, up on the eave, down into the trench to the door. The snow squeaked as Abe shoveled, then pounded on the skin door. "Chop the ice along the bottom! Hear me?" Jerry scrambled for the hatchet. "Now get back!" Torn by wind and muffled by the skins, his voice came in mad. I hid behind the water barrel. Abe and Enuk surged in out of the swirling snow. Ovals of frozen skin and drifted-on ice whitened their faces. I stared, longing for frostbite, the scars of heroes. Abe pulled his hood back and his curly yellow hair sprang out; his turquoise eyes shone above his bearded face. "Windy."

"*Alappaa* tat wind." Enuk was a few inches shorter than Abe. His wide face was stiff, his goatee iced. The men grinned and shook snow off their parkas and whipped snow off their *mukluks*. They eased ice off their whiskers. Iris danced barefoot between them, smiling and scooping up snow to throw in the slop bucket. I wished I could move like her, light and smiling. Behind the water barrel I stood on the dirt and the damp mouse turds, excited at having company.

Enuk's gaze swung and pinned me down. "Hi Yellow-Hair! Getting big! How old?" His face was dark and cold-swollen.

Travelers all carried names for me, like the first-class mail. None were the ones I wanted. I inched out beside the blasting stove, my eyes down. "Five." It was hard to look at Enuk—or any traveler—in the eyes after seeing no people for weeks. It was hard to speak and not run and hide again. Enuk's frost-scarred face betrayed mysteries and romantic hard times that drew a five-year-old boy with swollen dreams. He was muscled in the forearms in the way of a skinned wolverine. He didn't eat most store-bought food, except Nabob boysenberry jam. When he was out hunting with his dog team and snowshoes he carried a can of jam. He'd chop it open and—after dried meat, or frozen meat, or cooked meat—around his campfire he'd suck on chips of frozen jam. He also carried his little moosehide pouch. Inside were secrets; once he'd let us hold gold nuggets, lumpy, the diameter of dimes. We handed them back and they disappeared in the folds of leather. The day I turned old I was going to be Enuk. Small discrepancies left footprints in my faith, such as the fact that he was Eskimo and I seemed to be staying *naluaġmiu*. But years lined up ahead, promising time for a cure.

Our last human visitor had been Woodrow Washington, a month before. Woodrow had a mustache and one tooth on the bottom, one on top. They didn't line up. Not near. His closest worldly ties were with the bottle, and that left him narrow and shaky. Though he hunted like everyone, his concentration and shots tended to stray. When he showed up, Jerry always hid the vanilla. Sober, he was nice and extra polite. "Tat Feathers boy, he suicide." Woodrow had brought news and stayed only long enough for warmed-up breakfast coffee. "He use double-barrel, backa their outhouse. You got fifty dollar? I sure need, alright?" Abe gave him the money. Abe leaned on his workbench and rubbed his ears. Harry Feathers was—or had been—a shambling teenager with blinky eyes and acne. He talked to Abe when Abe was snacking our sled dogs in front of Feathers's post office. It seemed as if maybe nobody else listened to Harry.

Woodrow had been disappointing company. We had only what money was in the Hills Bros can, but I blamed him more for not spending the night. And not bringing our first class.

Jerry served boiled caribou pelvis, in the cannibal pot, and pilot crackers, salmon berries, *qusrimmaq*, and the margarine that travelers had left—without the coloring added. Abe didn't allow something for nothing; yellow dye was poison; the color of food was nothing. We all carried sharp sheath knives forged out of old chisels and files and used them to cut at the fat and meat on the pelvis bone. Afterward, for a while I forgot my shameful blue eyes and yellow hair when Enuk leaned back on the bearskin couch. He hooked his thumb under his chin. His gaze slid away, beyond the leaning logs of the back wall. His pleasant face might have said *aarigaa taikuu*, but what he did say was, "Tat time it blowing same like tis, up Jesus Crick I kill my dowgs." I wiped my greasy hands on my pants and climbed onto his words as if they were a long team to pull me away to the land of strength and adultness.

He whittled a toothpick out of a splinter of kindling. He let the chips spin into the darkness under the table to mix with the caribou hairs and black mouse turds that carpeted our hewn floorboards. Eskimos weren't like Franklin and Crazy Joe or other *naluaġmius* who occasionally came upriver; Enuk's story was just to fill the night and he wasn't afraid to let silence happen between words. Time was one bend of open water to him and he hunched comfortable on the bank, enjoying what the current carried.

With the stick, Enuk picked his teeth. He had most of his teeth, he said, because he never liked "shigger" or "booze." I didn't know what booze meant and was scared to ask, vaguely convinced it might be something frilly that city women ordered out of the first half of the Sears catalog. I sat on the chopping-block stump and stared up into his face.

Abe threw a log into the stove. Sparks hissed red trails up around his shaggy head and flicked into darkness against the low ceiling poles. The poles around the five-gallon-can safety hung with dust tendrils from past smoke. Smoke and the oily odor of flame spread in the room. Abe filled a kettle, making hot water for tea. Mice and shrews rattled spoons on the kitchen boards.

"Wind blow plen'y hard tat night I get lost. Freeze you gonna like nothing." Enuk nodded at our bellied-in plastic sheeting windows behind his head, white and hard with drifted snow. A dwindling line of black night showed at the top. "My lead dowg, he been bite my dowgs. Al'uv'em tangle in'a willows. I leave 'em, let'um bury. I sleep in ta sled, on *qaatchiaq*. Tat night I never sleep much."

He chuckled and glared. "You listen, Yellow-Hair? Can't see only nothing too much wind." Enuk's bottom lip was thick and dark and permanently thrust out. I laughed, shy, and slapped my grubby red feet on the cold floor and tried to push out my too-thin lip.

In the corner on Abe's spruce-slab bed, Jerry and Iris lay on his caribou-hide *qaatchiaq* playing checkers. "Rabies," Jerry murmured. "His story's going to have rabies."

She pinched him. "It's your turn." A shrew ran on the floor. Enuk's black eyes followed it. He picked up the block of kindling and waited. Behind the wood box shrews whistled.

Jerry dragged a moose-antler checker over her pieces. The tops of his were marking-penned black, Iris's red. "'Kay then. King me." They wore corduroy pants. The corduroy ridges were eroded off the knees, thighs, and butts. Iris had two belt loops cinched together with twine to keep her too-big pants up. Abe didn't encourage us to change clothes more than once a month. More than twice a month put a burden on everybody. He wouldn't say no, but the house was low and one room—the only place to get out of the weather for miles—and the faintest disapproval could hang in the air.

The corner posts of Abe's bed were weather-silvered logs, the tops bowled from use as chiseling blocks and ashtrays. Above the foot of his bed, his workbench was messy with empty rifle brass, pieces of antler and bone, rusty bolts, wood chips, and abandoned paintings, the canvas and paper bent and ripped by his chisels and heavy planes. Abe Hawcly was a left-handed artist. He was also our dad. But we kids didn't know to call him anything generic or fatherly, only Abe. Travelers called him that. By the time we realized what normal people did, years had hardened into history. Calling him Dad felt worse than shaking hands.

"Enuk. Here." Abe slid a mug across the uneven boards to the middle of the table. He rubbed his sore knee and sat and rolled himself a cigarette with one hand. "Kids, don't worry about schoolwork tonight." He waved his match out. Two joints of his ring finger had been swallowed by a whaling winch in Barrow. His hands were thick and red, paint dried in the cracks. They carved faces on scraps of firewood and drew whole valleys lurking with animals on cardboard boxes.

"Ah, *taikuu*." Enuk slurped the scalding tea that would have seared a kid's mouth into mealy blisters. "My dowgs be funny tat night. Lotta growl."

Another night passed in his story.

"How old were you?" My words tumbled away like a fool's gloves bouncing downwind. Blood stung my cheeks. Interrupting seemed worse than pissing your pants in front of the village schoolhouse.

"Hush, Cutuk," Jerry said. Iris giggled and pretended to bite her nails, both hands at once. Abe had a piece of caribou-sinew string in his fingers, and he began pulling loops through loops. A lead dog formed. He turned the wick down on the lamp. Storytelling shadows stretched farther out from the moldy corners. The wind gusted. The door was half buried. I pictured those yellow metal nuggets. Wondered if they were in Enuk's pocket, and how young he'd been when he found the first one.

Enuk sipped. "Cutuk, you gonna be hunter?" He flicked my arm, unaware of the stinging power of his thick fingers. Tears flooded my eyes. "Tat's good. You got one 'hol life. Tat's plen'y. Gonna you be tired if you alla time try hurry."

Abe smiled. He pulled a string. In his hands the lead dog vanished.

I shrank low and twisted broken threads in the knees of my pants. At least he'd used my Eskimo name. Clayton was my white name—a mushy gray one. I had taught my ears not to hear it, until people learned it didn't work. *Cutuk* meant fall. Not fall when the berries were ripe and the bears were fat enough—fall like dropping down out of a tree without planning. Except in Iñupiaq it was spelled *katak;* but none of us or Enuk had known the spelling. The way Iris sounded it out had stuck. It was no first-pick name, misspelled and not even easy to say, but Enuk bestowed it on me before I could campaign for a better one. So I justified it into greatness by pretending it had special come-from-behind potential.

"Night time, still snowing I hear lotta growl. First light gonna I dig t'em dowgs. Right there, blood in'a snow. When I fin' my leader, tat one try bite." He ran his fingers through his shoulder-length hair. One of his ears had a hole up near the top as small as a goose's windpipe. Gray hairs curled through. "Five dowgs. Good size dowg team back then time, not much food on ta country. Not like now gonna t'em white guy dowgfed in'a bag. I shoot three before it turn dark. Right there I know tat gonna be real bat. Tat was nineteen . . . nineteen thirty-something, before Kennedy and Hitler fight. Could be I'm twenty-five tat time.

"Cutuk. Peoples got not much shells tat time not like now. I got jus' only one shell. I go 'head shoot t'em last two dowgs."

The glory of Enuk's words melted under a warm spell of reality. I pictured my pup Ponoc, grinning his sloppy puppy grin—he collapsed under the boom of a rifle. Blood sprayed Ponoc's silver face and ran out a red hole, steaming into the snow like the last rabid fox Abe had shot. The corners of my throat grew wet and needed to swallow.

"How many nights I wait. Even I make spear from spruce. Then I see hills. Right there," Enuk shrugged, grinned, and gestured, his huge fingers cutting straight across his other palm, angling up, "I take off on snowshoe. No dowgs. Could be they already let me gonna crazy. I see wolv'reen. Right there. Real close. No ammo in ta pocket. Long time ago gonna plenty hard time we always have. No ammo in ta pocket."

Enuk sat for a minute, then shuffled over and dumped his coffee grounds in the slop bucket by the door. The grounds plopped on the dishwater frozen in the bottom. He reached up to a peg behind the stove for his parka and *mukluks*. Reminiscence no longer softened his face; the telling was over—the story, like old stories I'd heard at the Wolfgloves' house in Takunak, started in the middle and ended somewhere along where the storyteller grew tired.

Enuk shook water droplets out of his wolf ruff. I tried to contemplate the way I knew grown-ups did, to poke at his words with sharpened thoughts. I wondered if he'd restart the tale the following night—or in a year. I felt I should comprehend something profound about shooting dogs, but I couldn't get past thinking that the books on the shelf over Abe's bunk, the soapy dishwater and coffee grounds in the slop bucket—and our team sleeping buried down by the river—all were blatant proof that we owned too much, lived too comfortably. I needed tougher times to turn me Eskimo.

Our low door was built from split spruce poles, insulated with thick fall-time bull caribou hides nailed skin-out on both sides. The hinges were *ugruk* skin. "Better chop the bottom loose," Abe suggested. He reached in the wood box for the hatchet. Enuk pounded with his big fists until the condensation ice crumbled. He yanked inward. The wind and swirling snow roared, a hole into a howling world; the wind shuddered the lamp flame. A smooth waist-high white mirror of the door stood in his way. Chilled air rolled across the floor. Enuk leapt up and vanished over the drift into the night gusts.

Chunks of snow tumbled down. I had a flash of memory—summertime, green leaves. Enuk, and a strange man. The man had combed hair. And a space between his teeth that he smiled around and showed us how to spit through. He cradled an animal in calico cloth. *A baby porcupine!* The man seemed to be Enuk's son Melt. But how could that be? Melt was mean and smiled like indigestion. Mixed up behind my eyes was that baby porcupine dead in a cotton flour sack, a ski plane taking off, and me crying, unable to convey the tragedy of my blue Lego spiraling to the bottom of the outhouse. These memories seemed valuable, as unreplaceable as that Lego had been, but the roar of the wind sucked my concentration into the dark.

Abe scratched snow aside trying to close the door again. "Need to use the pot?" he asked.

Iris did and I did, and we hurried. There was nowhere to hide—it was how Abe had first explained the word *vulnerable*—with Enuk coming back momentarily. Breaking trail to the outhouse would have involved digging out the door, getting all dressed in overpants and parkas, finding our way, digging out the outhouse door, trying not to crap on our heavy clothes. Then tracking snow in the house; wet furs; trying to get the door closed again; firing up the stove. Abe didn't encourage any of it. Embarrassment counted as nothing. It mattered to him as much as the color of margarine.

Abe slammed the door, and again. His hair and the collar of his flannel shirt were floured with snow. He grinned. "Glad I don't have to go to work in the morning."

"What he gonna do?" I asked, instantly ashamed of the excess of Village English in my voice.

"Check the dogs." Jerry clacked checkers together, matter-of-factly. "Abe, can an animal catch rabies and get those symptoms in one night?"

"Maybe not. That virus takes a couple weeks to infect your nervous system." Abe picked up the book he'd been reading that morning—*The Prophet*—turned it over, peered at the spine thoughtfully, and put it back down. Abe eyed his thumbnail and bit it. "I had to shoot a rabid moose that charged in the team, long time ago, in the Helpmejack Hills."

"Does a person forget their friends?"

Iris crossed her eyes. "Jerry'll never skin another fox's face."

"I bonked that rabid one that scared you," Jerry growled, "chewing the door. You were going to stay inside until Abe got home."

A second rabid fox had screamed insults to our sled dogs and snarled in the window at his warped reflection. After that incident my imagination encountered them all winter, during the bad-mouse year, foam dripping off their narrow black lips. Nights mice and shrews streaked across my pillow and gnawed at my caribou-hide *qaatchiaq*, and I lay awake doubly frightened that something as invisible and unaccredited as mouse spit could carry such consequences.

Jerry chewed his cheeks, cataloging Abe's answers. Jerry remembered poems, songs, definitions. I believed that he wanted to be the healthiest, the smartest, and the best, in case our mom came back. He was all that, and had black hair—things that I thought should come to him with smiles.

Iris's eyes flashed. "Guys, I say that's what happened six years ago. Abe caught rabies! He thought he was walking to the store in Chicago to buy tobacco, next thing he noticed a new baby, lots of snow, and us kids gathering *masru*. He's maybe still got 'em."

I looked down, ashamed; I hadn't seen a city. Jerry didn't smile. "You win." He rolled up the birchbark checkerboard, with every other square peeled to make the board pale white and brown. Under the dull roar of the wind, in the leftover silence, I had a sudden flash—Jerry was thinking our mother may have caught rabies.

A gust shook the stovepipe. Abe shut the draft on the fire, lit a candle to place by his bed. He pissed in the slop bucket. He rubbed his knee. "One of you kids lay Enuk out a *qaatchiaq*." Steam rose out of the bucket. I stood up, rattling the lamp on the table, disturbing the shadows.

The door burst open. Enuk jumped in. A thought startled me: *Would a person tell if he had been bitten?* People might run away. Someone would stand across a valley and sink a bullet in your head. What if a dog bit me and died later; would I have the courage to tell? Enuk rubbed his hands together close to the stove. He grabbed my neck from behind. He laughed near my ear. "What you're laying out *qaatchiaq* for, Yellow-Hair? You gonna *nallaq*? Nice night, le's go hunt!"

TWO DAYS PASSED. The wind fell away and Abe shoveled out the door entrance. We climbed up the snow trench into a motionless thirty-below day. The old marred snowdrifts had been repaired and repainted. A scalloped white land stretched to the riverbanks, across the tundra to the orange horizon. The cold sky seemed crystalline, dark blue glass, in reach and ready for one thrown iceball to bring it shattering down.

In our parkas and *mukluks,* we kids ran back and forth examining the new high drifts and sliding off cornices. Abe helped Enuk find his sled and they dug at it. The snow was hard, and it chipped and squeaked under their shovels. They iced the sled runners with a strip of brown bear fur dipped in a pan of warm water. They were careful not to get any water on their *mukluks.* Iris and I stood together while Abe and Enuk harnessed his seven dogs. Jerry stayed in the safety of our dog yard. He mistrusted strange dogs. Often they snapped at him, though he never lost his temper and clubbed dogs with shovels or rifle stocks the way other people did. I vowed when I grew big enough to handle huskies I wouldn't miss a chance to help a traveler hitch up.

Enuk stood on the runners with one foot on the steel claw brake, his hands in his wolf mittens holding the toprails. The dogs lunged against their towlines, yelping to run. Our dogs barked and scratched the snow. There was little room left in the yowling for last words with company. Enuk said something and nodded north. We stepped close. "Next time, Cutuk? Be good on ta country." He swept away, furrowing snow to dust with his brake.

We hurried out on the river to watch him become a black speck and disappear far off downriver. Dark spruce lined the far riverbank. In my mind I could see the village and barking dogs and the people there, and Enuk's grandchildren, Stevie and Dawna Wolfglove, with their mother, Janet, to kiss them and make caribou soup with yellow seashell noodles.

Jerry kicked snow. Abe put his hand awkwardly across my shoulder. I flinched. Abe and Jerry and I didn't touch—unless it was rough, tickling or king-of-the-hill wrestling over a cornice. Abe turned toward the house. "If the trail stays firm . . ." He wiped his nose. He liked us to be happy, and we usually stayed that way for him. "Maybe next month if the trail's okay, we'll go to town? Nice to have a traveler, wasn't it?"

I tried to ignore the splinters of comfort at the thought of people. I was going to be a hunter; the toughest hunters traveled alone. I kept my mouth shut and broke the tiny tears off my eyelashes. Abe hated whining. He believed that excess comfort was damaging, that whininess was contagious. Stern lines would gather at his mouth and grooves would form above the bridge of his nose. "You an Everything-Wanter now?" he'd growl. And then I would wish for my mother with her black hair and flashing eyes.

But the truth that made me squirm?—she'd left me few memories. All I was certain I remembered of her was that man January Thompson, a fat Outsider, a wolf bounty hunter with a blue and gold airplane on skis, bouncing on the ice, lurching into the sky. I pretended a memory but in the tiny honest slice of my mind I knew I had cannibalized whole hindquarters off Jerry's stories. Jerry was almost five when they left the lower States. "We came in Abe's blue truck," he'd say. "The license plates said North to the Future. You were almost three, Iris. 'Member?" That was all. But it stung. That history didn't include me. The Hawcly past before the Arctic was another planet, a sunny place of Sunkist lemons and green grapes drying into raisins—instead of meat drying into meat—a place that I'd never walked and couldn't put roots to even in memory.

Jerry once told how my mother had a yellow car, with a built-in radio. I wondered why so many of the stories had cars. Did all the cars have radios? When he related these things, Iris and I squeezed together on the bearskin couch, curious about that stranger down in the States who wasn't coming back, but somewhere still lived. It was all strange, but seemed normal, too, the way she was a fairy tale that kept fogging over, while Enuk, even vanished downriver, stood in my life as sharp as a raven in the blue sky.

Abe and Jerry and Iris tramped up to the house. I lingered in the dog yard, playing with Ponoc and the others. They stared downriver, howling occasionally, forlorn and dejected about not following Enuk's team. It was a chance to play with the dogs without getting scratched and licked off my feet. I ruined it by slipping Ponoc a stray chip of frozen moose off the snow near the dogfood pile. Sled dog brains kept to narrow, well-packed trails of thought, and food lay at the end of all the trails. They howled and gestured with their noses, wagging and protesting the inequitable feeding. My heart grew huge for them, my happy-go-lucky friends, always delighted to see me, prancing and tripping over their chains. How endless the land would be without their companionship.

Suddenly I saw the dog yard empty, the strewn gnawed bones, the yellow pissicles and the round melted sleeping circles, all drifted white; only the chain stakes remained stabbing out of the snow like gray grave markers. A mouse ran out from under the meat pile, dropped a turd, and disappeared down a round hole. I backed away from the lunging dogs. Maybe they were already infected.

Ponoc bit a wad of caribou hair off his stomped yard and tossed it playfully in the air. His pink tongue flicked between his teeth, his mouth muddy with hairs. I spat between my teeth. Maybe in my huge future I would have to shoot a whole team of my own dogs. The thought of the years ahead flooded hot in my chest. I raced up to our igloo, to my brother and sister and father, there eating *paniqtuq* and seal oil and red jam. Food that would make me Eskimo.

TWO

WHEN I WAS TEN, on a night shortly after the sun returned, a pack of wolves raided our peoplefood pile. Along the bank to the east, beyond our pole cache, the wolves worked over it all except one frozen caribou—a skinny carcass that we too were leaving till last. Our dogs howled and barked in the dark. By first light at ten o'clock the pack had vanished, leaving a pawed circle of meat dust and cracked bone chips in the reddened snow, and tracks leading in too many directions onto the windblown tundra.

The faint scent of clean dog hung in the clawed holes. Abe hunched down, kneading his yellow beard, happier than if he'd discovered gold in the gravel at the bottom of our water hole. Snow clung behind his knees to the creases of his overpants. He examined a wolf turd, long and gray with twisted caribou hair. In his hand the shit looked as capable of magic as a tube of Van Gogh Basic White.

"Should have come out to check the barking," he muttered. "Like to have the scene in my mind." He stood and stared off north, spraying a square of his powerful imagination against the sky. He often leaned against trees, absorbed in the pastel glow of evening. "Been years since the wolves took much from us. Usually too wary. Hope we don't get people-company next couple days."

A raven flew overhead, heading north. We eyed it.

"We're low on meat." Jerry melted his cheek with a bare hand. Black hairs were sprouting on his jaw. I itched with distress when his hand wandered to the icicles on his downy mustache. "Wolves're always coming by. Why's it a big deal?"

I kicked the snow ground, embarrassed for both of them. I was ten years old, behind schedule on shooting my first wolf. "Let's go after 'em."

Abe didn't hear.

For the next two weeks Abe read on his bed. Suddenly his book would drop and he'd rise, practically walking through us to his easel. He worked in oil. The turpentine fumes left us breathless and lightheaded. Tubes of his paint had frosted to the wall under his workbench, and he swore. He glared over his shoulder at the dim light, paced, peered, his mouth puckered. At night he tossed on his *qaatchiaq*, lit candles, rose to sigh at his work, and one night he tore the canvas free and stuffed it in the stove.

The second painting became a staked dog team, witnessing a pack of wolves borrowing caribou. Each dog's face held a different expression. Some merely whined, sitting, suffering the thievery patiently. Others stood on their sinewy back legs, lunging against their chains. Their mouths were outraged barks. None of the dogs were of our team—they lived in Abe's past or in his imagination. A black dog closest to the wolves jumped so hard his chain flipped him upside down, and Abe painted his curled claws, hinted at the wiry gray hair between his toes. Nine wolves leaned over the meat, cracking bones in their triangle molars. The painting had a dark silvery feel, a feeling that the wolves were friends, with each other, and with the night. I thought Abe's paintings of wolves were better than his other paintings.

During those weeks the fire in the barrel stove often burnt down to ashes. The cold waiting beyond the door and walls hurried in. Our last caribou shrank to a backbone, neck, and one shoulder. We peeled the back sinew—for thread for sewing—and made frymeat out of the backstraps before boiling the backbones. Abe didn't care what was for dinner. He sipped his tea and answered some of our questions, not all of them. We asked few. He was in a place for artists; we didn't know the language. We kids simply knew Abe wouldn't hunt and kill meat until something changed. We were allowed the few .22 cartridges to shoot ptarmigan and rabbits and foxes—if we could find any—but not allowed to take the big rifle or its ammo.

Jerry and Iris and I sling-shot mice gnawing in the food shelves, and split wood and chipped five feet through the river ice and hauled buckets of water. We heated water on the stove and scrubbed our gray laundry in the galvanized washtub, mopping with a shirt at water that came out the leaks. The two windows steamed up. The black water we hauled outside and poured down the slop hole. Steam rose and the ice popped and crackled. The second week we splurged and hauled extra buckets and took baths in the washtub. It was my turn to use the water first. That meant I had less to kneel in because we kept the last kettle boiling to add as the tub cooled. Abe squatted in the tub last. His fingers and forearms were smeared with paint. The surface of the water grew oily. He stood naked by the fire and dried.

We studied our schoolbooks, administered exams to each other: spelling, phonics, math, English, biology. With his hands floury from making bread, Jerry drew circles, explaining cells and cell walls, mitochondria and osmosis. On the bearskin couch we read books out of the library box and flipped through *Harper's* magazines, scrutinizing glossy pictures advertising giraffe-legged women smoking cigarettes and sleek gray automobiles called Cougars.

"Someday I'm going to have a Chevy truck," Jerry declared.

"Don't be boring!" Iris bent his fingers off the page. "I'll have an ocean-blue convertible. And smoke Virginia Slims!"

"You never seen ocean. Except in Crotch Spit. That was frozen. It doesn't count."

I kept quiet. I was the one born in the native hospital in Crotch Spit. I'd never seen a real car—only the dead red jeep where kids in Takunak played tag and bounced on the burnt seat springs.

We put the magazines up and scraped caribou hides with the *ichuun*. You always scraped with another hide underneath, to pad the skin and keep the *ichuun* from tearing holes. We then spread on sourdough, folded the hides skin to skin, put them under Abe's *qaatchiaq* to let the sourdough soak in overnight, and later dried and scraped the skins again to finish tanning. The windows dripped condensation. Outside in the twilight, big snowflakes fell. We hauled in wood and kicked the door shut tight and stuffed a jacket at the base of the door to keep cold air out. Abe lit the Coleman light. He pumped it and hung the hissing lamp from a nail on the ridgepole. Shadows twirled and came to rest. We got out an early-fall hide that Iris had sourdoughed earlier. The hair was short, thinner, and soft. We scraped it and worked the skin in our hands until it was tanned and white. Jerry traced new insoles for all of our soft-bottom and *ugruk*-bottom *mukluks*. Iris cut them with Abe's razor. In silence we sewed ourselves caribou socks, then swept up the hairs. Abe hunched over his easel, silent. Caribou hairs clung to his sweater. Outside, the snow piled up.

"Should I boil meat?" Jerry murmured. Iris and I soundlessly raised our eyebrows, *yes* in Iñupiaq.

Jerry put leg bones and water into the cannibal pot. While it simmered, we used Abe's powder scale to measure 4832 gunpowder, and reload .30-06 ammo with the Lee Loader. Iris sighted down a completed cartridge. "Boy, fresh moose heart would be good, wouldn't it?" She covered a grin, swinging her gaze to Abe.

"Look!" Jerry said. "You forgot to prime this one. You're *wasting!*" We glanced at Abe. *Wasting* was the baddest word in our family. Jerry bit the lead. He pried the bullet out and dumped the gunpowder back in the scale. The bullet copper was dented but would still be good enough for finishing off a caribou if it was too alive to get with a knife. "Here! You're not supposed to get the inside of the primer sweaty, 'kay?"

I crossed my arms, checked my muscle. Actually, we had plenty of food: seasonings and sugar and fifty-pound sacks of flour, powdered milk, rice, and beans. Jars of rendered bear fat for shortening. Most of a quart of vanilla. And there was a keg of salted salmon bellies, and piles of *quaq* in the dogfood cache. We could eat that. It was good with seal oil, and in the seal oil were our prized *masru* and pink *tinnik* berries. We wouldn't go hungry.

IN LATE JANUARY, Abe took his rifle off the peg behind the stove. We kids scattered for overpants and parkas. He blew dust off the bolt and scraped his thumbnail along the stock where frozen snot or dog spit had dried. His hair and beard were unruly. His turquiose eyes squinted with a grin. "Iris? Feel like coming along?" He nodded and laid the gun on the floor across his parka and mittens. Jerry and I slumped. Abe boiled water, filled his thermos, and slid it into the caribou-hide insulating tube. We fidgeted, out of the way, while Iris got bundled and ready.

They hitched the team and went east, hunting for an acquiescent moose to contribute both dog food and people food. The caribou herds were far south in their wintering grounds. It was cold—cold enough that the kerosene had jelled and wouldn't pour into the lamp—and the dogs did not lunge to run.

Afterward, Jerry wandered back inside to rewrite a letter to his pen pal in New Zealand, romancing her long distance. Mice rustled and scurried on the floor. His pen rustled the paper. He liked to write letters and poems. And his diary, too. I figured he was faking talent. We kids didn't say it—that would be bad luck—but we hoped we'd inherited a little of Abe's specialness. We grew up watching our dad; for months on end he was the only one to watch, to teach us about our world, and tidbits of the city world. We watched his left hand, the one with good genes, hoping to recognize the first twinges in our own hands.

I hauled armloads of wood. Jerry went out to cut meat for dinner. The house was quiet. The table and chairs and floorboards seemed gray, dingy, and bare with no one about. Curiosity pushed my honor aside—I slid a thumbnail in where the edges of his diary's pages were smudged. My eyes scrambled over the words . . . *only you who watched mothers fly away, after the cold will be my sisters and brothers* . . . I dropped the book. Quickly I placed it back on the table. I laced my *mukluks.* Fumbled into my parka. Hurried out behind the woodpile and pretended to scan the tundra for life.

Jerry hung the bow saw on a nail. His *mukluks* squeaked on the snow. He carried sawed caribou ribs inside. They were skinny ribs, thin and with signs of wolf lips and shrew turds on them. He came outside, no jacket. His brown eyes looked rolled back like a village dog held down by its last six inches of iced-in chain. "That's mine." There was red meat sawdust between his fingers. Jerry's big square fist swung. My face seemed to crack open. Behind a snowbank I leaned over. Blood hung in coagulating red icicles off my nose. I tried to forget the words in the diary. And the jealousy that Jerry might have what I didn't—a share of Abe's gift.

Iris, too, had something. Something completely different, though. It wasn't something you could talk about. One spring a white-lady social worker skied down the river towing a plastic sled. She was from the distant big city of Anchorage, and how she got upriver we didn't know. She wore bright blue windbreakers and windpants, and had a black backpack, an orange aluminum foil space blanket, and dehydrated space meals and Swiss chocolate bars. She was very beautiful and had heaps of wavy brown hair and didn't seem to get cold. Her name was Wax Tiera, and we adored her though we suspected her of being an alien. The odd thing was, the day before she showed, Iris cleaned the entire igloo in a way we had never before done. She swept away caribou hair and dust, washed the floorboards with steaming soapy rags, organized Abe's paints, used the splitting maul to knock down the spike that froze in the outhouse. She had scrubbed all day, washing the outsides of mason jars, laughing excitedly, squinting nearsightedly into corners.

Another time, two falls ago, before Freezeup, Napoleon Skuq Sr. came upriver in his spruce-plank boat. Nippy had a big eighteen-horse Evinrude. He was proud of it. He boated up every couple of years, his fall trip. Sometimes he brought a cousin, sometimes his sons, Junior and Caleb. Nippy wore a leather skullcap. His eyes around the edges were bumpy and yellow. He arrived drunk, spent the evening telling Abe how to hunt and trap, and traveled on in the morning. Within a few days he came back downriver, his prop dinged, the boat weaving slow in the first ice pans. Caribou legs poked over the gunnels of his boat. He spent the night again, and this time Nippy's hands had a tremor as he pulled his Bible out of a cotton sugar sack. He spread it soft and sagging on his thigh and under the wick lamp preached about Jesus and sin and a bush that you couldn't put out from burning. Then he told Abe some more of his hunting stories. He bragged about his son graduating from Mt. Edgecombe boarding school in Sitka.

"I thought your son died," Iris said softly. Nippy swung his wet eyes on her. "Maybe you thinking somebody else." He was sitting on the bear-skin couch, on the shoulder end, where the hair had worn the least. He glanced into the soup pot, served himself the tenderest fat short brisket bones. He scooped a plop of cranberry sauce on his plate. Iris stood up from the Standard Oil Co. wooden Blazo-box seat that pinched your butt and squeaked. She scraped her gnawed bones into the dog pot and went to fill kettles on the stove to heat water for dishes. After Freezeup, when the ice was thick enough to travel, word came that Caleb Skuq had been stabbed behind a bar in Juneau and died. No one told the whole story in front of Iris, though everyone in Takunak knew it, and they glanced at her differently.

ABE HAD LEFT the unruly puppies, Plato and Figment. They were interested in my bloody nose. I hung around the dog yard, chopping out pissed-in chains and the third-of-a-drum dogfood cooker. The top was sharp and rusty where Abe had cut it with a sledgehammer and his piece of sharpened spring-steel. I ignored the bite of the cold and wandered in a fantasy of myself shooting a charging moose. Jerry's pen pal wish-girl lay shrieking in the trail. Broken leg. He couldn't get to her. Calmly I shot. The girl blurred into the dark-haired woman on the front of the JCPenney catalog and had no difficulty jumping up to kiss me repeatedly.

Suddenly Plato sniffed. She barked, and with a worried tail stared north. A flock of redpolls shrilled up in the birch branches and vanished in a gust of small wings. Off the high tundra west of Jesus Creek slid the elongated black speck of a dog team. *Travelers!* It didn't matter who, if we knew them or not, what they looked like. Or how much they ate, snored, farted—even if they spoke only Iñupiaq, or Russian. Only that they would talk and be *company!*

The speck separated into seven dogs and came across what we called Outnorth Lake or Luck-a-Luck Lake or The Lake, depending on the season and the conversation. Enuk mushed up the knife ridge that formed a narrow bank separating the lake from the Kuguruk River. He kicked his snow hook into an ice-hard drift. His dogs flopped down, panting. I sank my hatchet into a dog stake and ran to his sled, gripping the toprails.

"Hi, Enuk!"

He gazed stiffly out of the frosty silver circle of his wolf ruff. He broke ice off his gray mustache and eyelashes. Then he grinned, as if trying earlier might have pulled hairs. He smelled of campfire and coffee. He took off his rifle and hung it carefully off the handlebar of his sled. His gaze flicked over the tracks left by Abe's team. I stayed respectfully silent while he rubbed the frosted faces of his dogs and bit the iceballs off from between their hairy toes. It was annoying and white to talk too much or ask questions, especially when a traveler first arrived. Shaking hands, also, was a sign of being an Outsider. Enuk wore new tan store-bought overpants. On one hem was the red chalk of frozen blood. His sled tarp was lashed down, too tight for me to poke under without being nosy. Sled tarps had always held secrets, brought packages, presents, fresh meat, store-bought cookies. Old and ratty didn't matter—sled tarps were the biggest wrapping paper of all.

"When you leavin', Enuk?" I asked finally.

"Pretty quick."

"How come? Spend the night."

Staring north, he pursed his lips thoughtfully. He nodded. "Maybe gonna I spen'a night."

"I wish!"

"If I know, I woulda' bring you-fellas' first class." His squinted eyes roamed the snow-covered river, willows, and tundra, probing for the tiniest movement of life. He swung back to me. "Anytime they could get you." I eyed his sled. What was he talking about? Bears? Spirits? "If they want you they get you, anytime." He noticed my eyes on his tarp. "Ha ha, Yellow-Hair!" He kicked a fast *mukluk* at me.

He unlashed the tarp and spread it open. "I get lucky." He nodded toward the mountains. "T'em wolves kill moose young one. Not too far." I didn't follow his eyes. The wolf was silver-gray and huge, twice the size of Enuk's huskies, its hair long and black-tipped. I petted the animal in wonder, feeling splinters of blood frozen deep in the fur. I recognized the clean dog odor. Broken ribs shone in a large bullet hole in the side of his chest. I saw the wolf stumbling, hearing his own bones grating, panting against death pouring into his lungs.

I shook my head to dislodge the pictures.

"Coulda have more, alright. Only thing, smart one in'a bunch. He let t'em others run." He looped his stringed overmitts behind his back. Barehanded, wary of the blood, he kneaded the wolf's thin lower legs. "*Alappaa!* Freeze. Hard gonna for tat way ta skin. I bring tis wolf inside. Wait for your old man."

ABE AND IRIS RETURNED without meat. We ate the skinny ribs Jerry had boiled. Skinny meat was a sign of a poor provider, but Enuk ate with relish. Afterward he skinned the wolf. When he finished, he folded the skin fur-out. On our floor the naked wolf grinned permanently in the weak lamplight, his teeth and tendons white against dark red muscles. The stomach was hard, and fetid smells were beginning to come out. Enuk had only a little blood on his fingertips. There was a slit in the wolf's throat. "Let his spirit go other wolf," Enuk said. "Gotta respect."

"Do you like wolves?" I asked.

Iris and Jerry peered over the tops of their schoolbooks. Their papers were spread on the wooden Blazo boxes that we made into desks—and also cupboards, shelves, seats, muskrat-stretching boards, and more.

"They got fam'ly. Smart. Careful. I like 'em best than all'a animal.

Your dad know. He make tat good picture. Gonna ta white ladies buy tat one more than any kinda wolf skin. Ha! Ha!" Enuk opened the door. Cold-air fog rolled in. He flung the carcass into the dark. The furless animal slapped on the packed snow out under the chipped eyes of the stars. In the dog yard one of Enuk's dogs barked nervously at the thump in the still night. An echo rolled back lonesome from the timber across the river, and the dog challenged it with three quick barks.

"Yep, Yellow-Hair. Tomorrow you take your old man." Enuk grinned. "Go out back way, hunt moose." His eyes flicked to his knife, and I wondered what else he was thinking about and whether it was killing more wolves.

"We might." Abe smiled and looked shy about something. He wiped blood drips off the floor with a holey sock rag. His cheeks and nose burnt with red ovals from frostbite that day on the trail. Iris's face was marked red, too. They hadn't seen the right moose—a barren cow, a moose that would have fat meat and its hide fair for snowshoe *babiche*, sled washers, cold-weather *mukluk* bottoms.

"We might look again tomorrow." Abe folded the cardboard he had laid out for Enuk to work on. "You do a real nice job, Enuk." Abe sounded as if he would have an impossible time skinning even a caribou legging. Abe had taught me to skin and dry foxes, perfectly—better than any fox I'd ever seen skinned in Takunak. Their pelt was papery, difficult not to tear with the sharpened metal tube *ichuun*, difficult not to tear when turning the dried skin back fur-out. And though we often used only the thick warm fur for mittens, he made me skin to save the toenails, tail, eyelashes—out of respect to the animal whose life we'd taken.

Often, Abe helped me make birch and *babiche* snowshoes that few in Takunak remembered how to make. Or one time he helped write a letter to the substitute president, Gerald Ford. But he would never pick up an axe like he was tough. Never talk or hold a gun that way. Never brag, "I'm goin' after bear." Any bear we got walked up on its own and still Abe didn't want to kill it. Around travelers, Abe's modesty trimmed off too much of the fat. Apparently things started getting out of balance back with his dad. Tom Hawcly had been a sport hunter, a menacing species to have in any food chain. He left our grandmother in Chicago and roamed off to Barrow to be a pilot, the owner of two Super Cub airplanes, and a guide for polar bear hunters. The story was exciting enough, and romantic—up to the part where they found him smeared dead on the sea ice. People along the Kuguruk River hated sport hunters and guides as much as they did schoolteachers. Frequently they were one and the same. I was thankful that Barrow was a long way north. And that people thought of white people as having no relatives.

Enuk finished skinning out the paws. He talked of shooting his first wolf when he was ten. His dad had taken him to check a *tiktaaliq* fish trap. A lone wolf was there on the ice gnawing yesterday's frozen fish blood. The wind was behind the wolf. Enuk's father handed him the rifle.

I listened to Enuk's low voice and lusted to gun down a whole pack, to stockpile prestige. Somehow, I had to learn to stop worrying about wolf pain. Abe had to stop molding me into an unhero.

Abe slapped his pants, fumbled in his big pockets for tobacco and papers. He glanced over the table and workbench, and eventually gave up. To Iris he said, "Otter, boil water? When Enuk's washed up maybe you'll make a splash of tea?"

Iris set her math book on the wood box. She smiled at Enuk. The frostbite was pretty across her cheeks and nose. "Nine times eight, Cutuk!"

"Huh? Seventy-two."

"Twenty-one times eleven."

"Two hundred and thirty-one." My thoughts softened; I pictured happy otters playing, sliding along day-old ice, stopping to nuzzle each other.

Iris dripped the dipper on my head as she danced barefoot toward the water barrel. She peered close, to focus out of her weak eyes. "Cutuk? Why, Yellow-Hair Boy, you looked mad as a wolverine in a trap."

I flicked her leg. The religious poster—the one Abe tacked out in the outhouse, the one the Gospel Trippers had left when they passed through last winter—said a family was supposed to say it: "I love you,"

I whispered, at my hands, too softly, the only time in my life. Iris, with her black hair and surprising blue eyes, full of smiles where I had storms, she never heard. She was in her own thoughts. What were they? I should have asked, but kissing, saying the word *love,* and talking about feelings weren't what Hawclys did, and I was embarrassed and went outside for a few minutes in the dark, to stand barefoot on the snow and listen to the night beside the naked wolf.

THE STOVE DRAFT FLICKERED orange lights on the peeled poles of the ceiling. The orange melted through my eyelids to clutter my dreams with flames. Pitch smoldered, sweet and resinous on top of the stove.

Enuk lay on his *qaatchiaq*. His legs stretched out of sight under the table. Iris's black hair curled across my face. I brushed it aside and pulled our pants and shirts under the covers to warm them. I gripped the corner of the sleeping bag tight to keep the chilly morning out. For years Abe had promised to order me my own sleeping bag. Like Iris's glasses, it was another thing we'd have to go out into the world and find for ourselves. Iris took up more room this winter. She was bigger. Her breasts were growing, disconcerting to me when I accidentally brushed them.

"You elbowed me really hard in the eye last night." Her voice was sleepy. She wore one of Abe's flannel shirts, faded and thin. She smelled of flannel, candle wax, and soft skin.

Jerry's bed was head to head with ours along the back wall. I wasn't sure if he was awake on his caribou skin. It was dark in the room, except for firelight. Abe banged the coffeepot on a round of firewood. He swore softly when a chunk of frozen grounds crumbled on the floor. He toed the grounds against the wood box. Iris leaned her chin on her wrists. "Daddy slobbest. What will he do without us?" Her words made me shiver. Firelight glowed on his broad white chest and arms. He crumpled a painting, stuffed it into the stove. The stiff paper caught and flared. For cash Abe made furniture to sell in Takunak, and occasionally he mailed one of his paintings to Anchorage. Never his best. I lay fantasizing; he was an outlaw artist with a notorious past, his name would be legend in the places I traveled.

His bare feet rasped on the cold boards. Outside darkness painted the windows black. The roar of the stove grew, and frost in the safety dripped and hissed. Kettles began to whine. Enuk yawned and rose. He wore jeans and a white T-shirt. His body was stout and muscular. The sun had never seen it, and his skin was smooth and pearly brown as a young man's, except on his thick hands and face where weather and time had stained their stories.

They sipped coffee. Abe lit the lamp. He took the cannibal pot off the stove and put it on the table. We knifed out hot meat and gravy and ate it with bread and the frozen sliced canned jam that Enuk brought. A fly buzzed, one wing frozen to the ice on the inside of the window. The door was frosty around the edges. It was still dark outside. The dogs howled.

Enuk put down his cup. "Today I get old."

Iris pattered her fingers on his shoulder, as unconcerned as if he were a shelf. "Are you a hundred?"

I watched her hand. Jerry was watching, too.

"Jan'wary twenty-one, nineteen hunnert an five. How many tat gonna? Seventy?"

"Seventy-one!"

"Not so many. I still hunt best than my son."

"My birthday was the fourth," I said, thinking how perfect it would have been to be born seventeen days later, on Enuk's birthday. "We're not sure we celebrated on the right day. That day was warm and it snowed sticky; you remember, was that the fourth?" I trailed off. The mouthful of numbers felt white.

Enuk ignored me and retrieved his frozen wolf skin from outside the door. Cold-air fog rolled in. He eyed the skin for shrew chews. His leather pouch lay beside his mug on the table. It had sounded heavy when he plunked it down. "You fellas have tat." He nodded at the can of jam. "Cutuk, t'em mooses waiting. You gonna hunt?"

I studied Abe's face for a sign.

"It could be cold." He sharpened his knife, three flicks on the pot, three flicks back. "Real cold."

"I'll put my face under the tarp when it freezes."

"Tat a boy!" Enuk said.

DOWN AT THE RIVER it was minus a lot. My nose kept freezing shut on one side. The dogs uncurled and shook frost off their faces. They stood on three legs, melting one pad at a time while the other three quickly froze. Abe's leader, Farmer, stayed tight in a ball, melted into the packed snow. Her wide brown eyes peered out from under her tail. The hair on her feet was stained reddish brown. She was a gentle dog. I coaxed her to the front of the team where she shivered with her back arched, tail under her belly and pads freezing. Abe and Jerry harnessed the big, hard-to-handle dogs. The snaps were frozen. The harnesses were stiff and icy and hard to force into dog shapes. Our dogs weren't accustomed to company; even cold, they showed off to Enuk's dogs, tugging and barking, tangling the lines.

A quarter mile downriver, Abe waved a big wave good-bye to Enuk. Abe geed the dogs north, up the bank below the mouth of Jesus Creek. The snow on the tundra was ice hard, scooped and gouged into waves by wind. It creaked under the runners. Morning twilight bruised the southern sky. Shivers wandered my skin. I yanked off a mitten and warmed frozen patches on my cheeks. The cold burnt inside my nose. My fingers started to freeze. I wondered what thoughts walked in Abe's mind. I felt as cumbersome and alone as a moon traveler, peering out the fur tunnel of my caribou hood, beaver hat, and wolf ruff.

Farmer led toward the Dog Die Mountains. They were steep mountains, the spawning grounds of brown bears, storms, and spirits. They beckoned like five giants, snowed in to their chins. Occasionally we crossed a line of willows that marked a buried slough or a pond shore, and a dog or two would heave against his neckline and mark a willow, claiming any stray females in the last ten thousand acres.

"Is that a moose?" I said.

The dogs glanced over their shoulders, faces frosty and alarmed at my shout.

"Might be a tree," Abe said softly.

My moose mutated into one of the lone low dark trees that grip the tundra, hunkered like a troll, gnarled arms thrust downwind. Abe had more careful eyes than I did; they grabbed details, touched textures, took apart colors. I slumped, cold on my caribou skin, stabbed by love for my dad. He didn't have to say "might be a tree" when he *knew*. Plenty of the dads in the village would holler, "Shudup. You try'na scare everything again?"

On a ridge, Abe whoa'd the dogs. He took out tobacco and papers. His bared hands tightened and turned red. I looked away, pretending for him that they were brown. He was too naive to know that red fingers were not the kind to have. The smoke smelled sharp in the smell-robbed air, comforting. The southern horizon glowed pink and for a few minutes a chunk of the sun flamed red through a dent in the Shield Mountains, like a giant flashlight with dying batteries. The snow glowed incandescent. I sprinted back and forth, melting fingers and toes. Abe glassed the land.

"Hmm. There she is."

Through the binoculars the moose stood silhouetted, black as open water. We mushed closer. A deep moan floated on the air. Abe braked the sled. He shushed the dogs. They held their breath, listening. Then the pups yowled and tugged, the scent stirring their blood.

"Must be that cow missing her calf," Abe said.

"They can sound like that?" I'd heard loons laughing manically, the woman-screams of lynx, ghoulish whimpering from porcupine, but I hadn't heard a mourning moose. I was proud of Abe, proud of his omniscient knowledge of the land.

"Never heard anything like it before," he said, pleased.

We jounced on.

"Abe, why do you think greatness is bad?" My question startled both of us. I stiffened, mortified. He snapped ice off his mustache. "I mean—. Burning your best paintings. And acting like you don't know how to hunt when travelers are bragging."

When Abe spoke, he used his historical-problems-with-the-world voice. He had a degree in art and history; Iris often teased that his degree *was* history. "This book I'm reading, the author argues that our heroes aren't heroes at all and have traditionally—"

I stopped listening and watched frost-laden twigs pass. Abe liked to mull things over until he got them complicated. A discussion with him was like rolling a log uphill in sticky snow. Ideas glommed on. I started to offer ten-year-old facts, but the dogs sped up and we dropped into a slough and lost the trail of the conversation when the team piled up on the leftovers of the calf moose. Backbone, hair, hooves, and the head with the nose and eyes chewed down, all scattered in a red circle. Fine wolf trails and deep moose trenches mapped out the battle.

The dogs bit at the frozen blood and woody stomach contents. Abe bent, careful not to let go of the sled handlebar. He touched a clean wolf paw print. "Soft," he mused. "Been back to finish her up."

The dogs raced west, up a narrow slough. "Abe," I whispered, "should we maybe not shoot that ma moose? She's had enough bad luck. Didn't you want to shoot a barren cow, to be fatter?"

I wanted to get out of the overhanging willows before she charged. The snow was soft and deep. Anyone knew moose were more dangerous than bears. Especially on a dog team. As a child, I had been petrified during the night with fear of a moose dropping in our ground-level skylight. The thrashing black hooves would crack our skulls. The wind would sift the igloo full of snow. Shrews would tunnel under our skin and hollow us out, and when travelers found our bodies we'd be weightless as dried seagulls. Abe nourished the nightmare, shrugging, conveying the impression that, sure, given time, my prophecy was bound to come true. Abe was that way. Realistic, he called it.

He ran behind the runners, dodging willows that tried to slap his eyes. He panted over my hood. "Might be the only moose in fifty miles that doesn't care either way."

I knew I could argue with him, and he'd leave the animal. He'd welcome the discussion—and the chance not to kill. I shut my stiff lips. Willows whipped past. Abe climbed on the runners and rode. He cleared his throat and whistled encouragements to the dogs. I squinted in frustration, thinking, *Now I'm definitely not going to get to shoot.*

"My parents split up after the war," Abe said. "People didn't do that back then. That-a-girl, Farmer. Haw. Haw over. I was thirteen then."

In the sled I stared at my *mukluks*. Shocked—not that his parents divorced, but that he was telling me. His past was always as distant as the cities.

"I came home from school one day, in trouble with Sister Abigail for saying I trusted animals more than people. Dad's flannel shirts were all gone from the floor and the backs of chairs. I knew without those shirts, he was gone. He went off hunting fame or fortune, I guess." Abe sounded like he was telling himself the story, too. I stayed silent, pretending indifference. Those seemed to be the manners I'd been taught; I just couldn't remember learning them.

"Even in Barrow, I usually drew animals instead of shooting them. I would've liked to be a hero. Of course I wanted to be one. It just felt . . . phony. Wearing the clothes. Strutting and flexing. Shooting some poor creature. It just wasn't me."

Had he told Iris this yesterday? Probably not; she didn't have my mouth that had always wanted to know how to be someone else.

"I propped the Super Cub for my dad, the day he crashed. Kind of a heroic thing to do?"

Willows slapped my face and the crook of his arm. Snow sifted down my neck.

"The engine sounded funny. I could have said something but Dad would have hollered to stand clear. Guess life's like shooting a caribou, huh? You want a fat one, but if you end up with a skinny one, you don't waste it."

"People leave a skinny caribou, Abe. Or feed it to the dogs and shoot a sledload more."

"You kids!"

We plowed out of the willows, onto a lake. I saw her across the ice; she stood on long graceful legs, huge black shoulders. The backs of her ankles were pale yellow; along her flank stretched a white gash in the hair.

Figment hollered and lunged, cheering the other dogs on. The moose cantered into low brush. The brake ripped furrows in the snow. The sled slid across the ice.

"Stand on the snow hook!"

I jumped out with the hook. It bit into the packed snow. I held it down with knees and palms. The moose waded in deep snow, disappearing into the willows. Abe raised the gun and shot. The moose went down, and WHOMP—the bullet hit sounded like an air-dropped box of nails. Fresh meat! I forgot my frozen cheeks. But not that I wanted to be the one to shoot. Abe wasn't going to change. He didn't believe it made any difference which hunter pulled the trigger. Since he was already an expert, of course he always shot.

A FEW YARDS FROM THE DOGS, I stood beside the steaming gut pile. Under the snow, the lake was solid six feet down, and I pictured lethargic pike and whitefish squeezed in the dark silence between mud and ice, waiting with cold-blooded thoughts for winter to go away. I felt strong withstanding the cold.

Up close the moose was alarmingly big. Abe and I loaded the huge hindquarters and butt on the basket sled. He hurried off to break willows, the springy sticks shattering like glass in the cold.

"Making stick towers to scare the ravens?"

"Get dry wood. I'll start a fire."

I discovered with dismay that one of us was staying with the remaining meat. Abe stepped away from the newborn fire and cut snow to clean his bloody knife.

I pretended to break the ice off my eyelashes. I peered about nervously. A couple of the dogs whined and tugged at the anchored sled, their feet and noses freezing, their hearts anxious to run toward home and dinner. The rest had curled up, conserving warmth. I longed to go, tented between the companionship of my father behind on the runners and the huskies panting faithful in front.

"I'll try to make it back 'fore too late." Abe planted the .30-06 stock-first in the snow. He stepped carefully, keeping his moosehide-bottom *mukluks* out of the circle of blood around the kill. "At home I'll have to lash on the gee-pole. And my skis." The gee-pole tied onto the front of the sled and Abe skied behind the wheel dogs—in front of the sled—and used the pole to steer when the load was heavy or the trail deep. I hefted the gun. The weight was powerful. The cold steel seared my bloody fingers and I knelt and thawed them in the pool of blood coagulated in the moose's chest. I wiped my hands on the coarse fur, slid my mittens on.

Suddenly all the dogs held their breath. Nine pairs of ears swiveled north. Abe and I turned. Across the distance floated shivers of sound: wolves howling. Abe straightened up bareheaded. His hair, aged gray with frost, slapped me with a glimpse of the future. We scanned the horizons. Finally, he took off his mittens and cinched the sled rope. Abe hated loose loads the way he hated whiny kids. "Nice to hear the wolves," he murmured. "Country's poor without them. Cutuk, it means there's other animals around."

I shifted, uncomfortable with him using my name. Abe had heard and seen hundreds of wolves over the years since he'd been a teenager in Barrow. He didn't shoot them; why did he care so much to see more?

Plato raised her muzzle and poured a perfect howl into the frozen sky. The other dogs joined in a cacophony of yips and howls that swelled out over the tundra. "Shudup!" Abe growled. He whipped the billowy gut pile with a willow. It made a hollow crack. We'd empty the rumen and take it and the fat intestines home for dog food, second load. We'd leave the lungs, windpipe, stomach contents, and some blood that the dogs didn't gnaw off the snow. The team sat, rolling their eyes apologetically.

"Don't hurry," I mumbled, casual. I glanced down at the gun. Already loneliness was settling like outer space pushing down the sky. The arctic twilight would fade and Abe would be under the stars before he slid into our dog yard.

He threw a caribou skin to me to lie on. Handed over dried meat and a chunk of pemmican with currants, dried cranberries, and caribou fat. "You don't need to shoot any wolves. You hear? We still have a piece of a wolf skin in the cache." His face twitched with sudden guilt for leaving. I opened my mouth to encourage the feeling, but he'd stridden back to the runners.

"Okay! Getup there! Hike!" Away they went, the sled heavy and the dogs heaving with their hips out to the sides and their tails stiff with effort. In minutes they had disappeared to a black dot on the tundra, silhouetted by the orange horizon that lay along the south pretending the sun had been up half the day and burnt that strip of fire.

I held my breath. Listened to the silence. The land at cold temperatures waited in molecular stillness; sound traveled far, though very little of it lived here anymore. My heart boomed. My ears filled with a waterfall of ringing. The land's thousand eyes watched. I knelt and tried to concentrate on the fire and the smoke, sweet with the smell of warmth and company. A noise startled me.

From a lone spruce on the far side of the lake a raven cawed. "Caaawk," I answered. I glanced behind. The watchful bird cawed again, urging me to leave the fat meat to him. I saw him standing on my face, feasting on my eyes. I saw him on Abe's face and I hummed quickly and fed the fire.

THE PASTEL SKY HAD DARKENED. In the south a last strip of orange and greenish blue lingered. The walls of blackness grew and leaned close over my head and joined. An icy east breeze thinned the smoke. The night cold was a monster now, merciless, pinching my face with pliers, sneaking fingers under my parka. It didn't seem possible to keep my cheeks thawed, and they froze over and over again. The flames sizzled the two-foot-long moose ribs I speared on a stick, burning the crisp fat while the ends froze. In the flickering light my pile of dry willow shrank. I scratched my neck to steal glances behind. The raven had gone.

When the ribs were nicely burnt, I gnawed on the meat pressed between my mittens. I worked a bone clean, tossed it into the dark. Back home it was Jerry's day to bake bread; probably he was sliding loaves out of our oven box in the bottom of the barrel stove, rapping the brown bottoms to hear the hollow done sound. I wished for a hot slice, and walls behind my shoulders, and Iris's teasing squeezes.

Jaws crunched a bone.

I dropped the rib and snatched the rifle. The dark was made of dots, walls of eyes. A scream tore the night.

A fox! Was it rabid? I hissed out a hoarse fox bark. Silence rang back. I barked again. To the left I heard a soft thump. Then running feet and the quick sounds of a chase. My stomach tightened. The wolves had come!

If the fox was crippled the wolves would eat him. I wished bad luck on him until I remembered that Enuk would say he could wish the same on me. Above, aurora wavered, green smoke ghosting in the dark, quick pale brush strokes, the bottoms tinted pink, twinging up in the black. The fire had sunk, hissing and steaming down on the lake ice. I knelt forward to salvage some coals. Smoke stung my eyes. Snow squeaked. The darkness moved into shapes. Slowly, I turned my head. Behind stood more.

The *chik-chunk* of the rifle loading sounded as loud as river ice booming. I aimed over the dark shaking sights. My thoughts scattered down terrified trails. The pack couldn't have forgotten that a man had shot one of them yesterday. Now I would never get to be Eskimo, or see a 747, or know for how many years President Nixon had to go to jail. I tried to place myself in a future story to milk heroism out of my bad luck, but all I saw were clumps of bones and yellow hair. A voice I hadn't heard whispered, "Shoot! *Shoot!*" I gripped the gun. I was ten. My chance to be Enuk! People in the village would know it the next time they teased, "Catch any weasel in your trap, Cutuk?"

The steel trigger froze through my fox mitten liner. I yanked back. The gun lurched. The black wolf I'd aimed at sniffed his paw.

The safety. I flipped the lever. Now Abe's disappointed face floated in the way. I looked over the barrel, tried to aim. The northern lights had dimmed. It was harder to make out shapes. Abe wouldn't cuss or even kick things around. He would help skin the wolf. That was the thing about Abe, he'd help someone else before he helped himself. The thing about me was I couldn't accept that all people were not like that. I saw

Abe as a boy, searching for his dad's shirts. I clicked the safety back. The wolf lifted his nose and howled. The pack joined.

Fear and elation skated on my skin. Were they cheering? Or voting? I felt cruel for lusting to kill one. I had eaten; I had a warm wolf ruff on my hood—but the gnawing inside was jittery and big, a hunger to kill and be great for it. It wasn't good, it was mean, but it felt glued all over inside me.

The harmony ceased. The wolves stood, listening. Finally, miles east, upwind, across the tundra, I heard the snap of branches, and fainter still, runners squeaking on cold snow; eventually came a low mumble that I knew as Abe's encouraging "Atta boys. Good girl, Farmer. Haw over now. Haw over."

The wolves circled, their claws tacking the hard snow. I aimed, barehanded now, my fingers burning on the metal. Under the green luminescence from the sky the wolf pack fanned out north across the lake. The animals I'd wanted to kill mingled and faded. That wolf—how many miles and years had he walked under this smoky green light? Walked cold, hungry in storms, wet under summer rain; walking on this land I'd always called *my* home. He knew every mountain, every trail along every knoll so much better than I ever would. And the wolf, I only knew him dead. I didn't want to be an Outsider. Not here, too. How was it that I'd never considered carefully that an animal would know infinitely more about something than I could?

The whisper of their feet disappeared under the sounds of the coming dog team. Two people pitched and clawed inside me. One whispered in awe: "They were so close." The other mocked: "You dummy! Ten years old, same age as Enuk, and *you* didn't shoot." My fingers screamed in the pain of warming. I hunched over them, humming to hide the anguish. Abe had said to watch, but he was a painter. He read books and watched the sky too much. Enuk said to respect the wolves, but he'd have shot as many as he could. Even the last one. Under my skin, so well I knew, in the village "could have" meant nothing without the mantle of a dead animal. I wanted the stars to drop some silver stranger, an alluring alien like Wax Tiera, to tell me what I should think. But there was only the dark, the cold, the miles and miles of snow.

THREE

THE MOON IS BEHIND THE LAND, *narrow and nothing to hunt by.* The pack moves south in the dark, spread out in pairs and alone, toward the kill. Tension is in the pack, a missing sibling, and quick snarls. A wolf noses through a line of willows. Pale light ripples overhead. He drops onto a lake. Three big pups trail him. They stop often to nose each other and sniff mouse tunnels. On the lake they stand, their long gazes pointed at a dancing orange hole in the night, and the scent of smoke and blood and man and dog. The wolves circle. A fox streaks past. The pups give chase in the dark.

The pack halts out of the flick of firelight. They sniff the man's sweaty fear and the charred bones. They hear his quick breathing. The large wolf tastes something else, a scent sealed into his puppyhood and the loss of his mother. The scent makes him yawn in apprehension. After a time he leads the pack away from the danger of this kill. Past their own kill with man's scent there now, too. Away into mountains.

FOUR

BRUCE LEE ARRIVED in moving color on the back wall of the Takunak church house in February 1978, the year I turned twelve. Takunak had been converted by missionary Quakers, but everyone under seventy, regardless of whether they spoke English, lined up at the cabin door to be baptized into the glory of ninja. Mr. Lee's style of instant gratification leapt the language barrier and left John Wayne piddling in the dust. He was an overwhelming success—the movie took in two hundred and thirty-nine dollars. Three glass windows in the school were broken the following night with throwing stars of frozen Cream of Wheat.

A week later, when, unaware, we mushed into the village, I felt the ramifications of Lee's acceptance into Iñupiaq culture.

We traveled to town two or three times each winter to deliver Abe's artwork—furniture and paintings—and to pick up mail and gossip, gunpowder, powdered milk, and mail-ordered vanilla extract for snow ice cream. Necessities. We tied our door shut, iced the runners, and hitched up the dogs. We got on the trail as the first twinges of morning twilight painted the Shield Mountains. "Take your mittens off a minute," Abe suggested, reminding us to go barehanded until our hands went numb, to shock the blood into flowing hot in our fingers for the day.

Two bends west, the river was deep with fresh snow that wind hadn't shifted and settled. Jerry, Iris, and I took turns spelling Abe. Two of us snowshoed in front of the team, breaking trail. The other ran behind. Only one of us got to ride on the runners, and often that person had to run, too. Frost whitened our furs and the dogs' faces. I froze my face as much as possible, getting ready to look tough and hunterly in town. At dark the first evening, we cut a dead sapling for a ridgepole and green saplings for spruce boughs to sleep on, and pitched our wall tent where the winter trail abandons the river for three bends. Thoughtfully, Abe pressed the faded canvas of the tent between his thumb and finger. Iris leaned against my shoulder smiling. "He'll be boiling bone glue, brushing size and ground on our tent," she whispered. "It'll only be a matter of time until he needs canvas and cuts it up to paint."

Jerry set up the five-gallon-can stove and pipe. We spread out caribou skins and ate blocks of pemmican and melted snow and threw dried whitefish to the dogs.

The following afternoon, amid the clamor of hundreds of barking dogs, we slid into Takunak, hideously uncool bundled in our caribou parkas and *mukluks*, black bear and wolf ruffs, down overpants, beaver hats, wolverine mittens, fox mitten liners, wool long underwear and balaclavas. Log cabins and a few plywood houses hunkered along the north shore. Fish racks were pitched along the shore, half buried and glinting with tin coffee-can lids on strings, spinning in the breeze to scare ravens and not doing a very good job. A hundred and fifty people—including the only two other white boys I knew—lived in Takunak. The village was securely connected to America (when the weather was good) by a weekly mail plane from Crotch Spit, a town on the coast. At the highest point of the ridge the log church squatted beside the frame schoolhouse. The close positioning allowed the church to siphon electricity uphill from the school generator. Abe usually made some comment about the high-voltage donation, throwing a different light on schoolteachers' bad reputations.

He geed the dogs up the ridge to Feathers's house and post office. He stomped the snow hook in and unbuttoned the sled bag. "Have some *paniqtuq*." He handed us kids dried meat to chew. Abe pulled his parka over his head and laid it on the tarp. His Army sweater was messy with caribou hair. He disappeared inside, carrying our library box and a sugar sack of letters. A Coleman lantern was burning inside. Around us, chained sled dogs shrieked and pawed the snow. Jerry stood with an axe handle swinging in his mittens, vigilant over our eight dogs. "Lie down," he growled. He was nervous and not attracted to the village the way Iris and I were. He had the good brown eyes and black hair, but his continents of interest—the wilderness and the Outside—lay in two opposite directions from Takunak, and Jerry saw no common borders.

The dogs stretched at his feet, panting, their ears up and fatigue forgotten in the thrill of town. Iris and I huddled close to each other, talking with our eyes on the ground.

"Maybe the Jafco catalog came."

"Maybe." I toed a splintered board, nails up on the packed snow. We felt sliced by hidden eyes behind cabin windows. Behind a cache—and heaped sleds, machines, caribou hides, fishnets, and broken chain saws—we could see a cabin, Nippy Skuq's. Farther east, beyond a thicket of willows, stood Woodrow Washington's upright-log house, and along the ridge more cabins we didn't know, and heaps of machinery and fifty-five-gallon drums. Through some mystical arctic grapevine, everyone in town knew we'd arrived. Everyone had a curtain cracked in case we had a spectacular dogfight, unusual mail, or a wrong way of walking.

Abe stepped out and lowered an armload of packages into the tarp. "Box of clothes, from January Thompson. You'll have to write and thank him."

I looked at pictures in my mind, this friend of Abe's, this wolf-bounty man, January, fat and with a shotgun in his hairy fingers. Had he been a friend of my grandfather's? Had he learned from him how to fly airplanes, and taught Abe?

"Abe!" Iris moaned. "Don't you know we're embarrassed here in town to wear salvaged Army clothes?"

"Salvation Army. Not the military." Abe grinned down at the moose-*babiche* sled ropes he knotted. "The mail plane had to turn back yesterday. Tommy Feathers says it's supposed to land pretty quick. You kids like to go over and watch?"

"Yeah! Let's!" Iris and I said.

"Wait. There'll be lots of people," Jerry cautioned. He chewed the string on his hood. "Just reminding you."

I pictured the crowd at the airfield, and kids throwing iceballs at my head. The De Havilland Twin Otter like a stiff frozen eagle sliding down the sky, legs out, its tunneled stomach ready to regurgitate strangers and Sears packages. And everyone staring at us, because everyone was part of the village except us, and no one had ever learned not to stare.

"Some kinda luck!" I tried to sound confident. "We got here just in time."

WE SLEDDED TO the upper end of the village and stopped at the airstrip, behind the last cabin. Our dogs curled there, resting while we tore open the mail, letters and yellow envelopes containing units of our correspondence schoolwork. We skipped the teachers' handwritten encouragements, glanced at the grades, and stuffed them back into the sled to peruse at home.

"Do well?" Abe asked.

Figment writhed his head back and forth, slipped his collar, and stretched gingerly back toward the sled, wagging for a bite of *paniqtuq*. Abe's blond hair was tousled, his mouth full of the dried meat. One of his front teeth had a piece of meat caught in it. He had a stub of pink pastel chalk in his mitten, sketching on the canvas sled tarp. He glanced at Figment. He raised his hand, palm down. Figment pointed his nose at the snow, glanced beseechingly one more time at Abe, and curled up.

"All As." Iris giggled between her mittens. She swung her eyes at Jerry. "Sorry."

"C in math." His voice was deep, his windpipe strong and smooth in his neck. He liked some of the high school courses but hadn't yet discovered an excuse for the existence of geometry. I was in eighth grade and felt the same about all schoolwork. Abe claimed that people in other parts of the world would fight to have an education. I didn't argue, but in my experience with people—Takunak—it had always seemed they fought *instead* of getting an education. I had skipped two grades: one because Jerry taught us everything as he learned it; the other because Woodrow Washington Jr. had broken into the post office when everyone was across the river waiting for a forest fire to pass Takunak, and he'd thrown my first-grade supply box down an outhouse hole. By the time mail got through I was halfway into Iris's second-grade lessons, frozen to the wall from the year before.

I jogged back and forth to get my blood moving and warm; in town the importance of never appearing cold far outweighed a school grade from a stranger in a place called Juneau.

"Better off learning what you want to know." Abe swung his leg over the toprail. "Don't let anyone with a degree talk you into happiness insurance." We stared at him, and then kicked snow, embarrassed. A drone came out of the western sky.

"There!" Iris spotted the speck. Above the cabins, smoke from stovepipes rippled, strained thin by a cold east breeze. "They're coming!"

Who would *they* be? Maybe the yearly dentist with his grinders and pliers. A hippie with a Kelty pack. Or people returning from jail or from shooting ravens in National Guard war games. The Twin Otter roared overhead, an alien bird deciding if we were fat enough to eat. The town dogs loosed a stirring ground wave of howls. The dot turned in the sky. Villagers boiled from houses and the school. Kids raced up and leaned at the toprails of our sled, spitting, stepping carelessly on our load of mail, camp stove, and gear. Our dogs wagged and stretched back. The kids jumped away.

"Hi Jerry. Hi Iris. Hi Cutuk," kids said. In the village young people said *hi* and someone's name, all as one word.

"Hi Cutuk. Bywhere you fellas' mom?" a small boy asked.

"When you go around here?" another boy interrupted.

"Today." We spoke uncertainly, not recalling all of their names. The kids wore bright tattered nylon jackets and cold stiff jeans. They would freeze before maiming their profiles with furs and skins. It wasn't a good feeling, the way everyone knew us. We were white kids, had only a dad, and lived out in what they called "camp"—but few knew even from what direction we appeared. Out of town simply meant out of touch, out of money, the opposite of lucky. No family from Takunak lived in "camp."

My cheeks were red, in the village a shout of weakness. I fingered the frostbite burns on my nose, hoping they had darkened into the scab badges of a hunter. I pulled my caribou parka off over my head, squaring my shoulders, exhaling as if I was sweating. Abe glanced up. He stuffed his chalk in his parka pocket. "Don't get chilled."

"You wanna fight?" asked Elvis Skuq Jr. "I'll let you cry." He had permanent residence in my earliest memories of town. From the time he'd been a small boy he'd enjoyed packing my face with snow and whipping my mittens off with a stick, laughing at my smarting red fingers. A scar ran from his lip up under his nose and, I'd long thought, on up to his brain. He was sixteen and towered over me.

The plane banked and lined up with the airfield. "From where you come?" Elvis repeated.

"Upriver," Jerry mumbled. I spat out caribou hairs that had wandered out of my hood and collected in my mouth. The plane wheels touched the snow. As it swept down on us, Iris and I jumped behind the sled.

"Aiy, sure *iqsi."* Kids jeered and dark-eyed adults smiled at our naïveté. A kid whipped my ear with a piece of knotted rope. Laughter came from behind us. A snowball dissolved against my neck. The props roared, warbling with power as the pilots adjusted the pitch. The turning plane flung a wall of snow over the crowd. Around me villagers faded like ghosts. The props whined to a halt. Everyone surged forward. Stevie and Dawna Wolfglove waved. I stood, a member of a group, all of us united in anticipation.

Woodrow Jr. slapped me on the back. He was in his twenties and carried his son on his shoulders. "How's the trail from your-guys' camp? You come to town to fin' Eskimo girlfriend?" Beside him a pretty woman smiled, her brown face and dusky lashes shining inside her white fox ruff. "I sure want your eyes, Cutuk," she said. "You should go be my son." People laughed. I examined the ground, shifted nervously, pictured myself belaying Woodrow Washington down Feathers's outhouse to salvage my education.

The airplane doors swung open. The pilots stepped down, white-faced and cold-looking with their radio earmuffs, aluminum notebooks, and Colt .45s on their belts. Villagers unloaded the boxes and mail bags.

Dawna stepped close. She smiled. "Hi, Cutuk. When you come?"

"While ago." I looked at my mittens. Dawna had a heart-shaped face. Her wide eyes seemed to beg an answer to a question no one had heard. Her hands were bare and pulled into the sleeves of her white nylon jacket. She wore faded jeans, perfectly frayed around the bell-bottoms. Dawna was fourteen and had recently changed in ways that I found embarrassing to snag my eyes on, and impossible not to. Before last year I had thought she was dumb—the pastime she enjoyed most was cutting up Sears catalogs to make collages, and looking at the photographs in women's magazines, wishing about cities far from Alaska. Sometimes she looked at the pictures upside down. Her dad, Melt, got mad when he caught her doing that. He ripped the magazines out of her fingers, cuffed her head, and threw her collages into the stove. "Don't always sometimes try to think you're something else," he shouted.

I figured that, being Enuk's granddaughter, she should want to learn to scrape skins and sew.

She leaned forward and put her hands on the cold paper of the stack of brown boxes and peered past them into the interior of the Twin Otter. Her fingers were long and brown. One of her little fingernails was unusually wide, and she kept it tucked out of sight. I thought that one fingernail was the only imperfect thing about her whole person, all condensed into one point, a mere mosquito bite of badness, and I was jealous because my eyes felt wrong, my hair, my speech, my entire skin felt wrong.

Everyone inched closer to the plane. I fantasized that Abe would step forward and offer to start the airplane. Why wouldn't he do such things? He must remember how. It would be so easy for him, and I would have friends after that. But Abe was kneeling, biting ice off Farmer's feet, nodding attentively as twenty-four-year-old Charley Casket bragged how to shoot wolves with a .22 Magnum.

"You got any catalog orders coming?" Dawna whispered.

"Only what Abe ordered—things we *need*. Vanilla. Paints. Sled bolts." Vanilla wasn't sold in the store. People would buy all of it the first day and get drunk.

Dawna's laughter pealed out. "Bolts? Like washers and stuff?"

People stared. Dawna didn't flinch. She was the only one in the village—besides Abe—who didn't seem to care all the time what everybody thought. Dawna's gaze flicked the crowd and caressed the last mail handed from the plane. Commiseration flexed under my ribs, and I cherished the feeling that we had a desire in common. A longing, for something, too exotic even to know how to name. Something better than sled bolts and vanilla.

"You wanna try race?" asked a boy. He was my size and had the wide friendly features of a Washington. Kids stood expectantly. I glanced at Dawna, and across at Stevie, talking to Jerry beside our dog team.

"'Kay, then," I said, trying to avoid two prominent town taboos—acting scared and sounding smart. We raced to the schoolhouse. The boy wore fast, light tennis shoes. "My *mukluks* are too slow," I panted as we walked back. It had been close. I knew I could easily beat him if we traded shoes, but no kid here would be caught in *mukluks*.

"*Aiy*, try blame."

A group of big kids surrounded me. "You wanna fight?" someone asked. Elvis and his younger brother. I sped up.

"You're *naluaġmiu*, huh?" Elvis sneered.

"I dunno." *Naluaġmiu* meant white person; the Eskimo dictionary didn't list it as a dirty word but everyone knew better. All conversations with Elvis were to the point—usually that one.

"*Aiy, kinnaq.*"

That meant dumb. My face reddened.

"Sure try fool!" Kids jeered. "*Aiy!* He sure get red!"

"You wanna fight, honky?" A boy yanked my wool hat down over my eyes. I dragged it back up, but the elastic was old, stretched and saggy. Whatever *honky* meant, I must be one of those, too.

"What's six times six?" asked Lumpy Wolfglove. I smiled, relieved to recognize him. Lumpy was seventeen and in eighth grade. There were three things about Lumpy: he was good at math, he was a great rifle shot, and he liked to torture puppies and mash their heads with hammers. He was Stevie and Dawna's part-brother.

"Thirty-six." Iris had taught me math for as long as I could remember in the winter evenings when it was too dark to do anything and Abe wouldn't yet light the lamp because that would waste kerosene.

"*Yuay!* How 'bout seven times eight?"

"Fifty?" I glanced around for smiles and shifted toward the airfield.

"You always know ninja?" Elvis asked. The boys waited.

"I don't know lotta Eskimo words."

"*Aiy!* Not even. So dumb."

"You're some kinda *kinnaq*."

Someone choked me in a headlock. I twisted his thumb. He grunted in pain and shoved me forward on my knees.

"Hi-yaa." Elvis spun. His boot blurred. It slammed to a stop against my ear. I skidded behind a snowdrift, other boots in my back, neck, and face. In my head his stretched-out brag, "No fuggin' problem." My mouth tasted salty. This part of town I was familiar with—this was the part I wanted to get past. I couldn't see the crowd and hoped none of the adults had seen.

A woman on the edge of the crowd shouted. "Hey, what you try let them boys do? Don't always pick fight." She turned back to the airplane. My eyes joined the laughing boys as they jogged away on the hard-packed snow.

AT THE NATIVE CACHE, Jerry offered to watch the dogs while Iris and I accompanied Abe into the store. For Jerry it was no great sacrifice—he knew shopping with Abe and without money had slim potential. And he was big and powerful and had the axe handle. Nobody would mess with him. Beside the door I rubbed snow on my swollen lip and flung the bloody slush under the steps. Jerry looked away. The storekeeper's Can't-Grow dog yapped from under the boards and gobbled the mouthfuls of my blood and snow. I growled and it ran yelping under the building. Inside the crowded cabin, a lit Coleman lantern hung from a nail on the ridgepole. Guns leaned behind the counter. The walls glittered with a miscellany of store-bought items: nylon jackets, Timex watches, fishing lures, sunglasses, aftershave. Carnation canned milk. Framed holograms of Jesus. Wolverine traps. In the center of the floor three men stood by the stove, talking, occasionally laughing at a joke kept behind the walls of Iñupiaq. I heard the word *naluaġmiu* and turned away from the fire.

In the back, two of Abe's homemade birch tables were on consignment. One had sold. Abe picked out sparse supplies that we couldn't order cheaper through the mail. He didn't enjoy being in a store. He believed most of what was sold here to be unnecessary clutter blocking the view to life, and he suffered the task patiently only because he didn't want to come back anytime soon. He was blind to the shiny watches and jackets that hooked Iris's and my eyes. "Hello," he said to the men by the fire. Abe liked them. He didn't count it as any of his business that Nippy Skuq nearly killed his wife once or twice a month, drunk and beating her; that Melt Wolfglove talked about white people as if he were the Eskimo gestapo; that Tommy Feathers shot every bear he ever caught sign of—even when they were skinny or had cubs—and left them dead because a bear had once taken their dried fish when he was a kid and his family had to go without. For one night.

Iris and I carried our parkas under our arms and searched WASHINGTON boxes for apples. Not even their faint clean smell lingered on the blue tissues they had once curled in. Iris wet one of the tissues with her mouth. Her smile looked strange, like it did when she was picking blueberries and holding a bitter green berry under her tongue to keep from eating every other handful when we needed to be putting berries away for winter.

She dabbed at the blood on my lip. "Nobody can see to the inside of us. Nobody's taking us apart like it feels, Cutuk. Smile. 'Kay? Think of that kaleidoscope Jerry made out of tomato paste cans. Remember the mouse turds he sneaked in with the beads? Think of a smile inside a kaleidoscope. Come on! Come on! Let's check for oranges!"

Tommy Feathers leered at her and wiped his chin. Iris dropped the muddied tissue back in the box. She found a last onion, composting in the papery brown skins in the bottom of a mesh sack. She led me to the counter.

"No apples?" she begged. She smiled prettily at Newt Clemens, the storekeeper. I wiped my lip on my fingers and stood awkward as bent wire.

"*Arii.* We got nothing. Sorry, *Bun.*" Newt's wrist stub showed smooth in his sleeve. He only had one hand. His right arm was thick. It could hold a rifle, people said. Before he'd shot his hand off, he'd been a real bad drunk, *guuq*. *Guuq* in Eskimo meant "it is said," a convenient word for passing gossip.

Newt glanced up. "You big boy small laugh. How come?"

I dropped my gaze and stood mute. What made a person shoot his hand off? Something bad. Maybe hate inside, but not enough to die? No one had picked Newt up off the bloody floor. He picked himself up and cinched a piece of fishing line around his blasted stump, *guuq*. Because of that pain, Abe said, Newt had stopped drinking and turned into a kind man. Abe said that pretty much showed Newt had been a kind man to begin with, otherwise he'd have gone the other way, like a dog that's a biter.

Newt shook Abe's hand. It was strange. A white thing to do. They grinned at each other like old friends. I decided they must have done things together, way in the past. They never hunted or camped now.

"Onion." Abe nodded. "That'll be good with fresh moose heart."

Iris kicked my foot. "The season's closed," she whispered. "That poster on the back wall says all the rules. Only one brown bear every four years. And there's a season on ptarmigan!"

"Yep. 'Sgood eating alright." Newt paused, "Here's your fifty for your table I sell. Then—" He hunched over the cast iron cash register, rubbed his chin with his round wrist end, and peered at the confusing numbers. Abe reached over the counter and put a Bit-O-Honey candy bar on our pile.

Iris lifted an eyebrow. "Cutuk. Something's wrong with Dear-Old."

I watched, wishing he'd grabbed a candy bar with nothing as natural as honey.

"Sixty-seven fifty, for tat grub." Newt squinted. "You got change? No cash in town." He had a stack of worn two-party checks in his powerful hand, ready to thumb them off for change if Abe had a bigger check.

Abe draped his arm on Iris's shoulder as he counted up the prices. "Shush, Otter," he said. "How much for the onion?"

"Le's see," Newt mused. "Little one. Dollar." He smiled at Iris and slid a pack of spearmint gum across the counter and under her fingers.

Abe stuffed the onion down inside his warm parka. "Two dollars a gallon for kerosene? Do I owe you fifty-six?" Abe's voice was slow, innocent, uncertain. Now that he'd added the figures and stated that, he wouldn't argue if Newt said no, you owe eighty-one. It would mean we couldn't order an extra case of apples in the fall, but Abe would not dispute. I ignored the exchange and read the tag on a silver-blue jacket. A realization was dawning on me, that this was a requirement to being cool and Eskimo: WALLS, Size M, shell and lining 100% nylon, $97. Woven into that manufactured material was a slippery secret to being Eskimo.

"Could be tat's right, Abe." Newt nodded. Pouches under his eyes wobbled.

Abe dug under his overpants, in pocket after pocket, to find his cash. The men by the fire watched. I locked eyes on the good jacket, pretending it meant nothing to me that white people weren't allowed credit.

OUTSIDE, THE LONG TWILIGHT had faded to blue-black dusk in the north and stars twinkled as we ran the team down the hill to the Wolfgloves'. Their plank house stood near the buried riverbank. It was a cold shacky house, stifling in June. In Takunak we stayed there, or else with the Newtons, who were schoolteachers. The Newtons lived in school housing and owned a record player, an electric coffeepot, and a cake mixer and used paper towels as if they were free. Their boys, John and William, were the only boys in town with Whammo slingshots. Jerry said that people in the States had Mr. Coffee electric coffeepots. I took that to mean all States kids also had store-bought slingshots for shooting squirrels and camp robbers, and more importantly for surviving scary slingshot fights in their villages.

Occasionally we stayed downriver at Franklin's island in his dark igloo with meaningless poems pinned to the posts, and one-pot suppers—rice and rabbit, or whitefish and rice, or boiled meat with rice—and the same for breakfast and lunch. No kids. No candy. Worse than staying home. Crazy Joe's cabin was a mile farther downstream and the size of a tent. It had a square hole in the front you had to squeeze through, like a cache—Crazy Joe's Birdhouse, Abe called it. Joe prospected, and never went anywhere without his rock hammer and magnifying glass. Joe drank a tablespoon of urine and ate a tablespoon of dirt every day to stay healthy and close to the land. It was handy; his floor was dirt. When he was in gold dust he spent his winters near the equator and with beautiful women who wore some kind of airy flat shoes where you could see their painted toes, *guuq*.

Occasionally in Takunak we stayed with the Spenholts, evangelical vegetarians from California who grew green alfalfa and mung bean sprouts under a purple battery-powered light. "The microEinsteins entering the window aren't sufficient," Larry Spenholt would explain. "Not as photosynthetically active radiation." His dark hair was swept back, voice nasal, eyes piercing. The Spenholts had an eight-year-old daughter, Rose, who cried if she had to go outside. She didn't let us play with her electric Legos. We were a waste of batteries.

The Spenholts were native-worshipers. Everything the villagers did was aboriginal. So special. But Larry and Song went silent if we mentioned skinning weasels or rendering moose kidney fat. They weren't the only ones in the village who believed white people shouldn't be allowed to hunt. The village council—depending on atmospheric conditions and cabin-fever epidemics—voted on random things that seemed a good idea to make illegal for white people to do: Own sled dogs. Haul firewood. Set under-ice nets. Build their own houses. The Spenholts were writing a book about living in the wilderness with the Iñupiat. Gossip said they'd be millionaires when the book got done. But they stayed inside a lot and didn't eat *patiq* bones or seal oil, so no one counted them as living here, just visiting.

Sled dogs barked and howled all over town. Our dogs raised their muzzles to inhale the sweet scents of love, food, and fights. Their tail sinews tightened; their eyes gleamed in the corners. They yanked sideways on the necklines, sniffing stupidly into other dog yards. Loose dogs ran out and held lightning skirmishes and growling matches with our confused team. Our dogs didn't know how to calmly pass another team or loose dogs, or even how to run past another dog yard. At the Wolfgloves' house, Abe smacked George and Figment with the axe handle and the team hunkered down while we chained them to willows.

Janet Wolfglove leaned out the door. "Praise Lord!" she shouted. "Go in!" She was a heavy gray-haired woman, always at home cooking and sewing and ready with a warm, squishy, motherly hug. It mortified me when she hugged me, but I liked her to do it. "Go in!" she shouted again, waving us into the messy, good-smelling kitchen. "When you fellas come?" She was wearing a heavy sweater and a silver cross, her face close to mine. I smelled scented soap, the kind that hurt your nose and told animals exactly where your traps were set under the snow.

"Today," I said. "Before the plane came." Two hours ago, I realized, startled at how minutes of pain and people formed mountain ranges across my past, memory peaks that normally took months to rise.

Melt, Janet's husband, spoke in Iñupiaq though he knew well that even his children couldn't understand most of the words. *Naluaġmiu* peppered his guttural complaints. We kids stood beside the stove, eyes lowered, chewing pieces of Iris's gum. Trying to avoid any *naluaġmiu*-like movements.

"*Adii*, you kids chewing loud!" he shouted.

Our jaws stopped. We all swallowed. The barrel stove glowed red, searing our overpants. The fling of warmth wasn't enough to thaw ice on the floor in the corners. Piles of socks, gloves, and clothes—and leaning guns—were frozen fast to the frosty walls. The temperature at the ceiling was breathtaking, fifty or sixty degrees warmer than the floor.

"Enuk go check his snares," Janet said, catching my searching glance. I nodded, too discouraged with my luck on this long-anticipated town trip to ask if he might return that night.

Stevie and Dawna surged in the door, laughing at a joke they'd left outside. Tommy Reason followed. Everyone called him Treason. He was curly-haired, a boy Janet had taken in when his mother burned in the plane crash at Uktu. His dad had run off, long gone back to the States, maybe dead. Once when Lumpy pinched a strip of his skin off with a vise grips Treason cried for a long time, more than a vise grips' worth. Treason didn't tease about us being *naluaġmiu*, or anything about hair.

My face was hot with shame. Places with people always came with this—the reminder that my family was different from people. We didn't say *hi* correctly, or stand right, chew properly—especially we didn't know enough about *fighting*. And there were so many people, and names, and faces impossible to remember. I dropped my eyes and vanished into fantasy where I'd created Elvis Jr.'s lip scar by hitting him so hard that newspapers out in Fairbanks printed the account.

Stevie dragged me into the corner. He kicked clothes piles out of our way. He nudged his glasses up. He was big-boned and stocky. His coal-black hair swept back, thick and wavy. Beside his family I knew I looked like a diseased seagull among glossy ravens. Stevie had been born thirty-eight days before me, but for most of my life I'd felt older than both him and Dawna—maybe because Janet enjoyed babies. Abe had strongly suggested we skip the "whining years." He had sewn the sleeves of our first caribou parkas shut so he didn't have to hear or worry about lost mittens.

"Junior fight you?" Stevie didn't ask who won. Stevie was like Janet. He had a way of smiling, unconcerned as a shrug. Kids who had wanted to fight him would ask if they could help feed his dogs.

"Yeah." I covered my lip. Dawna's mirror hung on a nail in the dark corner. Fly specks freckled my reflection. Worried blue eyes stared back.

Dawna giggled. "You fellas get your vanilla and nuts?"

Treason stood next to us. "Ever'body been try fight lots since that good movie."

"Which one was that?"

"Ninja one," Stevie explained.

I nodded, mystified.

"Cutuk, you want to see our new kinda snowgo?"

"What? You guys got a new snowgo?" I tried to clamp my expression, but the suddenness of the information smeared jealousy across my face. I wanted to hide behind the woodpile. Never in a hundred years would *we* have a motorized snowmobile. Abe didn't like engines. Maybe they reminded him of his dad's Super Cub. Not so many years ago only privileged people had snowmobiles: schoolteachers, Tommy Feathers, and a few others.

Stevie and I ran out without parkas. Stevie peeked in the window, cautious, making sure Melt wasn't looking out. It paid to be careful around Melt. Stevie led me behind the house. He flung aside a canvas tarp. He rubbed his hands. The snowgo crouched, silver blue in the sleek moonlight, a rocket waiting to burn across the tundra. He traced the name POLARIS on the cowling with his fingers.

"Not like that old Chaparral," he said in awe. "This new one always go fast." His breath rose in fat clouds. "It was have windshield, but Lumpy let it come off on tree. Dad sure wanna tie him to post and whip him. Only thing he's too big now."

A jagged crack ran down the front. I touched the glassy cowling and jerked my hand back. "I got a splinter!" A dot of blood darkened my finger.

Stevie gripped my hand. "That's fiberglass. Try see. Wait! We'll be blood brothers!" He poked his finger and squeezed it to mine. "Wish for snowgos, *bart*. Lumpy gonna try get Pipeline job an' buy one. Lotta people going Prudhoe."

Lust cramped my hands. I saw my long-wished-for equalizer, a mechanical creation that would transform me into a great hunter and an Eskimo. "We gotta go Prudhoe? What's Prudhoe anyways?"

"You drive snowgo before?"

I accosted my memory, attempting to adjust the truth—and avoid a lie. "No. Not yet."

"That's okay. You will sometimes. It go faster than any kinda dog, wolf, caribous." He shook his head. "Nothing can win it. Dad get wolf. He run right over it." We stared at the machine. Then he covered it and showed me the wolf skin draped frozen over the clothesline. It was skinned poorly; there were slashed holes and the lower legs and claws had been left behind with the carcass.

"We see lotta wolves up home, whole packs," I bragged in the dark, "but Abe never try kill 'em. Coupla' winters ago he left me one time to watch a moose we killed, and wolves—"

"How come?"

"How come what?"

"Why Abe never always shoot 'em?" Stevie pulled at his eyebrow.

"He likes them."

"What he always like 'em for?"

"I dunno. I—I think he just likes 'em."

"Huh." Stevie shrugged and flashed me a baffled look as he opened the door. In that moment it seemed preposterous that at home Abe's reasoning could have held its knots. Why couldn't he be normal and shoot whole clotheslines full?

THAT NIGHT WE HAD STEW that wasn't caribou or bear or lynx or anything ordinary; it came out of a big can that Melt brought when he wandered home from slumping around the Native Cache stove. Melt was short and well padded with a square head, perfectly adapted for sitting in the rocking chair Abe had made for him, while Janet cooked, skinned animals, cut up meat, and sewed. Whiskey had melted the teeth out of Melt's head and left a sinkhole of his lips. He dunked pilot crackers in his coffee and stuffed them in. He liked to preach sometimes at the church, when there was no pastor in town. He was grumpy except when he shared advice, weather prophecies, or his hunting stories—those things brought out a generosity in him. It was clear that they were better than any another person might own.

He was proud to serve that canned soup made from States cows. Anybody who didn't see the Dinty Moore label would have assumed from the way he hollered at Janet and opened the can himself that he'd journeyed down to Baltimore, Illinois, or Park Place and hunted those cows all himself.

Abe didn't like the soup. But he raised his eyebrows politely. "Salty," he mumbled as if all beef by definition was salty. The meat smashed under my teeth, same as the potatoes. I wondered what a beef did to get its meat large-grained like moose and still mushy as boiled ground squirrel.

My cut lip stung. I set the bowl on the floor to cool. Stevie and I practiced setting his new Conibear trap, made to snap on an ermine's head and kill it instantly. We forgot we were old and began trying to snap Dawna and Iris, since they seemed to be having more fun than we were, reading a magazine and whispering over the pictures. Jerry sat with the adults, hunched to one side, holding his soup over a Sears order blank he was filling out for *Aana* Skuq. People came in the door steadily, when we were in town, to have Abe make out Sears orders for them, or explain unemployment papers or taxes. Jerry did it now, relieved to have something to do that made sense to him.

Stevie snapped the trap on Dawna's foot. She screamed. "Stevie, you dumb thing!" She whacked his head with a rolled-up magazine, hard. "*Adii,* Mom. Stevie always bother."

"Ah shuck, you!" Melt hollered. "You kids go play out!" He pointed at the door. I couldn't tell if he meant it. In the village, people yelled and swore equally at kids and dogs, and neither obeyed. That strange memory flashed, of Melt, young, quiet, friendly, cradling a baby porcupine in our doorway. With a space between his teeth that there was no longer any way of verifying. Had it been a dream? People didn't change that much, did they?

Stevie sat on the bed with his face turned away, chuckling. Dawna stared at me, her eyes beautiful under black lashes. She wobbled the small mole on her cheek. She wore a pink hooded sweatshirt. The collar was torn around the eyelets. Her neck was smooth and brown. Her gaze looked laughy, but different somehow. I wanted her to be the first person I ever kissed—after I learned how.

She shook her magazine. A square white magazine-seed dropped out.

She wrote on it and let the paper fall near my knee. The writing was upside down. I turned it around. Now it was backwards, inside out. I flipped it over and read where the pen had pressed through like braille. *Cutuk, don't listen to that* kinnaq *thing. You're my friend and I wish you were my honey.* The words were curly and small, unbelievably valuable. I hid the paper in my pocket to read a thousand times upriver.

I didn't want to go outside in the dark; I slinked back to my stew. It had frozen along the edges. Janet giggled and brushed my arm. "Shh." She dumped it back in the pot and gave me a warm bowlful.

Abe unpacked our sleeping bags to warm by the stove and got out the lynx skin he'd brought for Janet. Lynx prices had risen to two hundred and fifty dollars at Seattle Fur Exchange, for rich women's coats, and when Abe got an envelope with a check for four skins he pulled his big traps. We still mailed in fox and rare marten skins, but now if he accidentally caught a lynx he gave it to Janet to use in mitten liners or to let Melt sell. When I was a baby he had traded Janet furs for sewing warm clothes for us, before she taught us to tan skins and sew, before she took us in.

Janet lit another Coleman lamp. It flamed and sputtered. She flipped the generator lever and pumped it rapidly. The mantle glowed, hissing out harsh shadows. "Look, *Bun*," she told Dawna. "Abe bring. *Aarigaa.*" Dawna smiled fleetingly, not even pretending she cared. She stared at Abe, not the lynx. She and Iris went back to admiring skinny white girls in the magazine.

Janet was known all the way to the coast for the *mukluks*, beaver hats, and mittens she sewed. People paid more than one hundred and fifty dollars for a pair of her *ugruk*-bottom *mukluks*. Melt often took two or three pairs to Crotch Spit when he went to get drunk for a few days. Her creations were beautiful, the skin tanned white with sourdough or red with fermented alder bark. Her stitches were tiny, the garments sometimes sparkling with beads. I wondered if my mother could sew. In my stray fantasies where Mom found us and brought presents, there was no great amount of sewing. Probably she was one of the rich women now. Maybe that was why Abe didn't send out lynx anymore. I wished Janet would be my mother. My imagination loaded a full-color picture: Melt, out on the ice. Suddenly he plunged through and the black current swept him from view.

"Janet! Make fresh coffee!" Melt shouted, still alive, sounding as if he were hollering at a dog about to piss on his rifle.

Treason came in, then Lumpy stomped in from roaming the town. He smelled of factory cigarettes. Woodrow Washington Jr., Lumpy's young uncle, slipped in with him. He stood by the door.

"Washingtons need caribou," Lumpy told Melt. Lumpy was taller and thicker than Melt now. He stomped snow off his boots. Melt had always reminded people that Lumpy was Janet's son, not his. Now Lumpy was reminding him who was bigger.

A moment later, out in the night, the church bell rang curfew. Janet flung Lumpy a look. "Mom, I'm hungry," he said, ignoring her stern eye. He pushed my head. "Hi Cutuk." The soup was gone; Lumpy stirred up a glass of hot Jell-O. It was one of Janet's new glass glasses; at home we had only mugs, and broken-handled mugs for glasses. Lumpy said nothing about me being kicked. He didn't offer a sip of the sweet Jell-O.

"See that door?" Lumpy whispered. "We got real door, not homemade Kool-Aid kind like you fellas." I stared, as surprised as the time he ate a tube of Pepsodent when the town was all out of pop and candy.

"Woody an'em need meat!"

Iris and I flung each other corner-eyed glances. Jerry peered up and focused back into the catalogs. Woody Jr. shifted by the door. His eyes were bloodshot. "*Alappaa* that east wind," he said, and finally, "Melt, where's your cigarette?"

Abe patted his pockets. "Here you go." He drew out his tobacco pouch. Woody moved uneasily away from the door toward the different kind of tobacco.

Melt had stayed molded comfortably in his chair, tuned in to his shortwave radio. We kids dreamed of music and never heard any at home; Iris had been ready to ask Melt if he'd turn it up so the faint songs would reach us. He grumbled, flipped the radio off, handed over a pack of Marlboros. He found one boot. He kicked at the piles behind the stove, hunching over stiffly, searching for the boot's mate. "You kids! You lose my one-side!"

I hunkered low, discovering interesting aberrations in my thumbnail. Janet slapped Woody on the shoulder. "Cigarette, that's your food, huh?" She grinned with Abe, took a meat saw off the nail over the kitchen counter, and went out to cut a hindquarter off a frozen caribou.

Melt settled back into his chair. He tossed the boot back into a heap of clothes. "Goddamn kids."

When Janet came back in her eyes were bright and watery from the cold and she smiled radiantly. *"Alappaa!"* She handed Woody the unskinned leg. Loose caribou hairs clumped on the fresh cut. "Enough?" He nodded. "Nice-out night!" she told him. "I'm glad you let me go out."

WE WERE ALL ASLEEP, stretched like mossed-in logs, when the door creaked open. Janet had left the lantern burning on the floor beside the slop bucket; it cast a hissing circle of light. Enuk Wolfglove's frost-whitened form materialized out of a cloud of condensation that rolled in. He was dressed in furs and held a stiff red fox under his arm. The animal's frozen eyes squinted in death. I blinked awake and lifted my head off my ropey jeans-and-shirt pillow. It was cold on the floor. My bag had a rim of frost around the opening. I could feel cold air going into my lungs. I watched Enuk in awe, knowing with conviction what I wanted to be if I managed to grow up.

He pulled his parka over his head and opened the door and put it out in the *qanisaq* the way elders did. He cracked the ice around his eyes and mustache and stared down in the weak light. "Hello, Cutuk. Welcome to big city. How's your luck?"

"I got a marten last week," I whispered. "Finally," I added, remembering the importance of a hunter's humility.

Enuk nodded in generous respect, elevating me above droll twelve-year-oldness. The bridge of his nose was black, a huge frostbite scab. His cheeks were scarred black. "*Yuay*. Tat's good. I get only fox." He laid the rock-hard animal on the floor beside the woodpile, careful not to snap the tail off. He slipped outside and got the head half of a *quaq* trout.

"You want coffee?" Janet murmured from her and Melt's bed.

"Let'um. Naw." Enuk cut chunks of the raw fermented fish and dipped them in seal oil. They were so cold they smoked on the table. "*Aarigaa.*" Enuk sighed and grinned. Janet sat up. They spoke softly in Iñupiaq. Melt grumbled and rolled over toward the wall. Enuk squinted at him and down at his fish.

"A wolv'reen almost gonna eat that fox. Enuk snowshoeing *tupak* it," Janet explained to me. "It climb tree, alright. His gun have ice and can't work." Enuk asked a question and she spoke again in Iñupiaq. I heard my name and wondered, were they discussing my bruised lip—or only talking about something that had fallen?

Enuk cleared his throat, switched to English. "One time gonna I'm young man, I live in'a mountains. In igloo, like you fellas, Cutuk. Good place same like your camp. Lotta wolf, wolv'reen, link, any kinda animal. Only thing, *iñugaqałłigauraq* be there. They rob my skins. Meat. Caribou tongues even. Let me *tupak,* gonna all'a time." He chewed a piece of *quaq*. "I can't leave till I get white wolf. Tat one got face jus' like moon. He look inside you. Gonna anytime. Tat one, he hide easy, gonna see you."

Abe stirred in his sleeping bag. I glanced into the far corner. Dawna's eyes were open and dark, asking for answers to questions that weren't in the room. She hugged her small stained pillow under her chin. It was a store-bought pillow, without a pillowcase, and it leaked chopped yellow foam. Behind her on the wall was a taped and torn poster of the beautiful Wonder Woman. Dents in the shiny paper caught light. The eyes had been colored in with ink and stared, detached from the small perfect smile. I wished I could loop my fingers around Dawna's little finger, kiss her wrists; but I didn't know how to kiss and the distance across the shack was too exposed and cluttered with sleeping people who knew everything else about me.

"One night moon shining, I chop hole for water." Enuk held his hand two feet off the floor, measuring. His fingers were huge and dark, puffy from seventy-three years of freezing and thawing. "Not so thick ice. My fry pan have bad taste an' I gonna washing it. Something grab me. Right on'a neck. I'm plenty strong tat time. Almos' gonna I take t'em hands off." Enuk clenched his hands. His words twinged me with envy. Some Eskimos—like Enuk—inherited the not-too-distant survival days kind of muscles. Much stronger, it seemed, than white-man muscles.

His eyes had gone serious behind the black pools of shadow. His words draped shivers across my shoulders. I dreaded leaving the noisy safety of town and returning home to wilderness nights, vast silence peopled with prowlings in the dark.

"Tat thing let me never breathe. Then it give up. No tracks on ta snow. Tat's spirit. He fight me cus he's lost, travel long way from home. Maybe spirit same gonna like us. Mad when they mixed up inside."

He rubbed his neck and after a minute he grinned, letting the somberness flow out of the room. "Tat time I lose my fry pan."

"How come you never hook it, Enuk?" I murmured. My chin was on my wrists, the bag clenched tight. Enuk sat up where it was warm. His story seemed pointless; I felt dumb and slightly angry for not understanding why he'd kept me awake.

"I never try hook it," he said patiently. "Now I been gonna hunt tat place sometimes fifty year; *iññuqun*, spirit, *iñugaqałłigauraq*, they never always try bother. You tell me if you see white wolf. Your dad maybe he gonna try forget again." Enuk and Janet laughed. Enuk leaned back from the table. "*Aarigaa taikuu.*"

I lay my head down and struggled to keep my eyes open. Enuk's words sifted down in my sleepy mind. The day of cold air on the trail had left me exhausted, and being around so many people—most who knew us and we didn't know back—took so much energy. Just trying to talk right, not chew loud or get kicked; it made sense why Abe had left Chicago.

Enuk dug in his moosehide pouch and the light glinted among his treasures. My eyelids fell closed. An instant later he dropped a cold lump in my hand. A brown bear figurine, carved out of ancient mammoth ivory, stood on its hind legs, nose up, whiffing worlds off the wind. How old it must be! It meant so much, and I pulled it into my sleeping bag and held it that way, like it was alive, deserving of eternal respect. With its enchantment, and in the cast of Enuk's warm eyes, mean things and people could not harm me.

FIVE

ON THE FLATS *between river drainages, wolves span out over a mile of tundra and leafy green willow thickets.* The pups play and bite each other's legs. The wolves work west, bruised and hungry after spending the recent night—bright and starless as day—testing a cow moose and her young calf. The calf had appeared small and helpless, eligible to be eaten. It struggled, staying close under its mother's flank during the final battle. In the end, the cow's berserk defense of her young left a wolf wounded, stomped in the willows. The pack had closed on the wolf, killed it, and left the creekbed. The famished calf nursed.

Now the wolves turn across the tundra toward their den. They recognize each moose in their territory, test each regularly for weaknesses and vulnerable new offspring. Four of the pack are pups. Playful and only a couple months old, the pups are insatiable. Since May, the black male and gray female have claimed most of the available food for themselves and their litter. They are fat. The young adults in the pack are skinny and starved. Two have left to hunt alone.

Today a third wolf rests, lets the family go on. She stops, trots north, and rests again. Finally she travels, a hundred miles northwest in the first week. The sun never sets. The days are hot and flies buzz around her nose. The sunny nights trill with the call of nesting sparrows and waterfowl. Beaver move out into lakes to evade her. Muskrats dive and disappear. The wolf catches a ground squirrel, a few flightless warblers, a ptarmigan. Everything warm-blooded wanders under the canopy of swarming mosquitoes.

The young wolf swims wide rivers, climbs mountain passes, crosses green valleys ashimmer with cotton grass. In the lee of twin peaks she comes to a snowfield. Seventy thousand caribou stand crammed on the snow, nearly insane and forsaking graze to elude a portion of the insatiable mosquitoes. The wolf catches a slow calf and eats, yards from the mass of animals.

Her stomach is distended and tight. She moves sleepily into the alders of a nearby creek. When she awakes, the brush teems with wolves. The young gray wolf rolls on her back, shows her throat to the unfamiliar pack, makes obsequious sounds left over from her puppyhood.

The wolves growl, stand over her with their heads high. The young wolf is skinny, the marrow in her bones dark red. For lack of threat, luck, reasons unknowable—the pack does not kill the intruder. The group moves toward the caribou. Thousands of animals race and mill. The wolves down a limping bull with swollen joints and soft black velvet antlers. The herd accepts the cost, swells back on the snow to await wind. At the kill there are growls. Suddenly a fight erupts.

By the first snow the caribou's and the female wolf's bones are clean, almost white.

SIX

SPRING WAS MY FAVORITE time of year, and it took extra energy to stay in a bad mood. The sun came home to the Arctic and shone tirelessly on the shimmering world of snow. Midwinter diminished into memory and the Darkness of next winter seemed inconceivable. Warm smells rose from the black soil of exposed cutbanks; birds shrieked and carelessly tossed leftover seeds down out of the birches. It was a season of adventure calling from the melting-out mountains, of geese honking after a continent-crossing journey, of caribou herds parading thousands long on their way north to the calving grounds, sap running and every arctic plant set to burst into frenzied procreation. Spring was the land smiling, and I couldn't imagine my life without that smile.

But I was sixteen and stunningly lonesome. Iris and Jerry were gone. Iris's last correspondence-school course lay behind her in the untarnished trail of As. She waited only for paperwork to be officially free. The Rural Student Vocational Program had sent a plane ticket for her to travel to

Fairbanks, to apprentice for two weeks, as a teacher. A year ago Jerry had moved there; he lived with a girlfriend named Callie. To me it seemed ironically unfair—since I was eight and first read about Frank, the elder Hardy Boy, *I* had wanted a girlfriend named Callie. Jerry had probably found the only one in Alaska.

For weeks the April sun lengthened and then Iris returned—transformed—a joyous goddess with black hair curled in a "permanent" that apparently wasn't, but would last long enough. Her cheeks were flushed, her eyes a happier blue than ever, with three-hundred-and-sixty-seven-dollar contact lenses focusing them. For the first time in more than a decade she could see needles on the spruce. I greeted her the way I had greeted sixteen, with a practiced impassive shrug borrowed from Treason and a safe smile. Her face glowed with jubilation and the wonder of the Outside; mine was dark and hard with snow tan and a grip on leaking uncertainty.

"Fairbanks has eight-story skyscrapers at the university," she exclaimed.

We were out near the middle of the river chipping a new water hole in the ice. The water in the old one near shore had grown brown with tundra water eddying up from the mouth of Jesus Creek. The ice froze all the way down to the sand in places and we hoped we weren't working over one of those places. A moose stood in the willows, below the dog yard, breaking down branches, chewing the tips, leaving carnage. Iris wore an aqua nylon jacket she'd bought in Fairbanks and she looked as pretty as Dawna Wolfglove.

"One night we borrowed a master key from a junior. We sneaked up on the roof and dropped the ice cubes out of our root beers. Down on the concrete. My friend Robin found a five-dollar bill in the elevator."

I rested while Abe shoveled the loose ice out of the four-foot-deep hole. The moose plodded out on the river, crossing toward the far shore. Two more moose stood over there on the bank, long-legged, big ears up, and watchful.

"Oh," she saw my expression, "a master key opens any door at the university."

"Yeah? What's an ice *cube?*"

"They make ice in freezers, to put in soda pop, Cutuk. They sell it, too, in bags."

Store-bought *ice?* I remembered the sweet powerful taste of pop. Tommy Feathers had stopped for coffee when he was hunting wolverine. He tossed a bulged red and white can on the chopping block. "You'll have tat one springtime," he joked. He was sober; that meant he was laughing and friendly, not frothing about *naluaġmius* starving his family, stealing food out of his children's mouths. We had sat around inside waiting for it to thaw. We could have bought pops in Takunak but according to Abe, pop cost money, wasted aluminum, and was bad for our teeth. Nothing for something. Why not drink water? Now Iris was describing the high school friends and fun we'd always worried we missed out on, and I wondered why I hadn't bought myself a few Cokes.

Abe clattered the shovel around the ice walls of the water hole. He flung a last shovelful. "Go 'head." Under his heavy mustache he had the faint curl to his lip that a person wouldn't notice unless they knew him well. I wasn't sure if his aversion was to the tall buildings, ice cubes, or this change in Iris.

I picked up the *tuuq* and checked for fresh rock nicks in the sharpened steel bar bolted to the end of the pole. I drove it down into the dark ice at the bottom of the hole, superstitious and reckless, promising if the chisel punched through it meant luck, meant I would never give up on the land, on my dog team, on a life where water came from holes in the ice. The chips remained powder dry in the shaft.

"Ice is thick." Abe sat on a bucket and took off his beaver hat. His hair was sweaty and matted. Snow squeaked under the bucket. "Traveling might be good late this spring."

"We went to a swimming pool. Kids teased me 'cause I can't swim." Iris claimed to have roller-skated, ridden buses, eaten pizza—things I had heard bits of from Jerry's letters. Jerry was more impressed now with macro lenses and Bukowski poetry. "Oh," her voice dropped in mock gossip, "Jerry's got another girlfriend."

"Two of 'em?" I jumped into the hole and chipped at the bottom. Only my head stuck out the top, my shoulders level with the snow.

"No, no. He and Callie split up. Be careful, Cutuk!"

Split up: the words reverberated with romance.

"We went to a dance."

A dance! While Iris was gone I'd mushed my dogs north, climbed a pass in the Dog Die Mountains. I tracked and shot a wolverine beyond treeline, beyond landmarks I'd never seen or heard stories of. I skinned it there, awed and humbled by the towering fling of white mountains, white valleys, white land that left me feeling small as dust, daring as an astronaut. Days later on the way home, in timber at the base of the Dog Dies, a brown bear charged out of alders. The team tugged forward. The bear stood in their midst. The dogs pulled against necklines, trying to scatter. I shot from the sled. The bear fell, rose, and bounded into the thickets. Cautious and alone, I snowshoed in after the wounded animal and took the bear's meat home, fat bulging between the bed slats of my sled, me tingling with pride and hoping Dawna would be present when Enuk heard.

Now in the thud of one heartbeat it was nothing even worth telling. My first wolverine was a greasy pelt, the bear simply meat, jars of rendered lard for pie crusts and fat to store *masru* and *tinnik* in. As boring as breakfast. Iris had been dancing.

"Cutuk! Be careful! You're almost through. It's thin under you." She leaned over the ice hole. Her voice was small, worried now about my feelings. Abe cleared his throat. He unlaced the top and bottom laces on his *mukluks* and pulled up his socks. The heels were gone. I remembered him unraveling our socks when our feet grew too big, crocheting larger pairs from the yarn. Abe was fast with his crochet hook. He never allowed us to throw a shirt, a pair of pants, a jacket away without unstitching the zippers and buttons.

"I bought a radio," Iris said. "It's for you, to listen to next winter. If Abe can stand it."

I leapt out of the hole and cut my eyes up at her, squinting to hide the dread that rose in me like the water now boiling up the ice shaft. "Where are you going?"

"College. Next fall." The water overflowed the ice, soaking blue into the snow. "I know we talked about trapping and raising dogs together.

But I met friends! They're all enrolling! If you come the year after, we could rent an apartment together."

I chipped at the ice. My strong arms ached to drown these shadowy friends down our new water hole. They beckoned Iris to dance away, with no thought of our family coming apart. I pictured ripping those worn brass zippers out of rag jeans, the fling of dust, old lint, and snapping threads. Abe's coffee can was full of used blue and gray and black zippers, the cloth edges curled and unraveling. We were never going to use all of them now.

"I've got to finish school. I've got seven dogs to feed. I can't talk to people the way you do."

Abe rubbed his sore knee. He pulled the *tuuq* out of my hands. Iris stomped off a few yards in frustration. She stood so unaware of her comeliness, her dark lashes leading the light into pale blue pools, her nose straight and sure, knifing through doubt. Allegedly, my sister.

Abe chipped methodically at the ice plug still in the bottom of the hole. His feet were planted far apart to keep the slush off his *mukluks.* Small winged bugs rose in the water and crawled out on the snow. Spring water bugs. They were part of the season, something to watch for and laugh about when we drank water or mixed up powdered milk. Abe's face was wide and serene, open with listening, his eyes the color of the northern sky. Talking feelings in front of him felt jagged.

I mumbled to Iris. "I can't even walk good when people are around. They act different every time."

"So do caribou!"

"At least caribou make sense! Caribou don't act like they're all wonderful and better just because they got bell-bottoms or something."

"The bulls do in October!"

For a second we grinned at each other. "Just because you're good at hunting," Iris said, "doesn't mean you have to instantly be the best everywhere. You could learn."

"To do what, be a truck driver? A dentist? What?" Anger and pride thickened my voice. "This is where I belong."

"You sure that's true?" Her question echoed in my head. *Sure that's true? That's true?*

"Ah, that broke it loose," I heard Abe say. Suddenly the snow sparkled too bright in the hurtful magnification of tears. I scooped the buckets full and stumbled toward the house in the deep snow. Water sloshed against my overpants. My chained dogs, and Abe's, climbed to their feet, wagging and whining for attention and food as they did every day of the year. Jerry, Iris—even Abe—now everyone knew how to be in that world of cars, music, and store-bought ice. Even Lumpy Wolfglove learned when he got sent to Nome for shooting his initials in the school roof.

I left the water buckets on the drift above the dog yard and ran north, across The Lake, along the Jesus Creek trail, toward what I knew I loved: wild mountains that were the bones of the land, mountains that might always be there and would never love me back.

THE SNOW MELTED SLOWLY as spring spread its warmth. We had dug snow steps down to the door and the caribou-skin weather stripping was damp and soggy; we were at the top of the drift enjoying the long light of evening when the dogs struck up howls. Abe glanced up from his easel. He'd just come out from warming his oils. White was spread in his cupped palm. His big hands were thrashed and old-looking, shiny and shot with deep grooves. He worked at a painting of a flock of ptarmigan coasting west in winter's falling dusk. He should have been using watercolors, painting the spring evening. This air tasted and smelled bigger and better than winter, this was the alive time of year, but Abe was stubborn about exercising his imagination.

I ran down the snow steps, inside for my gun, not caring what the dogs had spotted. Iris surreptitiously studied her atlas, sitting on a high snowdrift on a caribou hide. With her new contact lenses she'd already spotted that a traveler was coming, not something for me to shoot and skin, and she'd slid her thumbnail into the atlas and drifted back into the current of her wish world.

I kicked blocks of snow, embarrassed at my panicked rush for my rifle and desire to kill. The dogs kept barking. My irritation jumped to the traveler for being so slow. A disfigured speck inched up the river. Eventually the speck turned into Franklin Tusso on snowshoes and his dog Say-tongue, together dragging their small sled built on wooden Army skis.

Abe and I walked down the bank and Iris followed. Franklin huffed into the dog yard. The sled creaked to a halt. Say-tongue lay down gratefully and bit ice balls off the hair between his toes.

Franklin wheezed and bent over at the waist and stretched to touch his white Bunny boots. He shuffled his feet to turn his butt toward us. "Hi, kids. How are you?" he asked upside down, peering between his knees. "Kids" might have included Abe. Franklin was twelve years older than Abe. Clothes hung off his body and knobs of him showed through. He was short and wiry, and the whitest man we knew—not in personality, but in skin and hair. Villagers had nicknamed him China-man. Sometimes he spoke Chinese to himself. Rumor said he'd once been a professor of Chinese linguistics from Hartford or Harvard. But nobody cared about that. He was famous because he had a cat.

Abe petted Say-tongue's wide head and pulled the skin gently. The huge malamute squinted in pleasure. Abe and Franklin were good friends, and because of that a lot of things didn't have to be said. Other things were repeated just because they were glad to see each other.

"Been slim for travelers." Abe squatted on his heels in the soft spring snow. "How many days it take from your island?"

Franklin straightened. "Well . . . three? His mind seemed to be jumping over each patch of overflow along the way. He'd probably paused on the trail, sitting sideways on the load, meditating on what he could make out of bent spruce knees he passed, twisted alders, birch crotches. "I like crotches best," he'd once admitted, oblivious to our grins.

"Enuk Wolfglove's missing."

"*What?*" I said. "Enuk's back in Takunak?"

"He was. Melt Wolfglove and Tommy Feathers and others have been searching the Shield Mountains with snowmobiles. Janet thinks Enuk went hunting caribou. They want me to head back to town if you guys know anything."

"I hope he never froze," Iris whispered. We glanced at her. Iris worried about freezing. She had bad dreams and woke up sweating and gripping my neck like it was a log overhanging the river. One night when she was twelve she dreamed she had a baby. While she was skinning caribou leggings for *mukluk* skins, the baby slipped outside. It was storming out and Iris ran out with bloody hands and the knife and she found the baby frozen to the ice. Its eyes had frozen, turned opaque the way frozen irises do. Two days after that dream, Iris and I took dogs and sledded down the shore to check our *tiktaaliq* hooks set through the fast-ice. The dogs led us to a caribou calf that had worn itself out trying to climb out of the river onto jumbled ice. The calf's front legs were frozen down, its fur coarse with ice. The stomach was soft, way inside. The eye was frozen, staring up. I started kicking it loose, to get for dog food. Abe had taught us, any scrap we found came home for dog food. But the dogs whined nervously. A few yards away, bear tracks as big as Abe's *mukluks* were pressed into the snow. Iris shouted to the team to turn around. "Come-gee! Come-gee!" We glanced at the cold black current beyond the feathery ice. Up into the metal sky. Into willow thickets. Brown fur shifted back in the willows. We raced home.

". . . 's gone missing before," Franklin was saying.

Blood hissed in my ears, spreading anger. How could Franklin be so casual? *I* hadn't seen Enuk in four years. He and Melt had a falling out, and Enuk hitched up his team and drove sixty miles south to Uktu to live with his daughter. Last winter he'd mushed here to visit. I'd been out camping with my dogs, traveling, not seeing anything except dozens of moose, admiring the country, bragging in my loud mind to Enuk. And missing him again.

I missed Enuk. I had whole books of conversations polished, ready for when he arrived. Now I'd shot caribou, my first wolverine, a bear, beavers, moose, swans. I needed his affirmation that being a hunter was enough.

Enuk could live beyond mountains in the next river valley, he could be missing; he couldn't be gone. Not without taking me.

"Winter was tough." Franklin's eyelids protruded, crinkly lean-tos above his gray eyes. "Every time I snowshoed in a trail it blew or snowed." Abe nodded. Franklin nodded. "My meat ran out during that minus-sixty stretch. Might have been reading too much. Thought I'd have to eat piss and dirt like Crazy Joe." He laughed a jerky laugh that made me think of Melt Wolfglove and hypothermia. "Fortunately, an old ladyfriend of mine sent a nine-pound block of chocolate."

We all looked at his sled tarp.

"Ran out. Mao Tse-tung here and I lived off that for weeks. I'd hear his toenails on the boards at night, then him licking and gnawing. Seemed to sit well with him."

Where could Enuk be? I walked over and petted our dogs. Nothing was new with Franklin. He sounded surprised, as if he couldn't remember running out of meat every winter. In the fall he worried about global overpopulation, and shot only one caribou. He'd eat it down to the leg bones. By then the herds vanished far to the south and he'd be out hanging whitefish nets in the willows to catch ptarmigan. The old women in Takunak snared ptarmigan with picture-hanging wire Newt sold in rolls at the Native Cache. White people were the only ones weird enough to hang a fishnet in the willows. Villagers shook their heads—*Crazy can't-learn white guy. Gotta shoot lot!*

"Wind and snow covered his tracks." Franklin untied his load and pulled open the tarp. "Sun, too. Searchers found melted-out dog tracks. No one else in the village hunts with dogs anymore. But you know Enuk, who knows what he saw or what valley might have enticed him." An orange paw stretched out of the tarp. Kuguruk dragged herself into the sun. Our twelve dogs rose on their chains.

Iris petted the soft cat. "You'd make a nice neck warmer." She bent the cat's wrists to see the thin clear claws extend.

The things in Franklin's sled were small, rusty, and needed new rivets. He made Abe look like an Everything-Wanter. His tent was handsewn from Egyptian cotton, his stove Army surplus—"the Red Army," Iris joked.

He dug in the load and glanced up. "Brought a letter from Jerry. I went ahead and read it." Franklin bent and blew snot out one side of his nose. "I don't know why he'd live in Fairbanks with the Pipeline going through there. You imagine waking up to the sound of *trucks?*"

After chaining and snacking Say-tongue we went inside and Abe offered Franklin a clean washrag and the basin. Franklin took off all his clothes and washed in the corner. When he was finished he stood naked by the fire and scratched, and they talked. I stood by the window, angry; they weren't even talking about Enuk.

Franklin turned his underwear inside out. He climbed back into his wool pants, chamois shirt, and wool socks. Abe pulled the cannibal pot off the stove.

We feasted on pot-roasted lynx. Kuguruk knocked over Abe's coffee can of turpentine; stepped in blue paint; roamed the dirt corners seeking the smells of a mouse that had died behind the slabs. I ate slowly, reading Jerry's letter about buying a camera and working a union job pouring concrete. Pouring concrete seemed sinful. What would Abe think? Abe scratched under his beard, pleased with the blue tracks on the last floorboard behind the table.

Franklin had bad teeth. He chewed noisily. He spat a lump of gristle in his hand and plopped it beside his plate. "Crazy Joe says Enuk's looking for white wolves. Said Enuk claimed he saw one. He just laughed when Joe tried to get him to tell where. He thinks Enuk wants to get into the pack before he's too old. He said something interesting. Said certain minerals would make an animal's guard hairs drop out, make a gray wolf look white." Franklin peered over the table. "Pass the cranberry sauce, please?"

Abe's face was red above his beard. He rubbed his ears.

Maybe Enuk had broken a leg or fallen in overflow. I itched to run down and hitch up and head to town that night, to help search. But Abe would say wait. The corners of the igloo went silvery black. I went out and slumped on a snowdrift. It was almost midnight, the sun low in the northwest. A spring chill was falling. I clenched my eyes, tried to reach Enuk telepathically. My head grew hot and the horizon spun. And then the snow was cool and black against my face.

An instant later I came digging up through grayness. My legs and arms were far down. I didn't call out. Nothing like this had ever happened before. Maybe I had cancer, or some undiscovered congenital gutlessness. I ate a handful of snow and then quietly strolled back inside.

Abe glanced up. "Villagers will find him." His voice was low, inky, the way it sounded only when he talked to Iris. "They don't give up." I looked away, uncomfortable with tenderness from him, angry at the way he forestalled any heroic action. He went to the kitchen counter and banged around more than he needed making coffee.

"What's that flavor in this cranberry sauce?" Franklin asked. I'd made the sauce and sliced some nutmeg into it. It irritated me, him asking now. I sat on my bed along the back wall. Jerry's old bed.

Iris zinged a rubber band into my shoulder and tossed her eyes. Kuguruk attacked the rubber band. "He put in a cup of fish eggs," she said.

"Huh. Whitefish eggs? Have to remember that."

I lay on my *qaatchiaq* and chewed back a grin. Iris was the best of us all. Dark and pretty, she could gut a caribou and talk to strangers, Eskimo or white. Or all of that at the same time. Somehow she knew how to move between worlds and find a trail that was broken. She was what I longed to be—laughter in a storm. But she was leaving this place of storms, trading it in on something. A constant supply of friends? Candy in every store? Fewer mouse turds in the oatmeal?

". . . what they want to force on eastern Canada. Between the Sara Clubbers and the developers, we're moving toward playground wilderness." Abe and Franklin had been silent for a minute, possibly thinking about Enuk, but now were quickly warming themselves around their mutual favorite subject.

"Could be." Abe got up and splashed their lukewarm coffee back in the pot and poured hot. He stretched on his bed, his elbow on his pillow, the coffee cup tucked near his ribs. "The world isn't going to have room for any Hawclys or Franklins. Or Eskimos."

They sipped their coffee. A newly arrived junco pecked in the moss outside the window. I felt envious of Jerry—not having to be here, hearing all this over and over again—and annoyed that they could so vigorously jump into the worn trench of their ecological prophecies when Enuk had been their friend all these years.

"Thing is, any cute furry creature will suffice." The Blazo box under Franklin creaked. "Gadget-ridden lifestyles, and they find it titillating to fret about *baby seals*. Jesus, the aliens are going to be impressed when they find us." They chuckled the chuckle of longtime friends who knew each other's rants.

I twisted a wad of caribou hairs into a weak rope. We'd learned how to read on out-of-date *CoEvolution* magazines. No Dick and Jane or Little Red Riding Hood vilifying the wolves. Abe slipped them in the firestarter box. He weaned us on oil spills, deforestation, global spin air pollution. I'd grown up fearing the coming hordes of Everything-Wanters, daily expecting to see mutated two-headed caribou limping past, contaminated by nuclear fallout concentrated in their favorite lichens—*Cladina rangiferina*—passed to us and further concentrated.

"Goddamn Sara Club," Franklin muttered, "'s a charade when they're the developers' best customers."

Abe looked uncomfortable. "Well . . . I guess. Hickel and Reagan would put the blade down and drive to the North Pole."

I lay on my caribou skin, as strong and useless and trapped as a teenager could feel. Abe was right, what could I find that the snowgoers couldn't? My overpants and *mukluks* hung over the wood box. My gloves and beaver hat were on the floor behind Franklin. My whole body was a muscle that ached to escape. I pictured developers as huge leaping creatures, frog-colored, long and mean. They leapt like green fire across valleys, chewing tops off mountains, ripping up trees, flossing with cables. The Sara Clubbers were gnat people buzzing in clouds around them, clubbing persistently with their gnat checkbooks. Neither noticed Enuk, weak and wounded, as they swept over him.

When I did rise, the knots in my jaw silenced questions. I strode out with my hat in one hand, my rifle in the other. Iris followed. She stood barefoot on the snow steps. The evening air turned her toes and nose pink. She peered up and down the river.

"Which direction?" I begged. "You probably know! Just tell me!"

Her eyes went wide, pained. I looked away, ashamed of my meanness. Her eyes glistened, floating her contact lenses. She shook her head.

I stuffed huskies into harness and ordered my seven dogs south toward the Shield Mountains. Then west, along steep bear-den ridges and willowy creeks. I had only my gun and axe, some rope and matches. *Try me!* I swore at the sky. I wondered if I was greedy, only wanting to find Enuk to hear his compliments, to glean the past from him. Cutuk Hawcly, the secret Everything-Wanter.

A maze of melted and sublimated tracks pocked the snow. Caribou trails, the fine web of ptarmigan tracks, moose trenches, otter slides; wolf, bear, fox, and wolverine tracks softening into indistinguishable circles. My dogs left no tracks on the night crust, and huge trails in the heat of the following afternoon. A herd of caribou ran and stopped ahead of us. Quickly I yanked the rifle out of the scabbard. The boom lanced across the distance. I gutted the caribou, sliced her liver and tenderloins, and stuffed them in the rumen. I fed my dogs the intestines and backbone and blood-shot head, then ate the liver and meat that the stomach contents had partially cooked. I slept there, rolled in the fresh hide, hair side up on the bed slats of the sled.

The third morning I awoke and sat up. Something was wrong. Was it smoke?

Snowblind!

And I knew all chance of my finding Enuk had ended here on the tundra. The mountains were lost. My corneas were raw and chapped, my fingers smoky in front of my face. I felt my way up the line of dogs, toggling towlines to harnesses and untying Plato from the willow I'd used to keep the team lined out. The dogs wagged and pressed against my legs and licked my hands.

The sun had betrayed me. Maybe it had done the same to Enuk, though that seemed unlikely—he had the good dark eyes. The sun now was the only thing left to steer by. It seemed cooler today, and I kept it behind until Plato found the river in one of the portage bends, and then Franklin's narrow trail meandering the north shore. I climbed dejectedly off the runners and into the basket of the sled. The dogs pulled me home with my head down in my gloves as the light through my lids grayed and snowflakes fell on the back of my neck.

COLD GRAY SKIES CAME BACK, and for three days snow fell soft and fluffy. Winter had returned; each flake buried whatever tiny trace the wind might have forgotten to paint over of Enuk's tracks, whatever the sun had neglected to melt. Woodrow Washington Sr., Nippy Skuq Sr., and Tommy Feathers showed up on snowgos. Melt Wolfglove had gone west, they said, to his staked mining claim in the western mountains, to see if Enuk was there. People were talking, *guuq*—Melt wanted Enuk's nuggets. Woodrow's jaw thrust out in an underbite; he mixed *p*s and *b*s the way elders did, English not their first language, Iñupiaq having a sound in between the two sounds. "Tat Melt Wolfglove already try think Enuk's ivory gonna pe hiss. Melt never always can't find golt, only thing jade rock too pig can't lift." The men laughed, though less than usual, and swallowed coffee, asked about the condition of the upriver ice. And continued on.

The third stormy evening, Iris whipped up ice cream with the light snow, powdered milk, sugar, vanilla extract, and a dash of salt. She beat it until it was creamy and light. Franklin licked his spoon upside down, scraped it around his bowl, and licked it again. He set his bowl on a shelf to use again for breakfast. Kuguruk pointed her stubby face up and searched for a way to the shelf.

"Think I'll stick around for Breakup," Franklin announced.

Company had forever been a wish, but now with Enuk lost and the months Iris would be home slipping away, I felt cabin feverish about a permanent visitor in our igloo. *He better not expect her to make ice cream every night. And wouldn't it be nice if he cut those yellow toenails?*

Franklin pitched his tent a quarter mile downriver. Most days he spent nearby, carving wood or filing an axe into a smaller axe, eyeing the file for a future knife, and mulling over the coming environmental disaster of the planet, as if by sheer power of worrying he would be granted an opportunity to bend the path of the developers.

Franklin told stories of living and traveling with hunters on the endless steppes of Mongolia, of dark-eyed girlfriends in foreign cities and eating bricks of chocolate while being a tank gunner in World War II. All were virtues that should have earned him permanent status as a hero, but doing chores he wore flat green gloves that fit either hand—he wrote MEAT on one side of the wrists, WOOD on the opposite—and because he didn't shoot many animals, and ranted about the interconnected consciousness of trees shared between their roots, he was only a crazy white, forever ineligible to be a hero.

AFTER THE STORM, the warm May days slushed the new snow. I slept afternoons, dodging leaks in the roof. Late in the cool nights, when the snow crusted firm and solitude stretched out, I hitched up my team and searched. Mile after mile, tundra, mountains, sloughs, more tundra. The dogs relished running. I wouldn't say what we searched for. That could bring a lack of luck. I wondered for the first time in my life at the uncertain cosmos ahead if I let go of this living-off-the-land.

The land glowed as smooth and hushed as I imagined a lover could be. I stood on the runners of my moving dogsled and sang softly, corny words that condensed in my head, about valleys and mountains and faraway girls and wind in the sky. The night sun slid orange pastels behind the jagged peaks of the Dog Dies. The scent of Labrador tea rose off the melting-out tundra. Chirping sparrows, robins, and snipes found the bare ground and rustled leaves with their mates, turning up sweet seeds and berries. *What would he eat? Was he melting out somewhere like a wolf-gnawed moose skull?*

Miles north, and west, in front of the center of the Dog Die Mountains, I whoa'd the dogs at a creek. The creek had swift open holes under cutbanks, and cave-ins that stayed thin and dangerous all winter.

There were tracks. Something had walked along the edge of a stretch of overflow. Green ice showed where the pads had pressed through the snow. Quickly I anchored my team. The tracks ran for a hundred feet, soaked up and frozen in overflow ice. A few yards from the end were a couple of short crosswise drag marks, possibly made by a swinging neck-line. The tracks were old and pointed toward Takunak. They could have been made in April, or last November. Trailing were two sets of larger, fresher tracks—wolf tracks. Or maybe all three were wolves.

Ponoc pissed on a willow. The other dogs sniffed each other's butts and rolled, uninterested in the old prints. I walked the tracks again, unsure. I did know I was only sixteen, and white, and everyone in Takunak knew how to sneer at information from that direction.

The dogs got comfortable and pointed their noses south toward a thicket, listening. I sat on the bend of my sled and chewed a block of pemmican. It was made from crushed dried caribou, dried currants and cranberries, with caribou fat poured over. The fat had gotten too hot rendering. It was strong, and burned in the back of my throat. I ate snow, walked the tracks again. They weren't enough. Not to tell Melt. Or anyone.

I roused the dogs. "Okay! Hike!" We went on.

IN THE LATE MORNING, as the lifting sun softened the snow, I pulled into our dog yard with two cow caribou on my sled. Warble larvae were knobby as marbles under the hair on the animals' backs. Abe came down with a rolled cigarette burning carelessly close to the stub of his missing finger. He nodded. He put the cigarette in his lips and squeezed a warble as big as the end of his little finger out of the caribou hair.

"Barrow, old people used to eat these." Abe held up the writhing larva. The warble was fat, slimy, and yellow with bellows sides and a biter mouth. "Explorers ate them for vitamin C. A forgotten health food snack. Try it?"

I shrugged, took it out of his fingers, and popped it in my mouth. It was soft, like eating someone else's snot. Not salty though, sweet.

Abe grinned around his cigarette, pleased. His hands were messy with blue. His turquoise eyes caressed the caribou, counting and naming the shades of brown and gray in their shedding hair. "How's the meat? Fat?"

"One. The other, around the bone." Around the bone was our joke. It meant almost skinny. Iris often teased that if I ever got fat it would be around the bone.

"How's the snow?"

"Overflow all the way across upriver. Holes bubbling by the bend."

He looked out over the wide white river, forked with tongues of greenish overflow. "I'll go to town. Check if Newt sold any of our chairs, and mail in that ptarmigan painting." I knew he meant his spring trip, where he went by himself. As kids we had grown accustomed to his spring gone-spells. But the fear that an open hole in the ice or some drunk with a rifle in Takunak might snatch him from us—that dread kept us restless, pacing out to the riverbank in the night sun, watching the trail for our Abe.

HE HITCHED UP AT MIDNIGHT. The air was cool, the sun sliding lines of orange and bluish light across the tundra to the northwest. "You kids take care of each other. Watch the stove." Every year the caribou passed south, the sun went away, the caribou and the sun returned—and Abe said the same words. "You kids take care of each other. Watch the stove."

He slid his rifle into the scabbard. He knelt and pulled the hook. The dogs raced down the river, yipping, leaving only toenail tracks on the night crust. Iris and I listened as the rasp of the runners faded. Down at Franklin's camp at the mouth of Jesus Creek, Say-tongue's mournful howl floated in the trees.

We went in and stoked the stove. I wondered what the news of Enuk would be. Maybe I'd been wasting time, and sadness. We swept the floor and the cracks between the boards and behind the stove with a goose wing. We banged the creosote out of the pipe to make sure it was safe, and put our sleeping bags out to air. Abe didn't mean watch the stove, only to be careful of fire, but we'd developed the habit; years ago when the spring trip started and we were small and frightened and Jerry had to pretend to be big and brave, we sat and we *watched* that stove.

Iris stirred cocoa in a pan.

"It'll be good to hear how Enuk made out," I said, fishing for her to say something.

She sipped. "I'll make a cranberry pie when Abe comes home. We've got lots of bear fat for crust. Abe said that bear came after you. Why didn't you tell me that?"

There had always been three of us during Abe's gone-spells. Jerry had been here, solid and safe, his brown eyes shifting and uncertain and taking care of the worrying, his big hands cradling loaves of bread, bonking the rabid fox with a snowshoe, swinging a moose hindquarter onto his shoulder, his serious voice saying "You can have my half of the gum" or "You can have my slice of apple" or "Want my pillow? It's nice and cold on the bottom." Next year Iris would be gone. I opened the stove door and savaged the coals. "If Abe is so content with books and his harmony living, why does he drink and go mess around in town?"

Iris's face froze, stunned and desolate. "You can love something and still be lonely. I was having great fun in Fairbanks, but I missed you guys, too."

"When you leavin'?"

She picked at the frayed knees of her corduroy pants. She'd been saving her one pair of blue jeans. "If I get enough scholarships, this summer. You know how buggy and boring summers are." Iris turned, "Come too! You could finish high school down there. We'd have so much fun. Cutuk, kids there don't stare and make fun every single second if you're white. It's amazing. They don't try to beat you up. Girls don't get pants'd regularly. They call that sexual assault and it's even jail for that. Nobody on campus even acted like they wanted to fight me."

"We've got twelve dogs, 'cause of me. Abe'll need help drying fish. If I leave"—my eyes cooked in the crackling heat from the spruce logs—"my whole life will seem like some old story Enuk told years ago. I want to hunt. And have a friend or two. Not to think about if there's enough animals or is it bad to kill them or what is 'living' and what's 'polluting.'"

Loneliness laminated my words and I spoke up, quick and hoarse. "Think the stove'll smoke if we leave the door open?"

Now all there was ahead to see was summer, and me, a lone teenager immured along the mosquitoey riverbank, staring across the flat current.

We dragged the couch in front of the fire. Iris's mouth was pursed and red. Our faces grew hot and glowed in the flames. Some time after the sun had come around to the east we leaned together. Slowly the tension melted out of our muscles. Even in sleep I was aware of Iris against my shoulder. The presence of my sister surrounded me. In my dream I was in love with Dawna Wolfglove. We walked in a city, our shoulders brushing each other absently, the way teenage friends did. She wore lipstick and her sleeves were rolled up her brown forearms. Buildings towered overhead. Iris trailed behind. My arm was around Dawna's waist and she leaned close, closer to me than anyone had ever been. I realized with elation that somehow I had learned how to kiss!

As I kissed Dawna, her face blurred in the dream and became Iris's. Dawna stood on the other side of the street. "You *kinnaq* honky," she screamed. "Now how can anyone love you?" Iris took off sunglasses and peered. "Too bad. Y-you fool!" she whispered. "Everybody knows people don't kiss that way." The joy evaporated. I stumbled onto river ice. Everyone was waiting: Iris, Jerry, Franklin, the Wolfgloves. Crazy Joe. All the villagers. Enuk in his furs. *Where had Dawna gone?* The ice sheet rumbled and a black fissure jagged across the white. *Breakup!* The ice broke into separate pans and people began plunging like net rock-sack sinkers into black water.

I jolted awake, every hair follicle on my skin hurting and cold. Franklin clomped inside.

"Ah! Good morning!" Kuguruk dropped out of his arm and rubbed against the wood box. Iris groaned, and I stood and sloshed my head in the cold water in the basin. The dream seemed plastered all over my face, emotions protruding like duck feathers out of a threadbare pillow.

Franklin cleared his throat and cracked the shell on an idea he'd been incubating. "Let's you two get a jump on your schoolwork! I'll get breakfast going."

Iris pulled me outside on the drifts. "Geez!"

For all our years of correspondence school we'd studied the lessons at night, after dinner, and only in the dark of winter, never after the sun turned back to yellow. And Iris was graduated.

I pointed. A split whitefish lay on the chopping block. "Franklin chopped open a dogfood fish for *suvaks*."

"He's putting them in the oatmeal!"

We giggled suddenly. We held onto each other's wrists. Iris was strong and I realized I was, too. The strength of youth washed briefly through my limbs. It felt wild and springy, and as we hunched over laughing I wondered could this be how other people felt all the time?

TWO DAYS LATER Franklin was frying one of his tasteless flat pan breads we'd come to call Iron Toast. Smoke roped over the kitchen counter. Iris paced. She stood suddenly. Sled runners grated on the river. Iris and I whooped outside, sliding down the bank.

Abe's cheeks and forehead were burned painfully from the sun-shot trail, and his teeth flashed as he grinned. His hair was tousled and matted to his forehead. He squeezed Iris's shoulder. "What's the panic, Otter?"

"We're pleased to see you, Abe."

"How's the trail? They find Enuk?"

We stood on the runner, gripping the toprail. Abe had a load and the sun had melted ice to droplets on his sled tarp. A willow branch was caught in his brushbow. Somewhere he'd had to portage around water.

His grin crooked to one side. "Nope. Been a month. You know how they don't give up searching. But, Snowmelt—everybody's slacking off until after Breakup." Abe stomped in his snow hook. The dogs stopped rolling and flopped on their sides, panting.

"They didn't find even his rifle? No sled? No dogs came back?"

"Sounds like he only took five dogs. There's a lot of sloughs they could have tangled up in. Maybe hooked their collars on brush. Or killed each other . . . starved. Guys found a few tracks. Mostly rumors are going around.

Some people say he was hunting wolves. Melt's acting like Enuk went over toward Melt's mining claim to be there when the snow melted off."

Franklin walked up, listening. He blew his nose, wiped his thumb on his pants. "How's Janet?"

Abe worked an icy knot in his sled rope. "Melt's been out doing what you have to do on a search." He straightened and glanced at the far shore. "Looking for sign of Enuk would occupy your mind better than seeing him in every fox bloodspot on the floor, don't you think? And Janet was closer to Enuk."

He didn't say more about Janet. We kicked snow, waiting for the tarp to open. Abe rubbed his knee. "When my dad crashed, the searching was a trip through hell." He pronounced the word carefully, like he didn't say it often, which was true. "It wasn't good when we found him. The engine was under him. The wings crushed his back. But at least the searching was over.

"Enuk, I've known him since January and I were forced down at Takunak in a storm." Abe spoke in Franklin's direction. They nodded at each other and turned to look out over the river. Maybe they were looking back through more years than Iris and I knew how to. Or more lost friends. We looked out over the river, waiting for his story. "We were flying the blue PA-18 up, for my dad. On skis. I was only nineteen. Enuk took us in." Abe smiled at the ground and coiled the loops in his bare hands. "He was honest. I'll always like to see his face. Even that time he moved in with us here for Freezeup and—. Well, anyways."

Abe yawned. He'd probably been up for days. "Pretty sky, isn't it? Want to help unhitch?"

Iris squeezed my sleeve. We turned the tired dogs and pulled the harnesses over their heads. They were gentle and hungry and visited my dogs and Say-tongue. Their feet were warm and some left bloody tracks. The snow had gone hard and crisp. A chill was falling. Maybe the last good traveling for five months.

Abe had brought a library box and the last school lessons I'd mailed in to Juneau, scholarships for Iris, catalogs, and a box of used, ill-fitting clothes that I wished I didn't have to wear—from January Thompson, the man Abe had been with, weathered down in a Takunak that was Takunak no more. I wished I knew the rest. Was there still a chance for my future to be so wild and romantic? How did Abe stay friends with this January slob who slaughtered wolves from an airplane—and flew my mother away? She'd only wanted a ride out, of course, but still. It seemed Abe liked something about everybody. He found that something and focused on it. I wondered what it could be about January Thompson.

In town Abe had bought nails, flour, twine, baking soda, a sack of apples, an invented fruit called a nectarine. When we finished unhitching and feeding the dogs, we took off our gloves and gathered around. He cut the nectarine into quarters on the toprail. Where his knife cut it tasted like dirty penny and rancid seal-hide sheath; the rest didn't taste real—it was that sweet and tangy. Later, I planted the big bumpy seed. Just in case.

We took everything except the apples inside and poked at the haul like ravens around a gut pile. "*Aana* Gladys Skuq bought that wolverine skin of yours, Cutuk. Four hundred dollars. One of our rocking chairs sold." He handed Iris a wad of bills to put in the Hills Bros can. She dumped the can on the bearskin couch and forked bills and coins out of the balding brown hair. The can pinged as she counted. Abe brought the sack of apples in. We pulled out our sheath knives and ate frozen apple.

"Nine hundred and forty-seven."

"Take eight then, when you go." Abe sucked on a hard chunk of apple. "We've still got a table and two chairs down in the Native Cache. A letter came from Big Dipper Gallery. They're making numbered prints of that wolf pack. I don't like that. We'll ask them to stop when you've had all the college you want, 'kay?"

Tears started dripping off Iris's nose.

My throat suddenly needed swallowing. Franklin shifted on a stump near the stove. He'd been sampling the Bacardi 151 left in Abe's bottle—the bottle that usually stayed out of sight and lasted untouched until next spring—and glancing distractedly at a book in Chinese, bare pages of scratches like lilliputian trees, tent poles, sandpiper tracks.

"Where you going, Iris?"

"Fairbanks." She wiped her eyes. "I'm going to college."

"Well! Good for you! When'll that be?"

Without hesitation she said, "First boat after Breakup."

OVERFLOW SPREAD PALE STREAMS over the ice. The tundra snow sluffed and the buried crumbs of winter poked out and formed a webby scum. Our roof leaked in a dozen places, pinging moss-tinted water into every spare can, pot, and dishpan. The dog yard collapsed, dropping us waist deep through the softening layers of sled-dog existence. We tapped birches and collected sap and boiled it into syrup. Bare ground spread as snow melted on the tundra behind the house and along the riverbank, and we picked the first fireweed and bluebell shoots and willow leaves and louseworts for fresh salad. We picked pussy willows to suck out the sweet nectar and lazed in the sun reflecting warmth off the snow. The new ground came alive with smells, and nights rang with songs of sparrows and robins hashing out territories and mates. *Kuukukiaq* roller-coastered high and invisible in the sky, the warbled howl of their wings in each dive claiming their nesting area, night and day sending out the call of spring. The water rose, and ice frozen to the bottom boomed free, cascading water like surfacing whales. Jesus Creek gushed in the night, cutting us off from downriver. We moved the dogs to the highest drift and watched expectantly as water surrounded our marker sticks. Open blue current sparkled. Suddenly summer was no longer a forgotten season.

One afternoon, silently at first, the whole river began moving. Inside we felt something in the air, maybe a dog pacing around his chain, maybe geese honking and lifting off as the ice pressed in, or that other sense we had never learned enough to name. We rushed out to watch. Breakup was all the holidays combined into one. We shouted and pointed and moved along the bank excitedly. Grinding, three-foot-thick ice pans peeled back snowbanks and crushed dog stakes and willows and trees. Ducks and geese flew the banks, landing in open leads and taking off again as the leads closed. Below Jesus Creek the tops of tall spruce twitched and shook as trees fought to stand against the power of the ice. The day filled with sunshine and smells, bird calls and the roar and shudder of a new season being born.

And as quickly the river ground to a halt, jumbled, creaking, tinkling, a monster waiting for more water. Two days passed. The ice sheet broke free. It thundered past carrying torn-out trees, black sandy ice pans, glacier-blue upside-down chunks. The pans thinned by the following evening and the wide silty water dropped daily until one sunny night in early June the first maniacal laugh of the red-necked grebe carried over the tundra. It was almost too late then to collect arctic tern and seagull eggs, and soon the run of huge sheefish would come upriver to spawn, and salmon would follow. Green diamond leaves were coming out on sapling branches. The sun shone out of the north, shining on the wrong sides of the trees, making the spruce across the river glow separate and dusty green. Melting-out frogs rattled the ponds and awakening mosquitoes hummed at our ears. Sweet spring was dead and the hot boring summer here, an eternity trapped along the river under clouds of mosquitoes like a writhing skin, black and stinging. Me, painting rancid yellow seal oil on the dogs' faces and Figment's testicles, trying in vain to keep the mosquitoes from taking away their skin. Tall green grass and leafy trees. Fishing for dog food. Cutting fish, drying fish, cooking fish. Weeks and weeks of eating fish. The grebe could laugh in his red throat; he loved fish and had long forgotten if he'd ever watched a sister fly away.

SEVEN

HUUUUUUUUUUUUUUUUUUUUOOOOO.

Whuuuuuuuuuuuuuuuuuuuuuuuuuuuuuooooooooo.

The voices carry themselves, floating on air, finally falling into timber, to echo and roll and fade like spirits. One downriver, two upriver, many across. Silence. Darkness. Moonlight lies on lines of river current, ponds, pools between tundra tussocks. Caribou step through dying sharp grass, splash shallow water, and stop. They listen, then trot along a sandbar. Hooves beat cold earth, drum under silver-touched night and the twin comfort and unease of that powerful pale eye.

A fish swirls; white ripples glint.

Whooooo. Whooooo. Whoo, whoo. Whooooo.

Mice carry seeds, squeak down tunnels.

Arrooooorroooooooouuuuuuuuuuuoooooooooooooooo.

All hoof sounds cease as predators peel back river, leaping and swimming, crossing cold wide water fast. Hooves pound back up a sandbar, thud a grassy bank; antlers thrash and crash through willows and darkness. Hundred-pound shadows pursue, flank, wait ahead—somewhere . . . seemingly everywhere.

A pike swirls and plunks, swallowing a swimming shrew.

Mice squeak.

A breezes stirs. *Naataq,* the great horned owl, glides across a valley. *Whooooo. Whooooo. Whoo, whoo. Whooooo.*

EIGHT

THE MR. COFFEE MACHINE HISSED and gurgled like a muskrat quietly drowning in the kitchen. The smell of fresh coffee lanced through the Wolfgloves' house, awakening me into memory mornings of a thousand campfires and home.

Most of the houses in town now had electricity from the diesel generators lowered by the Chinook helicopters. Janet didn't remember electricity every morning; I heard her sit up in their room, yawn, and fumble in the dark for her calico *atikłuk*. On my *qaatchiaq* on the floor I flipped the sleeping bag open to let the cool air tighten my skin. School. Iris had left a year and a half ago, and I had let that first winter slide away up at home, my correspondence books frozen to the poles under Abe's workbench. This winter, after Christmas, he'd asked: "What do you think about finishing school in town?" All Abe did was ask, curious. He didn't say please. He didn't ever say sorry. It was up to me to do whatever homework my dreams demanded. Now if I survived verbs and prepositions and onomatopoeias of my last English grammar class I could break through the willows into wide-open life. Whatever that was. Mr. Standle, one of the new teachers, said any life I chose would need grammar, but he was a States person, and it sounded like they spent too much of their lives doing the paperwork, getting prepared to live.

Today would be another turbulent day. Yesterday Nippy Sr. had used his daughter's welfare check and his monthly Alaska Longevity Bonus to charter a Cessna 185 to Crotch Spit. He landed back in Takunak feeling good, the only other passengers on the plane three cases of whiskey and eight cases of Miller beers. Last night there had been scary-fast snowgos and rapid shooting beyond town in the dark—Nippy Jr.'s Mac-10—and a kung fu movie on the TV, with hundreds of people kicked somewhere in the vicinity of death. Today, between classes, there would be reenactments.

Enuk hadn't been found. Charley Casket found a moose skull in the fall when he was looking for bear dens. The skull had a .30-caliber bullet rattling inside—Enuk's caliber, and other people's, too. Charley, who walked creekbeds and cutbanks searching for mammoth ivory, teeth, and artifacts, also found a dog collar—sewed with sinew, that might have been off a dog of Enuk's—washed up downriver on a sandbar.

In whichever direction Enuk lay, it was a long way from Janet's shiny warm new HUD house. Abe wandered into my mind; what was he doing at this moment, light-years from this new world of mine, from Takunak, school, and NBC Night at the Movies? Likely he was kneeling naked, knifing kindling for the morning fire, or reading *The Iliad* or one of my leftover chemistry textbooks in front of a stubby candle. The wax would be running onto a coffee can lid that reflected the light, and, with the sides bent up, collected the wax so Abe could make a baby candle in tribute to his god of the Unwasters.

"Stevie," Janet said. "Get up. It gonna be eight o'clock."

"Adii." Stevie moaned.

"Don't always holler, Mom. Please." Dawna's voice floated out of the darkness.

"Dawna, you shudup!" Melt roared from bed.

The doors were broken out of both bedrooms. The shouting reverberated out to where I lay. Melt was beginning a hangover, and still buzzing too, as the guys called it. "STEV-VIE! You getup and go school." Melt sat up from where he'd slept fully clothed on top of the covers. Nowadays he was like a bad-toothed brown bear in a wet den. Treason had moved up the hill to Janet's brother's, Woodrow Washington Jr.'s, because of Melt. He only came down to use the flush toilet. Woodrow's grandkids had messed theirs up trying to flush caribou bones. Now it was just a shit basin, stinking up the house.

Melt despised having a *naluaġmiu* living under his roof. Janet was the only reason he couldn't boot me out. Melt leaned against a chair. He switched to slurred Iñupiaq, forgetting that I was learning a few words. I'd lived here a month; he was telling Janet something about me going *maatnugun*. The thing I'd heard around town about Melt Wolfglove, *guuq*, was *Tat was Enuk's only son. He let him be funny and never try teach him nothing. Enuk was been too much watch any kinda white guy.* Which, as far as teaching their kids, described many of the parents in Takunak. Which also translated to, Enuk liked white people. Which was a low thing to say about a dead elder, really.

Janet held a candle. She peered down and gripped my forearm in her fierce and tender grasp. She asked kindly, "You awake, Cutuk?"

"Yeah."

"Coffee?"

I raised my eyebrows, *yes* in Iñupiaq, and she padded back with a steaming mug from the Mr. Coffee. My lips found the rim as she remembered the light switch and shattered the friendly darkness. I dressed into the distraction of a school morning, with stomach cramps from gulping Bisquick hotcakes and Carnation canned milk in bitter coffee, rushed searches through the twisted heaps of clothes behind the stove for a missing one-side glove, missing homework papers—missing Iris and the land where no rules, no clock, only weather and the beautiful sky ruled my days.

Melt stood by the door. He shoved Dawna against the wall. The thin paneling bowed. He crushed her wrists in his hands. "You bring ta paycheck home tis time. Don't buy ta weed like t'em other girls. Mom and me need money. We raised you up right from our pocket." He let go of one of her wrists and wiped his mouth. He tilted and yanked himself straight, bruising her arm.

I faced the door, shaking, longing to loop a wolf snare over his head and pull all the slack out. Melt reached under his gut to tug at his hip pocket. "Right from our pocket we raised you up." Dawna was inscrutable, only her eyes glittering. She tried to back away. A rifle leaning against the wall slid along the paneling and clattered to the floor.

"Aw shuck, you! You think you gonna be something else?"

"No!" Dawna's lips tightened out of sight. Each exhale shook her. Stevie and I had fists at the ends of our arms and no idea whether we were breathing.

Melt picked up the fallen rifle.

"Go!" Janet said.

The three of us lunged into the *qanisaq*.

"GODDAMN RAISING YOU ALL, RIGHT FROM MY POCKET!"

Dawna slammed the door. I pulled my gloves on against the pinching cold, swallowed a laugh, picturing the three of us, an inch tall and trapped in Melt's unwashed pocket. My leader, Plato, and a few of my dogs whined softly but didn't uncurl from their melted ice circles. They were finally accustomed to me walking past them to school every morning—not coming out to run them.

We strolled up the hill toward school. Moose tracks crossed the hard-packed trail—a cow and calf had braved town. Dawna lagged farther and farther behind, heading to her morning job at the school office. Halfway up the ridge a big pretty husky lay frozen to the snow.

"Jus' like one of Newt's," Stevie said, interested. "Nippy an' them fellas feeling high musta been shoot it." He kicked the rock-hard dog, twice, to break it loose. The way his leg moved reminded me of Melt kicking boots behind the stove. Dogs, in Takunak, had the rights and privileges of damp firewood—and little use now that snowgos had come. Stevie flipped the dog over. It squeaked and sawed the snow. The legs stuck out stiff and straight. The bottom was perfectly flat, still a little soft, and white around the edges with frost. We saw a bloody bullet hole in the chest, and a dark hole melted down into the snow. Behind my eyes lay the big silver wolf on Enuk's sled, long ago.

"Stevie, what did you fellas do with that silver wolf Enuk got?"

"Which one? He get lots. I dunno. Could be Mom sew it. Or mice wreck it up."

"How about all his stuff?"

"He never been have much. Melt *pakik* everything. Mom use lotta skins to sew gifts for all the people who help search and cook."

Our breath rose in white clouds. The brilliant new streetlight at the top of the ridge splintered the snow into shards of shadow and light. I looked toward the hidden Shield Mountains. Across the tundra, far out of the fling of electric light and its confusion, curled in comfortable uninterrupted morning blackness lay the world that would always be *real* to me. Foxes and wolves, mice, the cold trees and buried sedges, all ancient vital members of the land.

I shook my head to clear the Abe-ism.

Whack. Whack. Stevie twirled Lumpy's homemade broom handle numchuks, smacking the back of his nylon jacket. "I'm almost gonna be Bruce Lee!"

"You dream." We laughed.

I glanced back at Dawna. Waited until she caught up, and shuffled beside her with my head down. "*Alappaa*, huh?" I pretended to warm my face with my hand, pressing my nose, trying to train it to flatten down and be wider. "He hurt you?" In the frozen morning air I bent close. "Dawna?"

"No." Her smile bent. She pressed her face on my shoulder and walked leaning against me.

I moved slow across the snow, shocked to be touched, and not wanting to get anywhere nearer to school where she would not do this. In the distance a group of kids threw iceballs at crippled Timmy Feathers, warming up his day. Since Iris left, the summer before this last one, I'd longed for a woman to talk to. Young guys talked about snowgos, fights, girls, getting drunk; they imitated rifle discharges, bragged of caribou they'd "nailed." The talk was intoxicating, but what remained was the race to be tougher, no tranquil thoughts to get warm around.

Dawna's bare fingers sank into the side of my neck. She seldom wore gloves; she held her sleeves shut, as if she were simply waiting to leave this place of mittens and gloves.

"Cutuk, you know the nurse who came when I was nine? Alicia McBride?

"She was twenty-three. So pretty. Fellas all thought they were gonna make something about it. But she wasn't like that. She wouldn't smoke weed with my aunts. Alicia knew medicine, and good poems even. She never try let me eat porcupine shits like Melt does if I get stomachache. When I had hiccups she let me stare in her eyes and they go away. She asked me what I liked best. I said 'pictures.'"

Dawna stopped walking. "I think she liked herself the right amount. Like your dad, maybe."

I stared across the darkness, at the school generator shack throbbing under a cone of yellow light. *"Abe?"* Dawna had never talked about way-inside feelings—I didn't think anyone in Takunak even had them—and she never said Abe's name.

She leapt a few steps sideways. "Look at me!" She giggled. "Pretend I'm just a picture and say what you see?"

Dawna stood still. The morning night and streetlight shared shadows on her face, glinting her eyes, laying dusk caves under her chin. Frost jeweled the black silk of her hair. She stood with her knees close, slightly bent in the cold, her stiff hard tennis shoes pressed together. A smile lifted the top line of her lip, folding it back provocatively. Behind her the school waited, for me a terribly cold heated place, for Dawna a pasture of popularity. My chest was full of air and empty. I loved her. I wanted to hold her. The magazines and TV didn't know; beauty was Eskimo and brown and named Dawna Wolfglove.

"The prettiest girl ever," I breathed.

Her smile vanished. "I want to go away where people are not messed up. Don't try let it be tough."

"You're—" The words that came to me I could see were useless as lazy dogs and I let them go.

"You're the only one I can talk to, and you can't listen. My brothers, my aunts, my cousins. They're being losers."

I stared, dismayed.

"Alicia said I could follow her and go to college. But Melt threw her letters. Now she's somewhere and I don't know where even." Dawna glared. She shoved my shoulders like the welcome to a fight. She was lithe, strong muscled like Enuk, quick-tempered. On New Year's Eve she gave Elvis Jr. two black eyes. "He was drunk and tried to be funny to me," she'd said. Which meant he'd tried to pants and rape her. She shrugged when she told me, and stuck out her tongue and laughed.

"So what, I'm pretty? Just like everybody only wants in my pants. Is that all you want, Cutuk? You want to *nulik?*"

"Dawna! That's not what I meant." My face felt red, my voice thick with disgust. I laid an arm across her shoulders, clumsy with uncertainty.

"I need to leave around here!" She shrugged away. "This is some kinda no-place place to be from."

I trudged for the school. My safe smile on. "Where you think you'll maybe go?"

"Cutuk!" Now Dawna sounded like she cared. None of it made sense—didn't the whole town love her and think I was dogshit? Lower than dogshit. Dogshit was everywhere. Dogshit was normal. "I'll go Anchorage," she said, pronouncing it the way the religious ladies pronounced *heaven.* A twinge tightened my stomach. I heard Iris's same unhesitating tone, *First boat after Breakup.* And now she was down in Fairbanks, deep in her college lectures, scribbling notes. Her letters were scribbled notes, happy rushed things cluttered with friends. Meanness flowered inside; suddenly I hated Dawna, and the cities because they were coming, and already claiming the best of everything we had. I felt the pull to go, too. Abe had mentioned there used to be bars in Anchorage and Fairbanks with signs out front that said NO NATIVES. I didn't quite believe that he hadn't gotten confused as usual and really meant NO WHITES. I knew exactly how *that* sign would make me feel; the other I couldn't say. Probably just as mad. Hopefully not gleeful. Maybe it was true, and Dawna would feel what I felt whenever people aimed their eyes my way.

Suddenly I felt cheap. Had to spit, and shake my face. Dawna better *never* have to feel the kind of crushed stuff inside my skin. We walked on in the silent movies of our thoughts, our eyes flitting along the parallel grooves left by snowgo skis on snow compressed hard and white as porcelain.

THE BASKETBALL BOUNCED OFF MY FACE.

"How come you always never can't catch nothing?" Nippy Skuq Jr. had a gash across his forehead and a brand-new shiner. He stank sour. Booze sweat. I thought about telling him I didn't grow up with balls, but it didn't seem like the thing to say. His brother Elvis Jr. rushed across the snow court. I thought about telling Elvis that his mom had named him Junior, too—not after his wife-beating bumpy-eyed dad, but a fat-chinned singing white drunk, *in a movie.*

Elvis and Nippy weren't even in school anymore; they had dropped out and now their lives balanced between the bottle and the basketball rim. They'd joined the National Guard. For a month. Then returned with cropped hair and word of how they'd served in the Marines and been taught kung fu.

I started laughing. I couldn't control it. It happened when things were completely unfunny. My palm unconsciously wandered up, to flatten my nose.

Nippy shoved my shoulder. "'Cause you're *naluaġmiu*. Ha!"

"Don't be mean," Dollie Feathers cried. She was Dawna's cousin. Treason and her were "going out," *guuq*.

My nose watered. I backstepped, hands like flippers protecting my eyes. Kids gathered in the familiar loose circle. Elvis moved forward for the kick, the face kick we all delivered in our karate daydreams. Suddenly he was my size, no longer the giant he'd been all my life. I'd grown up hauling logs, holding back huskies. I grabbed his foot and threw him on the ground. My fists were square clubs that swung themselves. That face that leered at everything I had ever been—I hit it down.

I expected the usual boots, brothers, and cousins on my back, but Lumpy dragged me off, his thick forearm clamping my throat in a fancy headlock he'd brought us home from Nome's Anvil Mountain Correctional Center.

"Enough," he growled in my ear.

The ring of faces were sharp. Elvis came into focus, puffy and the corners of his eyes sticky with blood. The circle stared. "What you try to prove?" Elvis's sister screamed. "Nobody wants honkies around here. Go back to Dallas or someplace." She spat and threw an open 7UP can at my head.

I dodged it. "I'm not from Dallas." My voice sounded wet.

"Aiy!" Girls jeered and stepped away, like nervous herd animals, but acting nauseated. Nervous caribou, at least, had never been nauseated by me.

Little kids raced up to see what was going on. They skidded to stops, spitting and patting snowballs. There wasn't anything grosser than me to throw at on the playground. I didn't know which way to look, if I should blink more or less. If I should run, and which way not to catch a beating. I slumped there—only I could win a fight this badly.

"Elvis, you got what you been asking him for, how many years now," Stevie said scornfully. He leaned out a window of the school. His fingers were on the sill. His words were electric. I lifted my head, eager to beat up anybody else available, basking in the lee of scorn, for one time aimed the other way. And no matter where the years might haul us, I promised I would not forget what I owed Stevie Wolfglove for standing up for Cutuk Hawcly on the packed snow, gum wrappers, and spit ice of the Takunak school playground.

NINE

BEHIND WOODROW WASHINGTON JR.'S new government house the Arctic Cat snowgo gleamed on the snow. Woody flicked a cigarette stub away. "It got only"—he peered at the speedometer—"only four thousand mile. Not bad, huh?"

"The radius of the earth," I murmured. A ways to travel on a snowgo.

Woody grinned and shrugged. He had a slow smile that the women liked. "Maybe not that far I guess."

"Thousand dollars? How come you're selling it?"

Charley Casket walked up. He spat. We talked about the weather for a minute. He held out his hand, cupping a jade arrowhead. "Fifty bucks. You could sell it five hunnert, I guess. Could be more."

Woody ignored him and nodded toward his other snowgo. "I got new Panther. When I go Prudhoe everybody always borrow. Goddamn, when I come home all my good stuffs jus' be junks. My clothes even, ready for dumps." Woody wore an expensive leather jacket. A gold watch hung loose and cool on his brown wrist. He was a good-looking man and dressed like a catalog.

I knelt down, admiring the thick springs and shocks under the tracks. Charley gripped the throttle, wide open.

"Let that be," Woody said coldly.

Charley's hand dropped. "I gonna get new Indy six-fifty. Next month, alright. For sure."

Woody didn't respond.

I looked at pictures in my mind—riding up to the school Monday morning. Searching valleys for Enuk. Impulsively, I handed Woody my rumpled thousand-dollar Alaska Permanent Fund check. The state had started giving a yearly oil-money bonus to every man, woman, and child. This year, the second, had been three hundred and eighty-six dollars. Charley's eyes followed the check. I didn't bargain with Woody. Bargaining was white, uncomfortable. Regular people said, *I'll pay you when my check comes*, and if by then they arbitrarily decided the price was too high, they just didn't pay.

He ran his thumbnail along the zeros. "How I'm gonna cash this before I—*Yuay*, Cutuk! You never spent your last year's Permanent Fund?" Woodrow grinned. Only a white person was crazy enough to save a thousand-dollar check. For a year.

"I didn't have anything to buy. Abe wanted me to buy a wind generator. Or solar panels, but they're made by ARCO, too." I trailed off; Abe's fossil-fuel philosophy was meaningless here. I felt anxious to drive away. I had just turned eighteen but still glanced about, as if there was a hurry, before Abe stepped around the corner of the house, reminding: "What about your dogs? And the petroleum just to manufacture the *seat* on that machine . . ."

Woody stepped up on his porch and placed the check in his Eddie Bauer leather wallet. Charley pushed his gloves in his pocket and wandered west watching the ground go under him. I yanked the starter. The snowgo sparked to life with a throaty roar, full of its own dangerous power. My body seemed to expand with the vibrating machine. I felt young and lunging with strength, not only from the engine, but also the potency of buying. This was why people lusted after money. Why villagers seldom walked unless they had to.

I was still floating when I located Nelta Skuq, the gas pump attendant. She had slipped home from work and was with her parents, eating caribou soup, the bowl right up close to her lips. Her mom had a tremendous necklace of bruises across her throat. Nelta had equally tremendous hickeys. Her youngest brothers—or her kids; I didn't know which—ate strawberry Pop-Tarts out of a box. They all hunkered around a glowing hot plate. A Jesus hologram hung over the kitchen counter. The floor was unfurnished to the walls, the linoleum gouged and worn through to plywood. Around the worn holes, the linoleum had been stapled down with hundreds of staples. An empty whiskey bottle lay in the doorway to the toilet. Skuqs' toilet was clogged. With dog chain. Folks in town knew these things, whose flush toilet worked and who was back to crapping in a kerosene can. A whitefronted goose—what people called a luck-a-luck—lay on the floor as if he'd been shot that morning. A luck-a-luck was all about the open air of spring, and bewildering to see in February. It took effort to remember that this house and all the other HUD houses that replaced people's cabins had been sparkling new American store-bought houses three years ago.

"They buying gas today?"

"They are." Nelta continued slurping her soup. She had ten or eleven brothers and sisters. Some were in jail. The Skuq girls were making babies, handing them over to their parents, leaving no clear line between generations.

I leaned by the door, uncertain what to do with my feet, hands, eyes. Nippy Skuq Sr. leered out the cracked, duct-taped window. My snowgo was parked next to the two his family owned. He sucked at his one front tooth. His lips puckered up and down. "You get snowgo, huh, Cutuk?" I nodded, disbelieving of the speed of the village grapevine. He guffawed, coughed, hacked, and spat in a Hills Bros can. "No more live in camp. They get you now. Ha! Now you gonna alla time need big money for little part." He roared with gleeful laughter. "They get ta last Eskimo camp boy today. Ha! Ha! Ha!"

Nelta eventually filled my five-gallon can. The gas cost three dollars and fifty cents per gallon. Going down the hill I squeezed the brake. Nothing happened. The speedometer digits hadn't shifted either. Old Nippy was wise as the wolves.

AT THE WOLFGLOVES', I paced the snow, impatient for Stevie to get home so we could go hunting. Figment stretched to the end of his chain and sniffed the snowgo. He lifted his leg to piss on the ski.

"Get away!"

He winced as his frostbit testicles swayed. I felt bad, and a little shaky and uncertain about my purchase and what this new addition to the family was going to mean. Figment walked in a circle, came back and pressed his smiling head against my thigh. "Just when you dogs were learning to pass another team on the trail." I sat on the seat and petted his wide face. "What are you smiling about, fool?"

Janet opened the door. "Cutuk. Quit touching that snowgo. Go in and eat!" Sheepishly, I went in and sat down. "Take your jacket off." Janet laughed. Melt wasn't around. Janet's kitchen was a sweet homey place when she was alone. She had flour on her hands and was thickening soup. "How much you pay?"

"Thousand."

"Good. That's good then. How about that snowgo, is it good or is it funny?"

"I don't know. I need to learn. It goes faster than my dogs!"

"Way better, alright. But it gonna always pe pust." She served soup. "Stevie, Lumpy, Treason, they let me puy parts everytime they go anywheres. Melt teach 'em that way. She's worst," Janet said, confusing male and female pronouns that didn't exist in Iñupiaq. "Thirty-four dollars for new belt. Over hunnert for ski. If they see fox or something they don't care about nothing. They pust up parts cost more than any kinda fox. I don't know how come. They always sometimes can't think." Janet stared, serious, the way Enuk used to stare. She walked to the window and watched a hunter on a snowgo speeding across the river. I liked sitting here with her. I wondered if she was looking into the past, if like me she tossed through the questions of what had become of Enuk. I wanted to ask, but she heard my spoon in the bottom of the soup bowl and turned to the stove.

Lumpy kicked open the door. His face had frozen patches. He shook his gloves off.

"What you do?" Janet cried. "You *alappaa?*"

"My hands freeze!"

"Aachikaaŋ!" She poured warm water out of a kettle into an aluminum basin. "Here!"

Lumpy knelt behind the stove and pushed his big hands in. After a few moments he withdrew them and hunched over, stiff with agony. He put his hands back in and withdrew them, over and over. Every once in a while a loud "Aaaaagh!" escaped him, strangely reminiscent of the pain sound from the black bear Jerry had once shot.

Stevie kicked the door open. He and Dawna burst in. Dawna pulled off her hat and shook her hair. "Hi, Cutuk!" She smiled. "I brought you a valentine: Will you shine and shine like the alpine timberline and no matter how I pine always be mine?"

I blinked. A purple and pink heart hung in her hand. She lowered her face in sudden embarrassment.

"What you do, Lumpy?"

He wiped his nose on his shoulder and didn't answer.

"Her hands," Janet murmured.

Lumpy hunched lower.

"So cheap that Mr. Standle an'em," Stevie growled. He held his glasses close to the stove, melting off the frost. "They let them put my name on gym list again. Now they gonna can't let me play basketball tonight. I should just quit school."

Dawna pursed her lips at him and pantomimed a jump shot. Stevie blocked her in the shoulder. She screamed and flew backward into a pile of clothes behind Lumpy. I looked away. Everyone knew I couldn't play basketball. And even the elders believed that being a star on the court atoned for any amount of stealing, nasty behavior, or jail time. The valentine crumpled and skidded under Dawna's elbow. She stared at it, and pulled. The paper tore. Angrily she dunked it into a bucket of dog scraps. She kicked the bucket.

"Arii!" Janet said. "You kids! Cutuk, take Stevie, go hunt. Be careful."

I glanced out the window, aching to be out on the land, away from the confusion of the village, basketball, and wrecked valentines. If only I could ask Dawna to go with me, and we could go to some distant knoll and talk and watch the evening colors pastel the sky. But in Takunak men hunted. They did not take women out alone to *talk*.

"You bought Woody's Cougar, huh?" Stevie said. "Brakes can't work. It's good though. 'Kay then, le's go hunt."

We dressed and got our rifles and went outside. It was cold, and snow sifted out of clear sky. Stevie was unhitching Melt's sled from his snowgo when up on the ridge Tommy Feathers shouted, "SCHEDULE!" Tommy lumbered east toward his house. He had a respectable stomach and no butt, and one of the big mysteries of Takunak was how he kept his pants up.

Melt ran loose-jointed down the hill. "Open the TV! Open the TV!"

Stevie dropped the wrench. He pried his watch out of his jacket sleeve. "SCHEDULE!" He bounded up the steps.

I untied my beaver hat, looked wistfully at the sun dropping in the west, and followed him. The list of the week's RATNET satellite TV programs replayed for half an hour before the first show. There was one channel. It played only in the evening. But everyone raced to watch the day of hissing blue snow fade and the first words appear on the television screen. For two years—since the satellite demonstration project arrived—almost no one had run dogs, hunted, or hauled wood after 5:00 P.M. Lumpy and Woody had let go a pack of eleven wolves that they had tracked beyond the Shield Mountains, and frostbit their faces black streaking full-throttle home, to catch the supreme hero of the Iñupiaq Nation—*The Six Million Dollar Man.*

"Eight o'clock!" Melt bellowed. "Ducks of Hazard!" His breath smelled of cologne. He wasn't sober.

Dawna stood near me. "Not *Ducks.*"

"Shudup you!"

I sat down, sweating in my parka. I glanced at the dog bucket. My first-ever valentine was still afloat. In my head the fast music played, when Bo and Luke Duke slithered stupidly in their car windows and Daisy swished her astonishing cutoff jeans. Everyone stared at the TV. I snatched the valentine from the slops and wiped off caribou soup grease. The side with sparkles and the pink heart was dry. Some of the sparkles had crumbled off where it bent. They glinted on the dog food. My *qaatchiaq* leaned in the corner. There was no hiding place for anything of mine in this house. *Mail it to Iris to keep.*

"That's Thursday," Janet said. "Coming is gonna be tonight."

"Technical difficulties!" Everyone sighed.

"Tomorrow, too," Stevie said. "*Adii,* so cheap that satellite junk."

Dawna's wide eyes watched the words rise on the screen. Her fingers strayed to the ripped collar of her sweatshirt. She didn't see the screen or Janet's pop-can-ring chains draped above it, or the pictures of Washington cousins in National Guard uniforms on the walls. Nor the ice-rimmed windows. The town outside of scattered caribou leg bones, fish racks, and wind-shredded Hefty bags. She saw herself somewhere where no one knew the stench of unscraped hides and the terror of Melt. I knew; I transported myself away, too. I went east forty miles. She went somewhere a lot farther, and was braver because she'd never been where she was going.

"You want to go hunting with us?" I whispered.

She shook her head, not unglazing her eyes. I pulled my hat on, embarrassed for asking. Stevie and I went outside. The door hung on loose hinges and wouldn't shut. We chipped ice with my knife, quickly, before Melt hollered about the draft.

Stevie grinned and kicked my snowgo skis. He wore sharp-looking Sorel boots; me, *mukluks.* "'Bout time one Hawcly got snowgo. Fellas said you wouldn't. I knew you would."

His words caught a loose stitch in my memory and unraveled the years, Jerry and Iris and I hunching beside the Wolfgloves' stove, me sneaking glances at Dawna, Stevie leading us out, showing off Melt's new snowgo in the moonlight. I could see us standing close, the jagged crack down the cowling, the glint of the fiberglass splinter in my finger. *My blood brother!* But the picture seemed like a flash from a TV film of a stranger's life, not my own.

THE RED FEBRUARY SUN was setting behind Stevie and me when we drove up a bluff west of Jesus Creek and crossed wolf tracks. I'd unconsciously angled homeward—maybe with the idea of cacheing the valentine folded in my pocket—and now far in the distance I saw Outnorth Lake and the thin bank between the lake and the river where our igloo hunkered in the ground. How could we be here so quickly? Takunak had been on the other side of the galaxy from our home. Driving a snowgo was like being God. I rode in a bubble of sound that fed my thoughts until they grew and wandered giantly, picking fights and jumping rivers. The land was smaller, as if I could touch the mountains. I wondered at how trivial the entire Kuguruk Valley must seem to sport hunters from Anchorage, Fairbanks, and Crotch Spit, peering down from their airplanes.

Above Takunak we'd driven beside Abe's meandering dog trail, taken fifty-mile-an-hour shortcuts out of bends in the river, up over willowy banks and tundra draws. Moose cantered out of our path. Alder twigs burned inside my engine cowling. I inhaled the sweet smoke. The world was a new place on a snowgo. I loved it. Abe would hate it.

Stevie shut off Melt's Polaris. He glanced at the gas gauge and then down at the wolf tracks. He toed them with his heavy boot. "Wolverine?" He melted gray frozen patches on his cheeks. Tomorrow the patches would be black, not reddish like mine.

"Could be wolf." There were four distinct toes, the prints in a neat trot. The wolf ran silver in my mind. I laid my rifle on the seat and touched the snow in a print. It was powdery. "Fresh?"

Stevie shrugged. He wiped frost off his fogged glasses.

For years I'd listened to stories of men chasing down wolverine and wolves and other animals with snowgos and airplanes. The villagers on snowgos despised the wealthy white men in the sky with ski planes. I'd thought all the high-speed chasing to be bad; Abe quietly loathed it. But now the picture had new color and I lusted to roar north, burning the trail.

Stevie wiped again at his fogged glasses. "Uktu fellas gonna come tonight." He peered through the lenses and polished. "Play basketball. Have dance in town. Or maybe Uktu." He grinned. Stevie wasn't a star at basketball, but he could always locate a jug, or a bucket of home brew, and keep a party going.

"They're gonna drive up, play ball, then go clear back sixty miles to Uktu to have a dance? Tonight?"

"Could be. I dunno. Uktu got good chicks. Better than Takunak." His grin was flirty. He glanced at the tundra and spat between his teeth. "Pretty fun when there always be jugs. Seems like that's the only time peoples have fun. Some time I'm gonna have a store like Newt's. Only thing, I'll sell drinks, let everybody have a good time." He chuckled. "Not Melt and some them fellas who don't know how to drink."

Stevie didn't like fighting. He hid in the outhouse and read comics when Lumpy killed puppies and Melt was hitting. Now he walked around his machine, jumped on the bumper, and stepped back on the snow. He grinned at the ground. "Maybe you'll help me get store, same like Abe did with Newt."

"What?"

"Huh?"

"What are you talking about?"

"Mom say Abe give Newt money. He help him make order first lotta times. You didn't know?"

"How could that be? Abe never had much money."

Stevie shrugged and shoved my shoulder. "Shuck, maybe he did and he blow it up before you come around." He laughed, then peered at the wolf tracks and spat again. "Go 'head. Keep going."

"I thought—" I pictured Newt shaking Abe's hand. But this couldn't be true. White people weren't even allowed credit in the Native Cache the way normal people were. I glanced at the tracks, pretending more interest than I had. Treason should have come. He was twenty-two, didn't talk much, and already had a reputation as a hunter. Villagers spoke in admiration, *He can't turn back, bad weather even.* I knew more about tracks, back fat, stomach contents of animals than Treason; I wished I could learn how to want to kill them as bad.

"Yeah, I'll keep going, little further."

Stevie hunched over and peered at his gas gauge. "I got not much gas."

"You have a plastic? We could dump some of my gas in your tank. Enough to make it to the mountains and home. You don't need to pay me back." Newt waded into my mind. Maybe that was what Abe had said, *You don't need to pay me back.* Being generous felt good. And Abe did what felt good to him.

"Naw." Stevie pried at his jacket sleeve and got a peek at his watch. "Anyways, gonna be dark. Go 'head, ride around." He spun and roared away. But he steered back and idled. "You sure you'll never get lost?" I nodded, surprised at this unlocal show of care. "'Kay then. See you if you make it home *maatnugun*."

He vanished down our trail.

If meant *when* in Village English. But I was conscious in the chill and falling twilight that *if* was a concept born of starvation and frozen hunters and very definitely also meant *if.* I listened to his snowgo until it was a hum mixing with the hums in my head. Dawna would go to the dance.

I headed north. My engine seemed to make new and uncertain rattles and pings. Evening painted the sky green and gold and orange in the south. Sitting, gripping the steel machine, my hands and feet and face kept freezing, and I had to stop to thaw them. The wolf tracks zigzagged toward the mountains. I plowed through the willows of a buried creek, spraying shattered brush in front of the skis. Moose stood and waded aside. The wolf tracks swung west, across a few miles of open tundra, followed a slough, and again crossed open tundra. Still they looked no fresher. Ptarmigan sleeping sly under the snow poked their heads up in alarm at my passing. Stars twinkled in the deep blue northern sky. I felt foolish for not turning back, but tonight I didn't want to ever go back to Takunak.

The machine bogged down in a creek, the track spraying snow and chewing a trench under the snowgo. The drive belt smoked. I stepped off the seat, sank up to my waist. The snow under the top layer was corn snow, as grainy and loose as rock salt. How could I not have thought to bring snowshoes! The huge twilit silence rang in my ears. Suddenly I realized how incompetent I was with a snowgo. I had no tools, no spare parts or even rope.

I pawed at the snow. Was this the creek where I'd found the frozen dog tracks with drag marks? Tracks that might have led back to Enuk? I couldn't get my bearings with this kind of fast travel. It must be here, or somewhere a few bends upstream. The creek had had sinkholes, cave-ins, open water. I flailed back and forth stomping snow in front of the skis, breaking willows to jam under the track, hoping the ice didn't shelve away. Under the snow, water gurgled.

The snowgo lunged out on the first try. Quickly I steered up the bank, and south, panting, as if my luck was ticking toward zero on a stopwatch. I glanced into thickets for a shirtsleeve of Enuk's twisted on a willow. Or a jam can. A blaze on a tree. On a lake a gray shadow moved. And then in the fallen light it turned and ran like only a wolf. The Arctic Cat bucked under me, leaping over drifts, tearing at the snow. I had had no idea a machine was capable of such things. The wolf wove back and forth, racing for the trees. The headlight of the machine lit chipped snow flung by his feet. In half a minute I was beside him. His mouth was panting wide, his head pounding up and down with supreme effort.

I hadn't been this close since I was ten.

The foolish boy was gone. I knew what men did, how to do it. I let go of the throttle and, still moving, pulled off my mittens, aimed, and shot. My hands shook. I shot again. He ran on unhurt. With bare fingers I grabbed the handlebars. He was nearly to the brush. Again I was beside him. This time I aimed for the butt, the only part I could, and fired. The wolf tumbled and rolled. He came up snarling at his back.

He arched in the air, rolled behind a drift, slinging blood and snow. My stomach wrenched, recognizing this moment, this first slam of death, when an animal was suddenly writhing and wounded, already a creature with terror eyes and no relative on earth, no way back to perfection. I fired into the gray melee. He fell. His chin lowered to the snow. The wolf stared into me. Slowly his eyes died. They were still open. I walked up. The rifle hung searing in my hand. My eyelashes froze together. "Shit," I said softly. "Shit. I'm not going to do that anymore. Bad luck it had to be you."

THE WOLF WAS TIED across the cowling of the snowgo, a pure and continuous brag requiring no words. I drove around the village, drunk on my luck, the sorrow of killing softening under a warm rain of admiration. I kept stopping beside strolling people, asking, "Seen Walkin' Charley?"

Treason sat behind me on the seat. He was big and broad-shouldered—a hundred and ninety pounds—and I was glad for my fancy shock absorbers. He wore an earband, *Takunak* knit into it, and his hair was trimmed short, flat on top. Dawna had cut it for him with electric trimmers. It was a shade browner than everyone else's black hair. The girls went for his smile that faded away lazily, like he didn't care what might be up the trail. Maybe he'd learned it from TV, or from watching his dad and mom and too much else disappear.

"TV's broke," he said. "Alaska Satellite is wrecked-up, *guuq*. Charley got jugs of One-Five. He's selling for Crotch Spit fellas." His Zippo clinked, a toy under his big thumb. "What I heard anyways." He passed a lit joint. I drove one-handed and pinched it, inhaling. I'd smoked only twice and felt clumsy and obvious.

The weed mixed with the smell of wolf blood dripping and searing on my muffler. I squinted, trying to look tough. Smoke shot out of my mouth. Smoke—one thing Abe had not taught us to conserve.

"Think he'd trade a bottle for a wolf?"

One-Five sold for three hundred dollars a bottle. A wolf skin was worth five hundred. But that was to the old ladies. Ahead a figure appeared in the trail.

"There's your teacher, Mr. Long Handle," Treason said. "And that dog musher *naluaġmiu*. Hide the j." I squeezed the joint out in my glove and stopped the machine next to my teacher.

"Cutuk! How's the best student north of the Arctic Circle? My wife heard you bought that snowgo." Tom Standle touched my shoulder faintly. He had wide-set dark brown eyes and red hair and was over six feet tall and skinny; when he sat on a snowgo he looked like bent branches. He wasn't like the regular schoolteachers, trying to shoot the biggest animals, taking the heads home to snarl on their States walls.

"A wolf! You just get him?"

He's trying to talk Village English? After all that bunk about prepositional phrases and dangling modifiers? I nodded, not trusting my throat. His face kept locking in front of my eyes, too close, then far. Then Abe's face. If I said one word, he'd see I was stoned. Now the white guys were examining the wolf too much. They must smell the sizzling blood. They must think me cruel, roaring around with a shot-up wolf strapped across my snowgo like Jesus wired on the poles.

". . .'s a gray one." The dog musher, Ted Brown, was uttering. "I could have had five of those last week, if I wanted."

I looked away, embarrassed by the bragging—taboo to a hunter. He had bulgy eyes and wore black canvas imitation *mukluks* tied at the knees over wool pants and a knit hat with long earflaps—good warm gear, but Outsider stuff. His hands were smooth strong hands. Newt at the store had said he was an ivory picker and a dog racer—new in the village—and had promised Nippy Skuq Jr. he'd teach him to pan gold and run a sluice box when summer came. Around the Native Cache woodstove, Newt had mentioned that the white man had thirty dogs and an equal number of guns. No one could quite fathom such excess. "What they always do with thirty guns?" Melt spat in Newt's wood box. Newt smiled slowly. "They use 'em something to talk about." Tommy nodded and spat. Newt eyed the rounds of firewood. Later he'd have to handle them and all that spit. Tommy plucked thoughtfully at the black hairs below his lip. "He's from the Middle East, *guuq*. Wisconsin. He got not-much-hair wife. Always holler at her like dog."

What had they said about my mother?

Now Treason stood up. "Silver wolf. That's good one."

"Oh? How you tell best fur? The long back hair?" Abruptly, the man's tone had changed, gone to an overdone attempt at Village English so painful and common among Outsiders. He tilted his head. His hazel eyes were too agreeable talking to Treason. *Native-worshiper!* Suddenly I wanted to see Treason throw a punch into that white face. A tiny voice said, *Your face is the same color! And you're mean—you change your voice, too.* I swallowed and wished there were a different kind of place to go in the hundreds of miles of night. Wished I could be a hero like John Wayne in the Western movies, mount my horse and clatter off to search creek-beds for Enuk. But that was stupid. The land was dark, ice, deep snow, and the size of the moon. A horse would founder. I'd have to eat it, warm my hands in its heart, and walk back here.

Mr. Standle didn't notice that I hadn't spoken. Hopefully, he wouldn't start his Big Opportunity speech. *All my graduates go to college for one semester then drop out. They all come home. None of them make it.* What was "making it"? White people talked as if Takunak and the land were just a camping spot before college and the big shiny world.

Dawna and Dollie Feathers appeared in the glittering pool of street-light. They wore faded jeans, puffy nylon jackets. Dawna was chewing gum. "Say! You get lucky, huh, Yellow-Hair?" Her voice was throaty and hoarse. The admiration in her eyes bounced around in my chest. I wondered what part of the cities Dawna forgot long enough to admire a hunter.

"You fellas gonna go dance?" Dollie said.

Treason swung his leg off the machine. He raised his eyebrows. "See you at gym, Cut." He walked away, bored with too much talk. Dawna flashed a smile and hurried after him. In seconds they seemed far away, and close together. A wind was picking up. Snakes of snow smoked along the hard-packed drifts.

"See you, Mr. Standle. I have to go."

He nodded. I tried to wave, but Dollie was giggling and gripping my arm. She climbed on the seat. She had never touched me before. Did this have to do with the wolf, or the weed? Her face dimpled with the laughter that seldom left her face. Maybe she had to laugh; her brother was

Timmy, the village walking-impaired rock target. My face and fingers throbbed from the day's frostbite. I hoped I wasn't red under the streetlight. Or orange. I flattened my nose.

"Com'on, Cutuk!" She giggled. I recognized the smell of Dawna's shampoo in her hair. "Let's find Charley then follow Treason an'em to dance."

Dance? They just wanted to jeer the way they had my whole life. Beat me up behind the gym. Maybe Dollie only wanted a laugh and a buzz. She had never spent a minute alone on the land. She didn't care how it felt to find tracks, and follow them, until an animal appeared on the huge cold emptiness, forming those tracks. And then to race up the trail of that life to the very last track, and kill, leaving smooth snow ahead where there could have been a million more footprints if not for you.

I started the engine. "'Kay then. Let's find Charley." Anything to hold this slippery grip on friends. And erase the wolf that ran in front, snatching fleeting glimpses back.

We roared toward a place I hated, the physical and cultural center of the new village order—the gym.

NEWT'S OLD LOG CABIN was black inside as we shouldered through the racked doorway. Under the broken window a snowdrift glowed luminescent like a sleeping white dog. My eyes flashed with leftover light burned by the dance strobe. I tripped sideways and held onto Dollie.

"You okay?" Treason slurred. We all giggled.

Outside in the wind snowgos screamed past, the men on the machines drunk and searching for us, to buy or take the marijuana that we'd already smoked. They had cornered me in the cold orange electric light outside the gym. Maybe my stonedness showed the worst. I was uncomfortable—off balance, hands uncertain, eyes shifting—under the stares and glares and jokes. I had felt shocked loose of my past. People here would knock down their *aana,* beat a brother to mush, just to not be the only straight ones in this village while nearly everyone else was amped, baked, or buzzing. *"Sell one joint even, you cheap honky fuck!"* Nippy Jr. had jabbed his numchuks in my face. "We know you got." Yesterday he'd asked me to help him fill out a Big Ray's order blank. His brother, Elvis, and two other guys stood behind him against the gym. I traded them what was left of Treason's joint for a B9ES spark plug and a shove.

In the cabin, Dollie whispered, "I hope they don't stop."

Treason showed us the glinting outline of his knife. "Let'um." His hands had dried blood—mine too—from skinning the wolf. We were good at it, and fast. I was better, but too dense to realize that Janet and everyone would hear in the morning of my trade for the rum. I fingered a cut on my knuckle. I'd skinned the mouth and knicked myself with the blade. *Rabies!* sprang into my mind as the saliva mixed with my blood. I'd wiped my hand on my jeans, shrugged. Worrying about a virus, in Takunak, was not cool.

I heard the squeak of the cap on my Bacardi bottle and the weak slosh left in the bottom as it passed. I pretended to drink. The smell made my throat climb. Treason glugged long on the fiery 151. He leaned forward and fell, laughing and knocking us all sprawling to the floor. The bottle rolled away hollowly on the uneven boards. In the dark Dawna and Dollie giggled. Jealousy tightened my face. Treason mumbled, "Com'on, where you . . ." He stumbled behind the partition wall with Dawna.

The wind gusted. Snow sifted in. I stood up dizzily and reached inside my jacket for Treason's lighter that had ended up in my pocket. My eyes locked on the spark, blackness shot with spinning blue and orange chips. Somewhere, in this cabin, years ago, Newt had shotgunned his hand off.

Dollie brushed me. Suddenly she was in my arms. I put a hand up to touch her face. Smelled shampoo in her hair. Felt her soft throat and face. *Dawna?* Her lips found mine. My body dissolved into longing, leaving no cabin, no me, no last high school English class, no windblown Takunak. Now I was in the warmth, somewhere behind the back wall of reality. We tilted sideways to the floor. Our hands struggled with zippers and clasps. She pulled me down, and we were clumsily together, apart again, and finally together.

So this is it. This is *everything.* My shoulders shook, with relief to finally be part of the clan of people having sex, and remorse that I'd never learned to kiss first or hold hands. Under her clothes her skin was as smooth as plastic and hot, her arms strong and her tongue sweet. I had never been held like this, never felt surrounded by another person. As I traveled into the spinning strobing lights, I wondered, was it Dawna pressing against me? Were my elbow and forearm getting splinters from the same boards Newt's blood had soaked into? And was there some debt there that had something to do with me? It didn't matter. I'd wanted to hold Dawna's hand and kiss her. I wanted a girlfriend and love. I wanted a girlfriend and to be Eskimo, and to be loved, but none of that lay on the boards of Newt's old cabin. None of that.

TEN

DAY AFTER DAY *caribou pass on the ice of the creek.* Thousands straggle by in strings of five and ten and a hundred, stopping and fretting and checking the wind, always heading north. The methodical clicking of their hoof joints joins the canyon sounds of falling pebbles and plunking water. The spring smells, of warm rocks and spruce bark, meltwater and caribou hair and turds and breath, are sharp after the aromatic hush of winter. The night sun stretches long on the face of the mountain.

In the chill of the evening, a less-edible animal walks up the creek. The smell of this carnivore shouts danger. Up on a canyon wall a wolf watches. The wolf crouches and backs into her den. High in the rocks she is hidden, eyes in shadow.

Down below a man shuffles along the ice. He smells of smoke and dogs, seal oil, salmon, and himself. He comes without a machine, rare for a man. He carries no rifle. The wolf senses no hunt in his movements. She eases forward in her den, peers down. On the ice the man stops.

He seems to sense *her*—his stance says it. His stare swings, probing the rocks. Near her paw, a tiny chip shifts and a pebble bounces away. A puff of snow cascades down.

The man jumps. His eyes lift. For the first time in her life the wolf locks gazes with a human. She stands as still as only a predator will, life focused in her powerful stare. The man backs away. An instant of fear tightens the air between them, then he hurries down the pale green ice of the creek.

The wolf paces the ledge, whining, whiffing the air for her mate, gone hours hunting or, now, maybe hunted.

ELEVEN

OVER THE COURSE of an hour the slice of moonlight eased across the floor and worked up the post of Abe's bed. The white light seemed to slide on celestial rails designed with infinite purpose, and just before it slivered to nothing it reached Abe's eyelid. He snapped awake. On Jerry's bunk I narrowed my eyes, let my breath run long, and for no conscious reason pretended to be asleep.

Abe knifed wood shavings. He stacked kindling in the barrel stove and it crackled to life. He stood naked, the match pinched in his fingers, and rustled in the shelves for a stash of camping coffee, trying to avoid a cold morning trip to the cache for a new can of Hills Bros. He grunted in success. The match flicked out. The stove draft danced orange shadows on the walls.

I groaned.

"*Alappaa*. Got cold again," Abe said cheerfully.

I rose and stood at our new glass window that Iris had sent. Cold air played on my thighs. Outside the land sparkled under a million moth wings of frost. "Thirty-two below? Son-of-a-bitch!" Abe didn't appreciate cuss words. But I was twenty-one now and felt an infuriated need to prove *something*. "Guess I'll leave my snowgo home today. Plastic parts don't snap off the dogs."

Abe slapped meat in the sizzling skillet. He scratched under his beard. "It'll warm up, when the sun comes around. I figure in a few weeks we could go spring camping. Back in the Dog Dies. Once you're done trapping."

"I'm trying to catch one more lynx."

I sat on the couch. It was soft and deep again with a new brown bear hide I had tanned with sourdough. I lit a candle and opened the automotive mechanics book to my weasel-tail bookmark—"Theory of Combustion"—where I'd been studying last night. The weasel tail was dried. The fur was black on one end, then pure white. The last few hairs were yellow, where they'd once attached to the ermine's pee-sack. The book was overdue. It needed to be mailed back to Fairbanks with the rest of the monthly library box. I wished I had a car to tinker on. I'd taken my snowgo apart to understand the needle valve, magneto, wrist pins.

Abe examined a half-completed birch snowshoe on his workbench. "Lynx are close to shedding, huh? Geese will be coming soon. We don't need the meat." In the kitchen his fry pan started to smoke. He eyed his workmanship critically. The snowshoe was light, the wood pearly white with gray caribou *babiche* webbing shrinking tight as it dried. Somehow Abe memorized the intricate pattern for lacing the webbing.

"There's plenty of lynx," I said. "Prices are high. Geez, I'll let him go if I get a shedding one."

"Hmm."

"Okay, I'll pull the number-four jump traps."

Abe hurried back to the spattering pan, peered in, and forked the steaks. "You'd be surprised, if you quit going to town and buying plastics, you'd hardly need money. I think—"

"Everybody knows *what* you think, just nobody except maybe Franklin knows *why*."

I snaked my legs into my stiff jeans. Go for a long snowshoe, I told myself, or open a new water hole. Four more weeks and Iris would be home. Abe and I would get along again. We only needed to feel like a family. We hadn't seen Iris since last spring. If they hired her to teach in Takunak, I could jump on the snowgo or hitch up my dogs and go stay with her. Or walk to the village in the fall. *Qayaq* in the summer. Maybe she could teach me to dance. I had done the right thing, waiting here and not bolting to the rumor and intrigue of the city.

Now if only Dawna would return. The beat-up valentine had ceased to emit feeling; now I'd been using it for lynx bait. Lynx were curious creatures, and, dangling on a string, glinting and twirling, Dawna's valentine was too much to resist. The inside-out braille note on the magazine-seed—from when I was twelve, before the Wolfgloves moved out of their shack—I'd wrapped in a plastic bag and buried under the moss and blueberry bushes behind the house. For years I'd searched and never been able to find where I'd buried it. Its disappearance seemed a bad omen. All my memories of Dawna were threadbare and didn't cause the undersides of my ribs to ache anymore.

Abe cleared his throat. "Ah, sorry if I was harping on you."

"Huh?"

I couldn't remember Abe ever saying sorry. He didn't like the word. I glanced up. In the last years gray had mixed in with his hair; lines on his face had deepened to trenches. His thick neck was still red, but the skin was rougher and lines forked into each other. Two decades here, and more—one wife and two children leaving, a third roaming the hills like a porcupine-quill-filled brown bear. Abe hadn't complained. His eyes still twinkled. He found new things to run through his fingers, to paint and chuckle about.

I sat on a stump and untangled the dog harnesses that needed repair. They needed sewing often. When the dogs were excited, lunging to leave the dog yard, they chewed towlines, necklines, harnesses. We sawed new puppies' mouths with rope when we caught them chewing lines, and most learned from the terrible and excruciating lesson. The harnesses were greasy. One was store-bought, the rest sewn from yellow cotton or red nylon webbing. My hands smelled of sweaty dog butthole. My throat felt raw.

"Abe, sometime I think you're like that Thoreau fella, living some back-to-the-wilderness dream. I'm not. It's like I'm a species of one. For me this is plain life, and most of the time I feel like I'm breaking trail."

Abe grasped the frying pan and stopped. He looked at his hand for a second. He hurried over and lowered the frying pan on the table. I washed with hot soapy water in the basin. Dumped the brown water in the slop bucket. Abe had the head of the dogfood axe tilted near the stove, toasting out a stub of broken handle. The blade was nicked from chopping bones so the dogs could get at brains and *patiq*.

We ate meat in silence. Abe bit grease off the backs of his thumbs. He sat on the wood box and took off his sock and searched for a splinter that was stabbing his ankle. The heel had been darned with navy blue yarn unraveled from the arms of his old sweater that he had remodeled into a vest.

"There were a bunch of reasons I brought you kids here." He sighed and stared out the window. "Some kind of birds working out there. Crossbills?" His jaw moved. He started to speak a few times. "Pandora's box." He chuckled. He glanced down at his rough swollen hands. "To the old Eskimos the land was everything. They *knew* the land." His hands gripped each other. "I think I was thinking that there wasn't time left . . . to let you grow up and find your own wilderness. City," he rubbed his ears. "It's everything about insulating you from the earth. I didn't want to work some job just to afford to get out to the wilderness once in a while. You can't have both. I like life close to the earth. It's alive. The city made me feel wrapped up and a long way from myself. Heck, maybe I've just been selfish!" He smiled his big beautiful straight-teeth smile. He worked his sock back on and folded the cuffs of his pants into his socks. I glanced away, faintly embarrassed—nobody since George Washington did that with their socks.

He rose and fiddled with the draft on the stove. "A part of you maybe is going to always be across the river from other people. You might be in for hard times. People believe in city. They call it 'the real world.' Won't be surprised if you're not able to do that." He sounded curious, not sorry.

In the crook of my thumb I pressed my nose flat. It didn't seem to be flattening. A thought flashed in my head: *Abe would cry if he knew what I was doing.*

There was a pained look to his eyes and in the lines disappearing into his beard. A mouse rattled a spoon on the counter. Abe glanced at it. "My dad poached polar bears," he chuckled, "his proximity to nature."

He had never said "your grandpa." As if he had always insulated us from that man.

"He landed his hunters and drove bears back to them. And he was certain no one loved the land more than he did." Abe glanced into my eyes. It was hard to look into his powerful deep blue gaze. "To prove it, he took all sorts of pride in ignoring laws. Danger, too. That day, if I'd told him his engine sounded wrong, he'd have said, 'Stand clear! Go play with your pansies.' That's what he called my pastels. Said, 'You're gonna end up in Paris, painting pansies.'"

Abe laced his *mukluks*. They were soft-bottomed, cold-weather *mukluks* with black and red yarn ties at the top. Janet had four-braided the ties. "Pansies are tough flowers. They survive wind and being frozen. People don't give pansies credit." Abe stood. Just like Enuk's, his story was over when he got tired of telling it. Or maybe he didn't know how to tell it. He was a painter. I played with my knife, breathless to know more, but under the weight of some childhood prohibition. Maybe when Iris came she'd be different; maybe she'd ask questions we'd been inured not to ask.

"Pansies," I murmured softly.

Abe didn't say anything. Again the mouse rattled spoons. We glanced up and laughed together. In that moment, me hunched at the table fingernailing the empty skillet, him squatted on a round of firewood, taking his *mukluk* off one more time to research his sock for a splinter, we were closer than we'd been in my lifetime and half of his. Maybe during the night I'd advanced into adulthood, like a deep bruise that finally turned black and blue after the hurt; maybe now at last we were two men, not a dad and a kid. Still, I felt like a boy inside. Would that ever fade? Or did people just stop seeing it from the outside?

In the kitchen we heard tiny frantic hopping. The mouse that had been doing nightly turd dances on our bread had plopped into a mason jar. We grinned, thankful for the interruption. We peered down opposite sides into the glass at the furry face.

"You're going back outside." Abe slid his calloused hand over the jar. "Back to that life before white man and bread. Or was it white bread and man?"

Abe wasn't going to dump the mouse in the slop bucket or bonk it with a piece of kindling. I realized that I wasn't going to, either.

THE COLD SPELL BROKE, and in the last days of April our sod roof began leaking. We had dishpans and pots spread, pinging under the tea-colored drips. Iris had sent a wave of exhilaration in front of her arrival; we were lighthearted as we carried grub boxes and sleeping skins down to load on our sleds. Abe chuckled. "Drips, that's spring telling you to get outside. Bears will be getting the same message." We laced on our *mamillaks*. They were skin-out *mukluks*, sticky and yellow-black with old seal oil. The grease waterproofed the seams and protected the caribou-skin tops and sealskin bottoms from being ruined by water and slush.

Down in the dog yard, the dogs stretched, trying to lick the oily skin. We hitched up after midnight. Abe examined his leader's feet. She often had foot problems. She had pink pads; racers now claimed that dogs with black pads were tougher. Abe walked up to the house and untied the rope on the door. He came out with medical tape and bacitracin and bear fat, and rubbed it on her pads and taped his old socks on her.

The icy night crust ran hard in all directions. Abe geed his dogs for the steep mountains in the northwest, and I let my team follow across the rasping snow. A red fox sat and watched us leave. They were unafraid in spring, mating, and often mistaken for being rabid. Three moose stood across the river, heads high, curious. Ptarmigan rattled in the willows. The air was rich with tundra smells, and peaceful, and half a mile of silence stretched out between Abe's team and mine. Caribou trails veined the tundra and herds poured out of draws and raced away in front of our leaders. Ravens chuckled and echoed their secrets of death and food across the distances. My heart grew as the Dog Dies towered higher in the bright night. Somehow I forgot each time how much I loved mountains. They were friendly giants, transforming with the seasons, not a grain of judgment in them.

I ran only five dogs now. Ponoc, with his misspelled name, like mine, had died after a moose kicked him in the jaw, and last spring I'd had to shoot Figment. His testicles were pink and swollen from freezing for so many winters, and irritability kept him picking fights and growling through the nights. I walked him out on the tundra and he padded along, the same floppy-eared shambling dog whose only ambitions had been food and to slip his collar once in a while and maybe get laid or chase rabbits. Figment had never taken offense at getting drifted over at night or curling up in harness and waiting while I checked traps or snowshoed after caribou. Each sled dog developed a personality of its own, like a friend, and when I tied him to a tree he sat painfully, and patient, and when I pulled the trigger, all the memories of my friend flashed and cracked and the death in his eyes was that unearthly creature.

I stood on the runners. Looked at pictures in my mind. How had Enuk shot all the dogs in his team in that storm how many lifetimes ago? Far ahead, Abe stopped in front of a towering slate outcropping, an island in the tundra just before the shore of the mountains. He stomped in his snow hook. When I pulled up, he'd already cut poles and laid down sweet-smelling green spruce boughs to keep our *qaatchiaqs* off the snow. He was tying knots that were quick to untie, pitching the white canvas wall tent, using a dead sapling for a ridgepole so pitch wouldn't mar the fabric. I chained out the dogs. Got a fire going. On sticks we roasted caribou leg bones that we'd boiled earlier. The sun came around the eastern summit and warmed the morning and our shoulders.

ABE SPENT THE DAY IN CAMP, watching birds and sketching. I climbed the peak behind our tent and came down in the late afternoon, bushed, damp, and chilled. I hunkered close to the fire, letting the frozen legs of my overpants steam. Abe moved around the sleds, tossing dried salmon to the dogs, checking their feet, patting their heads. He folded the sled tarps closed. Coiled the harnesses and lines on the bed slats. Picked up our axes in case of a surprise storm.

He came back yawning. "Shoot a caribou tomorrow for dog feed, feel like it?"

"'Kay."

"I'm going to climb in."

We'd been up for nearly forty hours.

I poked the coals. Abe had moved the campfire onto a slab of slate with green branches underneath to keep it from plummeting down through the snow. The smoke stung. Burning mushrooms, or lichens. Or flies hibernating between the layers of stone. I felt tired, dizzy, and the mountain kept locking in my eyes, almost as if I were stoned again.

"Make another pot of coffee, if you want to stay up and dry your stuff." He knew I liked to push myself to see how long I could stay up in the endless day of spring. A chill was settling. A portion of my brain kept pitching over a cliff into sleep. I retrieved my stiff frozen gloves from a stump. Laced on snowshoes.

Behind the rocky mound where we camped, a canyon twisted up the narrow valley. I snowshoed into its mouth. I'd been here before, but something else felt familiar about this creek. I sniffed the air. A north breeze fell off the slopes and a bundle of alder seeds rasped across the hard snow, sailing behind the curled skeleton of a leaf. High on the precipitous walls, clumps of brush and a few wind-bitten spruce clung to the rocks like sentries.

The creek ice was firm walking, rippled with pearly frozen overflow and wet on the surface. I left my snowshoes wedged in a split fallen boulder. It wasn't wise to dampen the *babiche* by walking in water. Trenched caribou trails braided up the sides of the mountains. In the orange sun bowls high up toward the pass, I saw a string of dots—caribou, or possibly a pack of wolves—climbing north.

After half a mile the canyon narrowed and made a sharp bend. No sun or wind found its way down here. The air was motionless. Seams of quartz protruded from the gray slate cliffs. Tundra moss draped the rim of the rock. I stood for a moment, listening to my heart boom. A shiver rolled over my skin. Suddenly I was awake. Far under the ice, water gurgled. I stepped a few paces toward the shore, in case the ice collapsed.

My hair rose. At the top of the rocks, in a fissure under an overhanging slab of slate, the hollow black eye of a den stared. I hadn't brought a rifle! A sensation breezed through me, a recognition of this as an exact location, here on the ice and tonight, where my trail might end. Creatures that my legs couldn't outrun, my hands couldn't scratch, lived on the land. Hunting food, and proximity to other very different and very wild hunters—maybe this was the "alive" that Abe spoke of. I loosened my sheath knife and in my pocket fingered Enuk's carved bear, as if it might offer protection. Enuk poured into my mind: thick laughter, thumb and finger pinching a chunk of boysenberry jam, teeth biting ice off his dogs' feet. I stared around, as if he might appear.

On a ledge at the entrance of the den a cornice of snow cracked. I crouched. Down it tumbled, a cloud of falling frost. In front of me lay the snowy heap. Up in the rocks, in the shadowed mouth of the den, I saw the eyes of a wolf.

For an instant my bones were liquid. I glanced behind and backed away. On the shore, grown into the crotch of a small twisted birch, hung a section of green rope. I walked over, still watching the wolf, and reached for it. The nylon parted, sun-shot, dusty, and destroyed. I hurried down the canyon.

"CUTUK!"

I jolted awake, stiff and afraid.

Abe leaned in the tent flaps, a thumb in his suspendered overpants. Behind him a fire crackled. "Brown bear coming over. You like to see her before the dogs holler? She's got spring cubs."

"Yeah. Bear. 'Kay." I fumbled for my clothes and laced my *mamillaks,* glad nobody was asking me to spell my name.

Outside the tent, Abe nodded in the direction of the canyon mouth, not alerting the dogs by pointing. A hundred yards away, brown humped shoulders appeared. Suddenly a wide blond body stood. The bear's head swung, testing the air. Cubs bounced into view: one golden, one brown. Plato raised her muzzle to the east and sniffed. In the past year she'd cultivated a hearing loss, a combination of true deafness and old-dog obstinance. I picked up a stick. Plato swiveled west, still sniffing. Three dogs lunged up, barking. The other nine rose and only growled and whined.

"Shudup." I hunkered down and advanced with the stick.

"Ssssst." Abe hissed. He nodded, satisfied. "Never know with new pups, if they'll holler at a bear. Farmer was always good at letting us know one was around without going crazy."

The cubs shimmered in the sun. They stood, curious, one supporting itself on its mom's massive rump, the other with its claws on its sibling's shoulder. The family stared, open-faced and curious.

Abe leaned against a melting-out rock, sketching with charcoal on a cardboard flap. His rifle hung in the crook of his arm. His face was tanned and content. The bears settled on all fours, turned, and ambled toward the canyon.

Watching the adult bear's fur ripple, I couldn't help thinking of how happy Janet would be to have some bear fat, and fresh bear meat. "Be fun to have a young'un," I uttered.

"A kid, or a bear?"

"What? A kid? *No!* A bear cub."

"Could be lot of trouble." Abe shrugged. "You kids were fun." He smiled at memories. "Hard to believe Iris is coming home from *college*." His glance dropped to his sketch. The bears dipped from sight. I whipped the side of the tent a last time to remind the dogs to relax and be quiet. Abe poured coffee out of our blackened Hills Bros can hung with a wire bail. He sprawled on a caribou hide to enjoy the morning and his sketch. I melted snow in another can to make oatmeal. The air was warm, the snow softening. It was going to be a warm day, too hot to travel. We were stuck here until it cooled off. The first geese could fly over any time now. We'd watch with watering mouths and I might try a long shot with the rifle. First Goose was the grandest season of the year, a change after hundreds of days of caribou meat.

"Makes the day feel good," Abe commented, "seeing bear. Wonder where her den is?"

The night sprang up behind my eyes. I poked through images, trying to winnow out what I'd been scared of, trying to decide how to ask Abe how much he believed in spirits and other things not in my high school science books. I fingered scars on my hands, resolving to try to stop thinking about Dawna and people, and to learn more from Abe, more about the land, and my father. Something could befall us.

"You and Treason ever find that bear den you were looking for, below Takunak? Few Novembers back?"

I poked sticks into the fire and shoved my boiling oatmeal aside. I eyed the side of Abe's face. "No. I voted, though. We were in town that election day."

"I always use absentee ballots. It's simpler."

I stirred the pot. "Pretty simple in town. I voted for Reagan."

Abe rumpled his sketch.

He flipped the cardboard at the fire. He rolled over on his back and closed his eyes. He looked old with his eyes closed. There were veins above his lids that no one ever saw. As the cardboard burned, the bears stood out for an instant, every tiny line deliberate, flawless, the bears' expressions curious as they turned silver black and curled to ash. What, I wondered, were you supposed to think when your dad could fling away on a piece of pilot cracker box more talent than you owned in all the cells of your body?

"I don't know how America can worship its Western myth and stomach that actor, again," he said. "He would pave the last wilderness. And sell guns and Bibles along the roads. Without wilderness, what will all the gold and silver or uranium be worth? It'll be worth armloads of shit!"

Abe had never stated an opinion so indubitably. He'd been more an older brother—letting us feel and think and be whatever we chose. In the silence the oats bubbled and spat. "Saw a wolf up the valley last night," I offered. "In a den."

"Could be a female. She'll be denning up to have pups. Any time now." His eyes opened and sparked with interest. He leaned on his elbow. The sun was on his face. "Maybe we ought to move camp a little bit west?"

Around our fire lay a continent of wild land. I could speak any words I chose and Abe would listen because he was my best friend, but I was unsure of these questions inside. Dead-people spirits, intuition, and fears were another set of feelings Hawclys didn't talk about. And all I said was, "Maybe so."

IRIS LEAPT DOWN out of the Twin Beech. She wore a blue windbreaker over a heavy sweater and the color made her blue eyes glow. Her black hair was long and curly with a thin earband underneath. Her face was pale and red cheeked. She ran up and twisted her arms around my neck. "Cutuk! I decided you wouldn't be here. You can still travel? The trail's not melted? You brought your snowgo, not the dogs?" She messed my hair. "Quit smilin', boy," she said in Village English. In the crowd around the plane people chuckled. Iris hadn't changed. "Say something!"

"Shuck. I'm glad to see you."

"I know *that.*" She pointed out her luggage and thanked the pilot for the flight. "If you ever get weathered-in and need a place to stay, ask around. Probably I'll be living here."

He struck up a conversation with her, enraptured, like everyone, by her cheer and bright beauty. I hauled her duffle bags to my sled and wrapped them in the tarp. She ran up behind. "This all? Okay to freeze?" My voice sounded too everydayish—I wanted Iris to know what her coming home meant.

I started the snowgo. She climbed on. In my ear she said, "I got the job."

I kept my eyes on the trail. Strangely, I didn't feel anything in my stomach, my place of thrill and anticipation. A quick twinge of fear yanked the bottom of my brisket. Fear for Iris, surviving the Darkness and the drinking of this village.

"I'll tell you the whole story at home."

"I have stuff to tell you, too."

We were pulling up to the Wolfgloves' house. Lumpy opened the door and strolled out, back from his most recent outing to jail. He had lost a front tooth. His arms and shoulders bulged from weight lifting. He was left-handed and the fingers of that hand were gnarled, like they had been taken apart and put back together wrong. An Arctic Cat primary clutch had done that for him. "Hi Iris." He placed a cigarette between his lips. His eyes roamed her athletic body, his face empty of expression.

Charley Casket ambled around the corner of the old Wolfglove shack and adjusted his course our way. He shook hands. His hand was limp—the way Eskimos shook hands—but clammy, too. It dipped in his jacket pocket, came out palm open. "This was my *taata's*." In his hand lay a coarse caribou antler lure, with heavy copper wire hooked through it. The copper gleamed, uncorroded, fresh out of its plastic insulation. "Hunnert bucks. That archaeologist fella say he gonna give me five or eight thousand."

Iris squeezed my neck. She smiled. "This place was getting hard to believe."

"You bring weed, Iris? How 'bout le's trade for pin joint?"

"Com'on, Charley." Lumpy spat between his teeth, barely moving a muscle. "Get the fuck outta Cutuk an'em's way."

Inside, Janet got out black *muktuk* she'd been saving in her freezer. "Long time you have no this kinda, huh?" She smiled at Iris. "We're so broud of you," Janet said, confusing her *ps* and *bs*.

"I've been eating store-bought food for so long I'm surprised I don't look like a loaf of Wonder bread."

"Maybe you're almost Wonder Woman."

Everyone laughed.

"*Arii,* you always let us laugh. You'll live with us if you start peing schoolteacher. That way we'll see Cutuk," Janet cuffed me fondly on the head, "'cause he sometimes always forget us for long time."

Melt walked in. The room went silent. He nodded briefly at Iris. "You buy me salt?" Janet asked. Melt wrinkled his nose, *no* in Iñupiaq. Lumpy stood, dark and wary, staring out at the sunny day. He shrugged into his jacket, lackadaisically hefted his shotgun, and went out.

"I'm going Uktu!" Melt shouted.

"How come?"

"They're going over!" Melt put his arms in the sleeves of the fancy sealskin jacket Janet had sewn for him. He paused, grabbed two beaver hats she had just finished, and hurried out the door.

"We got no salt for the *muktuk*." Janet giggled. "Anyways, let'um."

"Where is Stevie?" Iris asked.

"She go Barrow. He, I mean!" Janet laughed at herself. "He watch them hunt whale. That's my son. I love him pest than anyone. He's a good boy. I wish he start hunting, alright. I don't know how come he can't."

We sat eating, talking. The deep snow. The warm winter. Did Iris ever see Dawna in Anchorage? "I worry for her." Janet sighed. "Maybe she's not going to her schooling anymore. I think Lumpy always let her send marijuanas. He sell 'em to help pay her apartment. She got *naluaġmiu* poyfriend, *guuq*."

I stared out the window, willing the conversation past Dawna. I remembered one trip home from Takunak, in a snowstorm. Abe had snowshoed out front, trying to lead the dogs into the wind. His eyelashes kept freezing shut. The side of his face was frozen. "Better find willows." The unfrozen half of his grin curved. We camped under our tarp in a drift. We lay in our parkas and overpants inside our sleeping bags. The dogs tried to gather around. We fed them dried *siulik* and ate some ourselves. It was good, except where the fat bellies had gone orange and rancid. Iris had tickled our ears in the dark. "You guys want to remember the Monopoly? Cutuk, start at GO." When we got home we dug out the door and fed the dogs, hauled wood and hung our icy clothes over the stove.

Jerry slid the wooden Blazo box that we called the all-of-ours box out from under his bed. He cut property cards out of school construction paper. I colored in green Pennsylvania Avenue, blue Park Place. Iris rolled back the caribou skins on our bed, chased off a shrew that gnawed underneath. Iris glued together six sheets of paper. Iris remembered hotel rents, Community Chest cards. For hotels we cut beaver teeth into rectangles. Beaver teeth were orange and white and four inches long where they had curved way down inside the beavers' jawbones, always growing new, for spare. A beaver couldn't afford to go without spare teeth. It made sense to saw them into hotels.

I remembered Iris and me when Iris was thirteen, stacking frozen whitefish on the flat dogfood cache. The river ice had recently frozen. Yellow grass-seed stalks still waved above the first new snow. A drone floated out of the distance. Out of habit we listened, in case January Thompson might finally bring our mother home, or even just a snowgo might appear, anyone with a face, to talk to, and to *speak*. Suddenly the sound swelled and we clambered up on the piles of fish to see farther. The plane came in low, following the river. It swept over, the roar crackling against the frozen willows like a huge tent of sound. We saw the tiny figure of the pilot examine us. The white top of the wing showed as he banked. "It's coming! It's going to land!" Iris shouted, shaking my shoulders. When we glanced again, the plane was turning east. It flew away to a dot, disappearing.

I leaned on Janet's window sill, looking out at the soft river. Who'd been on that plane? Iris raised her eyes to mine. They focused on some great distance. When they came back for an instant they were bent with concern.

"I thought maybe we'd go up tonight if there's a crust. If it doesn't freeze"—I shrugged and grinned, imitating Treason—"we won't make it."

"'Thought maybe?' You sound like Abe!"

"That's Abe Junior," Janet said. "But blenty different, too. He's still gonna change if he get older."

"Anytime you want to head home will be fine," Iris said. "I learned a lot at college, and made friends, but you don't know how I missed running the dogs. And warming up by the fire. And making ice cream. Oh, I can't wait to see Abe!"

"Him too."

IN THE EARLY MORNING, by the time we neared home, water had spread across the ice from the mouth of Jesus Creek. I left the engine idling and clambered up the fifteen-foot-high snowdrift along the north bank. The snow in the middle of the river had sluffed green with overflow—water soaking under the snow. But it appeared that the ice on the river hadn't yet buckled or shifted. It was still a quarter-mile-wide white winter highway.

I gestured. "We'll follow the drift here and check the creek." Two ravens flew overhead, traveling east, their wings panting. They rolled and dipped. Iris clambered up the drift. "Last spring I jumped my snowgo across the mouth when it was wide-open water. Just go fast!"

"You wrote to me about that," she said skeptically. "Gas is four dollars a gallon now, isn't it? I'm surprised you're not using the dogs. Don't forget I'm heavier now than I used to be, 'kay?" Her face dimpled. "Education weighs a lot."

"You were never fat." I shoved her toward the cornice of the snowdrift. She spun and grabbed my leg. She was still strong and fast. We rolled, wrestling on the edge. The snow was loud, crisp and icy.

"Watch out, boy!" Iris panted. "I'll let you cry yet."

We slid over the edge. She twisted on top, her hair in my eyes, laughing and riding me headfirst down the drift to the river ice. I scooped snow out of my neck and threw it at her. "Ride in the sled, 'kay?"

She raised her eyebrows, *yes*. "Don't want all your eggs out on one limb?"

"Are you making fun of me? That's two different expressions, isn't it?"

She shrugged. "Why not use two?" She sat in the sled. "I think I picked it up from January Thompson, the way he talks."

I glanced up quickly, curious. The machine was already idling. I drove until we found a slanted drift and shot up the bank. We continued along the top of the hard-packed snowdrift, weaving around willows that reached all the way up through the snow. Smoke rose above the buried igloo. Abe was making breakfast. Jesus Creek gushed with brown tundra water, its banks sheer and tight with willows. A cow and calf moose stood shoulders showing over the willows. The ice on the main river stretched solid, with a narrow black trench where the creek current boiled under. I considered going back downriver, out on the ice and around. But suddenly I wanted to show Iris how competent I'd grown at reading the subtle differences in ice conditions. I wanted to show her that staying here at home had educated me, too—to the nuances of the land.

"Cover your face and hold on!"

I squeezed the throttle. The snowgo shot down the drift onto the river ice, skimming on the crust. The skis skipped on the open water. The black channel was wider than it looked, but we would make it. The right ski wavered and slammed into the edge of the ice. A pan cracked and broke free. The snowgo and sled jackknifed. I flew and skidded headlong across the needled surface. Iris screamed.

The ice stunned me, but Iris's call lifted me to my feet. The sled jutted half out of the water, still hitched to the overturned snowgo. Iris was not in sight. My leg collapsed. As I fell forward I saw blood on the ice, and wished desperately that it all belonged to me. I heard dogs howling. I saw her. Struggling in the black current. Iris's eyes found mine. For an instant we looked at each other across a bridge full of anguish, and then she slipped under. "IRIIIIIS!" My mind crashed into steel. Nothing around me could gather its breath enough to be real. I crawled to the edge of the ice. Yanked out my sheath knife. Lurched into the water. The cold vised my chest, knocking the air out. I ignored it. I didn't deserve air; I didn't deserve to breathe. I stabbed into the ice for a handle and peered under. Blackness. Current tugged my body. My head turned gray inside from the pain of the cold and the enormity of what I'd done. I inched along, stabbing new holds, groping under the ice.

The sky spun, and out in the swirl Abe ran. He was black on the glaring white ice. His legs lifted so high. He moved so slow. My thoughts mixed like slush with words coming out of my mouth. Maybe I was screaming aloud or only whispering in my mind. *Dad. I love you. I'm sorry for being so wrong. This water will take me away.* My hand was an iron clamp on the knife. Under the ice my other hand was numb, refusing to obey, miles away, touching—clenching. *Cloth!* Dimly I could see her face now. My body became a single clenched muscle, between the knife in the ice and my sister in the water; for the first time in my life I was exactly strong enough.

PART II CITY

TWELVE

ON THE EDGE OF CROTCH SPIT, wind shook the Alaska Airlines metal building. It moaned in the eaves. In morning darkness jet engines whined against an east storm lancing snow down the airstrip. I whipped snow off my duffle bag with a glove. A dog without a collar appeared. I knelt to pet it. It grabbed my other glove, nosed under a metal fence, and disappeared.

"Shuck," I muttered at the bad omen.

In the terminal, locals stared as if I were a tourist or a serial rapist—the first, of course, being the less desirable. The fluorescent lights overhead were painful; my skin felt as thin as a shrew-tunneled *quaq* fish. I'd woken up high on Lysol on my twenty-second birthday, Stevie and Treason gone, passed out with girls who didn't make eye contact with nervous white boys. I stumbled along the drifting streets from Stevie's aunt's, Elsie Feathers's, house to the terminal. Houses were half buried. Snowgo headlights cut cones out of the flying grains of snow.

All week there had been twilight, darkness, and wind. And the blowtorch roar of the daily Alaska Airlines jets. Outside Crotch Spit were no trees, no animal tracks, only the snowmobile-hunted tundra and sea ice. The only trees were flung-out Christmas trees, some of them plugged into the snowdrifts of people's yards to look alive. Humans lived here off the slough of American government millions.

"Here you go, Mr. Hawcly." A ticket agent with black hair bleached orange on top, like a beaver's after a sunny summer, handed me my ticket. She'd torn it by accident. Superstition sprouted roots—quickly I jammed my hands into my pockets. Enuk's ivory bear was sandwiched there between dollar bills. Out through the giant glass windows I glimpsed the ice-crusted dog burying my glove.

"Mr. Hawcly? Mr. Hawcly? We're boarding. Through the gate, sir."

Mister made me sound like a schoolteacher. I wondered how Iris was doing, back teaching school after New Year's, in a village distressed that she was still single. The silhouetted doorway of the metal detector seemed to be the magic door in the Chronicles of Narnia, books a yellow-haired boy had once read at the kerosene lamp.

I hurried into the bathroom. Water surged up and down in the toilet the way it sometimes did at home in the water hole, when a wind was blowing. On the wall a poster listed Iñupiaq values: *Sharing, Respect for Elders, Hunter Success.* Someone had penciled in *Love for My Arctic Cat.* There was no sign of Fairness or Unwasting. I threw up in the sink. Lysol burned in the back of my throat. Behind me an Eskimo man entered and held up a yellow and green Remington Shotshell box hung with ivory earrings. Some of the ivory had spent time in the coffeepot—the way Melt transmuted new walrus ivory into fossilized mammoth ivory. In the big mirror I wrinkled my nose, *no* in Iñupiaq. He didn't understand; he saw too much whiteness to register. My eyes were wide, round, and dark blue. It left me ashamed and weak—how *naluaġmiu* I looked. I rinsed my mouth and face in chlorine-flavored water, flattened my nose, moved away from the sickening mirror.

Outside, I walked out toward the jet, pledging to be a different person, somehow, in the place it landed. On the building gutter a raven hunched eating something. A frozen banana! The bird was heavy-beaked, feathers puffed with cold. Its black eyes watched like an elder's, flat and declaring, *You don't know what you're doing.* Ravens didn't fly south or migrate, did they? They knew the country, were wise, could live half a century. Ravens were locals, indigenous, and moving to town, the same as people, addicted to later stages of the same junk, but without free health care. Maybe this one had watched beside my fire on that lake with the wolves, twelve years ago. Maybe later the same bird had circled overhead, seen exactly how adroit I was at killing a wolf. Maybe last spring it had seen what I nearly did to Iris. I respected ravens more than any other bird, more than most people. What was happening? Was I giving up on being Eskimo?

Beyond the towering wing tip the airstrip glinted with supernatural blue lights, so blue that an ancient tribe would worship that blue for a thousand years. Now passengers huddled in their hoods, shouting complaints across the gusts. The gliding snakes of snow were little storm children, childhood companions of mine, and I stepped across them, up metal steps toward the smell of old coffeepots and jet fumes, and an enchanting catalog woman smiling there in the butthole of the jet.

THE AIRPLANE DOOR WOULDN'T LATCH. A muffled banging came through. I pictured Stevie out in the wind pounding good-bye with an unskinned caribou leg. The man beside me said, "This is the kind of thing that always happens to me. You would not believe the experiences I've had."

My seat was between a yellow-haired man with a computer and a white-woman dog musher. She didn't remove her Alaskan credentials—a huge parka with a polar bear ruff and clinging dog hair. The natives in the plane ignored me. I wished I could say something in Iñupiaq but knew only simple words and phrases. Perfumes combated sharp soaps and the scent of dog shit. I heard myself hyperventilating. My arms were shaking. The trail that carried me here came in flashes, glimpses of sunny days after May; mean times for me though unremarkable against the everyday explosions of rage in Takunak, a native society under technology's bombing. *Snowgoing stoned . . . frostbite way out there on my skin where it couldn't hurt me. The aftertaste of aftershave . . . waking up itching in the grass with no shirt and nineteen hundred mosquito bites. Catching* siulik *all night in the sun along the river with Woodrow Washington Sr., him wordless and precise, showing how to clean and boil their thick intestines on a fire to make* siulik *gut salad.*

After Freezeup Janet Wolfglove had fed me boiled *tiktaaliq* livers, complaining when I wouldn't eat. Her kitchen smelled of fresh rolls. Out the window on the river ice a black log had frozen in. A good cache pole. As if anyone built caches anymore. And later, packing. *What to bring? My two knives, string, matches, an Army sleeping bag, a strip of sleeping skin; leaving everything else I'd ever known there on the north shore of the Kuguruk River.*

The jet moved. The man with the computer rocked his knees up and down. "Alaska Airlines is another company just trying to salvage the bottom line." I had no idea whether he was addressing me, his computer, or the seat back, or what a bottom line was. I pictured a heavy rope used for towing jets when they ran out of gas or wouldn't start.

The tube hurled forward, inhaling black sky. My throat swallowed itself. I clung to a knit seat cushion—apparently a life preserver—asking for insurance from a God whose Sunday premiums I'd never paid. We climbed sickeningly, and down into the blue-black twilight the wind and frozen sea fell. Behind my forehead something like a spoon pressed down. Stars shone beside us. Far off to the south the sky thinned to a hazy curtain of blue.

"Are you okay?" The flight attendent offered a toy pillow.

"Fine," I croaked, the village in my voice. "Fellas let me drink Lysol for my birthday. I'm hungover. I sure *tupak* to fly." Village English was a different way of holding the back of your tongue, crushing the words—swallowing the big ones, of course.

Her smile shifted and lodged like a forked pike bone had caught in her throat. In the next row an old woman was telling a light-brown white man about being spanked by missionaries, in boarding school. For speaking Iñupiaq. "Tat what I always see when I see white peoples," she shouted. I lowered my eyes, remembering running my dog team behind the Takunak church, sixteen and scared. Tommy Feathers roared around a curve on his snowgo. He swerved and plowed into willows. He kicked my dogs. "Goddamn you white shit! How come you be on ta way?" His heavy lips twisted. Booze breath stunk. "Get my gun and shoot you yet!" My rifle hung in its caribou-skin scabbard, ready as always. "Plato, come-gee!" Plato poked her nose under lines, trying to bring the tangled team around. Tommy had stopped at our igloo for all the years I could remember. He spent the night last December rubbing his huge thawing ears, laughing and visiting while Abe soaked moose *babiche* to repair his sled. Making *babiche* for snowshoes and sleds involved shooting and skinning a moose—or caribou—soaking the hide, and scraping it daily with a shovel until the hair slipped, then half-drying the hide and slicing it into perfect strips to dry and store. Tommy's sled was lashed with nylon twine.

"White shit cocksucker!"

Kids raced up. *"Qilamik!"* They swiveled the team around. Most of them had beaten me up before, thrown rocks, chased me with slingshots and pellet rifles. But here they were looking out for me like cousins. Tommy was an elder. There wasn't any direction to run from that. They understood. "Go!" The kids whistled to the dogs.

The woman in the next row crooned on. I sat stiff and straight in the middle seat, picturing a sun-shot wolf turd twisted with caribou hair—white shit—and trying to feel mysterious, a secret agent trained in all the kung fu of the land. It didn't work. Someone who mattered needed to assure me that I mattered. Enuk was gone. Who else was hero enough? I pried out the folded money in my pocket and looked at the faces. *Thomas Jefferson?* Iris was the closest thing to a hero for me. She'd suggested that I experience the city, make and spend some money without Abe nearby. She said she had loved the city but had started to feel tired out by it; she had missed Abe, the dogs, picking berries. And taking care of food.

With nothing else to do, I counted my money. Ten twenties. And a two-party check for five dollars and seventy-four cents. The earth curved beneath us, squiggly rivers, white lakes, dark ink spills of trees—a thousand miles of wilderness, flat and colorless and no relative of home from up here. Across the riveted aluminum wing, the sun glowed on splendid mountains.

The flight attendant handed out baskets of food. On a napkin I jotted a note. *Abe, It's warm in a jet. A beautiful tall brown-haired woman wants me to eat. Alaska Airlines wants me to drink their coffee.* I paused, wondering what Abe had been teaching us all his life. He seemed to have taught *Don't chase money, that's a cheap way to live. Don't kill animals for glory, that makes you the worst kind of bully.* But what was in between? What did he want us to *do?* After a minute I grew more generous. *Be happy* was what he'd tried to teach. But weren't people supposed to be best at what they were taught and practiced? Kids in the village were great at basketball and stoning swallows off the telephone wires. Somehow I'd spent my practice *wanting* to be happy.

She handed me a tiny bag of almonds, a plastic cup, a 7UP, and a packet with two aspirins. "For your headache."

Quickly, I shoved the money back in my pocket. I stared, awed by sweet and carbonated water, rogued cheeks and soft brown eyes. The city was going to be exciting. The two white pills lay in my palm.

She held out her hand. "I'll take that wrapper."

I hesitated, then stuffed it in my pocket and patted it. "Oh, I'll save it. For fire starter."

She smiled fleetingly, then moved down the walkway.

INSIDE, THE ANCHORGE airport building blurred into distance. A world inside, like Trantor in Asimov's Foundation Trilogy. Too many people moved too fast, most of them white; it was eerie. All different sizes and shapes of white people, their clothes so clean and their shoes so shallow. I held onto a wall. *Eskimos hate rushers. Wolves eat stragglers.* Something was wrong with their eyes. I glanced at their faces, and finally down at my hands. Was I invisible? The flight attendant hurried past, her fast high-heeled legs as stiff and cloppy as a walking caribou's. I wanted to shout *Wait!* But for what? For me to woo her with stories of shrews running over my face in bed, gnawing at the greasy duck feathers in our homemade pillows?

First I had to learn how to get out of this village inside walls, on carpet and tile ground. Janet had warned, "Don't get lost on that airport. *Aachikaaŋ* that blace." What had Iris said? "*. . . the road goes right past January Thompson's . . .*"

The air tasted tired. The ground under the airport had to be holding its breath. I walked, came to bears standing dead in glass boxes, shot by dentists. Doors were numbered, locked, alarmed, signed with NO. I walked the other way, averted my eyes from the bears, passed a bald eagle perched in glass. Rode electric stairs, arrived at electric glass doors. They opened, pleased to see anyone go. Who paid the electric bills?

Outside, the air echoed and thundered and stank. In the warmth, snow melted under a steel rail. The snow was different from the kind you'd scoop a handful and eat. Herds of people milled with purpose. They rolled luggage to cars, and rolled away. In all directions exhaust pipes puffed. Jets veering into the sky. Cars parked with engines running. Buses spewing smoke. A truck charged past my ankles, its stinky breath blowing my clothes. Sunlight leaked under the overhang, amazingly bright, and yellow. Could this be midwinter? Crotch Spit was still back in morning darkness.

I shouldered my bag. The snowdrifts were knee deep and greasy. I waded back along the pavement. People stared out car windows. Something had changed. From inside their cars I wasn't invisible anymore. Hiccups climbed in my throat—the noise and stink. Monstrous trucks roared and ripped the air a foot from my side. They blurred as they passed, warping vision, the most frightening and instantaneous death I'd ever faced. The road stretched impossibly straight, wet and painted black with white and yellow lines. No one else was walking. Maybe it was against the law. I ran, my bag flopping, my *mukluks* growing ruined. Webby scum clung to the caribou hair. Water sopped through the moosehide bottoms, up through the sheared caribou insoles. It was a dishonorable end for a pair of Janet's beautiful cold-weather soft-bottom *mukluks.*

Where the road forked, I stopped, reaching into my pocket for the address and map to January's that Iris had given me. My money was there; the slip of paper was gone. I glanced around, shivering a small chill of terror. It had been folded with my money. I looked back. A jet lumbered into the sky.

HOTELS WITH A HUNDRED windows loomed. The roar was constant. Nothing at home was this frantic; the closest thing was female mosquitoes, brave and fiercely competitive, trying to acquire blood before they died. Poles and signs reached like trees for the light—survival of the fittest, city style. Everything had words. Flashing words. As if someone had cut up a magazine, glued it on the sky. *Dawna must love this!* No reading the river, snow, ice, tracks—the city took it literally; reading sign meant reading signs.

I turned onto smaller roads. Cars were fewer and I waved each time one passed, hoping one would stop and offer assistance. An elderly lady waved back. The air quieted between the close houses. The houses had numbers nailed on them. Someone was keeping count. Music thumped. A chain rattled. I glanced behind. I had never walked across Takunak without fear, never run my dogs into town without keeping an axe handle or a chain handy, wondering which loose dogs would try to fight my dogs, or who would try to fight the white boy. Iris had made it sound as if I could be exempt from that in Anchorage.

I unclipped my bag and pulled out a strip of moose *paniqtuq* and my knife. Abe had smoked the moose, for January, and sprinkled on a little salt. I bit it, cut pieces off at my lips. Dogs barked. They sounded strange, like prisoners, the barks coming one here, another there, not from any whole teams. A deep-chested black and yellow dog padded around the corner of a house. It bounded out. Dollars and dollars worth of galvanized chain uncoiled. No axe or shovel leaned in sight. Only mailboxes, pounded into the earth. I leapt back. The dog hit the end of its chain. A woman opened a window.

She was inaudible over the barking dog.

I pulled sinewy meat out of my mouth. "Hi. I'm l-looking for a friend. Any chance you could help me?"

She smiled, fleetingly and taut. "What are you doing in this neighborhood? Quiet, Zoogy!"

I tossed the tough sinew to the dog. He sniffed, picked it up, swallowed, and tilted his head for more. "W-walking. I'm looking for January."

Her glance angled to my *mukluks*. "For January? Don't give Zoogy your nasty germs. Go back where you belong or I'll have to dial the cops." She cranked the window shut.

I blinked, closed my mouth, bolted between houses. Ran around corners, my wet feet slopping on pavement. Signs accosted me. TURNAGAIN. DEAD END. STOP. NO TRESPASSING. IOWA. 32ND. BEWARE OF OWNER. TURNAGAIN. A person in blue tights, yellow shoes, and a helmet rocketed past on a bicycle. "Hi." Its white teeth flashed in a grin. A man or a woman, I couldn't tell. I halted, panting. Over my shoulder I grinned too late. "Iris," I murmured, "*these* are supposed to be my people?"

Along a fence, boot prints led over a bank, down to railroad tracks, metal with hundreds of big spikes driven into square wood. In the distance and falling light, blue signs said something that started with NO. People tracks crossed the railroad and angled through birch and spruce. I shoved both hands into my one glove to warm them. Houses lurked in the trees, their windows never all out of sight. Miniature lynx tracks traversed the trail.

The trees grew thicker. I knelt down. Finally, just barely, all houses were out of sight. I decided to camp, to find January tomorrow. It wasn't much of a camp site—stomped snow, spruce boughs, and my *qaatchiaq* and Army sleeping bag. I was unsure about laws concerning building a fire even though dry dead spruce limbs hung, tempting. Where the cat's trail dipped under a limb, I buried some dried meat and set a snare with a piece of twine. Car sounds penetrated the trees. A bird flapped overhead, its wings panting like only a raven's. I jumped to my feet, forgetting the house windows, breathing quickly, as if I could inhale home and this raven and the smell of warm snow and wind up in those branches.

IN THE DREAM, wind howled. Plato writhed backward out of her harness. A truck bellowed past downriver. The truck's panel side had no end. It grew louder. Plato pulled, twisting out of her pelt, leaving it hanging in my hands. The skin was rotten. Putrid fur shed on my wet palms. Her naked carcass snarled and bit my fingers. I awoke clenched in terror. The ground shook, light and thunder filling the trees.

Slowly the rhythm to the roar told where I was. A long time later the train had gone and still my breathing heaved. Up in the sky, orange light leaked on puffy clouds, leaving night not night but something cataclysmic. The sound of cars had not quit. Where did they all go? Who were all those countless white people? What if a road were plowed through to the Kuguruk River? Agh, the end of America must have been horrifying for the Indians.

I lay on my back, careful not to knock snow on my *qaatchiaq*, my face cold and breath rising in clouds. *Alappaa.* How did Iris make this trip warm and with friends? Enuk's voice blurted, *Turn back? Gonna never starve little bit even?*

I pictured the creek with the wolf den, the shred of green rope hanging from the tree. I wondered if I should try to find January in the morning, or try to absorb some of the city on my own first. "Enuk, you never came to Anchorage," I whispered. "I'm lost double 'cause I don't know this place or the people. Maybe triple. Maybe I don't know who I am either. So don't haunt my head."

IN THE MORNING I hadn't caught a cat. I dug up the *paniqtuq* and ate it loud with ice crystals. My feet tingled, numb, my back stiff, everything cold and wishing for fire. It was colder today. I packed, trading the glove from hand to hand, thinking of Franklin. I wandered out to scary roads that left me stranded in merging lanes like a deadhead in Breakup ice; braved traffic that should have earned me medals; crossed roaring badlands of no clean snow. Buildings towered overhead, named after oil companies and banks. Downtown people walked. Some of the people were Eskimo, but their gazes stayed away.

Inside a glass storefront, sweating half-naked men and women raced in place. A man spread blue crystals on cement. "How's it going?" he questioned, friendly, then disappeared in a door before my answer. Oily slush coiled into grates in the street. Trees stood alone, dreary and dripping and surrounded, roots weighted under heavy stone. Stores sold breakfasts. Stores sold ivory figurines, postcards, smoked salmon in flat cardboard boxes—twelve ounces for twenty dollars. My dogs hadn't known they lived so rich. The storekeepers were not like Newt with his flat eyes and fresh gossip. "Leave your bag at the door," a man ordered. As my bag lowered, his eyes fastened on my knife. I pulled my jacket down. Being suspected made my muscles stiffen suspiciously. He picked up a phone. I picked up my bag and hurried out. Movie-star women passed, taking my breath away and leaving perfumed air in fading trade. Tremendous metal glass skyscrapers grew like square cliffs out of the street. Great lookouts to hunt from. Glass people up there, hunting what?

IN THE NEIGHBORHOODS I found a green mitten, right-handed. A woman was checking her mailbox. "Hi," I said thickly. My smiling muscles felt out of shape. I thought about asking to use her phone book but couldn't find the courage. I walked on, talking in my head. In all the miles no silence lived. Inside my thoughts, I realized finally that, more than in wind or cold or Breakup, the power and absoluteness of wild earth resided in its huge uncompromising silence. Anchorage conquered silence, left not a trace—more frightening, not even a memory. Silence the dentists could not shoot and put in glass boxes. Whatever was left when humans were done, silence would come home.

My feet were soggy and peeling and staying numb now. I ached for someone to talk to. Something was not right in my mind. Thoughts carried on their own conversations. They shot across my head using only the first letters of words. It was spooky, unbalanced, a head full of acronym thoughts shouting to other thoughts. Leaving me out. *LMO.* "This is not good," I said aloud. *TING.* "Surrounded by a quarter of a million humans, and the longest conversations you've had have been with a napkin and a ghost."

IN AN ALLEY, an Eskimo woman who looked like Dollie Feathers hunched eating pizza out of a flat box that would make a good dart board. She breathed on her hands to warm them. She resembled Dollie, pretty, though older and no giggles. I slopped past. Forced my mouth to open. "*Uvlaalluataq.*" Good morning. I kept going, eyes shifting.

The woman peered out of her sweatshirt hood. Her eyelids were scarred and would never again close properly. "Ha? That white boy that always can't play ball." She spoke in a monotone.

That easy you can see my two worst flaws?

She spoke Iñupiaq, and waited. "*Kaŋiqsivich?*"

"No, I don't understand."

"You do little bit. We used to been go Takunak sometimes for Mamas and Papas Tournament. I'm from Uktu. Now I'm living in Anchorage, how long."

Two men walked past in suits. We kept our eyes down, waiting for them to pass. "Is there a difference between a pistol and a revolver?" one was saying. "Sure," the taller man said, "a pistol is a twenty-two." A woman and a man followed behind them. "Do you know how debilitating that is," she told him, "when you don't have a ball in your mouse?"

Pizza wafted into my concentration.

"Have some. They gave it to me from the back door. I won't finish it. Can't get good buzz if I eat too much."

I raised my eyebrows, *yes,* that was true. I sat where the pavement wasn't icy. The pizza was thick with cheese, frozen on the surface but still warm way inside, like a fox that died in the trap. Her name was Hannah Wana. We asked who each other's parents were, the way introductions went in the village; who we were wasn't as important, and meant little without that information.

Hannah stood and dusted snow off her knees. Her legs were bowed. Her throat had hole scars. My head filled with visions of the Takunak airfield, the crowd around the mail plane. *It's time to swallow your pride, Cutuk.* It was time to call the Takunak school to talk to Iris, to ask her to give me more directions.

I sat and finished the pizza. *Pizza Hut.* I'd seen it advertised on the Wolfgloves' TV. Eating made me happy and I thought of Janet. When Janet fed me *tiktaaliq* livers she said she was proud of me. Abe hadn't taught pride. Pride had to do with country music, sports, joining the military and getting dead for some devious president. Pride was cousin to bragging, and required a support group. Nothing we needed or had. Nothing for something.

Iris would have something to say, something like "Absence makes the heart swallow your marbles."

THIRTEEN

ON THE PHONE he believed my lie. Under the airport terminal, where suitcases went around and around, my eyes latched onto his overhanging gut. This man had shotgunned wolves from the sky, *guuq*, and taken my mother soaring away before the back of my memory. All I felt was surprise—that a ski plane could lift such a huge, tall, fat person.

The airport did not close. I'd walked here last night, after Value Village closed—Iris's idea.

"I'm not moving to another village, Iris. I'm staying." *Until I prove I can make it.*

There had been a pause while her laughter bounced off the satellite and spiraled down to the earpiece, out of a past now hard for *me* to believe. "*Value Village*. A used-clothing store, Cutuk. Just admit it—recite after me: 'I will spend money on clothes. And a haircut!' Don't worry, I won't tell Abe! What do you want me to say to Janet? She asks about you every time."

"Tell her I'm getting a job."

In the airport bathroom, I'd flushed the toilet half a dozen times, stripped off my clothes, dipped the rag in, and scrubbed my naked body. The clean used jeans, shirt, and leather boots fit better than any January had ever mailed. I stuffed Janet's *mukluks* in a garbage slot. At the sink, I shampooed with free lotion soap, scraped my chin with my knife. I combed my hair back with my fingers. Abe didn't own a comb. Combing felt vain. A man in a soft leather jacket fiddled his perfect hair, stealing glances sideways. I had avoided his eyes and tried to walk innocently out the door.

January was old, not as handsome or tanned as TV elders. He wore unlaced shoepacks and an immense unzipped parka over his T-shirt. Maybe he didn't have a comb either; greasy hair clung in clumps around the back of his head like tundra grass. Fat had bridged a shortcut from his chin to his neck, and the whole mass wobbled, bristling with white stubble.

He glanced up, startled. "Ho! Goddamn!" He crunched my hand. "Cat my dogs if it ain't Tom Hawcly's grandson. Honest-to-gosh dead ringer." I gasped, peering at people, wondering if they were religous and against swearing, and wondering how did he recognize me, and what was a "dead" ringer? I pulled my shirttail over my sheath knife.

"Broad shouldered, hell, you must be eighteen."

"Twenty-two. How are you, Mr. Thompson?"

"Never better! Never better!"

He didn't look never better; he looked sad and sunken around the eye corners, a smile hoisted in between. "Glad you called. Ho, got your duffle already? That all you brought? Got any money? I happen to be runnin' low." The doors opened for his commanding stomach. "You're quiet. This is Anchorage. What you think?"

He walked too fast, talked too fast. Somewhere out in the maze of the city was one more person. When I felt caught up to the present, I would hunt Dawna Wolfglove and find out what was left of the past. But I was late again. She'd have boyfriends and music.

"I expected trash. And apple trees."

"Aw, there's trash. White trash and regular. You limping? Here's my truck. Brought a sweater if you need. Gimme a coupla' dollars, wouldya?"

I pinched off a bill and handed it to him, dubious, and careful of wind. He shoved it in his pants. A sticker on the back window read EAT MOOSE, 5000 WOLVES CAN'T BE WRONG. I smiled, pretended nonchalance, and climbed into my first car ride. The brown seat was slippery and cracked. I rested my feet gently over the area for hammers, newspapers, coffee cups, and extension cords. The engine caught with a flooded roar. We jounced away from a cloud of smoke, almost too thick and blue to disperse. Mountains rose above a line of haze, sharp and friendly on the horizon.

"Nice mountains."

"Agh! Hillside's full a rich bastards. Varnished snowshoes over their propane fireplaces. They wouldn't know how to lace the bindings. Kind a people take winter vacations to Florida an' convince the in-laws they're pioneers."

A bungee cord kept January's passenger door closed. The pavement blurred right before it went under the truck; at that moment it wasn't road anymore but a rock waterfall. January gripped the wheel in his giant hand. The back of his thumb was hairy. The smell of his Copenhagen made my tonsils climb. A man cut in front in a black sports car. January smashed the gas pedal. The truck backfired and bucked.

"Middle a winter, look a' that joker's tan. I miss Alaska. This territory used to be a frontier, not a goddamn athletic club."

The cars stopped, a river of red taillights. My brain felt slow, layered as a frozen onion. I needed a plan, a goal, probably a career. From what I understood, the first most important thing here was a job, then car, house, spouse, friends. Last came hunting and fishing, right beside opera or Ping-Pong.

"I need a job." I pictured the twenty-dollar bill crumpled in January's pocket, then Melt Wolfglove, *Raised you right from my pocket!* Melt had gone Out, to boarding school. Chemawa, Oregon, down in the States. Was that where he learned to be unhappy and cruel?

"Can you do anything?"

My self-esteem came like static over his words. It seemed as if he wouldn't believe me if I said "Piss all by myself," which here in Anchorage was not as simple as it sounded. "I can skin animals real well. And shoot. Build dog sleds? Abe said dog racing is getting popular with city people."

"Na! Job work." The old man bobbed his head. "Carpentry? You ever built houses?" The huge hotels were coming toward us.

"Peeling logs and stuffing mouse holes doesn't count?"

"Nawp."

"People ask me to fix their snowgos."

"Fix my truck maybe? How'd *you* learn to wrench? I know a fella fixes cars. John Gordiano. Tell you the truth, I wouldn't let Gordiano ream my dog's hemorrhoids." He fished something out of his lip and peered at it. "Snoose's gonna kill me. My wife died a cancer. I take pumpkin seeds, PABA vitamin. Prostate gland. Gotta get the PSA checked, you know?"

"Huh-uh. What? No, I-I haven't."

He spat specks off his lips. "*Twenty-two!* You look like him. When I met Tom in Barrow I was a youngster. Abe, younger'n you. Fresh from Chicago an' already lost that finger in the winches. Tom wasn't motherly. When he get liquored up: 'Boy don't need all his fingers if he stays on his toes.'

"That was the first time I saw Abe paint." January's loud voice disappeared and his grammer improved. "He didn't talk for days. It was three feet high on a piece of tent canvas. I still get shivers. Just this figure standing on the ice, facing the other way, hands hanging out of his parka. Shoulders crooked with the weight of the world. All grays and whites and a finger behind him red on the ice. Your eye couldn't do anything but go right to that finger and hurt. Wheww!" January shook himself. His loud voice came back. "Don't he want you going to college?"

My mind was on the fast ice, north off Barrow. Why couldn't I have lost a finger? Why couldn't I paint? A piece torn away, a scar to forecast all this imperfection, and this scream inside, out and dried on canvas. "Abe-I-Abe doesn't care what I do. Long as I'm happy."

January arched an eyebrow. "Well, now ain't that whitey might a him."

"Did my sister Iris come see you?"

"Sure she did. Nice girl. Real pleasant girl. Yep, she did." He hooked his thumb. "Lake Hood. Busiest float and ski airstrip in the world." Between hotels stretched a snow-covered lake with trees around the edges and steep-roofed houses across on the hills. "Recognize"—I blinked, startled; did he know I'd walked this road?—"my old Cub on the shore? That's the plane your dad give me, after Tom cracked up his other'n. Before Abe went to college in Chicago. Oh, I sent him bucks sometimes, when a bounty check come or I sold wolf pelts. You fly?"

Abe gave away an airplane? *Dead wolves helped pay for his education?*

". . . teach you to fly, the way your granddad taught me. That would make me proud. One small hitch, though," he chuckled wryly, "name a the I-R-S. They got me on back taxes."

If this fat old man knew . . . how my memory had engulfed that blue and gold ski plane like a tree growing around rope.

January braked in the middle of the road. His turn signal clicked. Cars boiled around us, impatient white people, honking their horns, none quite colliding. I grinned slowly—*honkies!* Damn, was I learning everything now!

"Need to buy gas here." January pulled in, stepped out, and grabbed a nozzle. There were six pumps, men and women driving in, driving away, no one overflowing. Accurate city people. Halfway down the pumps tiny numbers read 863,231, 235,982, and 799,514. I leaned against a pump. Maybe I could be a pilot. The tiny digits increased with every gallon pumped. Millions of gallons? I had walked this city; all of Anchorage didn't buy gas here at this one spot. It was incomprehensible, and I tagged along behind January into the glass store. Aisles were lined with Ritz crackers, Butterfingers, Tide, magazines—everything a person might need, and more I may never learn how to need. A blue and yellow can of WD-40 leaked on a shelf. I inhaled the sweet odor. A *taaqsipak* woman behind the register watched. Quickly, I replaced the can. Behind the woman a back room was stacked with shelves of bottles: whiskey, wine, beer.

I didn't feel allowed to look near a woman's chest, especially a *taaqsipak*, but a name tag was pinned there. *Lacey.* The name had a sweet sound. Her eyes were alluring and dark, her fingers graceful over the keys. Would she like me if I were an Alaska Airlines pilot? Probably not. I didn't know how to play basketball.

Real unpowdered milk was shelved behind more glass. I'd tasted it once when the firefighters brought a gallon home to Takunak. "Plenty a time later to pick that up," January said. "My place is a stone's throw up the street." He jingled coins in his pants and strode out. I set the milk on the counter and handed the beautiful woman my leathery secondhand check for five dollars and seventy-four cents that had passed around Takunak.

"What's this?" Her eyes were black with tiny brown specks in the white.

"It—it's . . . money."

She frowned and flipped it over to see the signature. *Nelta Skuq*. A man as huge as January stood on my heels. He looked *naluaġmiu*, but his cap read Cleveland Indians.

"Are white people allowed credit here?"

"You in the wrong store," she snapped. "We take cash. C-A-S-H." The man roared with laughter. I turned my red face. The carton thudded like a frozen duck on the floor. A thin squirt of milk beaded across my shoes. I dropped the check and raced out the glass door.

January fought the stick into reverse. He looked over his shoulder and backed up. "Decided to wait?"

I hunched low. Beside the truck, brown cropped grass showed around a heap of melting snow. I touched beads of milk on my shoe and touched my tongue. Why had Jerry remembered lawns from Chicago? He could have saved sweeter memories: kisses and songs, glass glasses of Carnation real milk from our mother.

January swung left and quickly right. The woman who had hollered at me for not letting her dog bite me—her house was a quarter mile away, Lacey's store almost across the street. For a moment it all pressed in like Takunak, but this was city, with thousands of other houses and stores. A thousand cities in America. A million friends waiting to be mine. This must be what they called freedom.

We slid to a stop in front of a row of movable homes, too close together for people to live in all of them. Some had to be caches. The brand name on January's trailer read FRONTIER. He didn't seem embarrassed by it. Across the road stood a whole village of peak-roofed houses. Two

Can't-Grows barked behind glass in the next trailer, a dented gray aluminum home like an airplane with the wings unbolted. A pretty teenage girl peered out. Her hair was long and blond. Something made me stare back the way Lumpy would. Her gaze trickled down my body. The rug-faced dogs knocked over cups and dishes on a table. I stepped out, exhausted and excited, my feet tingling and numb.

"Handy, you live in one of these movable houses. You can migrate any time. Have you been in this spot long?"

"Sixteen years." January splashed on the melting ice, slippery and warbled as frozen fish eggs. He arranged his crotch, cleared his throat, blew snot out one nostril. Behind the window came the sunshine of a smile from the girl.

"Home Sour Home," January said. "Com'on in."

FOURTEEN

A WIND BLOWS SNOW SOUTH, *a wall of stinging grains of ice riding into the sky the length of the mountain range.* Wolves hide out in the willows of a creek. They wade the deep snow, sniff rabbit trails, chew feathery meatless ptarmigan wing tips abandoned by foxes. They haven't killed a moose in weeks. The big male is dead, shot, the naked carcass windswept and partially drifted on the ice at the mouth of the creek. Occasionally, at night, wolves visit the site. Ravens have picked the eyes and back fat and streaked the area with poop. Two steel traps are set there, too deep, chained under the snow.

The remains of a second pack join the first. The leaders also have been shot. Social order, and the feud for territory, for now, are dead. Wind gusts overhead. Snow sifts down. Yips and howls sing here and there in the trees. Hormones commandeer blood and all the mature wolves mate.

FIFTEEN

UBALDO FLUCK WHACKED me on the back. The Toyota carb clattered on the cement. "Oops. You getting solvent DTs?" He laid the connecting rod he'd been polishing on a rag. "I'll go to the corner, get us a couple Cokes."

He ambled out the garage door into drizzle, his shaggy head and beard like a brown bear's, swabbing a swath of drops out of a wet afternoon. The snow outside was gray-brown. I breathed damp air and glanced at the sky. It was late March. Fat geese would be up north in a month. Their *iŋaluat* would be edible, empty from not eating during the long flight. Abe would be wearing his *mamillaks* soon, oiling them with rancid seal oil.

I sloshed the carb again, sprayed it with compressed air, and set it on the bench, wondering how much solvent soaking into your arms did it take to dissolve your brain? When Iris and I had skinned foxes our armpits smelled of fox the next day; when we skinned wolverine, we smelled of wolverine. Brass jet needles winked in the light. Linkages and vacuum lines contorted. It seemed impossible to remember where they all went. Every day I spent hours elbow deep in solvent, making junkyard parts shiny new for John Gordiano. He conveyed the impression that they *were* new. My arms tingled. My feet still tingled—trench foot—nerves rebuilding themselves after being chilled too long on the street. On the radio a man named Bruce sang. I floated on his voice, dancing in the dark, not able to start a fire without a spark. Somewhere in the city people did dance. At home Abe had faintly tapped his foot when the schoolteacher Ron Newton played his Yamaha guitar and sang "Country Roads." I never tapped anything; anybody would see I was doing it wrong. My bones were hard; hopefully it wasn't too late.

"Igloo Gigoloo! Here." Ubaldo kicked his boots. He was large and broad with invisible eyelashes and blond hairs curling out of his collar. Every noon he roared up on a Harley with cut-away pipes, straight from psychology classes at the university. He was twenty-eight, finishing a master's degree. Mr. Standle would say he was "making it." And me? If earning potential and popularity were it, I was neck and neck with good trapping bait.

We snapped our Cokes open.

"I stayed out late last night, drinking." I'd come down with an infection of lying—nobody believed my stories anyway. Apparently a hangover was a generic macho excuse, something guys bragged about that didn't involve a ball, or their balls.

A powder-blue Dodge chugged up the street.

"Uh-oh. That was one of mine." Oil rainbowed its wet windshield. I rifled through my brand-new auto jargon. *Slant six, three on the tree, fit four Mexicans under the hood*—whatever that meant.

The driver slammed the truck door. He was thin, orange-haired. Freckles overwhelmed his skin like invading dots. The engine drooled oil.

"You the one worked on my Dodge?"

I nodded, and that quick was back in the village, waist-deep in scorn, ready to ask if I should go die somewhere. Where would be best?

John strode out from the clutter of his A-frame house, office, parking lot for lost junk. He flicked a cigarette stub into a grime bucket. He never seemed to smoke, yet always had a butt handy for the casual gesture.

"What's up?" John was short, his arms thickly muscled. His jeans bound and rubbed inside his thighs. Holes wore through and his skin peeked out gray. The gray of a lifelong mechanic. His dad had been a mechanic. Probably his mom, too. If a customer weren't here, John would have spoken Mechanic English: "Fuck! What the fuck is fuckin' up?" I still couldn't say the celebrated mechanical description.

The man lifted the hood. The heavy springs squeaked. Oil sheened. His lips disappeared. "Just fix it right."

John inspected him with concerned nods, then automatically shifted the blame. His eyes were slaty. "You lapped this gentleman's valves? Do it all again. Now, please."

It started to rain harder, sogging the remaining snow. I stared at my solvent-whitened hands that might have been my mother's. There was nothing in them of Abe, standing here in a city, cowering over a job like a dog that wouldn't pull.

The man apologized. "Sorry, John, hey. Everything else, and then this crap coming down . . ."

I saw hard medicinal porcupine shits raining around him, plinking on his massively orange hair like pellets rapping down after shooting a shotgun straight up. Everyone had spoken, except Cutuk, camping behind his face. It was John who had insisted on reusing the old valve-cover gasket that had blown, instead of having the NAPA driver deliver a new one. I slipped the Coke can on a shelf, instinctively saving it for shims, took one more glance at the dismantled Toyota carb, and hurried through the rear door of the garage, out to an unloved piece of the planet, to dig for a gasket in the junkyard gravy of grease slush and rust and battery acid leaking from the carcasses and gut piles of dead automobiles.

John's dog, Rifle, was tied to a chassis. The red hood and front fenders had been leaned back on the chassis to form a lean-to doghouse. The dog was brown and black and grossly fat—a thyroid problem—its head like a bump on a waddling keg, too fat to shake. It made me sick. It wanted to be petted, and I didn't pet it.

UBALDO HELPED TORQUE the heads and Form-A-Gasket the "new" cover gasket. "We don't have any hours to write down today." Anything over book time on a rebuild John considered simply our duty, not time he was going to pay anyone for. That included making parts new. "You should go home. Shower—twice. Find a girl to spend your money."

"How do you ask girls out?"

"Just talk to them." Ubaldo shrugged. "It doesn't really matter what you say. It's more how you say it."

I pictured the mall.

He scratched his hairy chest. "Be yourself."

"At the mall? That only works for me when there's no people around."

"I don't know about the mall."

I leaned farther down to scrub oil off the firewall of the Dodge. "You're one of the nicest guys I know, Ubaldo. Why don't you come—"

"'Why don't you *come?*' What are you two, gay?"

I extracted myself from the engine. Joe, one of the afternoon mechanics, smirked into the lifted hood. His black hair glistened. His arms were crossed to exhibit hard, bulging biceps. He had graduated from high school in December and now was often fresh from the gym. Some days a woman in a tight pink jump-around outfit dropped him off, a woman so improbably gorgeous it made me feel like I had been transported into one of the science fictions that used to arrive in the library boxes: Cutuk the caveman, visiting a planet of goddesses who smelled like flowers. Joe had advised pretty much that. "Nice is boring, man."

Did Abe have it all backwards? Again?

Now I wiped grease off my fingers and tried to grin easy like Joe. "I'm still trying to figure out how to be gay in this city."

Joe buckled over. "But," he gasped, "you had it figured out before, right? All those great times in the wilderness, just you and your dad?"

I stared at them. The truck pitched as Ubaldo stepped off. "Joe, give it a rest." He sounded tired. "*Gay* is slang for homosexual. Someone attracted to the same sex? You know?"

"Where's that old guy?" Joe glance around. "Lance. He's definitely a little faggot. Comes up to about here. He can show you *all* about it."

My fingers wrapped around the torque wrench. For some reason I'd expected white people to be fair and logical; in Takunak the schoolteachers and construction workers and other passers-through had exuded confidence, the impression that their culture was founded on purpose, with science and God both behind it. Takunak—somehow it made sense that Takunak didn't make sense. The steel wrench was smooth and heavy. Good for cracking *patiq* bones. I wanted to crack some of Joe's.

"The day before yesterday you said village people were all gay."

"*The* Village People, ya freakin' moron!"

The garage smelled of cold used oil. I felt myself retreating behind my face, warming up on hate moving like synthetic lubricant through my veins. White-people chatter—without cognizance of football players, famous actors, or processed food, most of the conversations might as well be dogs barking. Except dogs barking meant something: bear on the tundra, caribou crossing, dog team coming . . .

". . . this beast on the blacktop," Ubaldo was saying.

I suspected what his words meant, though he didn't suspect the most important thing about cars that I didn't know. Even my garage-sale bicycle I still pushed out of sight around the corner of the garage before clambering on.

Lance Shaw strolled in. His eyes were water blue under a ball cap and black hair. He carried a Snap-on ratchet set. He waved big, not caring who waved back, smiling crooked white teeth. We all knew he was the only real mechanic among us.

"'Lo, Fluck." He nodded.

John leaned in the garage doorway. "Boys," he clapped his hands. "Fuckin' com'on! Fuck! We need to fuckin' hustle."

Joe bent close, charismatic again. "So what's it like to butt screw a penguin, huh?"

"What? There are no penguins in the Arctic. Don't you respect animals enough to even know which hemisphere they live in?"

"Shee . . . I seen 'em on TV. I bet you've corn-holed hundreds. Or did you have a sister that was easier? You eat pussy, don't you?"

Bone tunnels in my temples throbbed. I pressed the sides of my head, pictured Abe rubbing his forehead. Lance glanced up, straight into my eyes. He raised one eyebrow. His socket set dropped. Sockets bounced, tapping and rolling away. He dropped to his knees, scrambling after them. John shook his head, flicked a cigarette butt, strode toward his office.

"Why do you people ask that?" I muttered at Joe. "I finally tried it, 'kay? The meat's mushy, like ground squirrel. We like lynx. My dad always tried to get a lynx for Thanksgiving."

"Pussy for Thanksgiving! Ha, ha! 'Come here sister, it's Thanksgiving. Dad and me gotta have pussy for Thanksgiving.'"

A translation dawned in my brain and next came nausea. Enuk Wolfglove, Iris, Janet, Jerry, Abe—they welled up behind my eyes. They had been good people, good gatherers and hunters who cut their own meat, saved the sinew for sewing, built fires, froze their faces and scarred their hands simply for food. For all it mattered in Anchorage our lives might as well have been lived on the Discovery Channel. I slammed Joe against a wall. A girl-calendar fell. A box of oil smacked to the cement. The police would come, with their sirens and great black flashlights. Take me to jail. Maybe I could escape and leapfrog to *America's Most Wanted*. Joe stumbled and got his heels under him. Frustration lifted the torque wrench, to smash through meaningless slang, style, and combed hair, to something as reasonable as bone.

"Please." Lance peered around, making sure John was out of earshot. "I don't like getting splattered with brains." His knees scuffed cement. His words were like sockets bouncing at a great distance. "Not that there would be an excessive amount—" The air compressor surged on. Air stacked into the tank. The wrench slowly lowered to my side. The machine wheezed and clicked off.

"Tell Joe don't talk things I don't understand about my sister."

"Me?" Lance peered behind cardboard boxes of two-stroke crankcase halves protruding long studs. He rocked back on his heels. "Jock junior lifts weights, and *he's a mechanic!* You're some igloo-dude meat-eating bookworm. That's complex interpersonal communication! Ask Fluck, man. Why do you think he's doing his shrink residency in this garage?"

"Jesus!" Joe breathed. "Learn to take a joke."

"You learn to be careful. Where I'm from, when somebody gets mad, sometimes people don't ever look the same again."

Joe licked his teeth. He put his hand on the door frame and swung out. Ubaldo scooped Simple Green on his palm, busily. Lance mouthed an O that collapsed into a grin. His finger and thumb moved to his lips; he inhaled, pantomiming smoking a joint. He raised his eyebrows, nodding encouragingly, Wanna? I shook my head, put my tools in the trays, and moved to the Toyota carburetor. My keep-your-mouth-shut-and-be-nice training was losing compression. I didn't want to inhale marijuana. I didn't want anything in the way of stray truth. I wondered if this was how Abe felt when he did the painting of his finger on the ice. Tired. Like you'd gotten your dog team on a trail you knew to avoid, a far trail you never thought you'd come to, and now it was Snowmelt, too many creeks open to turn back. It made me smile, in a detached way, that I got mad, and Abe made art.

Melt Wolfglove got mad, Enuk hunted.

Suddenly my throat tightened, and I hummed to cover distress. Melt flashed in my head, the memory of the memory of him holding a baby porcupine. A younger man, and smiling. Memories shuffled. Woodrow's words sprang out, *Melt never always can't find golt, only thing jade rock too pig can't lift.*

JANUARY CRANKED THE FOOTREST out on his sunburned La-Z-Boy. The chair squeaked and groaned. He scratched his huge hairy belly under his book. The book told the true story of coliseums, roads, and cities on Mars kept secret by the government, *guuq*. Important pages he'd tagged with pink squares of paper. January tilted a magnifying glass on a photo, trying to spot undiscovered structures that the author—and NASA, apparently—had missed among the grainy dots. He sighed. His glance strayed to the ex-Six Million Dollar Man on his new TV show. "Hey, hey. Looka' Heather!"

I rinsed my hands and turned the faucet knobs closed. The smell of chlorine twinged in my nose. I started to use a paper towel but quickly dried on my jeans. *Lee Majors, The Fall Guy; Cutuk Hawcly, The Fall Boy?* I tried to picture January and Abe in the same igloo. Hunched on skins. Talking about Martian environmental problems? Giving away airplanes?

Lights swept the window above the kitchen sink as cars turned out of Party Time Liquor across the street. In Takunak the PTL would beat any PTA for attendance; Stevie would trade his numchuks, *Taata* Nippy his snowgo, Nelta her body. And me, what, more wolves? I poured a glass of unpowdered milk. Blissfully creamy—the best thing about Anchorage. The headlights swung shadows of January's dishes in the drying rack and slit eyes of the spatula along the side of the refrigerator. On the fridge's flat top was a dusty polar bear skull with cracked incisors. Framed pictures showed a broad young January with his hand on the prop of a plane; an Eskimo couple standing at the entrance to a buried sod igloo; and January's wife, pale and frail.

I knelt by the door and laced my boots.

"Thanks for doing them dishes." January spat into a Spam can. "You're a good roommate. You don't preach or shed." He started to set his book on the floor and thought better. The roof leaked behind the oil furnace and the water ran along the wall to pool at the lowest point in the trailer—under his recliner. "Don't know why I don't drill a hole in that floor. Where you heading?"

"Dimond Mall."

A cereal advertisement flashed on the screen.

"Ma used to let me ride the combine with my brothers. Until the war come." He spat. "They went and were shot down. I threw them schoolbooks in the coal stove an' run off to join the Army. Sixteen an' never been outta Iowa. The recruiting officer drove me home. Said 'Sarah, I brought your little Nazi killer. Make him some corn chowder.'"

I waited by the door.

"Four years later I sold my octagon-barrel .22, for cash, an' hitched the Alcan. Bound for Alasker."

"You met Abe's dad?"

"Looka' that photograph. In that birchbark basket."

The photo was curled and brown. Tom Hawcly wore a polar bear parka. He was tall. The puffy white fur made his legs underneath look skinny and his arms huge as stovepipes. In Takunak it would have made him look like a white-man Outsider, trying too hard to be local. But the man's eyes were confident and fearless. He was a bush pilot in the late 1940s and 1950s in the territory of Alaska. Of course nobody messed with him. I tried to feel proud. But nowadays villagers would mutter behind his back and put sugar in his gas—a white wasn't allowed to show that much pride without asking for every kind of trouble.

"Why didn't he change the spelling of our name?"

Hawk—or even Hawkly—would have been much more romantic. Such an effortless switch arriving on a frontier. From what I'd seen, nothing about being *born* on the frontier felt like arriving driving from America.

"You off your feed?"

My gaze dropped and crawled to the TV. A Doritos commercial flashed on, a scrunch-faced guy leaning on a car. Why was it deemed so important to recognize these humans? On TV the woman with the giant *milluks* was Dolly. George Bush spoke in a way that made it clear he wouldn't be a lot of fun to camp with. Sylvester Stallone was tough and cool and so shook up about that, that he couldn't talk. His stalking—abrupt lunges with a chrome knife glinting in his hand—was inept; even Elvis Jr. would have plugged him behind the ear, first shot. Me, I could have left him bleaching on the tundra. But that kind of truth didn't count. The big question was, what kind did?

"Next show's pretty good." January horsed the chair upright. He walked into the bathroom, nearly as tall as the door frame and filling the small space, and pissed in small spurts and farted, with the door open, talking, "I'll take you shoppin' na'morrow. If the rain quits an' them leaks ain't stopped, you give me a hand before you go to work, we'll take a looka' that roof. How's them fellas you work with? You tell 'em where you's from? You tell 'em you's a goddamn real Alaskan?"

"People don't care about that old caribou-hair stuff. They ask one question, about where to hunt 'big griz' or gold, then slip in something not nice about Eskimos. Talk goes back to Shirley and Laverne or their magic johnson."

"Ugh." He came out zipping his pants. "Take my Ford."

"I don't need to pollute air. Thanks, though."

"I notice—"

"I know. I don't know how to drive." The flimsy aluminum door swung against my collarbone. I hoped this didn't mean he'd forget about what he already seemed to have forgotten—taking me up in my grandfather's airplane, teaching me to fly.

A COLD DRIZZLE thickened the air. Anchorage's sky was a constant wool blanket. I rode down the hissing edge of Minnesota Drive. The overpasses and exit ramps were monsters, concrete brachiosaurs, their backs lifting trucks and cars, the people in the cars veering together, beside each other, close enough to speak, share a sandwich, or fall in love, for a few moments. My nose drowned in fumes. A man held a scrawled cardboard sign; WILL WORK FOR FOOD. Exactly what Abe had taught us to do. *You kids want to gut that caribou and hang it under the cache and then we'll go after cranberries?*

How badly did this man need money, here where money connected—or separated—everything? Distrust squirted under my ribs and immediately I didn't like it. *This must be how you get empty eyes.* I braked and handed him some rolled-up dollar bills; six dollars. "Here. Until you find job." He squinted dubious and unfriendly at my blue bike, white throat, greasy fingernails. Beside us, beside the highway, stood a stretch of unmolested trees—stunted black spruce—small and worried as if they wished to bolt before pavement ate them.

AT DIMOND MALL I locked my bike to a light pole, pulled the wrinkles out of my jeans, and strode into America. Multiple floors, lights, glass, glitter—invitation sweet as roses, with price tags and pretty-woman scorn waiting to thorn the poor and nonconforming. The mall was an aggregation ground for herds of young people. I moved along, longing for someone to invite me home for soup, the way people in the bush invited a stranger in, though that was begining to seem as likely as a caribou following me home to *be* soup.

Mirrors hung everywhere. Columns of mirrors, mirrors behind rows of shoes, doubling their number, doubling their customers' feet and needs. Everywhere my reflection lurked in ambush. Veins showed in my sinewy forearms. My jeans were stained, my shoelaces, my vocabulary, my history, stained. High school boys brushed by on either side like a creek flowing around a deadhead. They wore faded jeans, faded leather jackets, fronds of faded hair curled in their eyes. Their leather jackets—former Carnation contented cows—cost more than my best paycheck in two months at the shop. That didn't count the price of their jeans and socks, watches and hair. Humans Wearing Money—probably already the name of a punk band.

Cutuk, Enuk said, *you see gonna too much shiny. Too much shiny whoa-mun.*

Strange and ugly puppies wagged in cupboards behind glass. Someone had chopped their tails off. ALL ANIMALS AND FISH 40% OFF. Beside me a man and woman stopped. "Oh, so cute." She clapped her cheeks. One of the dogs was barking, faintly audible through the glass. The man groaned and grinned in my direction. "The worst four-letter word around a woman, S-A-L-E."

"Why do they cut their tails off?"

"They do that," he said.

I had no idea what to say, or if the conversation was over. People didn't really buy dogs and fish at the mall? I expected the next store: Babies for sale. Trees for sale. Land for sale.

But only more shallow shoes.

A shop sold photographs of eagles and bears, and wolves—two hundred and seventy-nine dollars, roughly half the price of a real dead wolf. The wolves looked combed and extra good-looking, movie-star wolves; could they live in Hollywood, too? At the entrance to a clothing store, two women storekeepers stood, piled with curly brown hair. Pepto-Bismol nails. Silver rings. They wore name tags: *Taffy. Shannon.* Who got to kiss a girl named Taffy? I'd fight a bear. Drink solvent.

"Good evening. Would you like to see our men's apparel?"

Did apparel include jeans that fit? The word *apparel* made me think of the chewed apple cores Abe taught us to save in an Adams Old Fashioned peanut butter jar of water, to let them ferment and salvage the last bit of cidery juice. But these mall women—like girls in Takunak—wanted nothing of that kind of hunger.

I hurried on, thinking of Dawna. What would she need? But no, that was the wrong idea here. What would she *desire?*

"Hi Cutuk!"

Leaning over the rail, across the ice-skating rink, waved Charley Casket. He beamed with recognition; no flat Takunak greeting, more like a traveler stranded on a sandbar, mosquito-bitten and starved to see another human. We shook hands, his limp and wet. His hand dipped in his pocket. I stepped back involuntarily. A big brown bear tooth lay in his palm. Bog soil had stained it pearly black. "Sabertooth tiger," he said. "Pretty rare. When you been come around here?"

"Almost three months. Finally get job." Instantly, I knew my bragging, like bragging about hunting, would have a cost. "They find Enuk?"

His eyes pulled away on a passing blonde. "Lotta blond girl."

"Thousands. Just like caribou way across the river at Breakup—nothing you can do about it. I got nothing they want."

We grinned. Suddenly I worried about hurting his feelings. Charley, with his lies and lack of machinery, with his bone fragments and fake fish hooks, was a professional at having nothing anyone wanted.

"You got *naluaġmiu* girlfriend?"

"I wish. How's everybody up home? How come you go Anchorage?"

"Janet an'em's good. That letter say I win car. In steaksweeps," Charley said importantly. "Trans Am, I guess. Jus' like Knight Rider in TV." He shrugged. His eyes were flat and expressionless. "There's nothing by that address. Even they let Mom send 'em seven hunnert bucks."

I bit a grin—"let" in Village English meant "make." *Tat trooper let Lumpy go jail.*

"I sure wanna learn to drive, alright," Charley said.

"Me too."

Charley Casket was thirty-five or so, missing teeth and some gray hairs showing up, and still lived at home, on a mattress in the corner. Talking to him, I stood straighter than I remembered. Something was changing. In Takunak I was on a whole lower level than he who was the bottom—my eyes apologetic for being round and blue, embarrassed and staying to the ground, making quick forays to faces. In Takunak, Charley was Charley, Cutuk was Cutuk, our positions frozen in for the winter of our lives. Anchorage was free from that, but held something larger and vaguely similar. In the village, the new rhetoric had been natives "walking in two worlds with one spirit." Too crucial and cool, clearly, to assimilate a lone member from the Not-Quite-Right-White tribe.

Dimond Mall scurried past. I didn't have one spirit walking two worlds. More like Siamese spirits crawling the crevasses in between. Charley was on the Eskimo ice sheet. But what was Eskimo? Native, nowadays, much more than a connection to the land, seemed to be the state of being uncertain of who you were, basketball and booze the only constants. Television, teachers, and tomorrow were white. Charley might search there forever and never find his face. The way mine was not on heroes at home. The whole societal systems of walls left me disoriented, disillusioned, wanting no part of so much judgment.

"Musta been trick," I said.

"Musta been trick." He offered the tooth again, then scooped his other hand in his pocket. His palm cupped an assortment of lint and treasures: a lead .44 slug, a weathered moose molar, a YKK zipper handle, an antler toggle, a rotted strip of wood, half of a flint arrowhead. He poked a couple times, pinched the toggle, and handed it over, nearly hidden between his thumb and knuckle. He glanced around. "Enuk's," he murmured. "Back part dog harness. Enuk only one always use that kind. Maybe your dad still, too, huh?"

The antler toggle was old and punky like wood. It was the kind we used, at the end of each towline, to loop through the loop at the back of each dog's harness—something we could make with what we had, free, as opposed to brass swivel snaps that cost dollars. Maybe Abe had given one to Charley. Maybe one had surfaced in the Wolfgloves' yard, pressed into the hard-packed dirt.

"Where you find it?"

"I always walk lots. I find things. Troopers gonna hire me for searches, alright. Find clues and do the underwater diving. They all know I was a Navy *Seal.*"

I handed it back, biting the grin again. Charley's maze of lies, like trying to follow wolf tracks through caribou wintering ground. How much did he believe himself? How much did he know? "Where did you find this?"

His eyes were dark, inscrutable. "I can't remember. I sure need hunnert bucks, *bart.*"

Woodrow Sr. flooded my head—seventeen-year-old memories borrowing fifty dollars out of Abe's Hills Bros can—telling of Harry Feathers committing suicide with a double-barreled shotgun. It was all so ancient, Harry too far back, no face anymore. I handed Charley fifty dollars. *Fifty bucks for half a friend in the crevasse. All friends half off.*

He stuffed the treasures in his pocket and grinned. "I gonna buy jugs."

"Oh."

"I'll wait at airport." He nodded, shook hands again, and sauntered away.

Charley wouldn't talk so friendly in Takunak. Bacardi 151 sold there for three hundred dollars a bottle. If he could pawn artifacts he'd take home a case, and for a day have something everyone wanted. Maybe a woman would even go with him briefly. Either way, in a week that party would be past. He wouldn't pay back the fifty.

Charley leaving and the return of loneliness lifted the floor heavy against my feet. It was time to give up here, once again, on a date; time to find my bike and start home. January needed company. He might actually get around to the roof in the morning.

Pay phones beckoned, promising a last chance at possibility. Dial tone acknowledged my one-sided conversation to Dawna, then beeped viciously. *Lying to a phone isn't allowed.* My spoon face leered in the polished metal coin box. The phone book was heavy with names. No Wolfglove. No Fluck, Ubaldo. Shaw, L. L., was there.

"Lance? This is Cut-tuck." I stammered about Dawna.

"Try four-one-one?" His voice came down the wires different, quiet and no mechanic banter.

"That isn't the cops?" He sounded sincere, but I was learning about these people.

"That's *nine*-one-one. Let me try. I'll ring you back."

I faced the mall ice-skating rink, wheeling with bleached beauties and nine-year-olds hopped up on Pepsi and Gummi Bears, out of control. The phone rang.

"Got your pencil, Igloo Gigoloo?"

I scratched the numbers on my thumbnail with the tip of my knife.

"Hey," he said, "give a call sometime. We'll get together, swallow some suds."

I hung up and dialed, wondering, did white people drink soap? *Melt drinks aftershave.* I was somewhat white and had drunk Lysol in Crotch Spit. The truth was I'd drink soap any day in Anchorage for a friend.

"Who's this? Sugar?"

"Who's this?" I returned the Takunak phone greeting. Who was Sugar? I envied him a name that dissolved so easily into English.

"Cutuk! *You're in Anchorage?*"

"I'm inside Dimond Mall."

Memories draped down—that smooth skin above her cheeks, tattered

Sears catalogs, snared ptarmigan with their eyes frozen closed, thawing beside Janet's stove.

"Stevie called collect from jail. I thought you were there. Him and Lumpy broke into some teacher an'em's house and drank their vanilla and NyQuil. They *iġitchaq* them *naluaġmius'* pet bird!"

"What kinda bird?"

"Wait . . . you want to go to the movies with Dave and me?"

Blood drummed in my ears. I'd rather go midnight solvent dipping for a Nissan needle bearing. I scratched the mouthpiece, tempted to manufacture a sudden bad connection. I needed to find the roads home to January's. Why had I called? Hadn't I come to meet a mall girl, someone from this world, someone who never had to know I had been *naluaġmiu,* and too shy to say *God* or *love,* or kiss?

"We'll meet you out front." Her words were city-woman words now, farther from the throat. Suddenly the mall stretched too vast, a glass prison, loud, and chemical food, light-years from any sort of land at all.

"'Kay then. I'd do anything to see—" The phone began beeping.

SIXTEEN

ORANGE SNOWFLAKES FLOATED down the sky above the streetlights and landed soft on my hair. The fresh snow smelled genuine. I missed stepping out every morning and having weather decide my day, dogs prancing in the snow, sky arching over unowned horizons, sustenance waiting out there: caribou or rabbit, muskrat or bear. The tiny wet stars brushed my face. Cars migrated along Dimond Boulevard. The March evening had cooled, and in the parking lot shoppers tilted their heads, covered their perfect hair with newspapers, and rushed to their vehicles, cursing winter for showing itself, then riding away seated in their heated metal boxes to houses bright with electric lights, hot baths on tap and a hundred songs waiting inside every radio.

A red Mustang II hatchback slid into the parking lot. *Gutless. Four-cylinder cake mixer.* Dawna was in the passenger window, appearing out of traffic, the way Enuk had out of storms. And me? On square stone sidewalk, hands in pockets, gripping an ancient ivory bear, guessing what Dawna and I had left to cross a city about.

She jumped out, her legs in acid-washed jeans, longer and thinner than I remembered. Her face thinner. Behind the wheel a white man with puffy eyes watched like *ukpik*, the snowy owl.

"Hi Yellow-Hair!" She said it all in one word, like in the village, and giggled and hugged me. The years weighted my arms with uncertainty. People exiting the mall glanced over. Hair tangled in my lips. "When are you going home? Mom send *niqipiaq?*"

"Janet sent beluga *muktuk*. I ate it."

"Ah you!" She slapped my shoulder.

The boyfriend peered out, forearms cool on the wheel. I wondered if he knew how to cut joints—I could cut his wrist joints in six seconds. Leave him handless as a village disciplined by Attila the Hun. I touched my knife, recently sharpened.

"Dawn. Let's go!" His voice was nasal, hoarse.

Dawn? Dawna was one of a kind. Eskimo. Not abbreviation material. I concentrated on getting into the back seat, angled and slippery, red fake leather that had never been an animal's skin. The vinyl smell hurt. I smelled an ashtray, too, and cigarette ash, and roaches. Dawna turned, her cheek crushed against the headrest. "We're going to pick up some stuff and head back to our place."

"I should have ridden my bike." Now suddenly I hardly cared if the bicycle rusted to iron compost, nourishing the light pole's metal roots. I examined Dave's neck. He seemed easy to hate—blow-dried brown hair parted in the middle, long in back. My mind played with a collage of city images. Dave had rich parents, both with mustaches. He worked in the Safeway dairy department pushing cottage cheese. His mother was a fingernail artist, with one-tenth the brains of a two-year-old wolf, a Bible and a diaphragm in her purse, and material desires itching like cold sores.

He touched the brakes, oversteering. The car swung. Maybe Dawna was in love with his driving. It was all so sickening. We passed centers, not the center of the city—Anchorage it turned out had hundreds, maybe thousands of "centers." My bike grew farther and farther away. A car leaned on the curb, crippled, waiting for wheel donors.

Dave got out. Slammed his door.

She swiveled around, her Seawolves jacket slippery against the seat. I wondered what a seawolf was, and why my brain wouldn't stop wondering about these things. A sea-bear would be a polar bear. *Stupid humans, naming their proud jocks after an animal, one that doesn't even exist.*

"My GPA got low."

"What do you eat?"

She giggled and shoved my shoulder. "I was going to be a photographer. In the darkroom? Dodging and burning? I sure like photography. I thought I was good, but that teacher said my pictures weren't very art. You shoulda' been here to tell me."

"Me? I wish I knew some art." *Dodging and burning?—sounds like war, not art.*

"Those professors, they sure always think they're something else." Her jacket made a nylon sound. Her features were scooped shadows and streetlight. Her nails pattered the headrest. "Ever try coke?"

"Coke? Of cour—. No. Not yet."

The car was silent. Her eyes had dark circles underneath and stared a lot farther away than the back seat. Her fingers curled along my neck, twisted gently in my hair. "Cutuk, I'm still waiting to see you smile like you don't care who else is in the world."

"So, you're gonna let me learn? Or are you coming out on the tundra where I already know how to do that?"

Dave sprang into the seat.

"Sugar have some?" she asked.

"Re-friggin'-lax, why doncha." He pitched away from the curb, not moving any direction I wanted to go. Streets led to streets. In front of a bank, under shrubs, little lights with black rings glowed like recently hatched UFOs. The alien city went by, frozen stone, glass, locked locks, and enough left-on light to last lifetimes. I hunched in the back, wishing the car had four doors; I'd give a testicle to jump into the ephemeral freedom of car-made wind.

DAWNA SLAMMED THEIR upstairs apartment door. She'd left lights on. On a four-drawer dresser the TV stood. A green couch faced the TV. Dave pulled the switch. "I wanted to catch Letterman."

A blue truck door lay across cement blocks. The window was rolled down, clothes heaped and hanging through the opening. No books—college textbooks or otherwise—in the room. No meat saw. No skins. To the left was a kitchen, dark paneled walls, lined linoleum. Dawna had never had time for kitchens. I wanted to escape there, to wash her dishes; it wasn't even work with water coming out hot and going somewhere by itself.

David Letterman flung a book through a good glass window. *The only book in the house.* Both Daves laughed. There was a rabbity resemblance. Maybe they were cousins, white people had them after all. The sofa was tired, the springs bony. A caribou skin would help, and smell like home. The house made self-important noises: hums, drones, whirs.

"You want pop?" Dawna leaned into the fridge. The silver bars of empty racks gleamed. A twelve-pack of 7UP lay in there, a Ziploc of *paniqtuq*, a yellow squeeze bottle of mustard. I raised my eyebrows. She tossed a can. I scrambled after it.

She grimaced. "*Adii,* I forget you always can't catch."

The village rushed back, all the shame of not knowing how to play basketball—or anything else that mattered—and having red hands doing it, instead of brown. The clean bubbly taste of 7UP brought new memories, the jet ride with the beautiful flight attendant. My fingers played with the lock on the truck door while I kept my eyes off Dawna's body.

She sat beside me. "So how you been?"

Dave glanced over, leaned forward, turned up the volume.

"I'm working as an auto mechanic."

"For real? Say! I'll let you fix my car." She pulled strings and fought a curtain open. "Ever see this kind with strings?"

"Maybe Abe's nailed-up flour sacks worked better?"

"Nay! There. That's my car."

I leaned across her. She didn't use Pert shampoo anymore. Abe slipped in with stray thoughts—what was he doing without me to shoot mice with a big rubber band? They must gnaw all night at our soap in the Darigold butter-can soapdish nailed to the wall. Iris had said on the phone that Franklin had left his igloo and moved up to stay with Abe. Would they get around to shooting enough meat?

"You gotta kick the shifter, but now that can't even—what are you dreaming?"

"I—"

Dawna and I giggled, the way we used to by the dogfood bucket, behind Janet's stove. We reached out and gripped each other's wrists. I felt myself falling into the pools of her eyes. Her thumbs sank in like Janet's, reminding me of her strength. There was no slipping away. And for me it was like pushing freezing hands into a warm basin—it felt so good but along came the agony.

Finally, I looked down. "Dawna, did Melt go to school in the States?"

She jerked out of my hands and stood. "Shuck, I dunno. Oregon someplace. Chemawa. Teachers cut his hair and beat him for speaking Iñupiaq. Indians beat him for being short. Everybody knows those parts, if you been around when he's feeling high. How come?"

"Just wondering. How about Newt Clemens? Where did he go to school?"

She shrugged.

"Is your car an automatic?"

"Our parents are inside us." She giggled. "Have to be careful what we let out." She stood sexy in tight jeans, hands brushing easy on her thighs. The rings on her fingers were supposed to be gold. The plating had worn through. "Dave, what's my car?"

"Chevy Shove-it." Dave pried his gaze off the screen. "Let's cut some lines and get amped. You want to— ?"

I recognized his pause, the hydrogenated version of my too-native name. Intoxicating music leaked through the floor from downstairs, a female singer, singing about the weight of a stare. Dave pried a square of newspaper out of his pocket. *Raising Dawna, right from his pocket.* He went into the bathroom, and, flexing extra, lifted the mirrored medicine cabinet off its clips. Bottles rattled inside. He laid it beside the TV. The picture on the screen flickered and cycled downward. David Letterman's feet stood above his grinning face. With his driver's license, Dave cut rows of powder. None of my Eskimo friends in Takunak had a driver's license. Outsiders, they always had licenses, and all their teeth.

My hands gripped each other. How feeble and pathetic, me subsisting on January's trust and a flight attendant's single-serving smile when everyone else was singing, dancing, driving. Dawna's eyes watched, insolent and unblinking, unapologetic for any distance she had left me behind. I saw the wolf again, running, paying the price of a bottle; and Takunak, a speck in the wilderness, modern as microwaves, yet hissing with voices from a brand-new ten-thousand-year-old past: *Kill every animal possible, every fur. Share. Avoid taboos. Don't get ahead. Never stand out. Live now.* Takunak: generous and jealous, petty and cruel and somehow owning us; owning our decisions; calling us home to assassinate our ambitions. How strange my past, even farther back into the earth—the buried caribou-skin entrance, flickering lamplight, dreams and the conviction to hunt the land for them—and now the only thing familiar, a Wolfglove I didn't know.

I considered clubbing Dave, tossing him out on the dead lawn, and holding Dawna in my arms. It seemed as reasonable as killing a wolf for Bacardi, as reasonable as killing my brain cells scrubbing burnt bent VW lift rods in solvent to sell as new. It was the spontaneous sort of action Lumpy wouldn't have to think over. But I only *thought* about it, and thought, in Takunak, was the least-respected bodily function.

They rolled a dollar into a straw. They concentrated, then gulped 7UP. I prepared to be casual. I might sneeze and scatter dollars to dust. I wanted to ask what it did. But coke was expensive; it better not make me feel cheap. The dust tickled in my nose. Then all the way up to my brain a pleasant pain spread in dots like the cut of fine glass. A small bitter gob crawled down my throat.

DAVE LAY PARTIALLY on top of her on the couch, brushing her neck with his mushy lips. Dawna Wolfglove was the only person I had ever kissed. Including family. On the dresser, a tiny pair of calfskin slippers winked blue beads, Janet's as a child, later Dawna's. Some of the stitches and beadwork had broken; the old sinew thread was brittle and needed to be resewn. Dawna probably had no skin needles.

I migrated to the carpet.

Huge yellow wrestling flashed on the screen. Words stood in line in my brain, a blizzard of babble. Dawna sat up. "You ever try Pralines 'n Cream?"

I kept my mouth shut, in case it was a common narcotic, or some kind of bent-over sex everyone else had had. "I'll fix your car." I hurried to the door and out before she could untangle herself. It was cold outside. Sitting around too much made me shiver. Or was I turning into a city person who thought cold was equivalent to bad? But no, I'd lived the scars on my hands, made all the down payments for my Eskimo future.

The Chevette was white. "Uh-oh. Bad luck on you. Get a *paint* job." Somebody had smashed it hard. The right headlight bulged like Stevie's eye right after Melt caught him and punched him six times in Wolfgloves' outhouse. Stevie had smoked Melt's Marlboros. The last in town. I brought him snow in the outhouse for his eye. "I'll get gun and shoot him yet," he said. I thought of Tommy Feathers's threats to me behind the church. "You're not like that," I said. "Everybody doesn't have to be like everybody." Stevie's eye was swelling, the lashes disappearing. His glasses cracked in his hands. I sat on the stained seat. I nicked my wrist and took some of his blood and gave him some of mine. We were best friends and blood brothers again, moonlight leaking in. Our breath froze frost feathers up under the roof. He bowed his head, let spit run out of his mouth. "That guy never tried to love nobody only himself." He wiped his lips. "Here I been trying." Offshore, the river ice boomed and echoed. The world outside seemed made of interminable cold. Stevie's glasses clattered on the boards. He put his hand on my neck. It was warm. "I'm gonna die from drinking. Doesn't matter. But you better miss me, Cutuk. And if Melt never try cry you let him learn."

But Stevie ended up getting us laughing, pointing down, pointing out the impossible diameter of one of Melt's old frozen turds. Stevie—and me—we should have cried, but we were too young that night to remember how.

Beside Dawna's car, I lit a match and checked the ground for dog shit. I slid under the bell housing. It was black with grease. I yanked wires off the neutral safety switch, bit insulation, twisted strands, then stood outside letting time wander away, wondering what the hell was I doing, wandering around this city like a loose dog swallowing crap?

Orange clouds hung overhead. Either Nancy Reagan had gotten at the nuke button or it was city night, not giving the sky any sleep. My mouth was as furry as it was an hour after eating lentils. A strip of the *paniqtuq* out of Dawna's refrigerator would taste good. Refrigerators made me think of summer, up north, my teenage years, eating fish and *igamaaqłuk* porcupine because nothing would keep for long in the *siġłuaq*.

I slugged the white Chevette. "Daw-na!" I slugged again. *Lumpy does what he feels, loses fingers and goes to jail if that's the price.* "Nothing works! Nothing is working! People are messed up!" My hand didn't bleed. I was disappointed and hunched over it until the canvas of my jeans grew icy. My damaged feet were numb. I trudged up the stairs to beg a ride to my bicycle. The bedroom door was closed. Everywhere my eyes settled I took them away and thought of the feel of fingers on a gun stock, of shooting, smashing, shattering. Quietly, I washed the dishes, then examined Dawna's photos, hidden, pinned inside cupboard doors. They were of people and buildings, a dog crossing in front of cars, a woman running on a neon-night street. Black and white; the contrasts were harsh, the faces hard-partying. Who could say if they were art? I believed them, and didn't know much else to say that about, so maybe they were. Bubbles tinked in a 7UP can on the TV. I finished it and lay the can in the trash, wanting to swallow all sign of traveling this way.

Outside, the middle of the night was damp, tingly in my nose. Gunshots would roll away hollowly. It felt wrong, having so far to go and without a gun. The doors to Dave's Mustang were locked. Spare light glinted off the chrome. Fresh snow lay on the roof, downy and perfect for snow ice cream. Iris would be out with a spatula gathering a bucketful.

A light came on upstairs.

In the Chevette, the twisted key glinted in the ignition. I sat for a moment, breathing in and out my rage at all the humans with their wasted warmth, and love locked out of reach; examining my desire to drive engines, and wanting honesty; wondering, was that something Abe had invented to amuse himself? Maybe I only wanted honesty and kindness to be precious because they were things I'd wasted time learning—like bear tracks and algebra.

The engine heaved over, spun, and fired!

The car bucked out onto the street. The wheels spun on snow. The throttle stuck. The engine made a continuous growl, a growl that said worn-out timing gears. Soft white street blurred under the hood. Twin tracks stretched behind. In the mirrors, the Mustang's headlights swung onto the road. The wheel stiffened. I fought it. The car plowed through crew-cut bushes guarding a stranger's lawn. Dogs barked. I hunched behind the hood and lifted it a few inches. The hinges squeaked. Dave's Mustang rocketed past.

"Man, did you ever not learn to follow tracks!" Elated, I held a match under the auto choke. I pictured grabbing up a rifle, chambering a round. I had been quick at moving shots. When the rabid fox angled across the ice toward my team, rasping, out of its mind, I swung and dropped it, neck-shot. *Don't shoot rabid animals in the head; the brain is needed to verify the virus.* My teeth grated as the taillights shrank out of range.

NORTHERN LIGHTS BOULEVARD led to ocean, gleaming, moonlit, windy gray. The engine revved and idled rough. I got out. Walked to the edge of the overlook. The breeze was chilly. I'd biked here. Tonight I wanted to find the other edge of the city, the north edge, where houses stopped and *land* started. Ice pans drifted in the current. Open water, we called it at home. More dangerous than bears. Out in the inlet, water slapped ice. Thickets of birch lined the shore, growing close, straight and pale, like patches of giant moose hair. Behind were the lights of the airport.

Down the deserted road, I gunned, full throttle, the car shuddering like an Apollo reentry vehicle in the movies. I was driving! Driving—how was it so straightforward and logical? It must be the drivers, the places they drove, and their irreverence when they arrived that remained incomprehensible.

Before dawn I backtracked away from jet lights in the sky, toward the mountains, carefully switching lanes, watching for police, waiting for traffic lights to be green and then some. I thought about wrecking her car, plunging it into willows, or sinking it in saltwater. But the pollution, the waste of resources, the meanness—I decided to repair it. I steered in behind January's truck. The engine died, dieseled, and shook the car. My feet tingled. The streetlights had dimmed, everything gone flat and dull. The door creaked open. Cool air poured in. My head lowered against the wheel, breathing shallow.

"Are you all right?"

The girl stood on the slushy gravel, inhaling a Marlboro Light. "Are you going to be sick?" She was from the trailer next to January's. Her long hair was damp. Her shirtsleeves too long. Her eyes wide set and friendly.

"Can I have a puff?"

She turned the butt deftly. "There's more inside. I could get you one?"

I took it from her fingers. "I'm more addicted to sharing than nicotine."

She pressed her sleeves against her palms and shivered. "Mom has a freight run to Bethel tonight. She flies for Markair Express. Rainy Pass is IFR. You want to come in?"

The trailer was cluttered with rubber boots at the door. Inside, calculus books splayed on a blue corduroy couch; cassette tapes were abandoned on the carpet. Something rubbery and tentacled was thawing in the stainless steel sink. Stevie Nicks's voice skated softly out of a bedroom. A circle of plywood lay across a green plastic garbage barrel for a table, heaped. The Can't-Grows sniffed and growled at my ankles. She locked the door.

I went to the creature in the sink. Looked in its frosty eye. Its eight arms draped across plates and cups with oily tea left in them, and halfway to the floor. "Okay to touch him? It's an octopus?"

"I hope you're not disgusted. Dad caught it last summer at Naknek. I decided I better cook it before it gets freezer burn. You probably don't believe me, but the meat's excellent."

"I believe you very much." Something behind my eyes turned orange as a map of Asia. "W-what's freezer *burn?*"

"You know, dried stale old flavor. I'm going to cut it up and simmer it in salt water. Apparently it's good pickled, too." She ran water and handed over a glass. Her hands were smooth, her fingernails all different lengths and coated with something glossy. "I'm Cheryl." She pulled up her sleeves.

"My name is, uh, Clayton."

We sat on opposite ends of the couch. A yawn poured in and out of me, then another. I concentrated on trying to remember my name. She talked freely—UAA, biology, calculus, speech, parking permits. She was *naluaġmiu,* blond, captivating eyes; how could this person be talking casually to me? Was this really happening? What would be the right things to say? Suddenly I wished Stevie were here, with his Band-Aided glasses and big grin. Together maybe we could impress her with something—stories of drunken behavior, shooting, and big sheefish that tasted excellent? Her lips moved. I liked watching the fringes of them form words. My brain tried to follow but pitched into a stupor. *Jerry and Iris playing Chinese checkers with .22 bullets in a yellow plastic Remington cartridge box, the lamp flickering, beaver tail and feet simmering in the cannibal pot.*

"—dental hygienist." Her hand patted my knee. "What do you think, Clayton? Don't say 'Stick your hands in spit all day?'"

"I'd hold them." I stood up, blinking in dismay.

"I'm unsure what I want to do, in college, I mean."

I caught myself, about to blurt, *You're normal and divine, and cook octopus, what do you mean you don't know what you want to do?* "I—January's going to get me up in about fifteen minutes to look at the roof. Somehow I have to get my bike at Dimond Mall. I'd better go." I stood at the sink, rubbing my eyes.

Her lips quirked to one side. "Your uncle owes the IRS fourteen thousand. That's what Mom told me."

"Is she coming home soon, your mom?"

"She goes to her boyfriend's."

"Your mom has a boyfriend?"

Through the window we saw January open his aluminum door, spit, glance around, and step out. The sky was brightening, the eaves dripping. He rubbed his lower back, walked behind his truck, peered in the window of Dawna's white Chevette, and spat again.

Cheryl murmured, "You ever wonder where he gets all that spit?"

I glanced at her. She returned my gaze, a teasing look in her blue-green eyes. Then we were laughing. We bent down, out of sight behind the counter.

"He's not my uncle. He bounty hunted, with that ski plane my dad gave him. Sometimes he sent boxes of used clothes. Do you have any ideas, how I could make him that much money?"

"Get on at Prudhoe. Or fly to Dutch, get out on a winter crabber. That's what my dad does." She straightened up and ran new cold water over the octopus. I watched, admiring the uninhibited way she moved. She turned and shook drops of water off her fingers. "Gotta be tough for that. And brave. It's very dangerous." She forced pans and dishes out of the way and rinsed two mugs.

"I'm not scared of things out away from people. Want me to wash your dishes?"

"Any time! I'm going to boil water, make us a strong cup of Ass-am Fag-fopi."

It had been a long day, a longer night, way too much inside my head again. "A cup of what?" I said, resigned to being ignorant.

She rifled a cupboard, held up a tiny metallic green bag. "Ass-am Fag-fopi, that's what Dad calls his favorite blend of Upton tea. Assam tea. The initials F-T-G-F-O-P-I stand for things in tea-fanatic lingo. Finest Tippy Golden Flowery Orange Pekoe something-or-other."

"Oh. Tea art?" I carefully stacked dishes aside. "Or is it tea mechanics?"

"You're funny."

"I'm trying to be normal."

"Really?" she said. "Why?"

"Isn't that what people do?"

SEVENTEEN

UNDER THE PLANE, new grass and fireweed shoots grew up around the skis. The chain locked in a figure eight around the prop was heavy, and spare links had been left heaped on the ground, killing a patch of earth's chances for summer. In the bright sky, planes droned, and on the water of Lake Hood floatplanes taxied, taking off and landing every few minutes—Anchorage sportsmen seeking "sport" or "game" or whatever it was they did on their piston-driven forays out to the wilderness. January had said this was the busiest floatplane base in the world, and that seemed plausible. The padlock was square and the sign read GROUNDED BY FEDERAL SEIZURE. He might have been making payments, but not fast enough.

Lance poked at the key slot with a filed-down feeler gauge, counting the infinitesimal bump of each lock pin.

"I'm unsure what I'm doing," I admitted, and heard Cheryl's words resonate in my head. We laughed for some reason—Lance and I. He was my friend. I hadn't had to drink soap. I'd never had a friend you could say anything to, and that felt much stranger than drinking poison.

"Six pins!" he murmured in admiration. "Your tax dollars at work." He dropped the feeler gauge into his toolbox, stepped down off the ski and untangled a Stanley hacksaw. "Now that's a key!" he quipped in an Australian accent. A string of cars whooshed past on Spenard. "You're not sure what you're doing? What, with Cheryl? And you really wish I'd just go out with her instead?" He grinned. His hair was messy, black horns sticking up. It was May and his arms rippled with tanned muscles. He was short and slim and looked much younger than forty-two.

"We're not 'going out.' She wants to be friends."

"Bummer." He sat on his toolbox. He twisted his head until his neck made a soft pop. He pulled a grass stalk, chewed it, and stared across the water. "You better plink-plank along to fourteen grand, homes. Compound interest and entropy never sleep."

"Entropy? Is that the force that keeps some people from getting around to emptying their slop bucket in the morning?"

He laughed, a loud laugh that ripped free like a raven's caw, irresistible; two men with fishing poles and hip boots, waiting on a pilot loading a plane with a king salmon stenciled on the fuselage, turned and grinned. More than most things in Anchorage, I wanted to learn to laugh like Lance.

A floatplane took off, the flat-pitched prop deafening. A second plane flew overhead. I glanced up warily, still not quite used to the fact that planes weren't going to poop from overhead like gulls. "I think I'm using January's plane for target practice."

He fingered tears in the fabric of the airplane, patched with weathered duct tape. "Maintenance not Thompson's strong suit, huh?"

"Strong suit?"

"His cup of tea?"

"He doesn't drink tea."

He laughed again.

I sat on my heels. "My jobs, making money?—that's all me

pretending. Money is everyone's connective tissue. It's their measure of success, isn't it?"

"What do you call success up north?"

"Hunting. Fat meat. And dead wolves. And winning at basketball, of course."

He leaned forward. "So that's better?"

"Shuck. I sure don't know how to feel that way about *money!* Like I said, I'm using January's plane for practice."

"Man, Scroat, you're way too serious. I need coffee for this conversation." He slapped dust off his jeans, walked to his truck, and shoved his toolbox behind the seat. He came back. "You don't want money? You just want money so people who like money will like you?" He shouted laughter. "Sprout some balls!"

We climbed in and bounced onto Spenard Road. Stray wires hung like roots out of a cutbank from behind the dashboard. An electrical short in the cassette player flickered the green lights in time to the beat. The sun was warm. The pavement dry. On the other side of the glass, the city was busy with a Saturday.

At the coffee shop we traded positions and he coached me into a parallel parking slot. Inside, he ordered cappuccino and I hot water—silver tea, Abe called it. *Something for nothing.* Chlorine flavored the water. *Nothing for everything?* He sprawled at a table. "So, the Igloo Gigoloo wants to be one of the sheep." He talked singsongy, encompassing the coffee shop with the sweep of his arm. "'Baaa! Is the herd going that way? Swallow inoculant? Breed? Baaa!'" Lance's laughs ripped out, bouncing against the ceiling corners. Customers glanced our way. I felt safe, and cool, canopied in his presence. Alone, I'd have been twitching, nervous and shamed, certain he and his friends were laughing at me. Laughter in Takunak, when I was present, had been that way.

I lowered my chin to my overlapped fingers, lowered my voice, trying to encourage his lower. "When we used to see a traveler coming, we'd run down on the ice. 'Hi,' we'd say, 'Com'on up. We've got bread! Crazy Joe brought yeast, and we had flour. We've got bread. We can make snow ice cream. You can stay as long as you want.'

"What I'm saying, Lance . . . it's confusing here. I'm trying to learn stuff without getting mean. Like my friend's dad where I grew up, this guy Melt Wolfglove. He's scary. Sometimes I even think about killing people. Well, there's so many of them"—I dropped my voice further—"environmentally, too, that seems the only conscientious career."

"Do it." He shrugged and sipped. "Melt Wolfglove? That's a name! 'Howdy. Name's Melt. Melt Wolfglove. I done come for the little lady.'"

"I said I'm trying to learn stuff *without* getting mean." I told him about Melt and the piles of clothes frozen to the walls, Dawna and the Wonder Woman poster, Nippy's rotten teeth and bumpy eyes, Newt's wrist, Enuk's wolves and his face and his leather pouch . . .

"So, what have you learned *here?* I know you don't know squat about mechanicing."

"A couple things about tea. Engines. People's the thing. I keep getting more confused."

Lance swung his gaze. Suddenly it was wide-eyed, hard and blue, surprisingly intimidating coming out of his small features. "You might as well accept it, this 'stuff' can't *be* learned. It doesn't make enough sense. You have to be *fed* it!"

People were glancing over.

"How do you tell which ones are sheep?"

"You don't. You figure out who you are. Let's get the fuck outta here."

"Who are you then?"

"I'm—" For the first time I saw him, crouching behind his shield of words. He raised an eyebrow, shrugged mockingly. "Welcome. I'm Replicant five-seven-four, your guide here on the Plastic Planet. I'm one million units of toll-free explanation. My human cover is that I was raised white trash in Seward, attended college at Evergreen, lost the brown-eyed love of my life to a Neanderthal fireman; I live alone, read books I can't comprehend, have expensive tools and a cheap Chevy. Enough? Who are you?"

"Oh, I don't know."

"Actually, I think that is something you do know." He tilted his head and I thought I saw what was next.

"There's nobody to talk to there. No friends like you. No coffee-shop conversations. Or girls."

"Ah, those thousand ships."

"Man, Lance, and you say *I* talk too serious?"

His glance flicked the clock on the wall. He drummed his thumbs on the edge of the table. His thumbs were coarse and grease blackened, and not equal in size. His left thumb was average, his right surprisingly wide and blunt. "Gotta go, baby. I have to go in and rebuild slave cylinders on that rusted Datsun. The jackoff-of-all-trades owner put in the wrong fucking brake fluid."

"I have to go hang. Nine hundred and seventy knots to tie. I'm hanging another shackle of salmon net for Cheryl's dad." I rubbed the first joint of my index finger. It was shiny and callused from three previous nets.

"Meet at January's? Around ten?"

"'Kay. That'll give me ten hours to hang."

Lance grinned sardonically. "How apropos."

"What?"

"You. Hanging for a living."

BEHIND THE TRAILERS, I strung out the first hundred feet of cork line with thirty plastic floats on it like giant white beads. Our nets at home had always had flat gray wooden floats, and caribou antler or rock-sock sinkers. Now, with a red marking pen and a strip of wood notched at eight and three-eighths inches, I marked where each knot would be tied. Then it was tie a three-hitch knot, pick up three meshes with the hanging needle, measure two fingers of slack, tie another knot, cinch it tight. Plus an extra double tie securing each float. Fifty fathoms of cork line, fifty fathoms of lead line, one hundred and five fathoms stretched of five-and-seven-eighths-inch webbing—just short of one thousand perfect knots. I wondered if I was helping the world, or just killing fish.

January came out gripping a cup of coffee. He watched for a minute. "Tie them tight. Don't take much for Dennis to get hay on his horns."

Cheryl walked up. She touched the blood vessel on my forearm. "Hi." She smiled up at January and retrieved a net needle loaded with #21 twine.

"Hello, May Fly!" January was pleased to have her attention. "How are you? Did I miss your birthday? How's your ma?" He flung his coffee grounds in the grass.

"Next week. I'll be nineteen. Mom got an extra section to Crotch Spit today." Cheryl started hanging the lead line, facing us across the net. I cinched a half hitch and glanced up as she did. Her eyes were the color of the webbing, sea green, flecked with black, like rocks on Jupiter's moons. I wanted to travel on them and camp.

"Aw!" January shouted. "Been a coon's age since I flew up Crotch Spit way! That's getting close to this kid's country!"

The webbing was airy and nylon-slick and the needles twanged softly each time a loop released. January went inside, and cars passed, and we talked occasionally, and worked in comfortable silence. "You don't have to help," I said. "I know," she said. "It's relaxing. I like menial labor. I like it out here." Idly, I thought about being happy, practicing being happy. This might be a good time. *If she'd just kiss me.* I concentrated on breathing. On the burn of the twine on my raw fingers. I wondered what happiness *felt* like. The thing that came to mind was being outside, with a friend. What did it feel like to January, or Abe? Enuk? Janet? Lance? Was happiness some blend—20 percent desire, 30 percent perspective, 50 percent circumstance—like Upton tea? With these fancy human brains—and Sears catalogs—was happiness doomed to be ephemeral? Why should Cheryl or dollar bills control the weather of my happiness?

We worked hour after hour. Streetlights flicked on, and headlights on traffic, and the net was done. Cheryl helped pluck stray grass out of the webbing and bag it so loose dogs couldn't tangle in it. We went in and slumped on January's couch and groaned and stretched our stiff backs, flattened feet, and sore red fingers. He handed us icy beers out of the freezer. Cheryl's warmth was close along my side. She was flushed and polite, and I couldn't believe any of this, and while she went home to change, I stood outside and breathed the cool fumey air, listened to the constant cars, and couldn't believe all the wires, all the many planes still in the sky, how often people changed clothes, or really any of it at all.

LANCE LED THE WAY into Blues Central's bathroom. He locked the door. Music leaked under the walls. The toilet was sticky with piss, and good toilet paper lay wadded on the floor. He thrust out a tube of hair gel. "Bought this for you."

"I thought it was bad to have greasy hair. Abe washed ours once a month, in the dishpan, all in the same water."

His laughter echoed off the porcelain. "Damn, Scroat! Didn't you say something about wanting to try everything? It is bad if it's your own grease. This is mousse."

I leaned against the sink, tipsy from the beers. The music throbbed. The gob of green sat in my palm slimy as loon poop. "Bucks, moose, beaver . . . cars named after Indian tribes. Everything means sex, money, or sports, right?" Gingerly, I rubbed the goo into my long hair. "I think it's all a sign of things that can fight and still get extirpated. I haven't seen any cars or football teams named Frostbite, Virus, or Death."

"You're tight," he muttered. "Relax into the rhythm."

In the mirror—blurrier than Dawna's in the old Wolfglove shack—a grin curved my inebriated face. My hair looked wet, darker. "'Hold level ten?'" I flattened my nose. "Do they have moose or 'rhinoceros' or something for styling your nose? I always thought if I could be Eskimo I'd be happy and friendly."

"Reaganomics. 'When we're all rich we'll all be generous. Until then fuck you and the environment you rode in on.'" He balled up his jacket. "Here. Hold her like she matters. First you're going to slow dance." He moved my hands. "Right hand just above her belt, left hand out, palm up. Isn't she cute? You tall guys get all the babes."

I gripped the jacket, one sleeve extended. "You're forty-two. Don't you have things to be doing more important than teaching me to dance?"

His arms dropped. "Apparently not."

"Oh. Was that an insult? Are you tired? We could quit."

He sashayed past. "The insult is that you limp around like you're the Lone Stranger. Don't you ever consider that most people are searching for the same things you are?" Out in the bar the song stopped. "Okay, dance with me."

I stepped forward, an inch. He was half a foot shorter. Slowly I curved my stiff arm behind his belt.

"Don't go all puckered. You here to learn? I learned in a bathroom." Lance batted his eyelashes. "Care to dance, cowboy?"

It wasn't merely touching another man—a mechanic from the shop, no less—it was plain touching. I remembered longing for hugs from Janet, and slaps of cool-handed friends, flinching whenever it happened. Lance held my hand gently. I didn't dislike it as much as I expected. He placed his other hand on my shoulder. "Relax."

"What do you mean, everyone is like me? I think the wind is a thousand times more interesting than basketball. I think most caribou are more deserving than most people." He twirled us in lazy circles. "Other people know what to say. I don't even know what to want. America wouldn't function if everyone was like me."

He rotated us backwards. "This is jitterbugging."

He demonstrated regular dancing, sort of rhythmic hopping, but he was impatient now, eyes narrowed and not paying attention. He claimed I was passable and unlocked the door. A huge stubbled man in Carhartts and a sweatshirt shouldered toward the door.

"Coupla little queers! Shoulda figured."

My eyes dropped to the floor. Lance turned, suddenly focused, the way he was when he was under an automobile. "You a registered dumbfuck? Or just practicing for the exam?" His voice was honest and interested, as if he were asking the specific gravity of battery acid.

The man wheeled in the doorway, hands rising. "What? What did you say, midget?"

"I said we don't need your compliments tonight, thank you."

Bewilderment played on the big meaty face. The man rubbed at his chest with both thumbs. Lance looked like a boy next to him. I stood palms against a wall, somewhere between giggling and getting out of the way.

The man squinted, and shoved into the bathroom.

Lance turned, lips tight and ugly over his tangled teeth. "See, Cutuk? We all want a few dead wolves, don't we?" He put his arms in the sleeves of his jacket, tugged quickly at the collar. "I am tired, you're right. Give me a call tomorrow." He walked away.

I stood confused. Then lonesome, suddenly homesick. *People—would it work better for me to delete* all *expectations?* "Maybe you need to think of them as caribou," I muttered aloud. A raven-haired woman was pressing past, Japanese and a perfect nose, breasts firm against my arm and back. She reached up and kissed my jaw. "Hi, gorgeous," she said brightly. The homesickness went out like a candle. Lance vanished in the squeeze of bodies taller than he, my thoughts of him now shifting, "friendly" and "cool" buried by thoughts that took more effort, something complex, dark, unpredictable, like ice—what cold current swept below? I missed the simplicity of his laughter and quick crooked-teeth smile. Why did I miss the superficial? *Because you want to be normal!* Suddenly I realized that standing here in Blues Central I looked absolutely normal. An all-American male, not too wiry, too blond, too white—unfortunately, that made the stuff underneath all the more alien.

Out past the band, Cheryl waved wildly at a table. I stood, marveled at her lack of self-consciousness, then moved toward her. It felt strange to walk toward a woman and have her smile in welcome. I could see myself loving this feeling. Staying for this feeling.

"—blues." She shouted in my ear. She wore a hint of glossy lipstick.

I swallowed beer, the bubbles pleasant. How did people hear in bars? They seemed able to talk through this impossibly loud music. Blues made me think of Melt's radio, of a drifting shortwave station and staticky blues around the barrel stove. Janet: Arii, *that kind. Old* taaqsipak *mans moaning about their babies.*

Cheryl motioned me to dance. She led to the edge of the sweaty jiggling bodies. My gaze swung in careful panic, expecting the roar of a hundred village jeers. Aiy! *He can't!* I felt myself backing up, out into snow, looking through clear walls at all these dancing people; they couldn't hear me and leaned close to their noisy friends, all laughing and linked by *their* nature: the Beatles and Cougars and Juicy Fruit of their shared generation.

Two women glanced over, smiled. The dancers were older than us. What had Lance said to do with my hands? I put my smoky arms around Cheryl. "You're blond and beautiful."

Her chin thrust out in a flirty pout. Her lips touched my ear. "Are those two incongruent?"

"Apparently not. You're the finest tippy golden flower—"

Her laughter sailed out, and a rare thing happened: I didn't want to be somewhere else. A *taaqsipak* elder was rasping out a song and the music slid and rocked and boomed, and carried me to pleasant places. Dancing was freedom. I felt tapped into the angles and crosspieces that held the universe together. Finally, I wasn't banging into them blind, but riding these angles I'd sensed had to exist.

"COME ON, CLAYTON. I'll buy you breakfast." Her gaze was the green-blue dawn of a promising day; it was 2:00 A.M. and I had my arms around her.

"I'm not excited to trade this for chicken eggs . . ."

Cheryl led the way to her truck. She lit a cigarette, handed me the pack, and unlocked the door. She talked of a Rabbit she'd owned previously. "That car had no balls."

A grin stretched my face. "Rabbits have very efficient balls. They come out through the belly skin in the spring when they need them."

She blew smoke and laughter in the truck. "I have fun with you, you know that? Tell me your Eskimo name again?"

"Cutuk."

"Cutuk, if you don't want breakfast, let's drive up O'Malley."

I looked out the window at how little we had in common.

"What should I do with my cigarette butt?"

"Just throw it out the window. Everyone does."

Somehow I didn't trust the trees not to have feelings, or friends, or power over luck. The shamans had left behind taboos that we inhaled with every breath in Takunak—not even aware of being infiltrated. I put the butt in my pocket. How could I explain to Cheryl the ways superstition sprouted when you were drifted under in a sod igloo in a million acres of night? Up on Hillside, she parked and rifled her purse to find gum. The city lay twinkling below in haze and spring half-twilight. Was this the "parking" that guys leered about? It scared me, peering down at the electric fungus of Anchorage spread across the earth. *Gonna plenty dark if their lamp finish,* Enuk said. Cheryl put one elbow on my shoulder and flung hair out of her eyes. I chewed, hoping not too loud.

A raven hurried past, flying east into the pass in the mountains. *Kaung-kung.* I rolled down the window, eyes following the bird. I'd read that only females made that sound. "Kaung-kung," I answered perfectly. "Huuuuuuuuuuuuuooooo."

Cheryl giggled. "All those years you spent in the wilderness, did you see wolves?"

My mouth started to open, ready to flood out the city lights with stories of home. But would telling be bragging? I wondered if I were a name-dropper. A wolf-dropper. Here, and everywhere, I realized I walked a slushy path between the battle lines of Cabela's hunters and nature lovers, and if she were half as cynical and judgmental as I, she'd find me a traitor, a double agent, an assassin of the wolf god, a meat eater, and a tree hugger, too. Abe would say what he felt. Dawna, too. Jerry? He'd keep his mouth shut. My head spun. I couldn't concentrate. I didn't want to lose this girl. Sexy and made up, able to cook an octopus—from a world far above the consternation of red fingers, a dog team that wouldn't pass, and not knowing how to chew gum.

"J-just ordinary wolves." My fingers laced behind her neck and drew her soft lips to mine. This courage shocked me. Her perfume coiled in my lungs. I wondered where Dawna was. Like she might be watching.

"Ordinary wolves?" Her eyes waited, mesmerizing.

"I mean, no Mowgli and Gray Brother stuff." I pictured the last wolf I'd seen, in the den above the rocks; and downstream in the willows, rabbits chasing each other, mating; wolves hunting rabbits who were not paying as sharp attention as something so anxious to pass on genes should be paying; and possibly Enuk, focused, snowshoeing stealthily after the wolves, also focused; and . . .

I kissed Cheryl. Golden hair hung a shimmering tent around her face, her shirt open and showing the arch of her breasts. She kissed back, satisfied to let the conversation founder. My arms felt strong and weak, trapped by her perfume, and I wanted her body more.

She started the engine, drove effortlessly the grid of streets to her dad's, led me through rectangle doors to her room in the basement, confidence in her fingertips that held mine, born in her every cell. My cells sown without confidence, fertilized with *naluaġmiu*-scorn. In the thin light and in her arms I was afraid. I might do it all wrong and she would laugh. She would tell her friends and they would laugh.

"You look so worried." Her palms roamed gentle under my shirt, touching my nipples and the ridges of my stomach. "I won't hurt you."

You would never know if you did.

And then we were kissing, and there was only the two of us and the faint smoky smell in her hair and the heat where her breasts pressed my skin. Something animal was in her movements now. Strangely, I understood this part of being human. We pulled open each other's shirts. Our jeans fell in faded piles. The sheets were cool, she, warm and voluptuous. I kissed her throat, breasts, and stomach, wanting to touch all of her skin with all of my skin. She surrounded me, confident hands, and waves and moans of desire swelling through her body. Me forgetting all, for the first time running, wading, swimming into the warm ocean.

ON A SUNDAY I met her dad, Dennis, a man with big scarred ears and hands scratchy with calluses. He explained what granola was, chewing over our shoulders, dropping stray toasted oats, while she explained how to boot a computer, process words, move a mouse. Dennis said he liked how I admitted the things I didn't understand, and offered me the use of his house while they were in Bristol Bay for the salmon season.

Later, Lance taught me more tricks to driving, and handed over extra jobs he couldn't take: repairing dishwashers, lawn mowers, Weedwackers. Clean, in overwashed "casual" clothes, I paused in coffee shops, eavesdropping, trying to emulate, acclimate, relate. I watched the caribou—the average people grazing through their days—men who griped about Tongass timber harvests while their engines idled; women with big dyed hair carrying Can't-Grows with shaved haircuts; homeless men asking for spare change and apologizing for needing it. Money moved through my hands. Most of it went under January's couch, though some bought parts for Dawna's car, nectarines, calls to Iris, and pouches of Drum tobacco. I lost the rolling papers and could buy more—the stores didn't ever run out. I let the faucet run when I washed my hands, and then felt guilty and dried them on my pants. It felt peculiar to be this rich. Lance showed me how to arrange my collar, how to shake hands like I meant it and didn't care at the same time. "Don't forget the strength in your thumb. Look people in the eyes. First impressions are how people decide who you are. *Details,* Scroat. That's the way the game goes. You wouldn't go to a job interview in your bathrobe, would you?"

"I don't know. I never had either of those."

"Agh." His lips covered his teeth. He twisted his neck back and forth impatiently.

But I had reason to believe he listened; he'd painted his truck glossy blue, stenciled in the name so it looked factory-made: CHEVY VIRUS. He parked it where he had a view of it and could chuckle when circumstances bored him.

Evenings, Cheryl and I met under the wings of my family plane that I would buy back from Uncle Sam for Uncle January. We unfolded the door, climbed in, and kissed until the windows were fog curtains. In the narrow back seat we removed and lifted enough clothes to soar the updrafts. I saw the tracks of my life snap into place: down the gleaming rails I saw a job, a friend, a girlfriend; and city me, throwing all the wrappers into one easy trash, no fire-starter box for the papers of my life, no dog pot for the meat and moldy bread scraps, no bucket for smashed peeled Nabob jam cans to be burned and buried. No Abe making me wash out used plastic bags.

Out under the wings, she held my hand and peered at the cable workings of the craft. The cable clamps were corroded and powdery. The aluminum prop was nicked, the fabric tattered. Suddenly I saw the plane wasn't even blue and gold anymore; it was closer to gray and dirty yellow. Cheryl went on explaining ailerons, ground effect, angle of attack—things I'd been studying in library books. She ran her hand along the trailing edge. Her fingers were long and strong. "Extended flaps," she murmured.

"Is that better?"

"Less air spillage. It's for short takeoffs."

For landing on wolves!

EIGHTEEN

***THE TUNDRA SHIMMERS VAST** and white under the May sun.* The scent of caribou drifts provocatively on the air, whispering of a herd hurrying north, of calves and pregnant cows—of meat after three lean weeks since the last kill. In the north, mountains serrate the sky. The final timber before the arctic treeline beards their slopes, and higher the speckled rocks and snow reach against the blue.

The wolf drops out of a fluid trot and swings sideways to snatch stray sounds off the tundra. The wolf glows black as a hole in the day. In her blackness she has learned to walk warily and listen.

A mouse-sized clump of snow settles behind the bole of a lone stunted spruce. A raven out of sight to the east caws over a thing alive. A drone that might have been an airplane drifts from beyond the southern mountains. Another raven with a second and different voice speaks of the same life to the east. And the wolf trots again. In her stomach she feels the faint satisfied fullness of her young pressing under her diaphragm. The fullness is an illusion that belies an increasing hunger in her. Now only her shrunken stomach cries for food. Before the next moon the cries will come from a circle of short-faced pups, looking to her for a share of life. In the steep mountains to the north, she and her mate have a good den, safe in the dirt above a slate cliff.

The scent of caribou grows until it swirls and titillates the fine membranes of her nose, giving the wolf energy, the scent a veritable food she can taste and draw strength from like the meat and blood to come. The instinct to hunt and kill rises in her. She breaks into a lope, swinging closer to the mountains with their narrow-walled tributaries and trees. This home is good; with the seasons the land ripens with game for those fast and hungry enough to kill. She moves in and understands the cycle of hunger and the hungry, always circling each other.

THE SURFACE OF THE SNOW grows soft in the warm day. The wolf feels the heat on her already shedding black back and on her thin legs and nose. Behind her stretches a line of tracks shouting freshness to those who listen to the smallest whispers of smell. Her tracks on the white tundra shout also to all who hunt with eyes.

The hair on her shoulders shivers a tiny subconscious shiver. Again she stops to listen. The drone, which had sounded like one of the many new drones in the sky, has changed. It swells and shrinks behind her—the gnashing scream of a snowmobile tearing across the snow. She bolts for the mountains. At seven years old, still in her limber prime, the span between her front and back feet measures more than six feet. She has been chased by the machine-hunters three times before, always part of a scattering pack. The first time seven out of nine were killed. A bullet still rides, an aching cyst in her hip. The hunter had chased her over mountain ranges for hours before it gave up, to return the following day and search again. The second encounter, the pack lost none; the third, her mate had been shot.

The wolf's legs recognize fear.

One smooth mile from the timber it breaks over a rise behind her.

She begins weaving. None of her litter mates had known to zigzag. Or climb for the rocks. They didn't have a second chance to learn. Now the machine-hunter comes, an impossible creature moving twice the speed of any animal on the tundra. It screams past, striking her flank a glancing blow. It slides to a stop between her and the mountain. She flees left—toward a line of spruce marking a creek. A hundred yards short of the trees the machine catches her again.

She lunges sideways. Again it stands in front of her.

She runs for the mountain. In front of her, snow chips and sprays. Behind come fast popping and the wail of air being torn aside. A bullet pierces her neck, cutting through the flesh. The land tilts up and she reaches with the last strength in her for the mountain.

She reaches the peak of the mountain. Runs down the far slope. Up a second mountain. The snow on the south-facing slope sluffs soft and deep. Scattered spruce pluck shedding fur out of her sides. Again the machine-hunter comes, still untired. Bounding effortlessly up the slope. Smashing like an uphill avalanche through brush and small trees.

It hits her square, flipping her upside down, crushing her under the weight and blackness of its huge ripping foot. Sky and blood fill her retinas. She rolls to her feet, hurt, staggering upward. Suddenly a cliff drops away in front. She leaps into the freedom of air and death.

The steep angle of the landing saves her. Stunned, she tumbles down a ravine, bouncing off rocks and trees. At the bottom she regains her crippled feet and runs again while around her whacks the metal rain.

NINETEEN

SUMMER SLIPPED IN under roily clouds from the sea. The geese had gone north without me. And Cheryl west, to Bristol Bay, helping her dad fish, and after the season, mending net and doing maintenance on their set-net boat. Lance went east to visit his mother in Ann Arbor, Michigan. I stayed, struggling not to be disappointed at my friends for leaving me in solvent, TV white noise, and the unsilence of Anchorage. One afternoon in August I stood scrubbing dishes in January's sink, my thoughts pacing, solvent fumes in my conscience—if I still had one.

Outside, Spenard Road growled with Lower Forty-Eight motor homes lurching into Gwenny's Restaurant, here to *do* the Last Frontier. A black Toyota with a steel rack pulled in beside January's truck, a pump shotgun in the back window, an eighteen-inch walrus *usruk* bone on the dash. The driver wore shorts. His legs and arms were tanned, his black hair sun-shot like a summer beaver's. An expensive-looking camera hung from a strap twisted around his hand. I raced out of the trailer, wiping soap foam on my jeans. We stood eyeing each other like two sled dogs that might have once been litter mates. I hadn't seen Jerry in five years. We were related strangers.

"You're big." He stood a couple inches taller still—six foot—and thicker in the arms and chest. He stood different, slack and rugged, though still wary. His chin was black stubbled. He looked like a man; he'd left looking like Jerry. "Iris told me you were here." Jerry kicked a rock. His tennis shoe was cracked and leaked toes, his T-shirt faded. "She's a schoolteacher, isn't that funny?"

"They used to always be from the States, weren't they?"

"Got a job for you."

"You're wearing shorts." I discovered my bare foot, aiming at a spruce cone.

"Goddammit!" January's voice came from inside the trailer.

"He's heating goat's milk," I explained. "To 116 degrees to make his yogurt. It must have cooled or boiled over. Acidophilus is going to protect him from Martian intestinal viruses that are going to make the planet shit itself, *guuq*."

Jerry smiled at the Eskimo word. "I remember that wolf bounty hunter." He squinted through his camera, focusing on me, or maybe the front of the trailer. His lips scrunched, red. One eyebrow showed over the corner of the camera. "He landed right after Mom started crying and her guitar got chewed."

"And he didn't come back?" I asked softly.

"He did. She went to buy a new guitar and go see her parents until the sun came back. Abe was supposed to take care of us. After the plane came back without her, I had to. Lucky we had a sod igloo. They're way warmer than a cabin when you're out of firewood." He was nonchalant. The shutter clicked. The camera swung from his hand again. "Fairbanks is way smaller than Anchorage. Less people fresh from the States dragging along their Everything and lawsuits. Hey, I'm a contractor now." His smile flashed and vanished. He hadn't forgotten the old way—humility's role in luck.

"I forgot how we used to talk. Remember, Jerry, we thought lawsuits were policeman clothes?"

He laughed, careful. Jerry had inherited Abe's closed-mouthness for the past.

Inside, January opened beers. We hunched forward, elbows on our knees, and pushed wet lines up the sweating cans. We talked about Abe, building a cabin farther upriver. Jerry cracked a third beer. I sipped my first, waiting for him to say something, something like: *How have you really been? Somebody show you how to talk City English carefully, so you don't say "I eat a lot of meat" or "I whacked my stick on a beaver"?*

"Where'd you get the *usruk?*" I asked finally.

"A Yu'pik laborer on my crew borrowed a hundred bucks. He gave me that as collateral. He sells them to the Koreans." He pushed his hair back. The top of his forehead was pale. A grin streaked across his face. "Don't they grind them up, January, for dick-hardeners?"

January snorted. "Now-a-days that's all them hunters chop off walrus, the three tusks. Whites ain't allowed to hunt seals anymore, no polar bears. Marine Mammal Protection Act. Kid, when I take you flying we'll head way up to the coast, you'll see headless walrus washed up for hundreds a miles. They look like blown-up rubber gloves. Thousand pounds each. Native politicians scream foul if you don't bow and call it subsistence. You boys ain't even allowed one seal for *mukluk* bottoms. Dammit, don't get me heated up."

My fingers strayed to my *ugruk*-skin knife sheath.

Jerry smiled uncomfortably into his beer. "Want to go up to Fairbanks, work a month? The wages are close to Davis-Bacon." He spoke casually, a boss asking an opinion. Sadness salted down. Weren't we supposed to turn out like brothers in the movie *Outsiders?*—teasing, arm wrestling, ready to cry and die for each other.

January stood and unwrapped the towel around his jar of warm gray milk. He nudged it. "Yog, you little friggers?" He slumped to the window at the end of the trailer, looked at the world outside, stooped and spat tobacco slime out the crack. Not all of it made it. "Gonna teach your brother to fly the Cub."

Why do you keep talking about flying? This is all the definition of dysfunctional, *pretending chains and taxes don't exist.*

Jerry nodded politely. He glanced out for the sun, the way Abe did when he was impatient. "So you like the city?"

"It's . . . okay. Hard to sleep at first. Houses are so loud. All the droning. Blowers and suckers and little motors. Like there's constantly travelers coming. I don't like crapping in the house. And the splash."

January shuffled in the kitchen, muttering, ". . . still Alaska. The kid's gotta learn to fly."

"I hate the splash," Jerry said. "Where I rent my cabin the trees are thick and I can piss outside."

"People don't realize how much that matters."

"Nope. I'll come by in the morning, 'kay? See if you want to go."

IN THE MURMUR of the night my loyalties slipped anchor. The more I weighed the decision, in all this roar and clutter my brother was one of the quiet things that did matter. When Jerry drove away, more years would go with him, maybe all the years we had left. January wasn't flying anywhere. I felt invisible again in Anchorage without Lance and Cheryl. Even Ubaldo had graduated from mechanicing to join the Peace Corps in Burkina Faso. For a couple weeks now I'd been seeing Dawna, a seen woman. *Seeing* was an expression I stole from TV, without understanding it. Like *sleeping together*—which I knew we were not doing—it somehow shaved the truth of a relationship down to an enviable lie.

But Dawna wasn't admissable in my court as a reason to stay. Dave still existed on earth. "I'm going to leave him," Dawna had said quickly, last night when I told her about Cheryl. "I'll go back to college." We'd sat in her car behind streaming windows in front of January's trailer. She hugged her legs, resting her jaw on her knees. Rain typed messages on the roof. "I just can't right now, I can't." She wiped her face on her sweatshirt. The wet left dark circles on the purple cotton. I leaned under the dusty steering column, searching for more wires that might bring her signal lights to life. The word *can't* banged in my head like a cracked piston. "You can if you want to." I arched upright and leapt out. Raindrops splashed down. I stumbled inside to greet the light and January's hale words, while the wet night swallowed Dawna, with no signal lights and no license.

Now I stacked library books to return: *Stick and Rudder, The Art of Flying Skis, East of Eden, Ice Station Zebra, From Where the Sun Now Stands, The Right Madness on Skye.* I wondered what books Lance read. What Abe was reading. I stuffed my duffle bag. I remembered Nippy Skuq, the Washingtons and Wolfgloves—suddenly throwing mattresses and pots and guns, kids and wife on a sled, or in a boat, leaving for the hot springs or the coast. Woodrow Washington Jr. handing his infant to Janet and hopping the plane to Fairbanks. Abe called it "Eskimo exit." It came as a surprise to realize it, too, had grown up inside me. I called John at the garage and apologized into his gray silence. Dialed Dawna. Her phone rang and rang.

I lay on the couch, then got back up and rummaged for paper. The letter I wrote to Cheryl didn't mention her plans to go to college in Cincinnati—only said I missed her, it had rained since she left, how soon after the boat was repaired would she return to Anchorage? The note to Dawna said I was leaving in the morning. Be gone a month or so. Dave, the blow-dried Safeway cottage cheese reshelfing expert, could frame it next to his employee-of-the-moment award and flick beer caps at my fall-down Iñupiaq name.

IN THE DREAM Enuk sat on leaves and sticks on the bank above Jesus Creek. He sat skinning a white wolf, occasionally shaking his head. His face was frostbitten. Dawna hid behind him staring into an upside-down Alaska Airlines magazine. A clump of white condominiums towered over our igloo. Cheryl and Lance and I knelt on the ice, probing the water hole with beer bottles. Tourists watched from the shore and pointed video cameras.

"You ta one should gonna been drown," Enuk commented. He tossed his knife in the air. The knife glinted, a 38,000-feet-up jet. The knife plunked into the water. Iris floated to the surface, slated with mud. Black holes gaped where her pretty white teeth had fallen out. I pulled the rags of her shirt down over her chest. The tourists rushed to steady their cameras. Treason's Ruger Mini-14 rifle was in my hand. I clicked the safety and fired fast at the tourists, aiming for heads and hearts, like knocking down dogfood caribou for the winter. The booms lanced across the tundra, whomping into bodies. My aim was true. But they kept standing back up—more closing in behind. I shuddered awake, gasping, clutching memories of the accident in Jesus Creek. Had Iris not survived? Was Enuk alive? Had *his* remains been found? I lay on the couch in the trailer night, afraid for my families, my skin as cold as creek water.

THE DRIVE NORTH to Fairbanks took seven hours, a long time inside the vinyl-smelling glass box of a car. We talked, catching up on the years. Trees stripped by. Wind punched the car. I drove fast, exploring the limits of my learner's permit, occasionally asking Jerry if I should shift up, or down. A sign read DENALI STATE PARK. "This tundra," I said, "it feels like home, huh?" It didn't quite. Inside a car was like watching TV. Home had wind and smells and birds arguing.

"What do you think of it down here?" he asked.

"Oh . . . it's nice how everybody doesn't stare, isn't it? I like that. A lot of stuff, it's a bunch of pretending, huh? You see the boards and good metal they throw away? Even nectarines, with one soft spot. Seems like we grew up the opposite. If something broke or got eaten, didn't it seem like that was the last one ever?"

Jerry's elbow popped and he rubbed it ruefully. "People pretend they're not animals. It makes them tired. So they pretend a whole bunch more. That makes them really tired." He grinned and peered at his arm, equally interested in the conversation and his elbow. "The biggest heroes are the biggest pretenders. Actors. The big pretend story is it'll-all-be-better-in-the-end." He grinned, "It's called heaven."

"Huh. Soon as I mention the Kuguruk, people want to know how to hurry up there to hunt 'griz' and sixty-inch moose. 'Need to get *my* moose. Gruh, Gruh, Gruh.' All manly—and what they want is the *antlers?* If they shoot something with big antlers that means their penis gets bigger? Why do they invent that kind of nonsense?"

Jerry scratched in his ear with his little finger. He flicked the wax out from under his fingernail and didn't say anything.

"People say they wish *they* could go live in a cabin in the wilderness. Is that true? Why don't they?"

"I say I'm from Chicago," he murmured. "It's easier."

Motor homes were pulling over. I slowed. A large beaver hunkered in the road. It balanced itself with its tail and bared its teeth at tires.

"Fairly orange guard hairs you've got," Jerry said. "Better stay out of the sun."

I steered around the motor homes and sped up. "Jerry, what's a cheer leader?"

"Cheerleader. One word. That's those football players' girlfriends who bounce during the game."

"Hey, did you know, Iris is trying to track down our mom."

He leaned forward, flicked on the radio. "She left us, Cutuk. Or I guess you don't remember. She used to sing and give me toy trucks with little doors that opened. Then she just—just went."

A chill trickled down my head skin. Had I inherited it from my mother—and assimilated it in Takunak—the running gene? Was that what I was doing now, running?

A rabbit streaked across the road. "Shoulda bumped him," I croaked. "Haven't had rabbit in how long."

"Me neither. Remember we used to dry them for dog food? We'd skin them one pull, gut them in ten seconds, then cross the legs to hang on the fish rack." He squeezed his forehead. Abe haunted his movements and the lines on his forehead—thoughtful grooves, freckled from the sun. "The other day I was remembering our old beds along the back wall, and the all-of-ours box underneath, full of mouse turds and caribou hairs mixed with all our best magnets and paints and slide rules. 'Member going hooking for *tiktaaliq?* 'Member that time we first saw a satellite?

We ran home across the ice, in the dark, not even thinking about open water. Iris said, 'Abe, we saw a traveler star!'"

"Abe said, 'Shut the door!'"

"Fresh rabbit out of the oven—Beth would let me cook him, too." Jerry liked cooking. He knew when leftover soup had enough seasonings for good gravy, when a pie crust had the right amount of bear fat and ice water. He didn't measure the yeast or salt or any ingredients to make loaves of bread. "I love that girl. I'm not scared to say that word anymore."

Suddenly I knew my brother was happy. It was like looking at a mountain peak across a valley of fog. Except my brother wasn't beside me—he was across the valley.

Road tumbled under the truck. "Every day the city is full of people I want to talk to, get to know. How do you do that?"

"Just do it. Most of them will run off. Some won't." Jerry sounded like a boss again, his words dropping like sacks of frozen fish.

"Like caribou?"

"I'll help you make wages, but if you expect insight into humans, you've got the wrong brother." He turned up the music. His coarse palm rapped on the dashboard.

Abe with a beat. Abe with rhythm.

JERRY REACHED HIS HAND down to help me out of the ditch. "Break time." I sprang out and wiped sweat off my eyebrows, embarrassed and surprised to touch his fingers. Twelve-hour construction days left little time to practice being brothers.

"Stick to it," Jerry advised. We walked away from the ditch. He chuckled dryly. "Here they respect time, and certification. Papers parka your career." We rattled across gravel to the newly built back porch. He was still serious and protective, always carrying something heavy in his hand, eyeing dogs, people, cars as if they intended to bite us—as if trees schemed to dunk snow down his neck. The cabin he rented on Wolverine Alley was dimly lit, hanging bulbs, the table stacked with books, Makita batteries, and his Nikon cameras. The shotgun leaned behind the door. Buckshot in the chamber. The safety on. Beth turned all the lights on when she came in and the air brightened with her presence.

Around the front of the construction site a murmur of voices and laughter came from the rest of the crew. The stacks of Douglas fir smelled of pitch, clean and sharp. "Jerry, don't you ever feel like you're making more houses for more people that need more roads? Helping the Everything-Wanters?"

He splashed tea out of a thermos. "You want a job or what, Abe?"

Thick stands of birch grew on the edge of the clearing, making me claustrophobic, wishing to see a caribou or a bear stroll into view—or even just to see a view. Jerry handed me sweet tea. Half a decade fell away in those moments; we were the same age.

"If I don't build houses, they're still going to be built. Only, by some Californian or Texan." He scratched a scab off the back of his big tanned hand. "'Member those enzymes we studied? While Abe painted? Maybe I'm luckier than you. I knew some of the details Abe left out. Here in the city there's little spaces between you and all things, and for every reaction you have to put money into those spaces. Like those enzymes."

"I know that."

"Up home water came from the river, heat from wood, meat from animals. City people trade that in for a slot in the money system. It's efficient, Cutuk." He bit into his sandwich. "In case you didn't know, that's why people work so hard and stress about pensions. Nobody here's slot is guaranteed. And it's against the law to step out your door and shoot something to eat, or cut down any tree. Or even piss on the tree!"

A smile crept around behind my face like a sneeze. Jerry and I were talking. We sounded like Abe. We thought we knew more. But minutes ago we'd discussed only gable ends, code, and T-111.

Men walked around the half-finished house. Jerry stood up. His face stiffened. Maybe he was relieved to get behind the aloof mask. "Com'on," he said. "Let's go to work." But it inked the edges of his words—for a moment I knew he felt the same relief I did, to stumble out onto the trail toward family.

THE BACKS OF JERRY'S tanned calves led me across the campus. He carried a crowbar; me, a bag of ice. The ice was why we'd come. My new shorts left me feeling naked from the waist down, my legs as white and anxious for cover as two yanked-out-of-the-river sheefish. Tanned university girls strolled by in halter tops and cutoffs, breathtaking, safe on the sunny side of style. I tried to picture Abe in shorts. Or Janet Wolfglove. Enuk's legs in shorts. The pictures were as laughable as Barbara Bush skinning a muskrat behind the outhouse.

We walked into the campus center. "We'll stop here a minute." Jerry's face focused like Abe's, suddenly remembering something that interested him, forgetting the crowbar in his hand. "Some anthropologist is talking about the Kuguruk." He led me into a lounge. A middle-aged woman stood beside large glossy photographs on a wall.

I know her face! I know that tundra!

". . . and my Iñupiat teachers never kill a bear unless the bear attacks a hunter or berry pickers, or children." Song Spenholt faced the crowd. In the lights she was jet-black hair, tanned face, silver dream-catcher earrings. Strangely, I remembered her hair light brown, and her face pale. "When my Iñupiat teachers did kill a bear they saved every part, and invited my family to the traditional feast. This, right"—her pointer swung to a photograph of riverbank treed with spruce and blue mountains behind—"exactly here, is an important archaeological site, four miles west of Takunak on the Kuguruk River. Soon it will be protected as a National Historic Landmark. Carbon dating placed hunting points and pottery shards and articles found here at *eleven thousand years old!*"

The small crowd ah'ed.

Jerry scratched his cheek contemplatively with the claw of the crowbar.

Her pointer wasn't actually at the renowned Kuguruk site, but miles upriver, on the island near Franklin's igloo, *exactly* where he'd built his initial crap pit too close to the cutbank and after the big Breakup of 1976 it had sluffed out *its* articles.

Outside in the sun, Jerry paused to pull a linty stick of gum out of his pocket. His big thumbnail scraped away tatters of wrapper. He bit it in half and handed over the other half.

"Gum?"

"Why don't we ever say anything?" I muttered.

He chewed, too loud.

"People at home chase bears every time they see a track! They leave the skin. If the bear's skinny or eating fish they leave the whole thing. They boil up bear for dinner, then go play city league, not have a feast for the friggin' white people. Except Tommy—he blasts every bear and saves only the gall bladders to sell to the Koreans."

Jerry pinched damp gum wrapper off his tongue. "Native worshipers. It's a designer religion. Part of talking about going off to live in a cabin, but staying in range of Kmart." He glanced in mild surprise at the crowbar in his hand. "We're white, better to keep your mouth shut. Abe doesn't like conflict—neither do Eskimos. They just swallow it and walk away. And laugh. So laugh, Cutuk."

"And get drunk," I growled, "and beat somebody up."

"That's *after* the traditional feast."

We laughed and turned toward the eight-story dorms. I knew the lawns from stories Iris had sent home. The students throwing footballs and Frisbees might have been the same ones she described. We stepped inside the brass-trimmed front doors. I tensed, expecting a security guard to stop us, or people to stare, spotting instantly that I was too ignorant and confused to be a college student. Jerry had agreed to come, even though he had things maybe the law could take. A laughing fiancée, a Japanese truck, an honest reputation poured into the foundations of a lot of buildings. The sack of ice cooled my hand. The curve of the Bacardi bottle showed through. The lobby was quiet and deserted. Jerry stopped at a candy machine. Wordlessly, he handed me a granola bar. We never seemed to take time for meals, and now Mrs. Spenholt and her anthropology flavored the oat bar rancid as dried trout belly.

Jerry led into an elevator. The machine fell at the top, and queasiness greased my stomach. We tiptoed up a half flight of stairs. Jerry inserted his crowbar into the door. He paused and tried the knob. It turned. He grinned sheepishly and motioned me through the steel doorway. We moved excitedly out onto the black roof.

Heat waves curdled the horizons. We peered over the eight-story cliff just as a university security vehicle was driving away. It braked and stopped. We eased down out of sight, like stalking Canada geese. A brown Ford passed on the road and the security vehicle turned and followed it.

I knelt and opened the One-Five.

Jerry sipped and coughed. "You drink this stuff?"

"In Takunak it seems normal." I realized we were whispering. "Here, I brought a Coke to pour in when there's room."

He flicked a leaf off his shorts, over the edge. It floated, fluttering down. He clanked the crowbar beside him and peeled off his sweatshirt. We took off our shoes and cut our toenails with our knives and sharpened the knives on the bar and put them away. A pair of birds sang piercingly down in the trees. "White-crowned sparrows," Jerry said. "What did we call them, spits?" I nodded, and we called to them. A puddle spread out from the bag of ice and water tongued west. "Building's not level," he pointed out. A raven landed on a Dumpster. We cawed and he tilted his head in surprise.

The sun was a burning eye; I stared until the sky blobbed black. I ripped the sack and scooped ice into Jerry's hands. Half of it was gone, melted, flowed across the roof and evaporated. Like my life, I thought. I was quickly getting drunk, mad at the city down below for taking the animals' beautiful land and turning it into ridiculous things: parking lots and strip malls, pensions, section lines, and new hairstyles.

I flung a handful of ice. Together we flung handfuls, higher, as high as our strong arms could throw. Store-bought ice. The cubes flashed in the sunlight. They fell, exploding in small dry disappointing puffs on the asphalt. Looking down it was obvious—like so much else on Iris's path, I'd come up this trail too late, at a cost too great. I was here, but I wasn't all here. I was rushing and earning, waiting and hurrying, but somehow not even here. My legs stuck out of the shorts, white. *What am I doing wearing these half things?* The stun of admitting to being lost whacked into me and put its hands in my guts, and it hurt. All the storms, all the mountains and rivers and hills—and here I was, finally lost beside a street with a name. I was less than a wolverine in the wake of America, and the sky and the ground and tomorrow and everything else grayed because I was nothing. *Is this what Melt Wolfglove brought home? Is this how villagers feel when the parade of pretty white social workers climb off the airplanes, step in the snow for an hour, and urge them toward college and careers, away from suicide, Lysol, and the land? All my longing to be Eskimo—did I get myself no browner, just the damaged parts inside?* I leaned out, watching the ice pulverize. A heavy pull tugged me—like an under-the-ice fishnet set in too much current—to dive slicing into the waiting pavement, warm and black and deep as forever. Suicide, nowadays, was as Eskimo as hunting. I could finally be one of the People.

Jerry flicked a lump of dried bird shit. We watched the white sail slowly down to the earth. "Why did Abe take us Out?" I asked vacantly. "I mean . . . I am glad we grew up with animals instead of wall sockets and Little League, but what are the stories no one tells me? What happened? Did we have a baby porcupine?"

"She was mine! She liked glue." Jerry smiled down at memories.

Birds sang down there.

"She ate the face off Mom's guitar. It wasn't spruce, those are the expensive guitars. It was a plywood laminate. Too bad, that was her favorite thing."

"No soap opera stuff? Abe didn't shoot off Newt Clemens's hand? Mom didn't run off with January?"

"Newt shot his own hand. Drunk." Jerry's lip curled. "Maybe it was because Janet went with Melt after Lumpy was born. Who knows." Jerry diverted the puddle with his toe. "We're the same as everybody else. Abe's mom sent him to Barrow, to talk his dad home. I guess she never questioned whether she'd lose her Picasso to the barren arctic wasteland, too."

"He went to college in Chicago. January said that."

"Sure," Jerry grinned cynically, "years later. He happened to suddenly have a spare airplane to sell to pay for it. But when he was done, back we went to the people and place Abe respected. He didn't care what other people did as long as he didn't have to be near them doing it."

"You're saying Abe killed his dad?"

Jerry's eyes jumped. "No! He worshiped the guy. Our grandfather was a free man all the way. He did what pleased him. Abe's the same, just kinder and gentler about it."

He swung the crowbar in a slow arc. *Our parents are inside us,* Dawna's voice teased. *Have to be careful what we let out.* I said, "That was thirty and forty years ago! It's almost Alaska history. What are we supposed to think?"

"It's almost none of our business."

As we talked we had moved. We were both standing, feet on the edge. The bottle in my hand. The ground waiting. The city revved down there, McDonald's and Exxon and other transplanted chunks of the States, and we stood up here, two strangers from caribou skins and boiled beaver paws, ice in the basin and bears on the roof. Jerry shuffled close. "Stay in Fairbanks. It's pretty good. You'll get used to all the rules." He pretended to pat my shoulder. My brother was no actor. He cared nothing for less than utilitarian movement. His hand was hard and tense. I knew he was prepared to grab me, to rip my skin apart with his nails if it came to that. It was a powerful thing to know. Powerful, though not enough to stay in this city for.

TWENTY

CHERYL'S CAN'T-GROWS' yapping reminded me of the Caplins, a white couple who moved briefly to Takunak when I was sixteen. Stevie gave them a puppy, to be nice, and to keep it out of Lumpy's clutches. The dog was black. Being political creatures and far from home, the Caplins named the dog what they thought was the word for gift in Iñupiaq—*Atchiq*. Come here, *Atchiq*. Roll over, *Atchiq*. From the beginning there was confusion, as the word only meant "to name." Being adults, and Christian, the Caplins didn't, the first day, learn the word for woman's part—*utchuk*. I didn't know exactly which part, just that people were laughing at white people again. Stevie wasn't enamored. The dog learned to slip its collar. Worse, the Caplins overpronounced Iñupiaq words and confused i's and a's and u's. Across town, Tom Caplin shouting, "AATCHUUUQ? AAAATCHIIK?" Lonnie Caplin over the village CB: *click, shhhhh,* "Has anyone seen my little black Utchuk?"

Billy Feathers finally shot the dog for keeping his dogs barking during a *Charlie's Angels* rerun. He stuffed it under a tarp on his sled. He couldn't take it to the dog dump. He ended up taking it out on the flats toward the Shield Mountains. Used it for trapping bait. Got two wolverine. Nelta Skuq thought he was quite a hunter, and he got her, too, though in Takunak that wasn't near as big a deal as two wolverine.

In front of January's locked door, I realized that all those people at home were so alive and talkative inside me that I hadn't questioned how they might really be.

I squeezed into his spit window. Dishes were heaped in the sink, set with egg and concrete yogurt. The table was forested with Kmart ads, newspapers, UFO anthologies, precarious Spam cans of snuff juice. A tube of toothpaste lay gnarled and open on the counter. With the Martians already among us, January didn't have patience to fool with a cap on his toothpaste. Beside me Jerry's spirit took up space, slowly growing silent and thin.

Hitchhiking from Fairbanks had been great, like seeing a hole in the city's armor you could enter where you could talk with strangers. Now, wheels hissed invitingly on the wet street. The trailer hummed—that sound of travelers in the distance, but none really coming. Cheryl's window was dark. Looking at it made me lonesome, aware of the heartlessness of change. She had left nine days ago, for Ohio, noncommittal on the phone about whether she wanted company or not. Dental hygiene. *White smiles.*

I knelt by the corner of the couch. Eased hundred-dollar bills out and mixed them with the ones I'd brought. Nine thousand fifty-three dollars. In aluminum foil, I flattened ninety bills, pressed the wrinkles out. A horn honked. Boot steps passed outside. The trailer creaked. I listened, moved window to window.

I wandered the rooms nervously, stuffing the money under things and retrieving it again. I hid it under the furnace and, finally, back under the couch. I dialed Lance. No answer. Dialed Dawna. Her number had been disconnected. Dialed Iris. Her phone rang and rang. Gloom rose through me like the stink of bad meat. Money and the telephone—I hated them—leaving you worse than alone, connected to a billion people with no way to buy what you really wanted and no one to call.

I unpacked my Army sleeping bag. Plucked all the new loose feathers and tried to think, here in the city's imitation silence. What mattered? I was supposed to be like Enuk and know; not like some trust-fund Californian who had the hard job of figuring that out. What did I really want? To be Eskimo? That dream had disintegrated. To be a hunter? To be funny, rich, have cars and girls? "One generic American dream, coming right up," I teased aloud. "Get rich and buy a house."

I paced. Out the window, the neighbor beyond Cheryl's was making a bird feeder in his yard, wearing a hard hat. I turned on the TV. Dan Rather's news: crimes, spills, and bodies. America: something, somewhere, south. The boss stepfather of Alaska. Noticing how fresh and pretty she was looking.

"Caribou soup matters. Feeding the dogs. Bears." Suddenly air didn't want to go back in my lungs. I missed it all! Hawk owls on the slop hole tree. The pastel of evening sky over the snow. Caribou clicking past. Ravens on the wind, cataloging every movement from above. The fire crackling in the morning. The smell along the riverbanks of grass and tundra and highbush cranberry. Fox tracks in fresh first fall snow. Ermine tracks by the *quaq* pile. Out on the river ice, otters nuzzling beside deadly open water. Wind moving the tops of spruce.

The trailer was dusky. I slumped down and idly turned over a newspaper.

WOMAN FOUND STABBED.

There was a photograph—of tarps hanging in trees below the railroad tracks, a tattered couch, a campfire, and a clothesline. *An unidentified Eskimo woman with multiple stab wounds was found Thursday near Fish Creek, according to Anchorage police. The woman was believed to have been sexually assaulted prior to death . . .*

I snatched the phone. Punched numbers. "Who's this?"

"Hi Cutuk!"

"Stevie? Whacha' doin'?"

"Sitting in dark. There's no electric. Nippy's drunk, he been *alapit*. They was never let him sing in church so he busted into AVEC and shut off the power. Day before yesterday Tommy Feathers Junior hang himself. Kids saw him. They couldn't lift him. Nobody tell you? Fifteen years old." Stevie sneezed. "Uh-oh."

"What else been happening?"

"Caribous crossing. Real fat ones. That dog musher, that Ted Brown fella, he find ivory tusk by Igisuktuk. With Honda. Hunnert thirty-seven pounds. People are complaining alright. That's not his land. Here. Mom wanna talk."

Janet shouted, in case the phone line wasn't large enough. "Hi, Cutuk! When you going home? We miss you, son. *Arii,* Melt been pass out right now. I hope he never *miġiaq* again. We're doing good."

"How's Abe?"

"Abe got no sons here! He sure get gray."

I scraped my fingernails clean along the inside leg seam of my jeans. "Has anybody heard from Dawna?"

"Dawna peen go Uktu, how long. Flossie's real bat. Lucky he been sick long enough, I get most of the presents sewed for her funeral." Janet giggled. "She's letting Dawna listen to her old stories. That's good, you think?"

"Janet. Who died in Anchorage?"

"Ah! Hannah Wana! He's Feathers, adopted to Uktu. To Mildred Wana. He been go Anchorage how long. That was his real brother, who suicide around here," she said, mixing male and female pronouns again. "*Arii!* T'em young ones! You should go home."

Stevie's voice came on the line. "Say, Cutuk, when you come, bring me coupla' jugs!" There was the sound of a slap and "*Arii* you!" "Let'um then, I jokes."

Reluctantly, I lowered the phone and let five hundred miles of mountains spring back up and put my head in my palms, breathing carefully, allowing credence to the irony of bad coincidence. *If there were a God, this would be a test. Am I going to get drunk or pack?* Iris was probably cooking caribou *patiq* bones in soup for the men in the tribal building making the casket and, while it simmered, helping stain boards pretty for the cross. In Uktu—and in how many other Eskimo villages?—they would similarly be dealing with their deaths. January and Lance? They had simply stepped out somewhere. Dawna took a trip home. Cheryl was doing what she needed to do in the "real world." And Hannah? Hannah arriving at that end of the trail we didn't allow ourselves to think clearly about, no more tracks ahead.

January would return, drive up any moment. His front left brake would grab, his truck pitch slightly to the side—I still needed to fix his brakes. He'd get out and spit and wave, kind, and happy that I was back. He'd turn on the TV and poke in the freezer for moose or caribou meat that had been frozen too long.

I jumped up—tonight desiring something less predictable than conversation in a trailer—and snaked out the money. September darkness was condensing outside. The bright summer had gone and stars scraped through. Up north, after the long day of summer, the first black snowless nights made people afraid. Janet would be whispering stories, Melt and Woodrow and everyone keeping their shotguns loaded. Spirits and bears and *iññuqun* were out, the inky blackness rustling.

But who was I fooling? Spirits and bears and *iññuqun* didn't walk electric Anchorage. Cities were about remote control; they cleared out bad luck with the trees and brush and planted streetlights. Paved the dark nights and spirits. I checked my jeans and shirt for mud or stray snot and raced toward the airplane, glancing back. My heart faltered. The street up from January's trailer had two names. The big green sign on this side read IRIS STREET. Where had my eyes been? And I called myself a hunter? A sharp reader of sign? If I believed in "meant-to-be" I was doing fine after all, sensing some snowed-in trail like Plato used to.

The problem was, I didn't believe. Hawclys found their own food, sewed their own torn skin, and put stinkweed on everything else. Hawclys believed in themselves—and the inevitability of failing themselves—surrounded by nature too big and unpredictable to imagine controlling; they were responsible for their own lives, as far from welfare, suburbs, and "meant-to-be" as any place had ever been.

The ski plane was gone.

The chains were gone. The ground underneath the skis had sprouted its grass, vigorous and still growing. I stood for a moment, tossing possibilities, and what I didn't understand but already knew—something inside of me was a compass, as sure as the compasses in caribou and Canada geese. I sat on my heels, examined my hands and underneath them my dreams to fly my grandfather's airplane. Every flight plan pointed north. Soaring above the land, into the past that didn't exist. Glancing down for the tiny black line of Enuk's team that didn't exist.

Cars purred past. Along the shore, water slapped and plunked softly. The memories of Cheryl's and my time together here swirled in the dark. I'd done it; I'd found jobs, friends, an amazing girlfriend, even my brother, and a bunch of dollars. *Now you can go home where real things happen! Have a dog team, hunt, find Enuk's trail.*

I paused, then turned, and, one foot in front of the other, followed Spenard Road, one last hunt into the heart of lights. The moon was full and clouds were sweeping by. There were dark pocks in the moon's bright face.

A BURLY BLOND MAN questioned me in the *qanisaq* of Chilkoot Charlie's. "A learner's permit? No driver's license? Where are you from, Russia?"

"Close." Song Spenholt flashed in my head, smiley with prevarications. "Up north we don't have roads."

"No roads? No chicks? What do people do?" He guffawed. "Okay, go on in."

Sawdust was on the floor. Fishnet hung from the dark ceiling. The stools were made of cutoff logs and beer kegs, the tables from wooden wire spools. Out through a back door was a country band; inside, two louder bands. The people shone. I'd never seen such narrow women, such muscular men, with such young faces, and weak hands.

"One-fifty-one, please."

The bartenders ignored me. I glanced up, half expecting a NO WHITES sign. Beside me, on a bar stool, a crewcut man whistled. "Wrrrt! Hey! Man here with a hundred-spot, so dry and rich he's croaking." He twisted around. "Bobby. I'm from Texas."

"Cutuk." We shook hands, shouting in each other's faces, like foreplay to a fight. Bobby shrugged and let my confusing name blow away in the rock and roll storm. Shots came, and a stack of change. I swept the quarters into my pockets. His eyes were friendly and brown with freckles flung underneath. I recognized a drug, this spending money and making friends, and not being alone with your thoughts. My cells welcomed the alcohol and the angles inside the music. I smiled and glanced at women—everywhere Aphrodites—and touched the thousands in my pocket. How could I turn from this, back to the immense silence and cold? How could I stay and stand the way it all felt paid for by the land? I gazed around, wishing. *An Everything-Wanter with everything!*

Bobby bent close. "I'm only seventeen. My daddy works on the Slope."

Prudhoe!

He asked the usual questions about the Arctic, then told about a friend in Matanuska Valley who had fourteen snowmobiles, and a little toboggan they dragged behind, loaded with cases of Budweiser. Shots came. Bobby watched my hands take out money. He mentioned taking a spin. I raised my eyebrows. Lights were sharp and threatening to spin. The place had become crowded, people pressed like fish upright in a bucket. For a moment I panicked—*where was the door?* "Just push," Bobby urged. He squeezed a woman's black-skirted butt. He grinned and pretended to wave to a friend. The woman wore a metallic blouse, like some sort of alien goddess, and leaned close enough to me to kiss, her eyelids silvery as smashed moths. "Watch out, asshole, or you'll be sorry."

"Thanks, I'm already aware of that."

Bobby's car was a blue Mazda RX-7. I flipped pages in my library-book memory. *Wankel rotary engine.* Couples stood cooling off after dancing. Bobby's wrist flicked as he shifted. He used the brake and throttle hard. "Let's cruise Fourth." We were at a light. The night raining now. Neon signs flashed and taxis rolled away from DWI-scarred curbs. "I hear you can trade a bottle for ivory. Hey, what's Eskimo pussy like?" He pounded the steering wheel. "Is it, like, cold and shit?"

Hannah Wana's dog-chewed face rose behind my eyes. My throat lifted. I breathed, inhaling the essence of the car—the engine, the plastic dash and seats, the stereo—letting this inanely expensive freedom wash under my skin. Men shuffled the sidewalks, fists deep in their pockets, wading into a permanent wind. My pockets were stuffed with money. I twisted around; was that Elvis Jr.? Rain swallowed the figure.

"There's a fight!" Bobby said.

A palm cracked on a face. Bitch-slap, in Mechanic English. "Hold on!" He veered left, left again, around the block. I slumped low in the seat, carsick. The door latch slick and cold. We could roll by. But Bobby rolled down his window. The tires hissed. The air cool and damp. The night street flashed wet neon. The man was big and heavyset, vaguely familiar. Woodrow Jr.! Beside him the woman's head was bowed. Drizzle glittered on her black hair.

Bobby bent forward, leaned out the window. "Now you two rub noses and make up!"

Woody had a bottle. He flung it.

Bobby stomped the gas pedal. The car twisted and lunged. "Yeehaaa!" The bottle shattered in the street. I hunched against my knees. Had Woody seen? The woman wasn't Dawna but so easily could have been. She'd been struck by one person and racially insulted by another. I was old acquaintances with that pain raining down. *What is it with lucky people?* I tried to concentrate on how to convince this white stranger how truly amazing Eskimos were. How truly amazing the arctic landscape was all by itself without Prudhoe, roads, and cases of Budweiser. Where would I start? With words? Or my knife? Suddenly it was so elementary. I leaned his way and stuck my finger as far down my throat as it would go. The shifter and stereo got the second round.

A DRIZZLE MISTED THE LIGHTS. The air was pleasant. In the lee of a skyscraper, I spat and ducked into a phone booth and dug out handfuls of quarters. It was all so magic; Iris answered on the fifth ring. She was groggy but listened to the story. She laughed over and over. I smiled huge in the dark, and imagined her doing the same.

"You give him money?"

"Shuck no!"

"How about Woody, did he recognize you? You know, I rent my cabin from Woody."

"I'm not sure."

"Sounds as if you're doing as well as I am, teaching." She yawned. "My gosh, the papers I grade!"

"What? Is it a lot?"

"That too, but no, it's my students." Her voice grew serious. "They have such a rough go. Nelta Skuq, she's got nine kids, you know; she just got her AFDC check and split again, who knows where—Nome? Anaktuvuk? Fairbanks? Her thirteen-year-old, Mary, is on the CB asking for diapers."

"Mary's thirteen?"

"She's pregnant! And here's Miss Hawcly, assigning a paper—one page on her favorite experience. Mary writes one run-on sentence about the Bulls. The errors were in perfect vernacular. So I asked the kids to write about their worst experience. Mary writes another sentence, this time about a fly that got in her Coke and she almost drank it. She's been raped, Cutuk! By her brothers and uncles, and who knows who. Who even knows how many times. She's been beaten and abandoned and passed around since she can remember. And she writes about a fly in her Coke? Most of the kids don't write anything. They throw stuff and bounce off the walls, or zone out and be drones. There's no intellectual curiosity. I shouldn't be whining to you. It's just hard."

"Iris, I worried about you. Only . . . since I left I've been living some strange egocentric existence. I'm caught up in all this . . . stuff. Can I send you something? I have money now."

"How about a pizza and a beer?" Iris giggled. "How about if you came home?"

A police car rolled past the phone booth. The brake lights flashed red, and then it continued down the street. "Maybe. I don't know if I can live in Takunak, with everybody staring and complaining about white people."

"Oh, that's spilled milk under the bridge. I know what you mean, but good people are everywhere. Think about Janet. She'd love to have you here. Down there it is easy, in some ways. But something felt a little bit missing. Guess that's why I'm here."

"I feel wrapped in plastic. I thought it was the food."

"I think it probably is the food," Iris agreed. "I'd make you snow ice cream. And roasted caribou leg bones. The Canada geese are still here fattening up on blueberries. Abe brought me two. He came down in his plank boat."

"Abe has a boat?"

"I bought him a little ten-horse motor. He sawed spruce boards and made a river boat. He and Franklin have two solar panels now, too. And a shortwave radio. They listen to BBC and Radio Moscow."

"That's crazy!"

"You should see it."

"Maybe."

I WALKED AWAY from the mountains, toward the distant thunder of a jet taking off. I realized I hadn't eaten since the night before in Fairbanks. The One-Five left history in snatches and fragments. Fairbanks squatted fourteen hours back, behind mountains the size of years. Homemade songs jumbled in my brain, the corny words ringing hollow in where my past was peeling off the walls of my skull. Bruce Springsteen would laugh, or vomit into his spruce guitar.

I pictured Dawna in Uktu, drinking dark liquid—one-night homebrew—with dark cousins. On the street I pushed my hand into my pocket and touched Enuk's bear. Could the old thing be bad luck? A thicket of willows grew beside the road. I brought back my arm and flung. "Let go when I tell you," I told my hand. The bear stood in my palm, sniffing the night. Maybe down in the ancient ivory the spirit of an extinct mammoth glowered, still mad at humans for extirpating his species. I flung again. My shoulder popped and my hand opened in pain. I panted, tremulous with shock. The tiny bear glinted in the streetlight, cracked against a branch, ricocheted into blackness and brush.

No raven flew overhead, no gust of wind in the trees. The planet turned east as I walked west.

BY THE TIME I found January's trailer the sky was graying with dawn. Inside, I stood shivering over a metal slot where heat blew out. *Alappaa.* I missed cutting dead trees to burn in the barrel stove. I rustled in his freezer, found a chunk of caribou. On cardboard I cut shavings and chewed the raw frozen meat. Out of the open bedroom door January yawned. His coarse fingernails rasped coarse hair.

He shuffled out. He was naked and his hazel eyes were puffy and confused. When I was counting friends and coming up with zeros, I hadn't considered January. Something slid friends into the "not quite" slot. *We just work together. He's Abe's friend. She probably doesn't like me.* All the time I should have been thankful for January, alive and here to share the city with. I should have fixed his brakes.

He leaned against the counter and scratched his head. "Damn, I miss my hair. Among other things!" His gut hung huge. He glanced wistfully out at the morning coming over the next trailer.

I leaned back from the table. *"Aarigaa taikuu."* I wiped my hands on a paper towel, pried out the aluminum foil. Opened it on the table like a brownie.

"Ho! How long you been rat-holin' that?"

"Since you told me about the IRS."

"Guess I best find my trousers."

"It's for your plane. To buy it back. I wanted you to teach me to fly."

"Goddammit, kid. They confiscated it. My plane's all gone. Probably in Arizona by now, being flown by some friggin' fed counting wetbacks."

January grimaced. "Goddamn old age ain't all she's cracked up to be. Wisdom? Shee! Memory loss more like it. And the government stealing you blind, when you hardly got a pot to piss in." His voice was thick and rumbly. He rubbed his gray caterpillar eyebrows. "That Cub . . . winter before statehood, me an' your dad headed to Barrow. Them's were the good old days. That Super Cub was *brand-new.* People don't know what that means nowdays. Abe an' me flew dabsmack into weather. Thought we'd crack up putting down on the Kuguruk. Goddamn brand-new Super Cub!"

The blower started and blew warm air. January's hanging testicles twitched as he breathed.

"Dogs, grandmas, everybody come out. Two white fellas I remember, skinny schoolteacher with a beard and a big fat-assed preacher with no beard. Wolfglove come out, invited us to stay in his cabin. More generous people never was born. Telling stories. Eatin' like you are there. Enuk had a big smile. I know'd what he was after. When the storm lifted I took him up. Where you put the stick in to fly from the back seat, Wolfglove poked his finger in an' banked me into them Dog Die Mountains. Tremendously strong guy.

"Later, when you was being borned, I flew back an' stayed with Abe. One time, I seen Wolfglove do pull-ups with one finger on a spike pounded into your cache pole. Tremendously strong! He stayed with your family in the one-room. Drove your ma bananas. That guy wanted to figure out why a white man who could fly would live Out, in a way even Eskimos wouldn't anymore. That bein' Abe."

January put a kettle on the propane burner. He leaned against the stove, waiting, his hand resting on the grimy handle of the kettle.

I sat on his La-Z-Boy and leaned back. I'd never tried his recliner before. With the TV on, this must be part of what they called "making it."

"One storm," I mused. "Well. We got nine thousand dollars. What do you want to do with it, January?"

"You're spendin' that chunk a change on your own narrow heinie."

"Actually, I was ready to throw it in the willows tonight. That or give it to a Texas kid."

"Maybe you best give 'er to me." He grinned bad teeth.

"Do people rent airplanes? I want you to fly me up north."

"Well . . ." January scratched his leg pit. He pushed out his lips, thinking and nodding, not able to keep from smiling a little to himself. He shifted the kettle. The water started to sing.

PART III **HOME**

TWENTY-ONE

***THE NORTH BREEZE** falls off mountains and whistles down a valley.* Curled leaves stir in the birches. Under the spruce boughs, dead needles release their grip and lance down. Snakes of snow smoke along the ice at the edge of the creek. The snow drifts behind tussocks, swirls into rocks and roots. It squeaks under the wolf pups' feet, soft and powdery.

The pups roll and kick their pantaloon hind legs in the air. They bite at their first snow. Slash upside-down noses into it, fill their eyes and nip their siblings. One by one they roll to their feet, shake, and follow each other, sliding clumsy and cautious on the shelf ice, until it cracks and drops them elbow-deep into the polished water.

The male pups are as big as their mother already, silver giants, flashing long lips full of inexperienced ivory. They will play and chase and help very little when the first moose goes down. They will keep their tails tucked subserviently while they eat enormous shares. The female is smaller, her legs and tail and face and hair shorter, white with black tips on her guard hairs.

Now the pups dig, claws ripping at the moss and soil, big paws flinging dirt and snow between their hind legs. They dig with playful energy. An animal's old bones reel out of the frosted ground. The wolves mouth the bones. Pink tongues taste dirt, ball and push the bones out. They dig longer bones. White and green and pink, painted by moss and lichens and bleached by sky. The big pups struggle in a three-way tug-of-war over a piece of old dried hide, growling and raking each other's eyes with muddy feet. The female sniffs the chalky bones and smells no food. She turns and trots up the slope, toward high rocks, and her parents and the scent of a ground squirrel.

The wind blows up here. Snow squalls drape the broad valley, dragging the first curtains of winter, and the sun shines a bright hopeful face on the heavy clouds. The pup and her mother lick each other's faces and ears. They lie down with their forelegs bent under their chests and watch the land turn white. The tundra stretches down the side of the mountain, rolls across hills and valleys, miles of distance, mountains and sky. Snow falls on the slate scree, covering wobbling leaves, sparse grass, squirrel skulls, and another season, painting a hue of hard beauty on the land, the wolves' home, for a hundred thousand generations before any of the colors of human.

TWENTY-TWO

THE FRESH FALL ICE cracked and the five dogs shied under a cutbank. In the snow and curled willow leaves under the bank, the team bounded along frozen humps of dirt, dodging stobs and dangling roots. The sled flipped on the ice. The rear stanchion snapped. "Gee! Whoa, Rex!" Lumpy's dog—now promoted to leader—cowered and heaved with curved hind legs, clawing further onto the dirt. I longed for old Plato. Dog mushers always remembered their leaders to be dauntless in storms, able to follow long-buried trails, though we all had rifles with broken stocks, from periods when those legendary leaders needed extra encouragement.

I was heading up to see Abe and to get my guns. That was about as far as my career plans extended. I hadn't been along this stretch of the river before. January and I had flown north to Takunak in August—he had taken months to get his license current. Finally, out of patience, I'd bought tickets for Lance and me to Phoenix, and we'd spent a month and eight thousand dollars getting private pilot licenses, having the times of our lives, flying.

That got January motivated; he passed the physical and did a check ride in a Cessna 172. By then the August rains had submerged the sandbars near Abe's cabin. In the sky I'd turned west, banked into the north breeze, made my final approach on the new lighted Takunak crosswind runway. And walked away from flying, possibly forever, as Abe had done.

January had left me standing in dust, beside the old duffle bag. Iris had been in Crotch Spit for a school in-service and it was Elvis Jr. who drove me over from the new airstrip. His left eye was scabbed shut. I rode behind him on his Honda four-wheeler; dust boiled behind us. His wrists were bare and brown and thin. "Here I thought you was in camp," he shouted. "You bring any beers?"

"Naw. What happened to your eye?"

"I *alapit*. Guys said my Honda sure fly and tree bump my face. Hey *bart*, I got wolf dog for sale. Eighty-three percent, man. You want to buy it?"

JANET LOANED ME her .30-30 carbine; Iris loaned a sled and one of her dogs, and Lumpy three more dogs. It was debatable whether his dogs had ever been off their chains. Or when they had last been fed. The dog racer, Ted Brown, offered an eight-month-old pup he didn't want. "Can't keep pace with my fast race team," he whispered, in front of the post office. He explained how he named his puppies by the litter, like Chinese years: the litter of the weather was Frosty, Windy, Cloudy, Stormy; the litter of the sitcom . . . The yellow leaves floated off the aspens above Takunak. My eyes roamed to the sweepstakes envelope in my hand: *Crat Hawker, You Could Be A Ten Million Dollar Loser.* "I made Uktu last spring in five hours," Ted said. "Spring crust is killer traveling." He squinted wisely.

I glanced into his hazel eyes, wondering when I'd become anyone worth impressing. A big man strode down the post office steps. He had pale blue eyes and no hair on top and he wore a cross. A preacher, an airport maintenance man, or a sport hunter? Or all three.

"Ted! I tell you how I nailed the Dog Die pack?" He looked smug. In the air was the faint turbulence of two egos occluding. "Last April, I flew over to reconnoiter, then I snowgoed to the top of a two-thousand-foot knife ridge and dropped over a cornice. Didn't need to fly over, really, I know the country like the back of my hand. That drop must have been a fifty-footer. Surprised the crap out of me. Sneaked right up on those bastards!" Foam specked the man's lips. "I could've wasted the whole pack with my thirty-round clip of FMJs. I only shot four. Next spring I'm going to get my brother up here, get him a wolf." The man swiveled. "Never seen you. I've been here for years. You ever shot a wolf?"

I quickly nodded good-bye to them and the old Alaskan pissing contest—who had been here longer. I walked away embarrassed, somehow vanquished. Ted was saying, ". . . Iris Hawcly, that little hotty schoolteacher . . . one of the brothers . . . I panned a gram of color below the Hawcly place . . . just took fifteen minutes."

White people—everything talked to pieces until all the pieces had numbers. *I get wolves,* Enuk would have said, *back by mountains.* It would have been someone else's duty to fill in the story and any heroism. Enuk seemed a long way back, and I missed him and that place. I shuffled envelopes in my hand. *Your preapproved American Express card, Mr. Crawly.* Behind the post office, Elsie Haft stood on a cowering dog's chain, beating him with an axe handle. Her toddler grandson stood observing in rubber boots and a Pamper, sucking a lollipop.

In Melt's Boston Whaler, Stevie boated the dogs and me and the sled upriver. The first fall ice pans were swinging downriver, too much moving ice to stop at our old place. Stevie grinned as pans gnashed under Melt's fiberglass boat. "I hope the bottom never open." His hair was bristly, an even half inch long. He had gained weight and had new glasses with lenses that turned gray in the glare off the water and ice. I hadn't told him—or anyone except Iris—about my pilot's license. I didn't want people talking, trying to figure out why a young man with a pilot's license didn't hire on as a mail plane pilot. Or get an airplane to hunt with.

Stevie helped chain the dogs, limb saplings, and pitch my tent on the bank in the willows. He trimmed the limbs close and watched as I tied the knots. He was thoughtful; it seemed as if he might want to stay. Finally, he sat on the bow of the boat, blocked the breeze with the collar of his nylon jacket, and lit a farewell cigarette. His fingers started to stuff the cigarettes into his pocket. He glanced at the white Marlboro pack and tossed it to me. "Cut, take my smokes. Maybe you'll need 'em. No nine-one-one around here." He grinned and shoved off into the tinkling floes without saying good-bye.

OUT IN THE RIVER, the current hauled big frosty pans groaning and crashing against the fast ice. Cracks raced to shore, twinging like the echoes of a galactic stomach. The dogs cowered. Wind had pushed drifts of snow into the hollows of jumbled ice and the dogs scooped mouthfuls and sniffed at caribou trails braiding up the shore. On the ice, I lifted the sled on its runners. In wheel position Lumpy's yellow dog, Mike, whined and yanked.

"Lie down!"

The dog never pulled. His fur was thin and still shedding. I lit one of Stevie's cigarettes, glanced at the cutbank, and dug in my pockets for twine to splint the sled stanchion that had broken. The Marlboro magic swirled Cheryl and Takunak in the cold air. The pocket on my old caribou parka held the compost of my teenage life: matches, string, corroded .22 shells, a peregrine falcon talon, a linty rectangle of Bit-O-Honey. The dogs lay on the concrete dirt, wet pink tongues out, brown eyes warily watching the unfaithful ice. In my inside pocket was a packet of pansy seeds, the only present I could think of to bring home for Abe.

When the sled was repaired, I surveyed our position; we were stuck at the lower end of a long cutbank, blocked by open current up ahead and willow thickets bearding the bank. The cutbank stretched up and around the bend. The dogs growled at each other and cut their soft hopeful eyes at the caribou hindquarter tied at the front of the load. "When that runs out, one of you is next," I warned. They stepped forward, wagging eagerly. I kicked at stobs, searching for something to tie the dogs to. Tucked under the bank, just above ice level, a curved log caught my eye. I grasped it to see if it was frozen in firmly enough to anchor the team. It was as heavy as a wet log, but loose and not wood. I knelt and scraped at it with a plate of ice. Dark blue vivianite dust flaked off. An ivory tusk! I spread my hands, not believing my luck, then glanced around, remembering my last mammoth ivory.

The big curved tusk weighed the sled heavily, and I rolled it back off the load and staked the dogs to it. I unsheathed my axe, climbed the bank and cleared trail through a sweaty mile of brush, and returned for the dogs. I heaved the cumbersome tusk on the sled, grinning, picturing Abe questioning my efforts over something that he would admire, and leave where it lay. I tried to coax the team up the bank; Rex scrambled to the top and the overloaded sled hung nearly vertical. Mike hesitated and the other wheel dog tugged him sideways.

"Go 'head!"

Rex peered over the bank and leapt down. The sled crashed onto the ice and plunged backward into the open water. I sank to my waist. In an instant I scrambled up, over the handbars and load, to shore. The runners punched into the river bottom. I stood on a lump of collapsed bank, panting. I flung dogs up the bank, then yanked at the brush bow of the sled, pulling it out half a foot at a time. "Hike! GO 'HEAD! GET UP THERE!" The sled rose, finally balanced and disappeared up in the willows. "Whoa!"

My heart pounded. I grabbed roots and clawed to the top of the frozen dirt. In the willows the dogs had stopped. My gloves were soaked. I flopped them across the tusk. They froze down. Barehanded and shaking, I rubbed snow on my pants. The water had hardly penetrated my new nylon overpants but had filled my Sorel boots. I rubbed snow on the dogs' legs to soak up the water before it froze. I unlashed the stiffening tarp, scraped out slush and water, and sat and wrung my insoles and changed to fresh socks. The grub box was wet and icy. Down below, the open water appeared clear now, the bottom steeply inclined. My breathing slowed. I rocked the tusk until it lay curve-up against a clump of willows, marked it with willows, checked my load, slid on heavy wolverine mittens, and told the dogs to go.

In another hour we were past the cutbank, traveling on up the ice, winding into the valley as the first evening planets twinkled. There were tracks of the fourteen wolves that I had seen yesterday. They had howled at my dogs and paced and finally curled on the ice until afternoon when they ambled into the mouth of a slough. Their voices had faded in the willows, and I howled to them, suddenly overwhelmed to be home, while Janet's voice whispered in my head, *Why you never shoot 'em?*

Rex's ears lifted. All the dogs tugged. Ahead, a small herd of caribou trotted toward us. I threw out the snow hook and pulled the rifle over my shoulder, checked the muzzle, and shot a young bull. Cows and calves flooded around us, scented the dogs, and veered onto the ice. Momentarily, the caribou stopped, wide-eyed, nearly surrounding me. The dogs barked and the animals raced back the way they had come.

Across the river a *naataq* hooted. It was getting dark. The dogs wagged and whined. Quickly, I gutted the caribou, realizing it had been two years; my hands knew what to do, and it made me proud. I cut slices of liver and stuffed it in the rumen to cook and eat while I worked. The dogs got all they could swallow of fat intestines while I snapped willows and built a fire. Coffee boiled in a blackened can, and the choice parts—the tongue and brisket—simmered. The sky grew orange and green in the south, blue-black overhead. I chained the dogs, ate meat and fat, slept in the sled with six onions.

We loaded up and went slowly on the next day, and the next, until the dogs sniffed wood smoke and sped up. At the upper end of a timbered ridge squatted a cabin. There was snow on the roof, icicles on the eaves. A cache stood nearby poking up out of the trees. Behind, mountains rose in sharp white triangles. It felt strong and good to be near mountains without names. Probably CIA satellites hunting the sky had numbered all thousand peaks—for national security—but it was these mountains, and their namelessness, that left me feeling safe.

Dogs struck up a warning. My team sprinted up the shore. Abe stood out on the ice, Franklin coming down a path. My dogs passed both, yanking along the glare ice toward their dogfood pile of salmon and whitefish, moose and caribou. I glanced at Abe. He wore an otter hat and between the hanging flaps his beard was gray. He didn't have mittens on, or a jacket, but a heavy wool shirt with long-underwear sleeves sticking out. A coffee mug was clamped in his fingers. His hand and wrist looked big, his shoulders thick. I stomped the snow hook into a crack in the ice and my dogs lay with their lips pointing at the pile of fish—except Magnum PI, the wiry little racer, who stood whining and tugging to go.

Abe and Franklin held the toprails, eyed the caribou in my sled. Abe sniffed the evening air the way he always had, checking for moisture and temperature, predicting the night weather without even knowing he was doing it. Franklin wore a green down jacket, black and greasy chested and patched with duct tape. He was stooped, his eyelids chapped and papery.

I turned to Abe. His eyes glowed, bluer than frozen sky. His face was craggy. His hands gnarled my shoulder. I could hold my head up, my smile up, but not my eyes. Part of me felt free and at home, back on the land, eating *patiq* bones and berries; the other part was wilted from too much cowboy coffee and culture shock. My skin felt thin and I didn't want him to see through to the hollow spaces and doubt. He swallowed and made a hoarse sound; he turned away. "Help you unhitch."

A huge sled dog shambled over. One brown ear hung out to the side like a wind was blowing. She had the deep chest, stiff hips, and ratty tail of an old retired working dog. She pushed her chin in my hand. "Plato?" I knelt, suddenly choked up, petting her soft eyes, and I glanced up, smelling the dogcooker fire, and icy leaves and cold falling air, and hearing mice rustling in the grass and grosbeaks cracking cones up in the spruce and ice piling out in the channel, and way across the tundra I felt the sun going too far down.

They chained the five dogs and led me up to the cabin. The steep twisting path passed an igloo—Franklin's—overhung with birches. The snow in front of his door was shoveled, but untracked except by mice. Abe's cabin was small with two beds along the back wall and a workbench in front below a glass window. I dropped my duffle and *qaatchiaq* and stood gazing at my father's life. Paintings and brushes and plane shavings mixed on his workbench. Now black wires came in the wall between logs—from the two solar panels Iris had mentioned, and a small wind generator—to a twelve-volt battery. Wire sneaked along the roof poles to a tiny fluorescent bulb. Abe's bed had two caribou skins stacked on it instead of one. The curled edges had been trimmed straight. A shelf above his bed held books: an atlas, a dictionary, *Endurance, The Iliad, Wildflowers of Alaska, The Bourne Identity, Lonesome Dove, Journals of Samuel Hearne.* Dusty aluminum foil tacked to the wall reflected light onto his pillow. Thumbtacked to logs was a postcard of the New York City skyline, a birch leaf, a lichen, one of my letters, a package of Coleman mantles; hawk feathers, chain saw files, and skin needles were poked into cracks in beams. A quote from Henry David Thoreau, printed in black ink, was speared on a nail, and a calendar photograph of a lynx in soft blue snow.

Abe flipped his easel out of his way and gently booted tubes of paint and cans of thinner across the floorboards. He rapped on the window. "Plato, back down to your doghouse. Go eat your fish." Along the wall beyond his bed, a bearskin couch was within reach of the fire. On the stove, a piece of antler rolled in a pot of boiling water. "Softening this, for a chisel handle." Abe peered into the steam. Franklin reached under a counter, got out a box of pilot crackers. He was completely bald on top now, his white fronds staticky and wild and he moved creakily, pretending to innocently nudge Abe's easel until I could see the painting. Under his tented lids he stole glances. Gray light came in at the window; at the easel, a wolf's face gazed into mine, the face thin, hungry, surreal. Abe stoked the fire and the flames threw quick light. The lines on the wolf's nose were tiny crosshatches. In the shadows of the cheekbones I saw my father's face. I stepped close, and chills rafted my veins. In the reflection of the golden orbs—were those the distant towers of New York?

Abe banged the stovepipe. I jumped. Creosote tinked down the pipe. "Lot easier living here than downriver in the wind," he said. "Deep snow, though. Gets tiring snowshoeing out our wood trails. Less animals, too." Abe was telling me something, without delving into the past.

"Why'd you move?" I said bluntly. "You like animals."

He sighed. His left knee cracked. "I was up Jesus Creek one day . . . watching wolves. A snowgo came and shot them with a semiautomatic rifle; he ran over some, wounded some, finally got all of them. It about got me mad at people." Abe grinned and rubbed his knee. "Not good to feel that way. You feel better when you like everybody."

I wondered if the hunter had been Treason, or the loud talker at the post office; it could have been anybody. Lance burst into my head: *We all want a few dead wolves, don't we?*

"Abe's been working on that for months." Franklin nodded at the easel. His chin shook. He pulled a piece of used dental floss out of his shirt pocket and flossed the teeth he had that touched. He wadded the gray string back in his pocket.

"Don't throw this one in the stove," I said.

Abe swiveled suspiciously. "What would you do with my wolf?"

"I like it." I was lying. I'd find an address in Chicago or somewhere where people cared about painting; I'd find out if Abe had the talent January claimed, if he had had open doors and still walked away. It was almost none of my business, but it seemed to matter.

". . . maybe the best I've ever painted," Abe said. "Iris thinks so, too." He splashed hot water over coffee grounds. The roasted aroma filled the cabin, seeping into the moss chinking, mixing with the pitchy firewood turning white and frosty, thawing beside the stove. He handed me a mug and slid the sizzling cannibal pot onto the table. The pot was black with grease, Abe not the kind of person to ruin cast iron with soap. I ran my thumbnail around the rim; it clicked into an old chip where Iris had hit the pot with my blue hatchet, chopping out broth. The hatchet lay beside the wood box. I shook my head, trying to align the years, the Taco Bells, exit ramps, rabid foxes, and this old pot.

"Built a cabin this time." Still Abe didn't sit. He rustled on the kitchen counter for clean mugs. His finger stub was stiff and sore-looking and didn't curve with his big hand. "Not as warm, or as cool in the summer, but sod igloos you have to rebuild every twenty years, and I didn't feel like building the last one when I was eighty."

Franklin puckered a grin and softened a cracker in his coffee. "Have some, Cutuk. These are our last pilot crackers."

By now, I knew they must be out of new reading material, too. I opened my pack and spilled out their junk mail, slippery as a washtub of fish. Franklin sorted greedily, his thumb claw gripping a Victoria's Secret catalog. "What's this? Sears and Roebuck got a new daughter-in-law on their cover?" He opened it in the middle and leafed back and forth in both directions, feigning minimal interest.

"We have a plank boat, with Iris's ten-horse." Abe dumped our lukewarm coffee back into the pot and poured hot. "The impeller wore out. I made one out of a boot heel, but I didn't want to get stuck the summer seventy miles downriver if nobody had spare parts." He and Franklin shook their heads. Stuck in Takunak, watching four-wheelers and airplanes and Oprah—for them too close to hell to risk; they could wait until winter and dog-team down to town.

Franklin lowered the lingerie catalog and flossed again thoughtfully. I knifed at the pot-roasted brown bear foreleg and dipped the meat in cranberry sauce. I felt bad for Franklin. He was old and those women in the catalog were so misty-eyed and inviting, and nothing remotely like that was ever going to happen to him again. Anybody could see from his mouth puckered around his teeth that he wished there was at least a prayer.

Finally, Abe sat on a stump. He cut hot meat and spooned cranberry sauce on a cracker. His forearms and hands were heavy, forked with veins, almost grotesquely huge and powerful. "Last box of pilot crackers." He chuckled. "We were saving it for company. Shrews chewed in the back and almost outflanked us." The cracker he lifted to his grin had an edge gone and the rasp marks of fine teeth, and it was something like love to see the humor he still took from almost being beaten by a shrew. His naïveté made my lungs catch. I looked up to smile on my dad—and shuddered in the yellow gaze of the wolf.

A WEEK AFTER I ARRIVED, Abe and I stood out on the ridge without parkas on, pissing. Franklin didn't give us a lot of time alone, never enough to crack into the past. I wouldn't ask any question with Franklin, a finger in Victoria's Secret, listening, waiting to practice atrophied parenting skills. Now he was down rummaging in his igloo for flour to make pan bread. *Iron Toast.* The echo of Iris's laughter made me smile.

"It's good to be home. Though the old days feel like something I dreamed up."

"When you're young, the hills are easy to climb," Abe said. "The good thing about getting older is they don't seem so big." He shook his penis and stuffed it back into his pants. "You were always my favorite."

"You talking to me?"

His eyebrows twitched in sudden embarrassment. They were thick and still blond. Iris was always his favorite. I nodded, not needing to change that, but words tumbled out. "You must be getting Alzheimerish. I wasn't your favorite. Iris was."

In his beard his lips smiled. "Where did you learn to discount yourself?"

"Where were you? People taught me different is bad, starting a long time before I did anything besides wait with the dogs." I stopped and dropped my eyes. This wasn't any chat I wanted to chat. *I've been places, Abe. I've flown in Boeing's jets, walked paved streets, and kissed girls.*

"Well, I'm glad you came home. I'm glad Iris came home. What did you end up liking down there?"

"It was fun to go to movies. Sometimes to a restaurant and order a BLT."

He looked puzzled for a moment, then raised his eyebrows—*yes.*

"Shuck, lots of it is hard not to like. Little packs of sweet salty almonds. Boy, they're good! Washing machines. Good lights. Amazingly comfortable seats that don't hurt your back. Not like sitting on firewood stumps."

Abe looked at his thumbs, listening, smiling faintly, and I wondered if he was waiting for me to be quiet.

"It's funny." I heard my voice speeding up. "Life down there is . . . like you're running before it runs out. Seems like people design great chairs then . . . then I don't know. Pay bills in them? They make shoes that are beautiful and expensive, and water gets right in them. Scientists—who knows what they're inventing or what poor animal they're collaring so they don't have to go outside to really learn about it. People hardly think about the animals. They argue about abortion, then get mad if you don't 'fix' your dogs."

I toed snow. "Abe, it's all strange. Preachers preach about doom . . . and you better give money for a reservation to heaven. Like this place is crap, and you can just leave? Like Outsiders act about Takunak. You feel bad for Jesus. He was such a good guy and all sorts of mean bunk is done with his name glued to it. They talk about gold streets in heaven. For what? *Melting?* People jet around the world burning fuel to spot rare sparrows. People helicopter-ski down mountains bigger than the Dog Dies and worry if their ski boots are the right color with their snowpants. When I think of humans as one big herd? I see winter coming and them scurrying around thinking about sex or losing their keys."

Abe rocked a thumbnail between his teeth. "Well," he grinned, "news says we are getting fatter. That's what creatures do to prepare for cold. Fat, that's their money in the bank." Abe wore gray wool pants with patched knees, a knife made out of a chisel at his waist, and a flight jacket with rips and patches, grease, pitch, and dried blood on the front and sleeves. "Early cold fall." His eyes were on the faraway horizon, playing the pastel sky. He was fifty-seven, and I was twenty-three. I thought about the last time I'd touched the controls of the airplane and wondered when his last time had been. Strangely, it seemed as if no matter what I did, I was zigzagging along his path. Maybe Dawna was right, maybe it was the curse and luck of offspring. The river and ice and tundra were pink and orange, lavender and blue, the way they had always been. An ache gripped my chest.

"Franklin and I picked two kegs of cranberries. Want to give a hand getting the rest of the meat?"

Still I stared out at the beautiful land. "The hardest thing has been to understand people. Why didn't you teach me?"

He stuttered in surprise. "Teach? How would I go about that?" His face was thoughtful. "So much else is more interesting to me than people. Figured to let you decide yourself what was worthy."

Our elliptical conversation and the weight of that lifelong obligation left me annoyed. I spat over the bluff, biting back swear words. "Where are my guns and my traps?"

"Fur prices are gone. The anti-trapping campaign took off in Europe."

"Bastards. What do they know?"

"Maybe the same thing we do." Abe had always spoken as if his words were unfiltered thoughts. Now the quiet in his voice was a strange and commanding thing. "We've seen plenty of fox legs shattered and torn off. Wolverine, ripping their feet off."

I glanced at the path, watching for Franklin. Trapping logic trickled into my brain: wolverine tracks were like lynx, but not so neat; foxes had two toenails nearly touching, on their front feet, that showed in their tracks; at fifty below a wolverine might stay in a leghold trap for a night while at zero it might last three nights before breaking free. Furbearers moved before a storm, seeking food. Now a dog shook down in the dog yard. Abe gazed at the river, frozen all the ways it flowed. The cold stood hairs up on his wrists. My heart softened. This was my father, after all, the anchor of my life. Abe's mouth opened as he listened to a raven in the distance. "Fog, over there against the mountains," he breathed. "It's cold enough now, winter meat will keep. Good! I'm glad you're here. I'm glad you're thinking about things."

Something thudded down in Franklin's house. We were quiet, our breath rising fat and orange in the dying sun. Franklin's moosehide *mukluk* bottoms padded on the snow.

"January said you could have been a famous artist."

"January Thompson? What a nice guy. No, I was just a student drawing wolves downing moose, instead of one naked lady after another. Later, at college, people stopped and looked. Sometimes I painted things they bought to lean in their garages, hoping I'd get famous. I didn't like being waited on. Linda liked it. I didn't." Frost had formed on the chests of our long-underwear shirts. "Let's go in and poke up the fire." Franklin shuffled up the path, a Hills Bros can of flour under his arm.

I couldn't see my dad and a garage in the same lifetime. "You could have given her the world!" I whispered in awe.

"Maybe you are confusing things," he said gently. "I did give her the world."

A RAVEN CIRCLED AND CAWED. I cawed back, and she led us north. She wasn't mystical or mysterious, just hungry and intelligent, and I liked to think we both enjoyed sharing sounds. The tundra was mottled with tussocks and snow, brown and white and yellow in the weakening sun. Mottled humps moved. Abe and I knelt and checked the wind. The big bulls were rutting, grunting and rattling their antlers in quick sparring matches, peeling their lips back and chasing cows and calves. Now, in late October, their blood and meat would be stinky with hormones. We crawled closer, glassing teenagers, four-year-old bulls, watching which ones still nosed at lichens instead of thrashing small spruce with their antlers. Snow melted through my elbows and knees, and refroze, burning pressed circles of frostbite. With a rifle in my hands the pain was distant and I made room for it. The raven waited. Behind the herd, heavy timber marked a creek. Abe crawled west, toward the spruce. I glassed one more time, memorizing the animals I wanted. He nodded slowly, fifty yards away, and lowered his cheek to his gun stock. The boom cracked across the distance, whomping into a caribou. A caribou lunged on its hind legs, warning the herd of danger, the same movement advising predators of its prowess. I fired. Echoes thundered in the trees. The herd split and poured west. Fifty animals raced toward Abe and veered. I shot another, and another, the instinct to protect the food pile taking over. Winter lasted a long time. Everything would be hungry for fresh meat before the caribou migrated back north. I gathered my brass cartridges and shouldered the rifle. In the distance, the herd paused on the skyline. In front of us, a few wounded animals kicked and fought to get to their feet. I circled, and jumped, pinning a bull's antlers and stabbing my knife behind his neck; across the tundra, Abe was doing the same. Blood flowed into the snow.

I sniffed it to check for rut. The caribou shivered. The raven watched. Against the white mountains I saw the black dots of her coming cousins.

It took a couple hours to clean eleven animals. Abe rolled them ribs-down to drain and keep the meat warm and start it aging. He was particular and exact about how his meat was handled. We dragged the gut piles aside and cut boughs to make *X*s over the kills and hung bandannas on a branch to keep the birds wary. Enuk's voice seeped out, *Don't shoot* tulugaq. *Gonna storm plenty on you.* Abe and I hurried home to get the dogs, our sacks heavy with tongues, livers, hearts, and *itchaurat.*

At the cabin Abe knelt and pulled a dog-collar ring lashed to a trapdoor in the floor and swung open his cold hole. "Stevie Wolfglove brought his sister up, during high water last fall." He bent and retrieved an onion. "She told us about Anchorage, being on some kind of drugs, in a darkroom? And about Flossie in Uktu teaching her to cut wolverine skin. Said they both leaned back to watch TV and when she sat up Flossie had passed on."

"Dawna came *here?*" I glanced around, embarrassed that she'd seen the likes of my meager roots.

"Reason I moved up here," Franklin mumbled over his coffee, "was come spring, snowgoers chased the caribou so bad the meat was worn out." His hair was wild and sleep still crusted in his eyes. "I never cared for the taste of a run caribou."

Onion smell filled the air. I hoped Dawna hadn't said anything that included me, but, of course, she must have.

"A lot of people can't tell," Franklin said, "but I never cared for the taste."

I sat on the floorboards, sharpening my knife, my thoughts wandering back, wondering how respectful the local ravens were, whether they were already beak-deep in the back fat of our meat. Everything wanted fat. Fat got you through the winter. Every conversation that had to do with meat, fish, and birds came around to when were they the fattest. Janet would be uncomfortable if I brought her skinny meat.

Abe cut *itchaurat* into the heated pan. The sides of his hands were crusted with dried blood. His face was flushed and pleased with the morning. He dropped two tongues into a pot to boil. Everyone's favorite part was the fat tongue. "Strange thing, Franklin," he said, "often the machines made it easier for me. The caribou forgot what a man on snow-shoes was. Remember before snowgos? The man who could get caribou all winter was a leader." Abe and Franklin sounded as if they discussed the year before last. Age was squeezing their years, grinding them into wisdom. My dad was an elder! How had I been so gullible and faithless as to believe an elder must be brown-skinned? ". . . snowgos, not TV, killed the old culture." He forked liver and tenderloin slices in the pan. Searing meat smoked around his head. "Sure is special, Cutuk, having an onion."

WHEN THE MEAT was sledded in, we cut the lower legs off at the elbows and knees, and stacked caribou on a low pole cache with the skin left on to insulate and protect the meat for the winter. The remaining animals we skinned and stretched the hides and legging out on the ice to freeze flat and smooth, then ripped them up to finish drying slow in the winter air. Freeze-dried, the skin came out thick and white; inside the house, it dried quickly, brittle and brown. The back fat we rendered in one pot; the softer fat, the poopshoot and kidney and *itchaurat* in a second pot. Abe cut up the meat and allowed the ribs, briskets, and backbones for soup to freeze quickly. He dug a hole in the snow and lay a fresh caribou hide in the bottom and stacked the quarters and loins in. He covered it with another hide and soft snow to insulate. Later, hindquarters were half-frozen, then shaved thin and the strips hung inside on long poles to dry into *paniqtuq*. The dry *paniqtuq* was stuffed into cloth flour sacks and stored in the cache—except what we pounded into dust and chips, to mix with dried cranberries and blueberries and pour rendered back fat over to make bars of pemmican. Some of the hindquarters and the backstraps he cut into steaks, while all the leftover bones were saved for soup, roasts, or eating the marrow raw.

After the meat, we cut dead spruce and hauled sledloads. The first thirty-below day I split wood beside the cabin, aiming for natural seams as thin as paper. The maul smacked into the rounds. The cold wood shattered. My muscles felt clean and accurate, uncramping after so long in sight of judging eyes. Abe snowshoed up, a frozen trout was under his arm. "Come in. Eat *quaq*." His beard, eyebrows, and wolverine ruff were frosty. Plato paced behind him and stopped when Abe stopped. She wagged a quiet greeting. Abe contemplated the piles of split wood.

Inside, when it softened enough to cut, we dipped the frozen fermented fish in seal oil and ate it before it melted. Abe heated water for tea with bread and jam. *"Aarigaa taikuu,"* Abe said and leaned back from the food. Twilight darkened into the early evening, and I rummaged in my bag, got out the bottle of One-Five I'd been saving.

Franklin went for his mug on the shelf. We sipped by candlelight while coals glowed through cracks in the stove. Franklin fiddled with the shortwave, and Radio Moscow came faint and crisp into the cabin.

"They've been dumping nuclear waste in the Arctic Ocean," he interrupted the announcer. "Our trout sometimes winter across in Siberian rivers. Who knows what we're eating. Look what it did to my hair!"

I lay on the bearskin couch with my feet hanging over. Frostbite tingled and itched my face. The men argued now, about global spin pushing pollution to the poles—smog from the Ruhr Valley and the East Coast—about the *Exxon Valdez* oil spill, and the pipeline pumping a million barrels a day out the crotch of Alaska. They were informed about the news, the radio no longer something perfidious and vain.

"How come you quit smoking, Abe?"

He untied a cloth sack of dried apricots. "Didn't taste good anymore." He chewed an apricot, fighting the hard fruit. Grin wrinkles curved from his eyes into his beard. "Did you think, air pollution?"

"Maybe."

I was getting melancholy, pressed by the heavy miles of dark outside, acutely aware of the fact that the last thing that had slept with me was a sack of six onions. An idea cooked in my head. I'd fix up our old family sod igloo. I'd use the money from the mammoth tusk to buy Dawna something expensive and beautiful. The dream from there faded into little floating ice pans of reality. What would I buy?

"Think I'll head down to Takunak to get my gear and visit Iris. Take me four or five days to break trail, especially if I pick up that tusk. Maybe a couple to get back to the old house."

The dried fruit gritted in my teeth.

"Organic Hunza apricots," Abe said. "Complete with gravel and camel dung. Aren't they sweet?" Under the flame I saw sand stuck to the hard fruit, larvae casings, and a coarse black hair. I held the hair up.

"Pakistani." Abe grinned.

"Yeah? I hope the dung was the *camel's.*"

Franklin clicked to AM. Johnny Horton sang, "*When it's springtiiime in Alaska, it's forty beloooow . . .*" Abe toed his overpants in front of the door to keep the cold from smoking underneath. "*Alappaa.* You be careful on the river ice," he said. Shadows flickered and leaned and leered in the cabin. Outside stretched the Darkness. I reached over and rummaged in my parka pocket, slipped out the packet of pansy seeds and tacked them to a log, with a tack that held the postcard of the city of New York.

TWENTY-THREE

REX REMEMBERED THE TRAIL from Abe's cabin. An icy wind lifted snow. It matted the dogs' fur, whipped their tails and ears sideways, froze to their faces and buttholes. The trail behind blew away, no longer existed. Takunak didn't exist, nor airports and stewardesses and cordless telephones. Only the frozen river, the snow, and the gray tarp of twilight. The storm, and winter itself, were giants, powerful, beyond anything humans could control. Their strength made me well up glad inside. I sensed animals as I never had before. Ptarmigan puffed into the wind—and I already knew they were there. Something pulled my eyes across the river: deep in the willows the long face of a moose watched our passing.

I found the cutbank, and my tripod of willows marking the tusk, and lashed it onto the loaded sled. I smiled again at my luck. The dogs heaved, and looked back, irritated with the drag. I broke ice off my face, melted my eyelashes open, and jogged behind the runners. Miles later, I looked back suddenly. Low to the ground and hurrying, a wolverine was crossing our drifting trail. I yanked off my beaver hat to listen upwind. My ears froze, white and hard as frozen fish sperm sacks. A raven's wings panted above. I stared around but couldn't find him in the sky. Was I carrying a mammoth's spirit again? I felt wild, unafraid; my father was behind me, and home out of sight down the trail. In the lungs of the storm, I felt free, unconcerned with any tomorrows, any price in scars I might pay.

When it grew dark and the sky and snow fell into one gray frenzy, I tied the dogs to willows, chopped whitefish for them, and stomped and dug a snow cave. I crawled in out of the wind and leaned a block against the entrance. It was quiet out of the wind. Snow sifted around my head. I ate part of one of the raw frozen whitefish with chunks of bear fat and slept on my *qaatchiaq* with my ears hot and throbbing.

The next morning, the storm had worsened, and I crawled out, dug out the dogs, and we went on with the wind at our backs. By dusk the gusts fell away and a few fresh stars twinkled. Moonlight came from behind a bank of retreating clouds. We halted in the old dog yard, and the dogs rolled and pawed ice off their faces. Trees threw arms and fingers of faint shadow on the snow. The igloo was buried under a huge drift. Off the mouth of Jesus Creek, a black slit of open water ran, the feathery edge ice lying on a current of cold black good-bye. I fed the dogs, ate, and rolled up in a tarp but awoke and strangely couldn't go back to sleep. The moon was out now. I got up and snowshoed over to Abe's old cache. He'd left our childhood snowshoes, small and broken, a bent *tuuq* and a piece of a shovel, trap springs, rusted-through enamel roaster pans, a Hills Bros can with corroded .30-06 brass in the bottom. I felt around until I found a bent nail in the cache post and pried it out with the shovel.

The ice whomped and boomed, settling under the new snow. I circled far around the open water. The air froze inside my nose. Across, near the south shore, I chipped a hole and scooped the slush out barehanded. *Tiktaaliq* were my favorite fish, camouflaged, long, dark, and prehistoric. I remembered they carried all their fat in their livers, and the feel of sticky fingers after eating their white flaky meat, and that foxes couldn't resist traps baited with their intestines.

Janet would like a fish.

Back on the north shore, Figment whined in my memories and dragged his chain around in a circle, keeping the cold metal off his frozen testicles. The water in the hole sucked up and down. Maybe a wind was coming. I lowered my bent nail, knotted on a piece of twine, baited with a strip of whitefish, and lay on my back, jigging with a willow limb. The wind had ceased. The night was black glass, huge and silent. "Mother Earth," I murmured, "how about giving me a fish?"

Ice thickened my line, cold grew in my bones, and current throb came up from the depths. The snow stretched unfocused black-gray, the water hole a blacker hole. If I had my nights right, it was November 20. The earth had been rotating me along for nearly twenty-four years. *Tat's not much even,* Enuk said. I grinned in the dark, remembering his story about *iññuqun,* a white wolf, and losing his fry pan through the ice. The stick tugged and turned heavy. I pulled in string and a fish writhed up and out onto the powdery snow. It flapped and rolled, half again as long as my arm, thick around the body and head, mottled dark green.

"Thank you, *tiktaaliq!*"

I clubbed it. The huge mouth opened, the sandpaper teeth pointing back toward its esophagus—a professional hunter—ready to guide young fish to eternity. The nail had scarcely hooked, and I rebaited it and lowered my line.

An hour passed with no further bites. Enuk knew a legend concerning all the different bones in a *tiktaaliq* head, exactly the way he knew every slough, every lake, every pass through the mountains. I couldn't remember the story; it was all mixed up in my head with ailerons, Chief Joseph, and Dodge three-speed transmission tooth counts. The temperature fell. Off in the east, aurora whipped and wavered, green and pink smoky strokes. Rex barked, and then the dogs howled; faint in the distance a wolf answered the dogs. Closer, another wolf howled, and another. When all were silent again, I howled. With no people to laugh, I let longing pour as perfectly as possible into the night. Howls floated over the trees—the wolves were coming closer. Hair lifted on my skin. Janet's .30-30 was back in the scabbard on the sled. I was glad I hadn't gutted the fish—letting that tantalizing smell escape into the air. I grabbed the *tuuq.*

Would they eat me? Shit me out on the land? White shit, in windblown places where animals knew secret trails and smells and whispers from the earth. I grinned fleetingly; in a Hollywood version of this life, my Indian name could be *Whiteshit*.

I listened. Maybe the wolves had heard more in the sound I made than I knew how to hear in theirs. It made sense; every day they trusted their very lives to their senses. I stood and looked down at the fish on the snow, and then further, down into myself, where truth was all messed and mixed up with uncertainty, shame, and the progression of paper history pretending or lying or forgetting to tell what was obvious. These genetic miles between me, the *tiktaaliq*, and the wolves did not mean that I was all alone here. Maybe a billion years back in evolution my great grandma jellyfish had run off with a reptile. The things out in the dark were my cousins.

My hands gripped the *tuuq* and the jig stick. The wolves passed on the ice. Feet softly padding snow. A click of teeth. Dark figures pacing, pausing, spreading in the dark. They faded downstream and the river ice boomed and echoed, the aurora pulsed, and I jigged my line, begging another *tiktaaliq* down below in his world, me on top of the ice, looking up now, counting satellites roving among the old stars.

WOLF TRACKS CROSSED the snowdrift over the roof, running north. The tracks were inverted white molds standing on spires scoured out by ice grains riding the wind, the ball of each toe rounded up where the pad had once pressed down. Anyone might read them as months old. I stood on the drift, inhaling twenty-below air, gratified that a north blizzard had rearranged the snow and made the wolf sign look ancient in the week since I passed here.

I'd visited friends in Takunak, spent Thanksgiving with Iris and the Wolfgloves, and this morning left the dogs in front of Iris's house and returned here quickly with Treason on snowgos. It had been impossible to resist his offer to travel with company, to travel in an hour what had recently taken me two days.

I glanced north again, across frozen Outnorth Lake to tundra and mountains. It had been easier, in a way, up at Abe's; here, now, I had to wonder, had I grown up under this snow? Who would believe that? Not me.

Posts spiked out of the drifts: wind-grayed cache poles, falling fish racks, and Plato's dog stake with the chewed top, where she'd hung by her teeth like a rabid animal on days when I made her stay home. Memories licked my face. My past felt fragile. The land might love me, but not more than one brown bear, one mosquito, one flake of snow. I could starve, get swatted, or melt.

Down in the hole Treason and I had dug were the remains of the glass window in our door—Iris's present to Abe and me—shot out. I knifed a lead pellet out of the weathered ridgepole. Number 2 shot.

Treason leaned on his shovel. He had taken off his beaver hat and Chicago Bulls jacket; his hair and sweatshirt were frosty. We were chest-deep in the hole, peering at the top of the door and the gnawed caribou-skin weather stripping. "Kids," he said. "Now'days they shoot anything." Treason wasn't as big as my memory. He talked about hunting, what he'd shot, what he hoped to shoot. He was twenty-nine and, like many village men under fifty, still partied when there was a jug, didn't concern himself with his various progeny, treated jail time as inevitable. Probably he knew who the vandals were. Secrets and gossip always leaked out.

The green nylon rope tying our door shut was knotted in four places, the fibers splintery with age. Somebody had taken the time to tie the door. I stabbed the shovel through the rotted rope, and the door racked but didn't want to open. Too much snow inside. "Things sure got old," Treason said. His cheeks had the fresh black frost scabs of a hunter, his teeth white in his handsome face. Somebody had busted his bottom lip, left him a fingernail-moon souvenir. I looked at my skin, dry in the moisture-robbed air, my hands an embarrassing red. My old bolt-action rifle ten yards away, hanging in a tree. Treason shrugged impassively. "Could be you better start over."

"I wish!" I crawled down and kicked my legs through the window. The snow squeaked and sawed under me. I dropped inside onto the floorboards. The igloo was dark and hushed, and a rank smell made me peer nervously into the dark.

"Hand me your lighter, Treas." His hand reached in out of the cold sunlight. The lighter was pink plastic, not his old stainless steel Zippo. How many lighters had he had and lost since I left? Everything went away so quickly now. How many snowgos? Guns? Women? *Dawna?* Janet had said Dawna went to church these days and worked at Prudhoe Bay. Maybe she would ask my religion. My mind joked, *My ten commandments start with be a nice person and end with don't work for an oil company.* I spun the flint, traveling back to Newt's cabin, wishing to start over, just holding her hand.

The igloo was black and eerie, the air musty with a familiar smell I couldn't place. The ceiling poles bowed from the weight of winter drifts; they hung with frost, a thousand ice moths. Something rustled. The air inside was forty degrees warmer than outside, just below freezing, and a chill brushed my neck.

"Watch for *iññuqun,*" Treason teased, though a hint in his tone was serious. He believed in them. Falling frost slivered light. Fingernails scraped on a board. Teeth rattled, something shivering. It moaned. I cupped the flame. On Iris's bed an eye glinted.

Treason jammed his AK-47 assault rifle along my shoulder. "Cover your ears. *Qilamik!*"

The flame went out, and I clicked the lighter, but it wouldn't catch. I warmed it in my fist. The flame flared and went out. "Don't shoot. I think—"

Boom. Boom. Orange blasts buffeted my face. Hot cartridges seared my neck. In shattered darkness the winter's diamond coat tinkled down, and I heard that second-oldest sound on earth, the slow sigh of death.

"TASTES BETTER IN SUMMER." Treason sucked broth off a shoulder blade and lay it on the table. The table rocked, three-legged now.

Around the room, posts were gnawed, the arms of chairs, and the floorboards under the slop bucket where as little kids we'd missed the bucket occasionally and piss had splashed on the floor. Porcupine loved salt, as did rabbits; we always pissed in the trail near our rabbit snares, for bait.

I had swept the ceiling, shoveled out the door, and checked that the roof moss wasn't touching the stovepipe, then got a fire roaring while Treason skinned and gutted the porcupine. Light and cold poured in the window holes. In the back, under our beds, colored construction paper from the all-of-ours box was plastered under moldy mounds of turds. A kerosene storm lantern hung from the ridgepole. A jug of kerosene sat dusty in the corner, beside a mason jar of rancid caribou fat. I pictured Iris slicing *itchaurat* and back fat, rendering it, and then whipping in berries and sugar and flaked fish to make *akutuq*.

Treason glanced around. "Guys mostly steal gas, booze, guns. Even CDs. Anything to have or sell. Sure *aaqqaa* in here, huh?"

I poked in the blackened coffee can and knifed a piece of back out of the soup. The broth smelled sharp and pitchy. I shook salt on the tender meat. Abe had left salt and sketches and stiff coils of homemade *babiche* hanging on nails, tobacco tins of bent spikes, charcoal stubs, matches. On the warped boards above the kitchen counter he had left pepper, a Ziploc of dried chives, a half inch of Worcestershire in a brown bottle. The vanilla bottle lay on the floor, empty, the cap flung away by thirsty intruders. Abe—trusting and curious—liked to leave chunks of memories hanging behind. He often said that was the reason some Eskimos left trash on the country—for the memories, and not to feel lonesome. You couldn't understand, he said, until you had been lost for days on the country *without* seeing a single sign of a human; then trash could look pretty darn good.

"Melt gave a baby porcupine to Jerry when he was a kid," I commented.

"Melt? He give somebody something?"

We chuckled, not looking up from chewing.

"That porcupine ate my mom's guitar. Now I guess we're eating its great-grandson." Something about it was too funny for us, and we dropped the bones and laughed until our foreheads touched the table. We couldn't look at each other without choking and had to sit shielding our faces from each other.

The stove crackled, heat spread slowly, and grainy snow on the floor didn't melt. We had thrown the porcupine hide into the fire, to burn the quills, to save foxes from slow deaths.

"Guitar soup. And here I sure was thought bear." Treason glanced around. Every movement he made was precise. He wore a sweatshirt and sweatpants under his black nylon ski pants. He leaned back and pulled a toothpick out of his pocket. "I'd camp in wall tent." He grinned. "For this winter. If you stay here, you better not go town. Everybody gonna laugh how you smell. Them girls wear perfumes, Cutuk. Takunak is nothing but new everything now'days."

"Like in that commercial—that woman says you better smell good or 'it's a turn-off'? You been to Anchorage, right?"

"Oh yeah. Lotta times. Three times. Always can't do nothing, only follow the road. Real nice to drink beer, though." He dipped his fingers into the can and pulled out the heart. He bit it in half. "Want some?" Warm soupy air came across the table. I took the heart from his fingers. The meat was black and pasty.

He peered out at the river. Out by the shovel, a pair of gray jays pecked feverish mouthfuls off the porcupine gut pile. Treason slid a .22 Magnum out of his jacket and rested it on the door frame and fired. The bird slumped out of sight behind a block of snow; its mate flew off. Treason breathed deep. Downy gray wisps of feather floated on the air. "Nice out. How much gas in your snowgo? Let's go home through tundra. Maybe find wolf tracks."

OFF JESUS CREEK, the open water had frozen. We snowgoed up the drifted bank below the mouth. My Arctic Cat still ran; Janet hadn't let anyone touch it. It steered loose and crooked—since the accident, and worse after Stevie's one adventure with it, drunk driving the weekend

Janet flew to Crotch Spit for a hospital checkup. "That same time Treason wash how many wolf and foxes in my Maytag." Janet had laughed. "Anyways, let'um, you're all my boys."

I glanced over the willows and up the creek. How many water holes had Jerry and Iris and I rechipped to avoid the brown water eddying up from this creek mouth? How many moose had we watched in these willows? How many foxes faded into these thickets? Iris had almost drowned here. And now Ted Brown, apparently, had found a trace of gold dust at the mouth, and would be back. I felt a rush of trespass and concern, knowing he would be back, with friends and big engines.

The snow stretched away, huge and rolling, the scoured drifts hard white waves. Mountains leaned against the back of the sky. Frostbite twinged my nose, cheeks, and forehead, and water spread and froze along my eyelids. Wolves reigned over whole valleys in those mountains, the way it was supposed to be. Take away metal, I thought, and humans were hardly different from animals, regardless of all the obsession over smells and body hair; substitute back fat and cached bones for 401(k) accounts, fleet-footed prey for fast food. Wolves were smart. They cared about their kids. Sometimes they ran out of places to run, made mistakes, and died.

And Enuk, what mistakes had he made? Did he know something mysterious and powerful from the last vestiges of the shaman days? The shamans—people in 1969 believed—had walked on the moon habitually, while the white men maybe only made up photographs of it. Had Enuk found a trail that science, the church, and the rest of us couldn't see?

AFTER HALF AN HOUR Treason stopped his Polaris. I stopped beside him. He melted his face and was silent for a minute the way you were supposed to be. He carefully opened a pack of cigarettes and let the cellophane blow out of his hand on the cold breeze. It crankled once, unfolding on the snow. He put a cigarette in his lips and flicked his lighter. "Couple springs back I lose black wolf in them mountains. Want to check it out?"

I stepped aside to piss, a smoking string in the miles of rolling snow. I stepped close enough to bend and scoop up the plastic. It was a distressingly white thing to do, and I didn't want to interfere with Treason's happiness. I wanted him to carry prestige home to the village, to Janet and the elders, but today I didn't want to see Marlboro wrappers on this snow.

"Fellas been going to work at Red Dog," he commented.

"Red Dog Mine?"

"Yeah, like Prudhoe, bywhere Dawna works, except it's lead mine. Biggest in the world."

"Lead? Doesn't that make your brain shrink?"

"Could be. Lotta fellas around here that won't hurt nothing." Treason exhaled and scanned the tundra. "Woody came home for R and R with brand-new snowgo. He's got a radio scanner. He heard a mail plane pilot talking about eight wolves downriver from town. He jumped on his Indy six-fifty, went and got 'em all like nothing."

I glanced at my black snowgo. The old bionic seat. "Does anyone ever snowgo north to Barrow?"

"Never, that I heard about anyways. Too far to carry gas. Enuk an'em walked there in old days, *guuq*. You should charter airplane if you gonna go Prudhoe to find Dawna. Could be five hundred miles, open country. She'll might be gone if you get there."

"Guess I need good money."

"You just now learn?" He grinned. "Your ivory, that'll buy you plane fare, round-trip to Disney Land even." His wrist flicked, rope-starting his machine.

He led me north, to the Dog Die Mountains, up into steep foothills timbered with memories, along a rocky cliff protecting a ravine where I'd found the wolf den. Unhappily, I parked and peered over. It was getting dark, the short day falling into the Darkness. The birch tree that had devoured a green rope was down there somewhere. Everything looked different—the ice level was lower, the big winter wind drifts hadn't matured yet, the creek was still open in places, flowing, black against the gray snow. I hurried back to my machine and followed his trail down onto the tundra. Treason circled and roared into a patch of spruce. He drove as if the skis were his flesh. His eyes took in a wolverine's tracks, probed timber thickets, watched a raven's hooded glances. He braked, touched the wolverine footprints, and raced away, faster than ever, his machine growling, chewing through brush. He was scared of nothing, not trees or drop offs or sinkholes in the ice. I'd forgotten—never realized how different it was Outside—here death was an accepted part of life, and fretting over the future as pointless as a dictionary.

His Romanian AK-47 hung loose across his chest. His eyes had a cheetah's stare, the fearsome focus of a predator. I struggled to keep up, suddenly knowing he *was* a predator, and an athlete, too. The Michael Jordan of the sport of hunting wolves and wolverine, moving in sync with ten thousand years of honed Eskimo blood and a hundred years of white technology.

I gave up following, and swung up the canyon. I fought the machine through new loose drifts. The snowgo tilted into the creek. I gunned across shallow open water, weaving back and forth across shelf ice. The ice buckled, a swift current tilted pans and they disappeared under the fast ice. Finally, I braked on the snow-covered rocks. The canyon walls blocked out the sky. A few yards away stood the little birch tree, and I walked in a circle, my hands shaking, the accident with Iris pounding in my chest. I felt sick, and questioned if I could make it back to the open tundra without sinking. In the distance came four shots, and I wished I could scream across the tundra like Treason and kill. If only it were that easy.

The green rope was gone. One of the forked limbs of the birch had snapped in a wind, and it lay partially buried. A huge black scar marked where someone had gouged out a wedge. Quickly I peeled back bark, tree scab, and pith. There was a narrow diamond-shaped scar in the crotch of the tree, a shape reminiscent of a dog-harness toggle. *Walking Charley?*

After a short while, I realized Treason might be searching for me. I roared out of the canyon, made it to the tundra, and circled the top of a small rise. His headlight appeared, flicking up and down, bounding closer. His beaver hat was off. His hair was frozen, his ears and nose frozen. His windshield was in shards. A spruce pole was lashed between his skis, holding them aligned. A cigarette hung in his lips and wind had burned perforations in the paper until it looked like a miniature machine gun barrel. I thought about the Marlboro Man; what a mannequin he was compared to an Eskimo hunter. Treason smiled big.

The wolverine was black and looked small tied behind the vinyl seat, frozen bloodcicles dangling from her mouth. We admired the thick fur and checked its length in our fists and combed the white circle above the rump. Rear claws to rear claws, a wolverine was one woman's ruff; front claws to front claws, one man's ruff; the rest parka trim. Treason was pleased. I didn't say anything about the rain falling inside me. He would worry; he'd think I'd caught Animal-Loverness in the city. A traitorous thing.

Barehanded he cleaned snow out of his cowling.

I toed the knotted-on tree.

"Busted my one-side steering. I lost him while I patched it. That tree throw lotta snow." He grinned, ignoring a grease smear frosting his knuckles. "Sure iced up my carbs. I had to melt 'em with thermos. Coffee never finish, though, if you want a shot?"

WE ANGLED AWAY from the mountains, west and circling beyond Takunak. The tundra beckoned, a thousand square miles of welcome. Shadows and snow stretched in shades of blue and gray and the Kuguruk River was an unshaven squiggle down in the flat tundra. We plowed across buried tributaries, awakening moose in the willows. They lumbered in the deep snow, tall walls of brown shoulders and silver scar-streaked flanks from the hungry wolf winter.

We angled across the fresh tracks of two snowgos. Treason grinned back and mouthed, "*Naluaġmiu* tracks!" I peered at the snowmobile trail. How could he tell? How could Treason so instantaneously read tracks that I should know how to read but hadn't a clue?

Across the river from Takunak, on the high tundra ridge running south toward Uktu, Treason sped up and roared at a yellow stake sticking up out of the snow. He grinned back. The fiberglass stake snapped in front of his machine—and whipped back upright. We stopped. My gas tank read E. In the headlight, I walked to the stake. GOVERNMENT EASEMENT. DO NOT LEAVE TRAIL. Yellow reflective stakes traversed the tundra toward Uktu, into the dim distance, a line so straight and forever.

I shut off my engine. Treason killed his and walked over, bundled in his beaver hat, icy and face badly frosted again from the flung snow and lack of a windshield. The light was nearly gone. "Government an'em paid us good. Twenty-five bucks an hour. Twenty-four something anyways. Real good job, putting them things. Better than *Exxon Valdez* even. What's *easement* mean?" He spat and melted his checks.

Iris's bright eyes flashed into my mind. "It's short for 'easier to bring pavement.'"

"Huh."

"This strip of land already belongs to somebody's road. They'll pay you to build it."

"Ha, they think me and you gonna could stay on that skinny line?"

Suddenly I understood how he'd so effortlessly read the snowgo trail we'd passed—the second driver followed *exactly* in the tracks of the first—the drivers concerned, out of their element, scared of the land.

Around our feet lay the beautiful land, enchanted in the twilight's weakening glow, cold, silent, unprepared. Suddenly the past was over. It would never come back to protect us. We'd been pretending as well any actors. The chasm between legends around the fire and surround-sound TV, snowshoed dog trails and Yamaha V-Max snowmobiles was too overwhelming, and no hunting, no tears, no federal dollars could take us back across. I felt an avalanche of grief, and momentarily thought I'd lost Abe, and Janet, too.

I pulled the rope starter, squeezed the throttle. My gas was gone. I couldn't make it home. I turned toward Takunak and hit the yellow stakes as fast as my machine would go. Progress against progress. Whatever progress really was. Maybe it was only the wind of going fast. The good frostbite seared my face. Beside me raced Treason, a best friend. Inside I burped porcupine. Sixty miles an hour. Sixty-five. Seventy. Numbers.

Leftover lavender from the horizon behind faintly lighted the land. In front the closest thing to my hometown squatted, beside gleaming white satellite dishes, in Pampers, on Pepsi, drunk, stoned, desperately addicted to dollars. I whacked another yellow stake. And another. One shattered and missed my eyes. And another. The rest lurched upright, perfectly upright, whipping like laughter.

TWENTY-FOUR

JANET'S DOORKNOB WAS GONE and a sock was stuffed in the hole. TV talk drifted out. I kicked my feet on the metal steps and went in; she would complain if I knocked.

"Cutuk!" She heaved herself off the linoleum and hugged me in her heavy arms. Her warm cheek pressed against my face. The lights and glare were stunning after miles of cold trail. Over her shoulder, a loud Mountain Dew commercial mesmerized me, flashing sexy bodies and music, water-skiing behind a horse. *Aana* Tessie Washington and *Aana* Mable Feathers sat on the floor beside the couch, sewing calfskin *mukluks*. Their faces were deeply wrinkled, sunken and beaming. The old women were giggly and tense, in the middle of a MacGyver episode.

Janet held my cheeks with her warm palms. "I'll make hot water!" Tessie and Mable smiled, no teeth. Stevie's little daughter, Daisy, stared wide-eyed from a high chair.

Treason stomped his boots and came in carrying the wolverine. The old ladies' eyes lighted and they heaved and tilted to their feet. They gathered around, clutching at the long hair and conversing in Iñupiaq. He laid the animal on cardboard behind the stove. "You should learn to hunt," they told me sympathetically. I didn't say anything. The windows were black—except the loud TV, a bright aperture to America. MacGyver reappeared with his porcupine hairdo. The ladies dropped the wolverine paws and scurried back to their places. MacGyver was under stress, in a hurry, wiring together a nuclear device or some such nonsense out of a washing machine and a Spam can key. I focused on my fix-it competition, MacGyver, trying to impress us with his ingenuity. Let him go a couple decades without a washing machine, he'd be walking around holding *that* up to the camera.

Janet handed us coffee. When the show ended, she lit a burner and heated soup. "I guess Melt's somewhere," she commented to herself. She put bowls on the table. "Go eat." A small skinny girl sat on the couch, gripping a Barbie doll by the hair. "Here's my brand-new girl, Whitney-Houston." Janet kissed her. The little girl's eyes were black stones. "Her mom die in Crotch Spit. Her brother been bumped her to death with Honda. Feeling high. *Arii.* So lucky they find this one okay." The little girl didn't shudder, cry, or even blink.

The CB squawked. "Meeting at Tribal Building. Anybody copy?"

The CB speaker garbled as villagers transmitted over each other, the volume so loud it made my teeth ache—a mike clicked on and off, a bored kid, sabotaging the village electronic connective tissue. "Don't play with CB!" an elder voice shouted. The mike-clicking intensified. "Fuck you," a voice croaked.

Treason moved around Janet's kitchen looking for something to crack a caribou *patiq* bone he'd pulled out of the soup pot. He whacked the bone behind my chair leg and put it across my bowl and cracked another. Janet stuffed marrow into Daisy's mouth. "*Aarigaa, patiq, Bun.* I wonder what kinda meeting? You kids better go explain for elders."

I sat staring dumbly at the fast images on the TV, replaying the day's events while knifing at the bone on my plate, swallowing meat that now could have been pieces of warm luggage. Around me, Janet was already clearing dishes, scraping bones and meat scraps into a dogpot, and then Treason stepped in from smoking, wrapped in cold-air fog. He stomped his boots. "Com'on Cutuk. Go check that native meeting? Door prizes," he grinned, "and you'll get to see *Taata* Woodrow's false teeth, before he goes out on the country and needs one for a screwdriver."

TREASON WAS LUCKY, though it was easy to discount the fact that if he grew his hair out it would be curly—not a good thing—and that his real mom was dead and his dad a nameless sperm donor; he won five boxes of ammo. *Aana* Hanna Skuq won a six-pack of pop, and her granddaughter, Elvisetta, in Pampers, won the pre-meeting grand prize, a drum of stove oil. Hanna took the fuel credit slip and gave Elvisetta a Coke. They were both happy, smiling, missing teeth.

The color TV, the important prize, was saved for after the meeting. The elders sat on folding chairs without taking off their parkas. The men had their mouths open, deaf from years of snowgoing and shooting. They hunched, elbowing their wives for information. Newt Clemens and Tommy Feathers and Woodrow Washington and others greeted me and asked after Abe. A good portion of the town and half of Uktu were at the gym, immersed in the Jimmy Skuq Memorial Basketball Tournament, in honor of Jimmy crashing on a snowgo, drunk. Jimmy, who one night had let half the dogs in town loose and in the ensuing dogfights broke into the Native Cache. Jimmy, who stole Janet's chain saw and ruined it trying to saw open the city office safe . . .

The native corporation speaker droned about projected finances. The corporation developed native land and sent out yearly dividends to Eskimos. It was big business now, being Iñupiat. The corporation had even invented a politically correct term for me: a "non-shareholder."

Charley Casket shrugged in the door. He spotted my non-shareholder hair and came over to sit beyond Treason. He reached across and shook my hand limply. His hand passed over an artifact, a strip of antler sled runner. Swarms of kids chased back and forth. "You kids go play-out,"

Hanna shouted. They ignored her. Another speaker took the place of the first. He was named Joe Smith. He wore glasses, a new haircut, tight jeans, and a gold watch with nuggets lumpy on the band. His hands were large and soft. "Funny-looking Eskimo," Hanna whispered too loud.

"I'm from the nonprofit arm of the corporation, and I'm here to inform you of our Cultural Edification Project. The project, or CEP, has been proposed through the regional elders, and a grant for one million dollars has already been procured."

I glanced at the antler, a porous gray artifact. Over the years, Abe had unearthed some strips of antler sled runner; surely, he'd left them behind on a window ledge or a shelf. They hadn't been there today. The room still rustled—overhead fluorescent lights twitched and twirled, throbbing pearl shadows. The elders' faces held the same expressions they had held at the meeting when strange rangers told them the National Park Service suddenly owned millions of acres of the best hunting land, in every direction. When anthropologists, archaeologists, and con men with computer credentials had come and held meetings and gone. The elders' expressions, meeting after meeting, for decades: "What in ta hell they're talking?" and "What in ta hell they're taking?"

A snowgo roared up outside. The door kicked open. Condensation and frozen snowgo exhaust rolled under the chairs. Elvis Jr. walked in sheepishly, thawing his face. Lumpy's 9 mm pistol slid out of his jacket pocket and thunked on the floor. He stared at it for a second, bent and picked it up. "... all recorded forms of Iñupiaq knowledge will be compiled on CD. This is in terms of libraries and universities—and, of course, what you the people know. We will then utilize informational assets to organize a strategy for teaching it." Lumpy didn't hurry putting the pistol in his pocket, glancing it over for a minute, pointing it randomly around the room. The native sitting behind Joe stood and translated for the elders. The elders listened, baffled, impatient to go home or back to the ball tournament.

I peered at the antler. Six hours had passed since Treason and I had left the igloo. Mice would be scurrying around in the last of the warmth seeping from the stove, nibbling any dropped morsels, huffing the spent cartridges. Charley leaned forward. "You find mastodon tusk?"

I raised my eyebrows, handed him the antler. "By accident. I was looking for a log to tie my dogs."

Charley's mouth formed a quick smile. Nothing else moved. "In good shape? How big?"

"I never weigh it. Eighty-ninety pounds? It's in okay condition. Just the tusk, no mammoth meat on it. I didn't find the tongue or anything." Treason and Lumpy snickered. I grinned and decided to prod Charley. "Today I checked on an old birch tree I found before. Ways up Jesus Creek. Back in the mountains. Something had been cutting it."

Charley's expression didn't waver. "I been show Ted Brown the country. He ordered airboat, same like white guys always hunt crocodile in TV. Use lot'a gas and go anyplace. He's good friend a' mine. Always give me jug."

Dismay tugged at my mouth.

On the other side, Lumpy nudged me. A bewildered grin flashed across his face. "What the fuck this fella saying, anyways?"

"They're gonna have classes, teach how to be Eskimo, just learn on your computer. Who knows, the new principal might get a better grade than you."

Lumpy's face stiffened. His face had grooves it never had when we were kids—frostbite and Bacardi wrinkles. His lip slumped in where his rotted teeth clung. He looked haggard, confused, and sick—exactly how I felt. Up in front, a *naluaġmiu* scraped his chair back over the gouges in the Tribal Building floor and stood. Everyone stopped whispering. Everyone knew what those gouges were. They were cuts left by quiet men working with Skilsaws cutting too deep, building caskets, after too many four-wheeler accidents and drownings, dying elders and suicides, in a town of 210.

"Good evening," he said. "First, I have to say how *glad* I am to be in your wonderful serene little village. I am also grateful to be able to meet so many of you and glimpse you living your traditional lives. I am here with Mi-tick," he nodded at Joe, "to make you aware of the sixty-four *billion dollars* available in grants to communities like yours."

The crowd laughed.

Treason muttered. "Com'on, let's go spark a bowl." He and Lumpy and Elvis rose and headed outside; each had a hand in his pocket.

The man glanced around quizzically, shuffled papers, and retreated into a forest of overgrown words and Accountant English. The meeting trailed into whispers and tittering. Back on the metal chairs, we chuckled at the man's pronunciation of Joe Smith's Eskimo name. We heard "my dick." We laughed, not because we were mean, but because laughing was traditional, it was something we were good at, and tonight we still remembered how.

"WHO WON THE TV?" Janet asked.

Lumpy opened her refrigerator. He squinted at the pots and containers. "How you know what the fuck anything is in here?"

Janet dropped the marten skin she was tanning. "What you want, son? That fish—take it off the way. Wait! I bought peef. I'll make soup." She put a pan of water on to boil, sharpened her *ulu,* and expertly chopped the sirloin into cubes and dropped them into the water. Daisy crawled into my lap. Whitney-Houston pressed beside me on the couch, encircling the Barbie in her arm. I felt the little girl shaking. I pulled twine out of my pocket, tied the ends, and made a caribou. *"Tuttu."* I pointed at my string. "That's *tuttu.*"

Daisy's big brown eyes glanced up under my jaw. "Care boo?" She raised a finger, red polish on her tiny nail, and made a gun bang and hit the string. I flopped the loops on my knee. "Boom. You shot him, now you have to skin him and take care of the meat."

"Again." She giggled. "Shoot it again."

"Mom!" Lumpy shouted. "My Kmart COD come?"

Janet bent over the stove, tasting the soup. She pointed. *"Takanna!* By the bed." Lumpy ducked into Janet and Melt's heaped bedroom and came out with a box. "So, how's them dogs I give you, Cutuk? How about Mike?"

Janet glanced up. "Lumpy never tell you? That dog's funny. When it was puppy kids put it forty seconds in microwave."

Lumpy opened the door, wadded his glove onto his bent fingers, grabbed his box, and went out.

Janet sighed. "I guess he won't eat." She took an Eskimo Pie out of the freezer, cut it with her *ulu,* and gave half to Whitney-Houston and half to Daisy. She clicked the TV off and sat down. *"Arii."*

The CB made gasping sounds. "Help me!" a young girl screamed. "Help me, somebody!" Her voice turned wild, a primal scream.

"That's Sara Skuq!" Janet leaned forward. "She was go Anchorage to bleach her teeth for school pictures."

"Sara!" Her mom shouted from a CB, somewhere, high, her voice hoarse. "Sara? You *shudup!"* The CB went silent.

"The meeting was about teaching Eskimo," I said quietly.

"You kids need to speak Iñupiaq. Better than last meeting, that white lady tape-recording women's traditional work." Janet giggled. "I told her, 'Women work, too much.'"

"Not words only. Eskimo everything."

A fly buzzed in the kitchen, wings frozen in the window ice. Outside, the temperature was falling. Daisy was still on my lap; chocolate and ice cream ran down her arms in big muddy drops. I felt more exhausted than I could remember; Abe and Anchorage hugely distant; the land somewhere not real. I got a rag and wiped Daisy's hands, then went and melted the fly loose. *Take advantage, mister fly, of your abilities to hibernate, and fly.*

I yawned. "I'm tired. I'm going up to Iris's."

"Cutuk." Janet peered seriously. "That pox. Lumpy get Aqua Net. Those boys been drink it. Melt even always drink that kind. You need to let them quit."

AN EAST BREEZE BLEW thirty-below air down the Kuguruk Valley. The Darkness was boundless, the bottom rim of outer space. Two houses behind *Aana* Mable's stood Lumpy and Stevie's house. Three Polaris snowgos and an Arctic Cat were parked on the snow, the modern machines sleek and predatory. Figures rushed into the cold-fogged *qanisaq*. Inside, the room was gutted, the faces blue in the TV wash. A battered television sat on a fifty-five-gallon drum, snowmobile shocks and scored pistons and a moose hoof piled beside it. Rifles and a shotgun leaned in a corner. A chain saw lay on the kitchen linoleum. The air smelled like cornstarch and gassy gloves, sour meat and cigarette residue.

Men sat on buckets, stumps, and a couch. Dollie leaned against a white guy, John, who hunched like a seagull trying to fit in with ravens on a gut pile. John was one of the marijuana salesmen the young girls occasionally brought home from Anchorage. He had thin red hair and big splotchy arms. His voice was nasal. "Yeah, man, I had this Ninja nine hundred." Motorcycles buzzed on the TV. Dollie smiled her dimpled smile. She had gained weight and her mouth had a stretched look, like she'd flossed or screamed a lot.

Stevie knelt, shaking a gallon jug. "Yellow-Hair! The six-dog Iditarod champion!"

"Four-and-a-quarter-dog," I said wryly. I sat on a bucket.

"Man, my Ninja was bad, man," John said. "I—"

Stevie's eyes narrowed. He pressed his remote. The motorcyles vanished and a documentary flicked on: Alaska natives hunting moose, the narrator whispering of respect given for every part of the animal, otherwise bad luck might befall the hunter. Stevie spat in a piston and grinned. "Fuckin' Lumpy better take care of his *quaq* moose outside." He pressed the remote again and blondes in bathing suits came on, twirling and humping around steel poles. Stevie thrust out the plastic jug. "Here you go, Grizzly Adams Junior. Maybe you're the last Aqua Net virgin."

A group of girls rushed in. "Stevie!" They tugged his sleeve. "Melt's coming this way! He *alapit*. Stumbling all over the place."

"Let'um, that guy can't know how to drink."

Big money changed hands. A group rushed out. Snowgos roared. I recognized a cough—Tommy Feathers sat on a gas can, passing a stained ivory pipe, weed smoke curling out of the bowl. Tommy was in his late fifties now, maybe sixty. Most of his experience was with alcohol, but he took advantage of his elder status at Search & Rescue meetings and funerals in church. He exhaled, slit eyes watching my hand on the jug.

"Don't have to," Treason mumbled.

I was tired. If only I could settle in and be part of the crowd. Haltingly, I passed the jug—and felt surprise. My hands had *never* passed a chance to fit in, never stepped willingly to the edge of the herd. The decision had come from somewhere in my head where I was unfamiliar with the territory. It was lonely here on the edge of the party, but the seconds ticking by had exotic clarity that I felt I might like, and I nodded thanks to Treason. He shrugged. "Going hunting tomorrow," he murmured. "Maybe look for wolves. Wanna *malik?*"

"Getting cold for snowgo, isn't it?"

"Let'um. I jus' wanna hunt. Nothing else."

The blond girls twirled and rocked their crotches. Lumpy slumped in the door. "Any hunter success?" Stevie teased. His lips glowed metal blue in the TV light. Lumpy's hand came out of his jacket holding his semiautomatic pistol, and he swung it, making a point of pointing it at John.

"Not that kinda hunter success," Stevie growled.

Lumpy reached in his other pocket and pulled out a wad of cash and two-party checks.

"'Kay then! Let's go Las Vegas, Cut," Stevie said. "Drink real beers like you're accustomed to." He pushed up his glasses. The earpiece was tied with dental floss. "I been to Point Hope, Point Lay, Point Barrow. What's the *point?*" He drank long on the jug. "Point Lay, man, I was there when they shoot sixty belugas. *Muktuk* on the ground even. Point Barrow Search an' Rescue got helicopter. Bring fellas home with polar bear and their snowgos just hanging."

I gripped Stevie's wrists. "Why don't you not drink any more of that crap," I whispered. "Janet's worried about you. Shuck, I'm worried about you."

He bowed his forehead against mine. "Cut, you shoulda stayed. Alcohol is my best friend now. I just love my daughter. I don't want Daisy to see me like this. My other kids, they already seen me party, how many times. I mean . . . I love you. You're my brother. I'm glad you went, Cut. You're lucky."

I pictured the softness of Daisy's little golden face. I braced myself against the wall—a partition had been ripped out there and dried blood was smudged; a smashed nose had left an angled trail to the floor.

"Stevie, we'll go, uh . . . hunting. Heck, I don't know what we'll do. Don't call me lucky. I don't know anything."

"That cocksucker Eskimo *naluaġmiu.*" Lumpy spat in a pop can. For an instant, I tensed, swiveling, thinking he was reading my thoughts, talking about me.

"You better not be talking about me."

"Fuckin' Crotch Spit people take alla government money that's for us. They sit around office play with computer and make sixty thousand. No school principal is more Eskimo than me. We know how to take care of the land. Not like white peoples. I can hunt anything, anytime."

The jug came around. The pipe came around. The strippers danced. No one spoke. I glanced at Stevie, nodded around the room, picked up my parka and beaver hat, and stepped out, into the *qanisaq,* and out to the snow. I stood, breathing out secondhand frustration and Marlboro smoke, breathing in clear cold air, staring at the boundless night sky. If Melt staggered up now . . . geez, I might punch him in the head, an early Christmas present for Dawna.

But only the aurora was out, stretching green gauze across the Milky Way. Green fire burned low in the east, behind the mountains, highlighting the peaks in eerie radiance. Under chain-girdled spruce, Lumpy's two remaining dogs whined. They were black shadows, their backs narrow and humped from starvation. The biggest one squatted, then turned in a stiff circle and swallowed its own steaming shit. A snowgo screamed at the other end of town, skis scraping the porcelain snow. I didn't feel like going back inside. I headed toward Iris's cabin. The east breeze streamed my breath away.

IRIS PUT ON her shoepacks and overpants and parka, and came out to help feed dogs. Light came out the windows of the cabin. We chopped caribou, frozen hard as soapstone. My team, and her other five dogs, barked and shrieked to be fed. Each time the axe struck, chips of meat scattered, and the dogs whined and wagged and kept vigilant track of the morsels closest to them. Iris swept meat dust, snow, and chips and chunks to each dog. When the last dog was fed, the cacophony ceased. They swallowed fist-sized pieces and made loud gnawing sounds, trying to crack the larger chunks.

"Oh, I like feeding dogs!" Iris said. She hoisted up the front half of the caribou and heaved it off the trail. I grinned. Iris was still strong. "Remember Ponoc, how he used to dunk over his eyes to gulp off the bottom of the dog pot?"

"Ponoc . . . yeah. This one's Mike. Turns out kids put him in the microwave. I can't fatten him up. He shivers and shivers and never pulls. I'm going to have to shoot him."

Overhead the aurora built and built, the sky twiching cold green embers. We stood with our heads as far back as they would go.

"God!" she said. "This is amazing. I bet they can see them in Chicago. Wouldn't that be funny if Mom's looking at them, thinking of us?"

Red rays began stretching down from the North Star; pink and green bands ran from east to west. Overhead a red gel grew, obliterating the stars.

"Do you believe in God?"

Two Can't-Grows bounced up in the dark, frosty and yipping and shivering. They went straight to the back fat under the carcass and gnawed at it. Iris knelt to pet the little dogs. "Oh yes!" Her teasing laughter rang. "Just look everywhere! God is in those who are what they eat."

I leaned against the sled, comforted to know I could speak feeble words and have Iris understand, and I told her about the yellow stakes, the meeting, Lumpy's pistol, his other dogs, and the drinking.

She straightened her neck, sheathed the axe. "Miss Hawcly's not allowed to go to Lumpy Wolfglove's den of iniquity. He is a terrible influence on my students. I don't even know how many junior high girls have gotten pregnant over in that house."

Inside, Iris opened the oven and set a lynx roast and baked potatoes on the table. She was pale and her eyes deep startling blue. Her arms were lithe and muscular. "It got dark and so late, I was wondering when you'd get here. I thought something had happened upriver." She had set the plywood table with a flowery tablecloth. In the middle stood a blue gin bottle with red and brown grass seed heads from fall.

"Uh-oh. What's this, Miss Hawcly, drinking gin again?"

She pinched my neck. "Treason gave me this lynx. I gutted it and cut it up quick. Long time since you've had lynx?"

Images of Anchorage clogged my head. "*Centuries.* Thanks, Iris." I sliced tender white meat off a thigh, dark meat off a shoulder. It was fat and heavenly good. Silently, I ate until I was stuffed.

"What's wrong," she giggled, "cat got your tongue?"

We stretched out on her couches and sipped decaffeinated coffee. Iris opened a box of mints and put a CD in the player. "This is Lucinda Williams. Doesn't that sound like a Takunak name? Lucinda knows how the story goes. Maybe she's from Uktu!"

"This is nice. I like your place, Iris. This is real nice. This town, I don't know . . . I walk around, and I feel the way I did before, except now there's no Dawna."

"Oh, it's the Darkness, Cutuk. We'll be over the hump soon, the sun will be back. You should call Dawna, or write a letter—she asked about you."

"She wouldn't live Out. I sure don't know if I'd live In." The couch was comfortable, and I closed my eyes. "I think I know how the guys feel. Real hunting is gone. Shoot, I'm wearing Sorel shoepacks. Trapping feels phony; things cost so much and furs are worth so little. Every time I get a grip on what matters, then I'm all confused again. A white-person career, with insurance? And a pension? Something is missing in me—that feels like being born a wolf and choosing a dog's life."

Iris set her cup on the worn plywood floor. The floor was cold, nail heads frosty by the door. She slipped her feet into beaded sealskin slippers and checked a blueberry pie in the oven. "Well. I've got a little white-girl career—there's problems, but that's life. I like it here. I'm with kids, I'm trying to help things, I've got a computer and a phone. If I wanted to,

I could catch a plane to Fairbanks. I can mush up to see Abe. So many caribou came through this fall they could hardly keep the airstrip open. Bears—" She sliced the pie briskly. "You know how people talk about Takunak and the wilderness being the middle of nowhere? I think this is the middle of everywhere."

"Sometimes I feel like I have something, some potential, like Abe," I said, "just right under my skin, all unfocused. What I'd really like is to do something for the country." I sat up. My hands were gripping each other. "I don't mean the American flag and the president. I mean for the *country*."

Iris glanced up sympathetically.

"I don't know what, that's the problem. I'm not going to join the Sara Club!"

Iris giggled. "We were so naive."

While the pieces of pie cooled, she poured boiling water in dishpans, one wash and one rinse. "You can be my running water—tomorrow run and get me some down at my water hole. I've lived so long without plumbing, I'm happy without it. I wash clothes and shower at the school, though. You're welcome to, too, Cutuk."

I helped wash the dishes, then we ate pie. It was after midnight and Iris had to get up early. We brushed our teeth, spat in a slop bucket. I unrolled my sleeping bag beside her on the bed, but every time we nearly drifted off, one of us would murmur or ask a question.

Iris yawned. "Dawna seemed tired of Anchorage. She talks about you all the time."

"What about you? Don't you have somebody you—"

"Cutuk!" she whispered, her voice full of dread.

"What? What's wrong?" I found her hands. They were trembling.

"Something bad. . . . It's going to happen."

"What do you mean?"

"I don't know," she cried. "It's that feeling I get. The first time was before January landed and took Mom. Now it just happens. Maybe it's just intuition, I don't know. I can feel it."

I hugged her shoulders and held her. "It's the Darkness," I said reassuringly. "It makes things seem all wrong. Try to get some sleep."

It grew very late, and I breathed deep and even, pretending. Eventually, we both hovered on the edge of sleep.

A muffled gunshot thumped.

In the dark, Iris moved, then went silent, listening. "What was that?" She leaned up on one elbow. She stood and went to the window. "What was that? Sounded like a gun."

She opened the door. Condensation rolled around her calves. Aurora flamed behind the black outlines of spruce. We listened to sounds in the crystal night. A dog's teeth chattering, trees crackling, the throb of the generators; in the leftover silence in between, snowgos suddenly screamed. And then the village siren wailed. We threw our jeans on, our parkas and snowpants, boots, fur hats, and gloves. On and on the siren went, a giant electric rabbit wailing in frozen darkness, calling Takunak together to be torn apart. Every dog in town howling. The northern lights dancing wildly. Stevie up on the ridge, crying like a tortured animal. *"WHY YOU DIE? WHY YOU HAVE TO DIE? WHY YOU DIE?"* And Lumpy on the snow, under the flashlights. His face fallen in. His trail ended here in the cold and night. Nothing as natural as death or even murder. Suicide. Janet limped up the hill. She put her arms around us. All of us. They were old arms, and fierce with love.

TWENTY-FIVE

THE FRESH SNOW *is new and clean, glinting under the stars.* Otter and mice, owls and foxes, and all the animals move, digging themselves out after the downfall, shaking off snow and searching for food. Their sounds carry in the frozen air, while their scents and breaths cling close.

Wolves travel down the river, spread out and hunting, taking apart the darkness with their consummate senses. The pack halts and swings south, catching the scent of a cow moose crossing the ice. The tall animal nears the shore. They circle, biting at her flanks and butt. In the willow thickets on the bank, the moose backs against a cornice and for hours holds off the terror with her black hooves. Ice fog forms in a long low cloud overhead. The snow packs down pink and finally red. Wolves lie and rest on the snowdrift while others lunge at the moose's hocks and nose. As dawn twinges in the south, the moose goes to her knees, and in their trenches the wolves move forward and tear mouthfuls. The moose rises again and then is down, kicking life away while the tired hunters open their feast.

THE PACK IS FULL AND STIFF, and the circles they melt in the snow are bloody. The oldest wolves, the leaders of the pack, raise their heads and stand as a black dot bounds down their trail. They turn and flee into willows. Their swollen stomachs drag in the snow. A wolf runs west along the hard snowdrift. Three scatter east and into willows. A young wolf stands—and drops as if clubbed from the sky.

The machine skims across the snow. The remaining pack runs. Booms stab across the ice, and a second wolf drops, biting at its back. A third collapses. The machine races past the moose kill, past the dead wolf and the dying ones. Wolves wallow in the deep snow and willows, the machine yards behind, pushing their fear-torn muscles, drowning their senses in its gnashing stink.

And then there's silence.

Tearing lungs. Booming hearts. At the trees, the running wolves glance back, their tongues lolling. The hunter unfolds and stands on the machine, clawing and chipping at its brown stick, its mouth small, its face flat on the front, eyes like an owl. The trees close behind them. The wolves weave and plod their way into the morning.

TWENTY-SIX

IN THE DROWSY June afternoon, distant Canada goose honks mixed with a Honda four-wheeler engine. On the tundra the last of the mating geese silenced their disagreement, in ecstasy or bad luck. I sat on the porch of Woody's government house, sharpening my knife. It had a wire edge.

Charley Casket sauntered over, yawning. "Thought you were that white guy."

I shrugged at the moot compliment.

The teacher, Delbert, had hired me as soon as I stepped out of Abe's old *qayaq* among the Breakup icebergs stacked in front of Takunak. He hired me to "watch" the house he rented from Woody, and feed the cat. Delbert was lanky and balding and had ranted about fetal alcohol syndrome. "Half the town's refried," he said, twirling his finger beside his ear. "My graduates aren't making it. Even the dogs here are loony. Some of the elders are truly great people." He shook his head. "It's the younger ones that haven't gotten to experience consequences because of the government squirting money on everything." His wife was pale and pretty with candy-green eyes. She smiled apologetically.

Iris was in Fairbanks visiting Jerry. "Watching" meant I would be between here and her cabin for two weeks keeping their pupils from breaking in and ransacking the houses. Delbert and his wife owned a blender and a microwave, a washer and dryer, cable TV, a SaladShooter. I was catching up on *Cheers,* and Dan Rather. The tundra was out there, the bull caribou fattening; but in this house I might as well have been in Sacramento, shooting salad.

I had put word out and gotten a short job. Billy Feathers was the current mayor and when Napoleon Skuq Jr. came home from Anaktuvuk, he had brought Billy four grams of weed, besides his personal stash, of course. Billy hired him to be cop. Nippy drove the cop van past the dump road and a long way over the tundra with two jugs and two high school girls. He showed them the size and extent of the law and also got the van stuck in a lake. I got paid to winch it out and make it run again, since he wasn't interested in the job without the vehicle.

"*Adii,* too hot, huh?" Charley held out an arrowhead. "Tom Standle was been looking for you."

The obsidian point was perfect—and shiny new. I'd seen one like it in Anchorage. A flint knapper from California had made it behind his carport.

"You get this at Kmart?"

"I find it," he turned, pointed at nothing in particular in the distance, "downriver. Quite a ways, alright." He seemed short now, from a generation before all these tall steroid-beef-fed schoolkids. Charley, lately, had sometimes been under the influence of Jesus, sometimes his old self, a quiet sampler of NyQuil, Old Spice, vanilla. He picked at a pink lake of frostbite scars on his cheek. "You sell that tusk?"

"Yeah, to a Fairbanks fella."

"How much?

"Thirty a pound."

Charley waited.

"Twenty-six hundred dollars," I said.

I'd made a list and mail-ordered supplies: a roll of Visqueen leaned inside, and axe handles, Coleman lanterns, dog harness webbing, ammo, rope, nails, four-and-a-half-inch whitefish netting, dried apricots, rice, salt. Chocolate to take up to Franklin, books, an outboard water pump impeller for Abe. I didn't tell Charley that I'd spent Breakup watching caribou and migratory birds return, and snowshoeing between patches of melting-out earth and songbird territories, alone with too many Abe-like thoughts talking me into the idea that actions—as small as a bird's song, as big as nuclear stockpiling—spread love and disturbance rippling through the earth, through all creatures. I didn't tell him that Enuk Wolfglove had once given me a mammoth-ivory carving, or where he with his sharp eyes and persistence could probably unearth it. I didn't tell him that I often questioned if I should have left the mammoth tusk right where I found it, or that I was saving all the money from it to buy Dawna Wolfglove something—when I figured out what.

". . . forty-five bucks," Charley mumbled, offering the arrowhead. Charley's merchandise—always a perfect barometer of the black market—was available today for the Takunak price of a gram of marijuana. I thought, I would have asked fifty, get some munchies in the deal. *You're hearing your honky genes, Cutuk.*

I wrinkled my nose, *no.* "What Mr. Standle want?"

"I dunno."

I walked with Charley toward the post office. The town was deserted, nearly everyone asleep until afternoon. Above the gym an electric sign read H ME OF T E TAKUN K WOLV S. Swallows clicked and chortled, mating up on the telephone wires. We moved slowly. Moving fast—especially in the heat of day—was a non-shareholder attribute. We passed in front of four satellite dishes anchored to the packed dust. They pointed at a low angle, taking a long time to lift their aim off the ground, Takunak's brand-new ears cocked south, listening to blips that spelled how to be a generic American village. Takunak didn't listen very well. Not listening brought more government grants, and most people wanted to be jobless when the caribou were fat and the berries ripe. The river flowed down below, blue and lazy, and across was the leafy wilderness, turning green and growing baby ptarmigan, moose, caribou. Baby butterflies and blueberries.

There was a letter from Dawna, and one from Cheryl. "Photo, Please Do Not Bend," Cheryl had written on the envelope.

"I gonna wait here today," Charlie said importantly. He leaned on the steps of the post office. "In case my unemployment check come." His hand wandered into his pocket.

Unemployment? Had Charley ever had a job?

I read Dawna's letter as I walked on. She had quit her job. She'd be in Uktu in August, then planned to fly home to Takunak. She sent a wild rose petal. Apparently, they were blooming where she was or had been.

Under glowing young aspens at the edge of town, Mable Feathers lived in her government house, and the Standles rented the drafty old cabin her husband had built overlooking the river. Piles of naily boards, wrecked snowgos, outboard motor lower units, and broken basket sleds littered the yard between the houses—a sign of wealth, longevity, and prudence. No one knew when they might need a washtub of busted snowgo undercarriage springs. Tom Standle led me into their single room. "Got that favor to ask," he said. A TV was on. The air smelled of Tide and herbal tea—apple cinnamon, the kind that smelled better than pie and tasted like sock water. "Like you to take an *Alaska* magazine writer down to meet Crazy Joe next week. Use my jonboat. Can you do it?"

I raised my eyebrows.

Aluminum foil and blankets were stapled over the windows to keep the pesky sun out at midnight. In the middle of the floor Sally Standle was washing clothes in a rectangular yellow Hoover washing machine. She offered Coke or tea. I didn't remember her so fat, triple chins and an axe handle across the sweat pants. A tall dour man sat cross-legged at the table.

"Oh, excuse me," Tom scowled. "Cutuk. James." We shook hands. Something about Tom's face wasn't pleased, and I wondered if he'd told the man that I hadn't "made it."

An orange cat strolled out, hunched forward, and licked its butthole. "Company's coming!" Sally shouted. She hollered that whenever her cat licked its ass. The way the ass pointed had to do with the direction the company came from, *guuq*. "Did you find a job?" she asked.

She was jovial and enjoyed pranks, so I told her I'd decided to go to Russia for work. "I heard you can support yourself over there selling condoms." I grinned down at my hands. They rested on a huge Bible. Hastily, I moved them. Jesus peered out of a circle in the cover. Bibles were strewn on the table.

James murmured, "Mrs. Standle, do you wish to make a purchase today?" *A Bible salesman? In Takunak?* The cat must have been licking its butt for weeks. Sally Standle's eyes twinkled. "The Rainbow Vacuum Cleaner salesman beat you by a month," she told James. "He sold seventeen-hundred-dollar machines to half the houses in Takunak. On credit, poor fool. No one even has carpet!" she wailed. "He put on quite the demonstration. Cutuk, you might enjoy incorporating that into your condom sales. Company's coming!"

The tea was scalding. Nothing that would be possible to swallow and escape. I had to laugh, talk about engines, and wait for it to cool—probably Mr. Standle's secret to sanity. Certainly Takunak's cure for summer.

IT WAS LATE EVENING, and sunny down by the river. Homemade wooden and new aluminum boats were anchored to the shore. Flies buzzed around piles of rotting sheefish. The river water had dropped and cleared up, and sandbars and mosquitoes were out. The writer, Alice Burne, was nowhere around. I leaned my rifle and a bag of apples against Melt's jade boulder. The ice had shifted the boulder a few yards downstream, and sand half-buried it. I sat and reread Cheryl's letter. A picture of her was folded in the letter. She wore yellow Helly Hansen rain pants, the suspenders forcing her breasts together, and yellow fishing wristlets; her hair was wild and her smile big and happy. She was in Naknek, set-netting for salmon, three months pregnant, and no longer with the father of her baby. Pregnancy made her feel great, she wrote, and already made her skin extra smooth and her hair thick.

My chest ached. She was stunning, and fishing! *But she's white and blond.* Quickly, I chided myself for my capsized racism, and for letting this amazing woman slip away. My thoughts leapt from her to Dawna and back. A self-deprecatory smile played across my mouth. I thought of the flight attendant on the jet to Anchorage, and those sweet and salty almonds, and for a few minutes I stared at the current going past, just to get time started again and not drown under my mistakes.

A cloud of mosquitoes swarmed out of the willows, sinking a hundred bites into my arms. Four-wheelers passed, drenching me in dust. Absently, I put a mosquito in my mouth, tasted the sweet tundra pollen on her body, spat her out, and tasted more.

"*Aiy*, you honky!" A group of kids passed, taunting a black boy, the Bureau of Land Management surveyor's son. The man was here for part of the summer, paid by the government to survey native allotments. Kids shoved and hit the small boy. He cowered, bewildered and scared, but not fleeing. I lunged to my feet, fists raised to smash small skulls. "*Hey!* Treat him"–I halted. They all stared.

The boy dusted himself off, smiled cautiously, and showed me his Swiss Army knife. The other kids stood beside him now, eyeing the scissors and tiny saw. "Hi Cutuk." A little five-year-old dropped his bike; dust puffed. "Hey, you always chew snuff? Want some?" The boy held out a round tin. "Have a dip. Got vitamin E—for Eskimo! It'll make you tough." I laughed loud, the way Lance would, though with no idea what to say.

Alice still had not appeared. I wandered over to the old Wolfglove shack. Gray boards had been pried loose, and in a tangle of Janet's handmade fish seine, unskinned caribou legs had been tugged through the crack and mauled by puppies. The old Mr. Coffee was upside down in the dust, shattered, its electric cord gone. I saw the cord tied in as part of the clothesline.

In Janet's doorway I paused, no fat meat or furs to carry in. What were these inconsequential jobs of mine? What did I want here in this techno-outpost in the wilderness? I was no tour guide. No drunk. No displaced factory worker on the Dan Rather show. I was an ex-hunter, trained on need, no longer needed.

Janet beamed. "Hi, Cutuk!" She wore a calico *atikłuk,* and sat on the floor beside an electric fan. She was splitting a willow for the rim of a birchbark basket. Whitney-Houston sat beside her. Tony, Stevie's four-year-old son, sat on a coffee can in the back corner, his shoulders tense, blasting away at video karate killers. He ran over and kicked my leg, showed me his muscle, and ran back to the controls. Daisy stood with her hand on Janet's shoulder, naked except for a clean pink Pamper and a wet strip of bark in her mouth. The fan blew her black hair back and made her small eyes squint. Janet pushed aside her rolls of birchbark, groaned, and hoisted herself to her feet. "You eat today?"

I wrinkled my nose.

"Get cold pop."

The refrigerator had Kraft plastic cheese, Banquet chicken, a bundle of dried whitefish in a Ziploc. I hauled out the dried fish. "You want *uqsruq?*" she asked. "You boys need to be fatter." Janet rustled in the freezer. "Hey girl!" She rushed back and pulled her *ulu* out of Daisy's tiny hands. "You gonna cut, little love."

Melt came out of the bedroom squinting and scratching his arms.

"Hello, Cutuk."

The fingers on his right hand were gone. His knuckles ended like a swollen pink spatula. Most of his toes were not in his Wellingtons, but gone on ahead to heaven or the Happy Hunting Grounds. Last winter, working in inexplicable alliance, Lumpy and Iris had saved his life. That night, as we huddled in a circle near Lumpy's body, Iris had peered at the faces, her eyes bewildered. "This is not it!" she whispered wretchedly. "There's something else wrong!" Slowly murmurs rose—*Melt! Where's Melt?* Melt, passed out behind the steep snowdrift against the Friends Church, had been in the process of changing from a liquid to a solid when Lumpy's actions roused the town and got him found and medevaced.

He heaved down at the table. I nodded, and peeled dried whitefish off the skin and dipped the splinters in seal oil. Melt yawned and scratched. He picked up a dried whitefish and bit off a strip. "Young man, your mom still never come home?"

His eyes were sincere. Melt had not been drunk since Lumpy died. The frostbite doctors at Providence Medical Center in Anchorage had done the best they could to thaw him back to his former self but hadn't been entirely successful. The new Melt stayed home for meals, perused *National Geographic*, and made Janet coffee.

I shook my head. "Iris is trying to find her, *guuq*."

"*Yuay*. Tat's good." Melt's voice resonated the way Enuk's had.

We chewed in silence. I glanced out the window. Watching for the writer, watching the current ease the river past. Not believing that our lives were the same lives we started with. The old Eskimo stories had held intrinsic truth, after all; they started in the middle of things and ended where the storyteller grew tired. Janet's kitchen was bright and comfortable. It was home, too. I'd had dreams die right here at the table. Cutuk, always clinging to the belief that he'd paid enough for being different, believing he was destined to be special. Mixed in with the fists and scorn, maybe there had been the expectation that because my skin was white I could void my past and go on. *Cutuk can hunt and do math; he'll "make it."* But I'd come from farther out, gone farther in. How could I have fooled myself? I was no less scathed than the rest. And in the end maybe that was all I needed to know. I didn't need to be Eskimo. I didn't need dead wolves or gold, airplanes or the other shiny things.

The phone rang. I picked up another dried fish and bit off a strip. Melt scooped coffee grounds. Tony sweated against the shouting electric ninja. I looked at the TV. The screen was slanted, the volume low. The recorded-earlier Oprah looked slanted, but I could see her looking serious about something. Some new problem down in the States. Something about sex, for sure. Teenage girls who have sex with their moms' boyfriends' dogs' therapists?

"Cutuk! That lady going down to water, *guuq*." Janet hung up. She smiled her big happy smile. "Maybe you'll let her pe your girlfriend, huh?"

The oil smelled sharp and fishy on my hands. Janet didn't know the world this woman lived in. Or maybe she did. Janet was a gatherer from a long way back. Janet knew everything.

WOODROW AND TESSIE WASHINGTON stood beside a washtub of whitefish, pike, suckers, and grayling. They were old and bowlegged. One of the pike flopped. The writer, Alice, stepped nimbly over the aluminum gunnel of Mr. Standle's boat and dug in her backpack for her camera. She wore crisp long-legged Levi's and a white shirt. "Wait! I want a picture of you with the traditional fishers, with those fish racks in the background." Alice was twenty-seven and had a load of curly brown hair that she had tossed back and forth during her four days in town. Every child in Takunak knew her name, every man was smitten, every woman suspicious.

She knelt and snapped pictures. I smiled apologetically at *Aana* Tessie. Alice got back in the boat. She wore a three-pronged piece of caribou antler on a leather thong around her neck and it nestled in her unbuttoned collar. In the emancipated mood I was in, I wanted to throw it in the river and kiss her.

"Catalog girl, huh?" Woodrow glanced over the river, his old eyes bloodshot and opaque with cataracts. "Long time ago, Tommy order tat kind. Jus' clothes come in ta box. COD. Ha! Ha!"

Aana Tessie shook her head. "*Arii!* Cutuk, you should let her take tat caribou horn off. Before it bunch hole in her *milluk*."

I shrugged, grinned at Woodrow, shoved the boat into the current.

It was a beautiful sunny night on the water. Alice was ecstatic about the wilderness she had discovered and the Eskimo culture, intertwined in peaceful harmony with the seasons and the mountains and the wind, and all the magazine stories she could write. Warm air blew by our faces. Occasionally we motored through pockets of cold air near shaded cutbanks. Cottonwood cotton floated on the water. The land was dry and wild rhubarb was already beginning to go to seed along the shore, and that meant the wild onions would soon be past, too, and the bull caribou would have dark velvety horns, and the bulls would be getting fat but would still taste like summer meat from eating greens; and salmon would be flooding upstream to spawn, and trout would follow, silver-blue and heavy with oil; and it all *was* truly wonderful, but something irked me about the way this pretty woman—who might never see the land we called winter—could swoop in and harvest our world with her camera and words and spoon it back as if only she understood its profundity.

Dawna had always loved pictures. My thoughts hummed with the motor. A camera! I would buy Dawna a camera! The twenty-six-hundred-dollar kind. I would fix up the old house the way I wanted it, and at least show her my roots. Maybe in her hands a camera could tell stories waiting to be told. It would be one way to start caring about this place, instead of acting—as people did—as if the white people were going to take it tomorrow.

WHEN WE MOTORED UP, Crazy Joe was kneeling on the rock bar in front of his canvas tent, filleting a salmon. He turned and stared. Alder smoke leaked out of his plywood smoker. Crazy Joe was small and stocky and had a fierce black and gray beard and black curls around the rim of his tanned skull. He'd come from Idaho, four decades ago, and never gone back. His pants were tied on. The crotch was ripped out and his testicles hung out. The material was all slimy and bloody there from him knocking mosquitoes off. He flung salmon strips in a brine bucket and ran toward us.

"You brought a *woman!*" He swung his bloody fillet knife. I handed him the sack of apples, and smelled the cloud of his notorious cologne. He sniffed the fruit. "Go eat, Hawcly. We got early salmon, the last two days running. Salmon heads all boiled, in the kettle. Give me an' the lady room." Alice smiled nervously. He towed her away, showing her his salmon smoking operation, whispering about the coffee can of gold dust he had hidden up a slough—the goddamn natives were after it, the goddamn gulls wanted his fish, the goddamn mosquitoes . . .

"... waste your breath asking the young fella anything. Abe Hawcly raised those kids with their heads in the Stone Age."

Alice turned and fluttered her fingers.

I sat on the rocks and ate a boiled salmon head. It was bright and peaceful here past midnight and I threw fish scraps to grayling that poked circles in the current.

I'd have to call Jerry, ask what kind of camera to order. Maybe Alice could help, too. "Joe!" I sloshed my fingers clean in the river. "I need that can of gold!"

"Boy, don't josh me around a woman. That's my winter rendezvous."

I strolled along the rock bar. Here and there were Bic lighters and Yamaha oil jugs and the blue spaghetti of rotten poly tarps, detritus that two decades ago practically would have been sign of aliens.

Later, as they walked back, Crazy Joe was still talking, telling her about a helicopter. "... a pod hanging below the struts ... subsurface. Probably our shit-for-brains governor, with a new plan now that someone's informed him he can't mine outer space."

I wiped my hands on my pants, moved noiselessly across the rocks toward them. "What do you think the helicopters are looking for?"

Joe swiveled. He pondered, bathing in attention from two directions. "I'm not certain," he admitted. "Something valuable, and poison. Uranium obviously comes to mind, these days." He straightened. "Probably zinc or lead is what it is."

He knelt at his campfire and blew on the ashes. I felt hollowness tunnel down my arteries and wondered why this was never enough—a man and his campfire. Didn't anyone want "economic development" to have an edge you could walk to and look at what the earth had so perfectly developed? Didn't people look at America and catch their breath, thinking, "Gosh, it must have been such amazing country!" Coals glowed, and he stacked twigs on and turned and filled a kettle from the river. "Make you folks a shot of coffee. I forgot my manners."

Alice's tablet was out. "Wouldn't mining on a large scale change the flavor of this valley?"

"The *flavor?*" Still kneeling, the old man put his chin in his hand and sighed. "You're a writer . . . that's right. The flavor of the water? The flavor of the fish?" Joe turned to me. "Hawcly knew. He built *above* Jesus Creek. He might act unconcerned, but he wasn't going to drink tainted water."

"Tainted water?" I uttered.

Alice's glance strayed to the river and back to the kettle. Joe flicked a peek at her backside. He straightened. "The Dog Die Mountains—you think that's just a name, no history there? You never think maybe something back there doesn't have a history of being healthy for canines? Dogs eat some minerals, they'll foam at the mouth. Guard hairs fall out. Come on, Hawcly, you know what a gray wolf looks like underneath the guard hairs. White. Pull your goddamn head out of the sand."

"I don't drink coffee," Alice said.

"When a batch of butt-sniffing senators are back there putting the golden shovel in some open pit mine, then everybody's going to say Joe knew it all along."

I smiled weakly at Alice.

She put her pen in a pocket and pointed her expensive camera at the far shore. In the late evening sunlight, along the horizon like iris petals, the Shield Mountains were velvet blue.

TWENTY-SEVEN

UNDER THE BRIGHT LEAVES of fall, I swept out the igloo, burned gnawed chairs and tables, and Cloroxed mold off the slab walls. The moss insulating the roof needed to be added to, and the slumped spots and marten and mouse tunnels patched. The sagging beams needed spruce post supports. Windows needed to be fabricated out of Visqueen, put in, and chinked.

The fall days were warm and the air smelled of highbush cranberries and leaves and the pitch of freshly peeled logs. My net along the shore caught salmon and pike, whitefish, suckers, grayling and trout. Occasionally a huge sheefish tangled in the small mesh by its square lips. On shore I lashed poles together to build racks to dry the fish. The chained dogs yawned and stretched and watched me cut fish, and cook dog pot out of the fish heads and guts, and lay trout and sheefish in the grass to get "stink" for *quaq*. They slept and awoke to bark, alerting herds of caribou that moved across the tundra. The animals were dark in their late-summer coats. I shot a few for meat and parka hides. When they went down in the dwarf birch they were hard to locate, smooth in their short hair and dark velvet antlers.

The fall days shortened and the nights cooled, and quickly the caribou grew white manes and their giant antlers peeled bloody and red and darkened like burnished hardwood.

In the afternoons, when the sun was warm, there were blueberries to pick, and after the first heavy frosts the cranberries ripened, and I filled wooden barrels with the plump red berries. Picking berries, I missed Iris and Jerry. Jerry had carried the World War I Enfield .30-06. Iris always had an unripe berry under her tongue to keep her from eating berries, and she carried the laughter.

I dug a new outhouse hole, filled in the old. Behind the house—where the bank sloped down to Outnorth Lake—I dug a pit and built a new *siġḷuaq* out of logs in the ground to store kegs of berries, jars of fat, butter, a bucket of *quaġaq* from Janet, seal oil, and a keg of salted salmon bellies.

Every morning I jumped off my *qaatchiaq*, made coffee and oatmeal, and heated leftover meat. I stretched the ache out of my hands and hurried outside to work. The sky was windy blue and scudded with cat-scratch clouds. The air was clean and the leaves smelled good. The animals and birds were busy preparing for winter. I kept a journal and wrote down what the land and creatures were doing. I told myself I needed to learn if I claimed to care and planned to help. I wondered if that was true or just sounded good.

Boats passed occasionally. Stevie had boated up to visit and bring my mail and the camera order. Another time, an aluminium boat banged into rocks out in front of the dog yard. "WHERE'S THE CHANNEL?" The men looked cold and eager. They motored closer. "Much caribou around?"

"Should be better back down four bends."

"How about moose? We haven't got our moose."

The driver rested his elbow on a powerful spotlight. They were drifting away, idling into the current. Friendly Crotch Spit men, dying to kill their moose, their caribou, their bear, their wolves.

ONE DAY A National Guard Black Hawk helicopter chopped over the valley. For a minute I questioned whether it was one of Crazy Joe's alleged helicopters, mapping subsurface minerals. The moose I'd watched all summer tucked in the willows at the mouth of Jesus Creek had grown huge antlers, and the flash of those antlers caught the helicopter pilot's eye. The thundering war machine slowed, turned, and swirled yellow leaves into the sky. It hovered over the willows of the creek.

In my binoculars I saw a man at the controls, peering down, then peering at dashboard buttons, marking this bend in the Kuguruk or entering the moose on a GPS. Maybe Billy was with him, or Nippy, or Dollie—half of Takunak was in the Guard. The helicopter racheted back toward Crotch Spit. My dogs howled. Thoughtfully, I hung the binocs on a limb in front of the igloo. A varied thrush raked leaves. He got me smiling, thinking birds must fake finding worms in this permafrost soil, pretending all that success in the rattling leaves.

A minute later the dot of an airplane appeared in the fall sky.

What is this? It must be Labor Day! Why don't they just call it Take-Break-And-Kill-Animals Day?

The plane circled. It didn't acknowledge my igloo, my smoke, my line of bright drying clothes. It circled the moose. The Super Cub banked and touched down on the bar below Jesus Creek. At the lower end the sand was soft and quick. The plane lurched suddenly onto its nose.

I rubbed my forehead, grinning, mulling mean versus generous thoughts, then put the *qayaq* in and paddled down. The water was glassy calm.

"We've got a problem!" the pilot shouted.

The man was big, a dentist from Anchorage, he said. "Get me to a phone and I'll give you a free root canal!" He ran in anxious circles under the towering tail. It was a photograph for Dawna: *Dentist with airplane.* Perfect

Alaskana. We heaved the tail down until the plane rested on three wheels. The prop was bent, but no other damage was apparent. I smelled the hot four-stroke oil and lusted to mechanic on the powerful engine. The man wore camouflage pants and a camouflage long-underwear shirt. I thought of the polar bear in glass at the Anchorage airport. Shot by an orthodontist.

"Biggest rack from here to Talketna!" He gloated. "Easily seventy inches. Buddy, it's right back in those willows."

IT TOOK ME all evening and the next morning to *qayaq* down to Takunak. Caribou swam the river. The sky spoke of wind, with lenticular clouds, and the willows and birches and tundra were crimson and gold beside the water, and the grass was yellow and bent, and mallards and widgeons nosed along the shores; it was all as haunting and beautiful as it had been ten thousand years before the evolution of sport hunters.

In Takunak a rush was in the air. Tommy Feathers was backing off shore, his boat listing and stacked with building materials to haul down to his native allotment. Three Washington brothers were climbing into a boat, carrying thermoses, SKS rifles, and a pair of Russian night-vision goggles. Two boys sat on a teeter-totter, watching me beach. They looked like street thugs, baggy clothes and shaved heads. "You a floater?" they asked listlessly. A "floater," along the Kuguruk River, was one of two things: a pale rotten spawned-out salmon floating downriver, or a fluorescent nylon–clad Outsider come to float the river.

I hoped I wasn't either. I was embarrassed to be white and therefore in need of a category, and wrinkled my nose, *no*.

They didn't hear. "You got cocaine?" I shook my head. The older boy spat. "You're so lucky. This town is the boringest place on earth. No roads. No good chicks here. Everything is native. So embarrassing. We're jus' waiting for the old people to die so we can go."

"Go where?"

"Where you're from. States. France—unless they build a refineries. Cheap gas would be good, alright."

A plastic Power Ranger lay half buried in the mud on his hands and knees, musclebound and begging. I stepped on the small of his back and stomped into Janet's, confused, the way she knew me best.

From Janet's phone, I called the troopers and the pilot's friend. Both phone numbers were busy. "Maybe rush hour season down there," Janet said. She wore rubber boots, sweatpants, and an *atikłuk*. "*Arii.* Now George Push sure wanna fight Saddam Hussein." She shook her head. "I don't want you boys to try go help." The air smelled like strawberries. With his stump hand, Melt proudly pointed out a scented Plug-In. "Cutuk, 'lectric strawberry!"

Janet put boiled ribs and seal oil, bread and boysenberry jam, blueberries and sugar on the table. There were new pictures of Lumpy beside her Bible on top of the TV. "Lumpy have five kids," she said proudly. "In Uktu." She pushed back her gray hair. "Cutuk! Dawna's in Uktu! Flossie's daughter been have baby girl and they give it Dawna's Eskimo name. Maybe she gonna never go home now."

The Super Cub on the sandbar flashed in my head. Whitney-Houston sat quiet, one hand on my leg, the other poking quilted buttons in the couch like linty navels. I put my arm around her shoulders and wiggled two fingers like rabbit ears. I pictured the cardboard box at home, with the black new camera and lenses lying in Styrofoam popcorn. I pictured Dawna a decade back, peering longingly at the brown parcels being tossed out of the Twin Otter's belly. Airplane words hissed through my head: "Prop wash," "Retarded right mag," "Grease those mains in!"

MY *QAYAQ* AND I rode home in a flotilla of three boats and seven men. The men were jubilant at the prospects: hunting animals, burning Search & Rescue gas, saving a stupid white guy. We roared up to the sandbar.

The prop was off the red and white airplane, a dome tent pitched, the moose's huge head and antlers upside down drying on the sand. I panted with sadness. This bull moose had hung around last winter, for company in the lonely winter, the way moose often did. During the summer I'd said hello whenever we passed along the shore of Outnorth Lake. Now a harem waited back in the willows, cow moose in love with this stud. Shooting him would have been as challenging and sporting as shooting a sofa. I lifted my *qayaq* out of Tommy Feathers's boat and walked to the skull. The skinned-out eyes and teeth scowled. Only the flap of head skin hung from the antlers, no thousand pounds of meat in sight. And I stood on the sand and wished, I just wished this fucking dentist could feel the other 364 days a year the moose had fought to live. How it felt to survive birth in the willows while brown bears waited; winter stands beside his mother against the wolves; survive years alone in wading deep snows, the willows buried, the tundra howling wind; survive the spring crust that dropped moose to their ribs while it supported big hungry bears; and the summer insanity of mosquitoes driving him to his eyeballs into water. All for the cool sweet fall and the chance of mating. While this dentist slept on flannel, mated whenever he felt a faint itch, bought bags of food at Safeway, and lived with a 99 percent assurance that his children would never be eaten. And planned his next adventure to kill an animal.

The men were cheerfully helping to install the propeller the man's friend had GoldStreaked north.

"This is a flat prop, an eighty-two forty-one," he explained. "Forty-one inches forward for every revolution. A fast prop like the one I curled costs two thousand bucks." He tie-wired the nuts expertly. "I'm going to save the whole head on Mr. Bigs. He's already cost me enough! See, I'm not sure about the crankshaft, so I'll need one of you to freight-collect that rack to me in Anchorage."

The men stared.

Woodrow Washington Sr. sat on the edge of his boat glassing upriver for animals, avoiding the talking. I sat on his gunnel. The pilot paced, pointing out boot holes in the soft sand. Woodrow put his binoculars down and offered me a Tupperware of *muktuk*, a side of *paniqtuq* ribs. We sat eating with our knives, dodging juvenile maggots in the thicker parts of the half-dried caribou ribs. It was relaxing to be near a composed elder. The black *muktuk* was fresh. Woodrow pointed his knife at an electronic gadget lying on his tarp. He chewed loose-lipped and swallowed finally. "Tat's my poy's elder-in-a-can."

I examined the GPS. "Will this thing point at Uktu?"

Woodrow turned his head and looked instinctively in the direction of Uktu. He pointed his knife. "Could pe. If Woody been open it over there. Go 'head, turn it on. Maybe you'll pe lost tomorrow."

The pilot's voice rose. "My crankshaft took a thump. This rack is heavy to tie to the struts. Tell you what. I was going to return for the meat, but if you'll freight that head out for me, you can keep all of it."

I stood up, before he offered hundred-dollar bills or porcelain crowns in my front yard. My voice was harsher than I recognized. "We worry about game wardens. None of us have hunting licenses." *Hunting* and *license*—the two words didn't go together. One was paper, and about distant Outsiders' rules. The other was the meat we were made out of. "You have to go with them and mail it yourself."

The men nodded.

"I take you." Woodrow stood. "Buy me twenty gallon." He smiled his beautiful false teeth. "Maybe Evinrude oil too, huh?"

The big man stood dumbfounded. "No licenses? You guys *poach* everything?" The men glanced uncomfortably at the river. He peered at his watch. "Okay. Okay. I appreciate you, Cut—how you say your name?—going for help the way you did. That was really something else. All of you. Here, you don't have to eat that stuff." He rifled his grub box and handed out sausages, mustard, canned ham, Coleman fuel, a science fiction paperback. He knelt and started meticulously salting and wrapping the moose head.

Nippy Sr. got hungry for moose ribs.

We tracked the blood trail into the willows. We heard the airplane engine stutter and roar as the man tested the engine. The animal lay big and brown as a woodpile, forlorn beside his guts, a yellow Kodak film wrapper, and no head. The carcass was hacked and dirty with leaves and sand, guts were spattered on the meat, flies buzzed. The men sniffed the sour blood and shook their heads. "Well. You got dog feed, Cutuk!" They laughed and strode out to gas up their motors.

The pilot filled sacks with sand to anchor the plane. As the boats idled into the current he was still shouting across the water, instructing me to swing the tail around if an east wind arose during the night. The boats roared upriver.

I sat, whistled with relief, and tossed pebbles into the creek. Sitting and thinking, the relief turned into ire. Eskimos' fame and favorite feature about themselves—besides hunter prowess—had always been shocking generosity. Without generosity, who were you? Nobody. Every day that generosity was strip-mined by Outsiders, many of them imitation hunters, most of them obscenely prosperous, until it had become harder and harder for us to come up with enough to even be ourselves.

"No wonder Abe gave away his airplane."

The sun was warm on my neck. Slowly, I felt like Cutuk again, the little boy in the big wilderness. Before this constant thirst hiding between coffee and alcohol, sugar and sex. I wondered if I had always been afraid. All my life there had been power out there that made the decisions. It hadn't been so apparent when no man owned the land and we could laugh at storms and hunt harder. But now everything was square and electric and came off airplanes. And we lived here not really knowing what the power looked like, who it listened to, or how it held its fork.

I was tired of it. I didn't believe in it. I stood up and brushed sand off my butt. "I'm not going to be a dog. I'll take the wolf's deal."

Abe's *qayaq* still lay in the sand beside the red and white airplane. Uktu was seventy-four miles southwest. GPS *guuq*. I dragged the tail of the plane around. I paddled to the house for the camera, let my dogs free, and went back and climbed into the cockpit.

Master switch. Mixture to full rich. Left magneto on. Starter button. The engine sputtered and fired. Sand blew under the wings. My dogs' fur blew back and they retreated. *Right mag on.* The smell and roar and wind carried me back to Anchorage: January taking off with me in the back seat, my hands on the stick and throttle, feet under the seat on the cable pedals. Now the sandbar stretched in front. It ended at the dark water at the mouth of Jesus Creek. The narrow fuselage shuddered with power. *Always walk your strip,* January said. This sand was the soil of my life.

I'd walked it plenty. I shoved the throttle to full. The engine bellowed. The plane gathered itself. Bounding faster and faster. I eased the stick forward. The tail rose from the sand. Sky and water rushed toward me through the shaded circle of the propeller. Sun glinted on the river. Dead ahead was where Iris had nearly drowned. I yanked the flaps. The Super Cub plucked into the air.

Water rushed under the belly. Down in it fish darted away over the sandy bottom. I pulled the stick back and the plane climbed. I tilted the stick toward Uktu, pushed the right pedal; the wing banked, and the plane responded, turning south, rising gracefully.

Far across on the north shore was the igloo and the fling of caches and fish racks and woodpiles, and behind, lakes and tundra. No boats were in sight on the river. Below lay maroon tundra and tiny bristled spruce and birches flagged in yellow. The Shield Mountains were ahead, hardly mountains anymore, now only stubbled hills with stone outcroppings, and beyond them an endless expanse of tundra. Ancient and new caribou trails cut hillsides and forked across marshes and up mountains, veins on the land.

I glanced at the gauges. Twenty-nine hundred feet. *The mixture!* I leaned it out until the rpm rose and started to fall again. Down below a herd of caribou fanned out, like hundreds of tiny grains of rice racing across the tundra, and I realized how much I loved the ground.

ON THE NORTH SHORE below the convergence of the Uktu and Kutny Rivers, Uktu squatted like a flyspeck in the vast wilderness. Government houses stood on metal legs in neat rows. The dump was behind the village and wind had blown plastic bags and trash in huge swathes across the tundra. The cemetery perched on a knoll half a mile from the dump. The airstrip lay on a bulldozed island in front of the village. A bridge spanned the narrow river channel between the island and shore.

I swept Uktu from the north. Dogs pointed their muzzles up and howled. I laid the wing over, skated around, and eased the throttle back. At twenty-one hundred rpm the plane floated. I played with the flaps to bring the tail up. I didn't know this village—where would Dawna be? Men and women and kids stood on porches, on the caked streets, and in boats.

Keep your nose down, January said. *Power is your friend.*

At full throttle I came in over the stovepipes. Houses and wires and faces ripped under the wheels. Nothing had ever felt so deadly and alive. I buzzed the length of the town. I could become addicted up here, swooping and diving until the dentist's gas was gone.

I lined up on the airfield. Confidence moved my hands. They pulled the flaps, eased the throttle. Willows flashed under the nose, and the plane wobbled and yawed, the tires touched and bounced. The plane veered, then the tail lowered and the rear tire dragged. The cowling blocked my view. I steered carefully onto the gravel ramp and leaned the mixture until the engine stuttered and died.

In the sudden silence, the ground and my thoughts felt distant and hazy. I pictured January and Abe landing on the ice in front of Takunak, meeting Enuk, thirty-five years ago, freighting in the future, whether they wished to or not.

Four-wheelers approached. I swung out on the gravel. People recognized me, shook my hand. A chubby boy grinned out of a small version of Lumpy's face. Dawna pushed through the circle. Her hair was short and fashionable looking, tinted with a hint of copper. Her cheeks had filled out. She was missing half of a front tooth. "I s-saw you driving a plane like a nuthead!" Tears flooded her eyes. "I thought you were going to crash and I'd never see you again."

I started to hand her the box, but then set it down and lifted her off the ground in an embrace. "Hi!" We laughed in each other's faces. "I miss you. What are you doing in this town?" I picked the camera box up and shoved it into her hands. "Here."

Her eyes squinted like Enuk's. She'd always been able to read secrets off my face. "Say, Yellow-Hair! Just like you fit your skin better, or something." She held the box as if it were merely a parcel I'd asked her to hold. "When you leaving?"

"I have to get this plane back. Now, actually." I climbed back in the front seat. People stepped away from in front of the prop. I paused, not wanting to leave her. "How'd your tooth come off?"

"My cousin." She touched it with the pink tip of her tongue, shrugged, and grinned. "That dumb *utchuk!* We were hunting ducks and she let her four-ten barrel bump my teeth. I have to get it fixed."

"I have to return this airplane. I stole it to come see you."

Surprise flooded her face. "I'll *malik!* Let me get my bag."

Landing with Dawna had not been anything I'd let into my mind—I pictured red and white wreckage strewn on the sand. *Double murder by stupidity.* I shook my head. "I'm not planning on haunting Janet, trying to explain killing you."

She wrinkled her nose and stood on one foot on the step and peered at the controls and gauges and the green plexiglass roof. "I dream about driving this kind." We locked gazes for a long second.

I pressed the starter. Wind gusted her hair. Slowly she stepped down, and I reached out and held the edge of her hand. "See you in Takunak, after Freezeup. 'Bye, Dawna."

"Maybe I'll steal a plane and come see *you!*"

I folded the door closed. Dawna waved and pouted with a smile.

AN EAST BREEZE rippled the Kuguruk River. I'd wanted to land west, to make fewer tracks—the irrational rationale of a groundlubber about to crash. The breeze would help, probably more than my inexperienced hands. If I landed without wrecking, and still felt the need, I could erase every track on the bar with a leafy branch.

I set the flaps and came in low over the water, raising and lowering the throttle, feeling the plane settle and the controls go mushy. I came around again. My arms were hard. Along the shore a gust rolled the willow leaves, pale sides up. A wisp of smoke stretched from the igloo stovepipe. I banked again, the stick clammy in my hand, and water raced under the prop. Then sand. A quarter of the strip was gone. I cut the throttle. The tires struck and the plane lurched into the air. The brown mouth of Jesus

Creek rushed closer. A tire hit. We bounced and rolled on both tires. January's voice said, *Christ, don't flip! Pull back!* The wheels gouged in the sand. A huge hand lifted the tail as I rammed the throttle and hauled the stick back. The prop roared. The nose dipped—and rose. I quickly lowered the throttle and taxied, wobbling and jouncing, back to where the plane had sat three hours ago.

I folded the door open and got out.

The breeze filled my lungs. The dogs gathered around, their paws and jowls bloody, happy and full of moose meat. I took off my shoes. The sand came up between my toes.

"There you go, January," I said. "Abe. Mom. Everybody, I fly."

TWENTY-EIGHT

A STRAND OF diluted sun fragmented to rainbows in my eyelashes. I'd been dreaming—Stevie and I were drifting downriver on a sheet of plywood, drinking hair spray that tasted like gin and tonic through tiny red double-barrel straws.

Outside the window, trees and branches and dead fireweed gleamed in thick morning frost. In the distance came the sporadic roar of ice grinding down the current. This was the fourth morning of Freezeup, the hunters had all fled back to their villages and towns and cities, and the animals had a few short days to sniff the blood of their wounded and dead before winter coldly filled in the season. Fall, with its leaves and insects, robins and liquid water, was hibernating. The land was folding its tarps, emptying its buckets for winter.

I lay on my back, staring at the aged beams and the spruce poles of the ceiling—a kid again, Yellow-Hair, rubbing his eyes, wondering at all these dreams he had had. The land hadn't changed, hadn't even blinked, huge and endless and wild. Storms waited to bury the house. A moose tried to get on the roof for companionship. Red foxes screamed hoarsely. Weasels and shrews burrowed into the peoplefood pile. Maybe Enuk would thread across the back tundra today on his dog team, and bring jam and tell stories of where he had been.

I got up, knifed shavings, started a fire, and made coffee. I dumped blueberries into a bowl of sourdough and put the griddle on. "Should you put *suvaks* in your pancakes?" I asked aloud. "Or save them for *ittukpalak?*"

After breakfast, I packed dried fish and crackers and candy bars, spare socks and matches and my Army sleeping bag. I carried my rifle over the pack. Ice pans swung down the channel. Gray jays chuckled and ferried mouthfuls from my caribou cache. A fox had left a winding trail in the frost on the shore ice. Mink tracks hopped along the bank between a brush pile and the fish rack. A lynx, too, had passed in the night, footprints as big and round as jam cans.

The dogs rose and stretched and sniffed the air, worried that they would be left home again today. I unsnapped their collars and they ripped back and forth, overjoyed to be free of chains, harnesses, and the sled. We dropped over the bank and crossed the booming ice of Outnorth Lake.

Jesus Creek was frozen in the wider, slower bends. I slid across on my stomach, gripping a sapling for safety. The dogs raced in front, slipping and falling, fearless and unaware. We picked through the tangled brush and climbed toward the high tundra. The tussocks were frozen heads, slippery with grass hair, the puddles between them hard. The Dog Die Mountains glowed dusty in the pale sun.

The tundra lifted to meet the mountains. Caribou herds grazed, endless lines of animals stretching into the distant north. They meandered south, their trenched trails forking dark across the mottled brown and white tundra.

AFTER SIX HOURS, I stopped where Abe and I had camped. Our tent poles still leaned in the crook of a birch. The tree had worn calluses where the poles rubbed in the wind. Silently, I apologized to the tree and lifted them and laid them on the ground. The flat rock we cooked on was clawed and cracked. I searched the ground, hoping to find a dropped spoon, a .30-06 cartridge, an Artista pastel. There were only the wind-blown cones, twigs, and snow, and sawdusty piles of old moose turds.

The dogs and I went on. Beside us the tundra of lichens and bushes and lone stunted spruce was still and silent. We came to big brown bear tracks, traveling the direction we were going. We climbed the first ridge of the mountain. Canyon walls dropped to willows, a partially frozen creek winding through the thickets. A moose towered down in the brush, his neck bent to the side, curious, and watchful, and I searched for a path down the rocks and descended to the creek.

Along the bank, snow had drifted in the hollows and rocks. Alders leaned over the ice, clawing at my hair, dropping seed clusters down my collar. That spring evening I had been five feet higher, walking up the drifts and pale green overflow ice, the frostbite scars not even beginning to season my face.

The creek curved. On the right it ran close against high slate cliffs. The bear had circled under the rocks. Cold air flowed off the shaded peaks. The dark den appeared above a clump of alders; a path wound around boulders and slate scree and on up to the entrance.

Caribou came down the valley, halting when they saw the dogs and moving up the rocks to go around. I took off my rifle and leaned it against a boulder. The dogs sniffed at it, and Mike started to lift his leg. "Agh! No!" He leapt away, cowering, then wagging nervously. I turned, intent on searching. The rocks were flat and slatey—heaps of them lay everywhere, shattered and shards, and across the narrow creek, near the broken birch tree, a lichened stick stuck out of the ground.

The dogs had disappeared, chasing caribou. Water glugged and percolated in openings in the ice. I shuffled onto the ice and worked my way down to a slower, deeper area to cross and investigate. The ice cracked and starred. I lay flat on my stomach, slithering toward the opposite shore. The ice was clear as glass, the air hushed, and I glanced up the canyon walls and at my rifle on the shore—if something wants to eat me, I thought, so be it, I'm not doing anything more useful than being a meal. High on the mountain, pebbles rattled. I shielded my face to peer through, down into the water and bright rocks. Tiny white and gray bubbles were captured in the ice. The rocks of the creekbed were beautiful, a foot below.

Behind a stump, current had swirled silt into an oval. I chipped ice with my knife, took off my gloves, and raked slush out of the hole. I whipped off my jacket, pushed my sleeves up, reached into the burning water. From the sides, through the magnification of the water, I watched big fingers brush silt. A cloud obscured the water. The current carried it billowing downstream. Two curved mud-colored bones arched above the sediment. I pried and pulled, and lifted the skull an inch. The current tapped my red fingers against someone's old old cheekbones.

THE TRAIL UP to the den was treacherous and steep. Rex leapt ahead, the other dogs pressed behind my heels, impatient but unable to squeeze past. Small gnarled spruce near the entrance had been gnawed dead by porcupine and quills littered the entrance to the den. A porcupine had chewed at the roots, dug an emergency exit, left heaps of wooden turds. The wolves had died, left, or been evicted.

The odor was reminiscent of the stink left by the porcupine in my house, and in disgust I called the dogs away and we went down beside the creek. Caribou clattered down the draw and halted, milling behind the lead cows. I shot a young cow, gutted it, fed the dogs, and built a fire. Gathering wood, I kicked a half-buried stick. A rotten and mossy bolt action .308 rifle rolled to the surface. Air flooded into my lungs. *Your gun! I found you, Enuk!* I peered out at the ice, toward the buried skull, and knelt in the snow, feeling curiously alone, suddenly eons from home—as if I'd roamed far into woolly mammoth territory. I cradled the rusted relic. The bolt was seized. The dogs hurried over, circling and curious, poking their bloodstained noses in my ears and face. "Hey, you have caribou-guts breath, get away from me." The damp gun stock twisted off in my hands. "Agh! Get!" I dug at frozen leaves, scooping under roots and rocks—in a clump of alders, a rusted tin can nicked my hand. I squeezed a few drops of blood onto the snow. The sky was growing dark. I listened. Faint footsteps crunched upstream on the ice. The dogs woofed and stared behind me into the brush. I went back to the fire and sat and ate fat and meat and half of a candy bar, and finally slept fitfully with the dogs close.

THE FOLLOWING AFTERNOON I climbed again to the discouraging den. I reached in and felt around. Quills stuck in my wrists and in the prancing dogs' feet. They whined, ran down to the creek, fed off the carcass, growling and arguing, and disappeared after a herd of caribou.

The tips of my fingers could touch the first depression inside the den and I scooped glovefuls, winnowing chewed branches, turds, and hair. Chips of ancient bone and heavy pebbles lay between my fingers. The eyes of a huge porcupine watched from the depths of the den. I glanced into a handful. Two dull yellow nuggets lay in my palm. I sifted heaps faster, raked out handfuls and prodded the stones and bones. My hands bled, burned from the quills, but no moosehide, or jade or ivory or more gold pebbles, appeared.

Finally, I knelt on the rock outcropping, brushed snow aside to sit. I held the gold rocks in my hands. "Well, Enuk." I pressed the gold against my lips. It was cold and stank of porcupine. My stiff cheeks lifted in a smile. "I missed you for a while there. I didn't know how to be alone."

Caribou passed below. I sat for a time. In the distance I thought I saw wolves, but it was only the dogs, returning unsuccessful from another chase, undaunted. I squeezed the rocks again quickly, as if I didn't want even my dogs to see their color, and flicked them into the dirt tunnel. "Here you go, porcupine. You be good on the country, too. Eat the whole tree for a change, don't just girdle it."

The dogs stared up from below. They raced up the narrow path, panting and cheerful, sniffing my hands, questioning what I'd found. I reached into my pack and pulled out a dried *siulik* and cut each a small piece. They swallowed their shares and wagged tails and tilted their heads for more. I chewed, and paused, listening. A howl echoed in the canyon. "Ssst." The dogs held their breaths. I pointed with my knife, across the canyon. High on the rocks a wolf stood. A second howl pierced the canyon, ringing off the rock walls, rising and falling away. The wolf paced on the outcropping, sniffed, and sauntered up the shale, moving higher, over a skyline and disappearing into a fold of the mountain.

Far across the tundra a dark thread of spruce marked a bend in Jesus Creek, near home. The sun was cooling in the west, dropping into a steely cloud bank. We were going to be heading away from it. The night would come and we would sleep somewhere. And the next day we would be at the igloo, and the tall grasses and fireweed would swish in the evening, and the snow would crunch under our feet. The fall air would be dense and cool, the light from the windows small and yellow in the huge blackness. I would throw *quaq* fish to the dogs. They would press noses out of the dark and tear the fish. Inside, the lamplight would be warm, while the stove sparked and the tea kettles sang. Maybe Dawna would see it, hear it, and love it. Maybe she would go as far away as airplanes could fly.

I handed Magnum PI the fish skin that I hadn't eaten, stuffed a Snickers wrapper into the pack, and lashed on the cow's hindquarters. I picked up the rifle and we started across the tundra.

TWENTY-NINE

A HOWL RISES *up the mountain, echoing in rocks, floating back down the slope to fade into the tundra.* The land stretches, vast crimson pastures, south to the river and beyond. East and west the land runs to the timbered terraces of the mountains. Caribou dot the tundra like lines of weathered quartz. A brown bear and her cubs are dark knobs in the distance, eating blueberries. They stop to wrestle, lying back on bushes in mock battle, their lips and tongues purple. The caribou wait, anxious, and then split into small herds and pour away. Ravens caw over the distance. A lone golden eagle tours the wind, patrolling the gravel porches of ground squirrels. In the willows of a creek, a cow moose and twin calves snap off the summer's fresh growth and swallow pale green branches. Far up the stone horizon, cut against the dizzy blue, a wolf pours her howl over the valley.

The air is cool and still. A line of gray in the west says snow, winter on its way. The caribou are too far out on the tundra to hear the wolf. The moose calves nose their mother's neck. The wolf stands, with lead in her shoulder, broken fangs in her jaw. Her guard hairs have fallen out from old age, left her white as a polar bear, and her yellow eyes stare on her offspring scattered below, and farther below, the human and its companions retreating into the land.

ACKNOWLEDGMENTS

WRITERS, MANY OF THEM, are people who might have been old Iñupiat—they have a generosity that doesn't make sense at times. They've helped me, and I don't remember half of their names. Peggy Shumaker was a beautiful professor at the University of Alaska, fresh from teaching convicts in Arizona, I think, when she complimented some feeble stories of mine and steered me toward Montana. There at the University of Montana, Kate Gadbow, Bill Kittridge, Peter Stark, and others offered help. At the UM journalism school, I was helped by cruel and excellent professors, ready to destroy a poor dyslexic student's grade for simply misplacing a comma. Dennis Swibold, Sharon Barrett, Nathaniel Blumberg, and all the rest—writers with fierce ethics, regardless of what the world thinks of journalists. I thank you now for the red on my sentences. And thank you, Adina, for traveling that road in my vicinity.

Thanks to John Weston and microbreweries—in that order—for my survival in Oregon. Frank Soos and Leonard Kamerling in Fairbanks . . .

and plenty more I should be able to recall. Thanks to Mary Williams for understanding as each season I arrive with less fat meat and more questions, to Chris Todd for reading the manuscript when he could have been running his dog team, and to Jim Dau and Cynthia Meyers for years of storing my computer discs in their sock drawer.

Thanks to Ruthie Sampson and Harriet Blair for their linguistic abilities and expertise with Iñupiaq translations. Any errors, intended or otherwise, are mine alone.

And, finally, those who come first. Thanks to my wife, Stacey, librarian extraordinaire and editor of all my writing, who even when our tent was cold during chilly summers and we were burning romance paperbacks never once requested that the manuscript be shoved in the stove where it could have been useful. Thanks to Emilie Buchwald, publisher and editor, the one person truly responsible for rescuing this story from sock drawer and stove. Emilie stepped out of somewhere when I needed her most, with the gift to blend the right recipe of encouragement with her masterful editing. And thanks to Sydelle Kramer and the Frances Goldin Literary Agency. Sydelle, my unwavering, wise, and always there agent who has never even met me. She is what I have in mind when I speak of generosity, support, and encouragement.

SETH KANTNER: AUTHOR BIOGRAPHY

TRAPPER, FISHERMAN, PHOTOGRAPHER, igloo-builder, and author of *Ordinary Wolves,* Seth Kantner lives in an America most Americans have never seen. Kantner was born in a sod igloo on the Alaskan tundra and raised simply on the land—wearing mukluks before they were fashionable, eating boiled caribou pelvis, and communing with the Iñupiaq, the native Eskimos of the region.

Kantner's acclaimed novel, *Ordinary Wolves,* draws on his own boyhood and young adulthood. The story wraps readers up in the Alaskan wilderness and draws them into the hopes and fears of Cutuk, the boy at the center. Much like Cutuk, Seth Kantner was raised and home-schooled in northern Alaska. He left the igloo for the city and attended the University of Alaska and the University of Montana, where he received a bachelor's degree in journalism.

Igloo and cache under full moon.

When he was a boy, Kantner's parents gave him a camera and taught him the basics of photography. He has been documenting his surroundings ever since. He says, "As a family we took about one roll of slide film per year (more would be a waste!)" Since then, Kantner's photographs have appeared in several publications including *Alaska Geographic.*

Seth Kantner's writing and photographs have appeared in *Outside, Prairie Schooner, Alaska, Switch!,* and *Reader's Digest,* among other anthologies and publications. His work reflects his devotion to the land and the animals who live on it, and his belief in the importance of wildness left wild. He lives with his wife and daughter in northwest Alaska. *Ordinary Wolves* is his first novel.

Q & A WITH SETH KANTNER

Q: Whenever we think of "Great Alaskan Novels," we invariably think of Jack London. Did his writing influence you in *Ordinary Wolves?*

SETH KANTNER: Very much so. Part of the reason I became a writer was Jack. He said when you spat or pissed it crackled and froze before it hit the ground. It never did that when I was a kid—it got to 78 below one time and it never did that! But the whole world believed it did because of London. Later I realized his descriptions of the cold and north were very good. Plus he wrote and lived and drank a lot—things I could at least relate somewhat to.

Q: How authentic do you think the popular image of Alaska as the wild, rugged, uncharted West is?

SK: Depends on your perspective—in the Brooks Range in a storm in midwinter, you could say it's pretty rugged. But a lot of folks come in the summer and fall; they have GPS and satellite phones. For $3.95 they can buy detailed USGS maps of every bend in every slough. Alaska, the Alaska I knew as a kid, is gone; the land is still here but planes fly over it relentlessly, carrying everything that Americans have too.

Q: How long does an igloo typically last?

SK: Maybe forty years at the very top. The one I was born and raised in is falling down. But if I'd kept living in it, it would be in better shape. Igloos don't like you leaving. They mold, get damp, the porcupines move in and dig holes.

Interior of igloo, with sleeping area (between pole and wall); skates hang overhead.

Q: Why did you decide to include the chapters told from the wolves' perspective? Do you feel you're anthropomorphizing or something else?

SK: Oh, probably. I like other perspectives—trees standing around rooted while humans brush past, ignoring them in their search for place and roots! The wolves were there from the beginning, and that's how I've written about them in my book.

Photo credit: Nick Jans

ORDINARY WOLVES DISCUSSION QUESTIONS

1: In the beginning of the novel, Cutuk, Iris, and Jerry express great excitement whenever they hear the sounds of "travelers" approaching. How is the idea of "traveler" sounds returned to later in the book? How would you describe the change in feelings such sounds elicit in Cutuk at these later points?

2: Throughout the novel, and especially during "Part I: The Land," Cutuk wants very much to become Iñupiaq. One outward, though unspoken, manifestation of this desire is his habit of flattening his nose. Another is his repeated wish for the material things—the nylon jackets and snowgos—that the younger natives in Takunak desire. But what he has learned from both Abe and Enuk is how to live the way Eskimos used to live. How, then, does he negotiate these two worlds as a child? How does he negotiate them after he's grown? And what way of being in the world does he ultimately adopt?

3: Why did Cutuk's mother leave? What effect does her leaving have on him? On Abe? Jerry? Iris? Why does the family so rarely speak of her?

4: Cutuk, Iris, and Jerry share an interesting relationship with their father, who is "like an older brother, our best friend, no dad at all," and whom they address as Abe, rather than Dad. Why has Abe chosen to have this kind of brotherly relationship with his children, rather than what we might consider a more traditional parent-child relationship? What are some of the effects of such a relationship?

5: What are some of the childhood values and lessons Cutuk learns from Abe? How do these values serve him once he goes to Anchorage? How do they fail him?

6: Discuss Cutuk's relationship with his two siblings, Jerry and Iris. How do Jerry and Iris compare with Cutuk in terms of their "comfort" with the world? How do their paths differ from Cutuk's?

7: What is the importance of Enuk in Cutuk's life? What is the significance of the carving that Enuk gives to Cutuk and what Cutuk does with it?

8: What surprises Cutuk about his interactions with white people—"his people"? If he doesn't belong to them, and he doesn't belong to the Iñupiaq, to whom does he belong?

9: Why does it become so important to Cutuk to learn to fly his grandfather's plane?

10: What is Cutuk's attitude toward money? What role does it play in his life?

11: Discuss Cutuk's relationships with the two women in his life, Dawna and Cheryl. How do his feelings for Dawna change—or do they change?—from childhood to adulthood?

12: What is the relationship between Cutuk's story and the short passages about the wolves? What does it mean that most of these passages involve scenes of the wolves being hunted down and killed? What is the significance of the scene in which Cutuk and one of the wolves see each other?

13: What is Cutuk's reaction to the state of things in the Iñupiaq village of Takunak? How does it change over time?

14: What does Cutuk mean when he says, "I'm not going to be a dog. I'll take the wolf's deal?"

SETH KANTNER was born and raised in the wilderness of northern Alaska. He attended the University of Alaska and the University of Montana, where he received a bachelor's degree in journalism. He has worked as a trapper, fisherman, gardener, mechanic, igloo builder, wildlife photographer, and adjunct professor. His writing and photographs have appeared in *Outside, Alaska Geographic, Prairie Schooner, Alaska, Switch!, Reader's Digest,* and other anthologies and publications. His work reflects his devotion to the land and the animals who live on it, and his belief in the importance of wildness left wild. He lives with his wife and daughter in northwest Alaska.

The Milkweed National Fiction Prize

Milkweed Editions awards the Milkweed National Fiction Prize to works of high literary quality that embody humane values and contribute to cultural understanding. For more information about the Milkweed National Fiction Prize or to order past winners, visit our Web site (www.milkweed.org) or contact Milkweed Editions at (800) 520-6455.

Roofwalker
Susan Power
(2002)

Hell's Bottom, Colorado
Laura Pritchett
(2001)

Falling Dark
Tim Tharp
(1999)

Tivolem
Victor Rangel-Ribeiro
(1998)

The Tree of Red Stars
Tessa Bridal
(1997)

The Empress of One
Faith Sullivan
(1996)

Confidence of the Heart
David Schweidel
(1995)

Montana 1948
Larry Watson
(1993)

Larabi's Ox
Tony Ardizzone
(1992)

Aquaboogie
Susan Straight
(1990)

Blue Taxis
Eileen Drew
(1989)

Ganado Red
Susan Lowell
(1988)

MILKWEED EDITIONS

FOUNDED IN 1979, Milkweed Editions is the largest independent, nonprofit, literary publisher in the United States. Milkweed publishes with the intention of making a humane impact on society, in the belief that good writing can transform the human heart and spirit. Within this mission, Milkweed publishes in five areas: fiction, nonfiction, poetry, children's literature for middle-grade readers, and the World As Home—books about our relationship with the natural world.

JOIN US

MILKWEED DEPENDS on the generosity of foundations and individuals like you, in addition to the sales of its books. In an increasingly consolidated and bottom-line driven publishing world, your support allows us to select and publish books on the basis of their literary quality and the depth of their message. Please visit our Web site (www.milkweed.org) or contact us at (800) 520-6455 to learn more about our donor program.

Interior design by Christian Fünfhausen.
Typeset in 11/15 point Jenson
by Stanton Publication Services
on the Pagewing Digital Publishing System.
Printed on acid-free 50# Fraser Trade Book paper
by Friesen Corporation.